TREE
OF
SOULS

The Blood Dagger:
Volume Three

MISTY HAYES

Copyright © Misty Hayes 2019

All rights reserved. The right of Misty Hayes to be identified as the author of this work has been asserted in accordance with the Copyright, Designs, and Patents Act 1988.

No part of this publication may be altered, reproduced, distributed, or transmitted in any form, by any means, including but not limited to scanning, duplicating, uploading, hosting, distributing, or reselling, without the express permission of the publisher, except in the case of reasonable quotations in features such as reviews, interviews, and other non-commercial uses currently permitted by copyright law.

Disclaimer:

This is a work of fiction. All characters, locations, and businesses are purely products of the author's imagination and are entirely fictitious. Any resemblance to actual people, living or dead, or to businesses, places, or events is completely coincidental. The products and names of companies and/or commercial items listed in this work of fiction belong to their respective owners and are not affiliated with the author in any way.

Tree of Souls - The Blood Dagger: Volume Three
by Misty Hayes

"Knock, And He'll open the door
Vanish, And He'll make you shine like the sun
Fall, And He'll raise you to the heavens
Become nothing, And He'll turn you into everything."
— Jalal Ad-Din Rumi

Dedication

For Becky Pruitt. I could think of no greater way to pay tribute to all the hard work you thanklessly put into this series. This story exists because of you.

Prologue

Alastair

New York - 1829

THERE IS A DIFFERENCE between bad dreams and nightmares. Bad dreams pass. Nightmares don't. The night he was turned, Alastair discovered that he didn't need to be asleep to experience a nightmare.

On the twenty-first day of November 1829, Alastair Iszler's world crumbled. At fifteen years old, he hadn't just been introduced to the existence of monsters—he had become one. Alastair wished he could take back that night, wished he could turn down the gangly-toothed man's offer of food and shelter, but his weakness had led him astray. He still recalled the way his stomach had rumbled—how hungry he'd been. All he had wanted was to get out of the bone-chilling cold.

Weakness.

Thomas Victor Wrentmore IV spoke of himself in the third person, pronouncing his name with a sort of obnoxiousness that only an egocentric could get away with. Once Alastair arrived at Wrentmore's lavish estate, he ate and drank until his stomach was fit to burst. He learned something that night: nothing is ever free, and if it seems too good to be true, *it is*.

Alastair felt disconnected from his own body as he watched Wrentmore rip his two serving girls apart in front of him. There was so much blood. In fact, Alastair's captivation by the pool of it at his feet would fill him with guilt for the rest of his preternatural life.

Those girls were as succulent to Wrentmore as meat on chicken bones was to a dog. He witnessed the maniacal grin on Wrentmore's face as he looked down on Alastair, the gore dribbling into his mustache. It was a look that said, "You're next."

That evening he met Sarah. She had eyes the loveliest shade of jade. He would obsess over those golden, bouncy curls and that perfectly corseted gown long after she was gone. Sarah was the last of Wrentmore's victims, besides Alastair. All he could remember was Wrentmore sinking his teeth into her neck. After that, he passed out from fright.

When he came to, Sarah was gone—presumed dead.

The tenderness with which Wrentmore held him, as if he were holding a newborn, coupled with the longing and hope and pride on his face, made the blood in Alastair's veins turn to ice. Then it thawed, transforming into something more volatile. *Hatred.* This was what true wrath felt like. Wrentmore's compassion for Alastair, with two corpses at their feet, would haunt him for a century.

There was a gleam in Wrentmore's eyes that he

hadn't understood until much later. So hyper-focused on the dark river of red standing out starkly against the hardwood floor, Alastair could only feel his pulse slamming wildly in his veins, and the thrumming of blood made his arteries jump out at his neck, like the beating of a drum.

When he breathed, his lungs burned.

"*Drink, boy.*" Wrentmore's gaze drifted to the two corpses at his feet. "I know you think you're dying, but it will pass. I have given you my blood."

Alastair stared at the slashed throat of the girl closest to him. She had been wearing a black choker with a silver heart pendant. It had looked so lovely around her neck. Now, it hung torn and tattered, draped across her collarbone like a leash. She was nothing more than a toy to him, he thought distantly.

"It will take your pain away. Drink all of it," Wrentmore told him.

Alastair's stomach churned with revulsion—and something else, something he would later come to hate about himself.

The pain was beyond anything he'd ever felt before. Fire tore through his belly, shooting up into his pounding heart, spreading through his body. His blood roiled in his veins. The sharp, coppery scent overtook his other senses completely. Alastair's vision blurred as tears scalded the backs of his eyelids.

He didn't want this.

Slowly, as if still in that nightmare, he ran a hand along his neck. A throbbing started up as soon as he felt the two puncture marks at his throat.

He tried to wrench himself out of Wrentmore's grasp, but his arms felt like iron bars.

"Shhhh …" Wrentmore cooed. "Someday you will see the necessity of my actions. The angel has deemed you one of hers. You have been chosen, my child. *She* is the new coming. The happening. Under her tutelage, we shall find rapture and dominion."

All Alastair wanted was for the pain to stop. But as soon as his gaze fell upon the two dead girls at his feet, his stomach did a flip.

No—that's wrong.

What he truly wanted was for the girls to live, to see them twirling and dancing in those pretty dresses once more. He remembered how vibrantly and brightly they had sparkled. Now the material looked like the color of rusted metal—dull and lackluster. He tasted the iron on his tongue—rich and intoxicating.

And then it hit him, that part of him that wondered what it would feel like to have blood running down his throat, soothing the uncontrollable thirst and ache within him.

Alastair had grown accustomed to hunger. It was a feeling that never really went away. It was a chronic pain that you learned to live with—consumed by it every day and every minute. He had gone to great lengths in the past to assuage that feeling of emptiness. He'd eaten straight off people's plates as they'd left their dinner table, grabbed leftovers out of the trash, fought other kids for scraps of food. But this hunger was different. This hunger would transform him into something he'd dread and despise. He'd do anything to make this stop. *Anything.*

So jarring was his anguish and revulsion at himself for these dark thoughts that he stopped struggling to get away from Wrentmore. And Wrentmore must have taken Alastair's stillness as a sign of acquiescence, because he loosened his hold on him.

Alastair didn't think, he acted on instinct, twisting savagely out of Wrentmore's hold with an animalistic strength he didn't think himself capable of—and fled.

Chapter 1

Larna

I SAT ON THE stone until it started to feel like a slab of ice underneath me. My clothes smelled like the burned ends of rope, and they were stiff with dried, caked-on blood. Alastair's body was still warm in my arms, his head resting in my lap. I couldn't even bring myself to look at him. *He is only sleeping*, I kept telling myself.

Through fuzzy, swollen eyes, I finally made myself look around. To look at anything other than Alastair. Sozo's office was a mess. Debris and plaster and smoke still lingered in the air, which led me to believe not as much time had passed since Sarah and Caesar's attack on clan Eleutheros as I'd first thought.

Corinth had been rushed to the hospital wing, but I couldn't bring myself to go to him just yet. As I shivered violently, holding Alastair, a deep numbness had begun to spread through me. If I let him go or got up, it would mean Alastair was gone for good. It would mean this was all real—he had died and left me here all alone.

The voices of the clean-up crew in Sozo's office

sounded distorted, as if someone were holding my head underwater. They also sounded as despondent as I felt. They'd lost people too.

My chest constricted. I couldn't figure out if it was a side effect of Caesar repeatedly forcing my heart to stop and then start so he could do it all over again, or if my heart had died the moment Alastair had.

The cots Corinth and Dave had rested on had been removed. They'd cleaned up Corinth's and Alastair's blood. Everyone was too afraid to ask me to move, or to touch Alastair. I was pretty sure it was the wild-eyed, on-the-verge-of-a-breakdown look on my face that cautioned everyone against approaching me.

I thought about the most pain I'd ever endured in my life—being turned. I'd trade a lifetime of being turned, over and over again, for not losing Alastair. *Please take me instead.*

Two young workers wearing all black filed in with a stretcher and laid it at my feet, ready to take Alastair away from me forever.

My eyes flared up with my *Sight.* "*Don't even think about it.*"

The fingers on my left hand were numb and stiff, balled into a fist. It wasn't until I uncurled them that I realized I still had a firm grip on Alastair's pocket watch. It was still happily ticking away, mocking me with its heartbeat. It wasn't fair.

Alastair died to save Corinth. Alastair died to save Corinth. Alastair is dead *because of Corinth.*

A soft weight dropped onto my shoulders. I pulled a hand up to feel warm leather and then glanced down, noticing the black sleeve of a jacket. Alastair's jacket. My heart fluttered distressingly. I'd almost forgotten Alastair had taken it off before attempting to save Corinth's life.

Gabriel Stanton slid gracefully down beside me, crossing his legs underneath him. "You have to let him go."

His voice wasn't unkind. In fact, it sounded sympathetic. I should have thought about why he would do something so … thoughtful, but I couldn't bring myself to care. I didn't even voice my protest at him being so close to me. Strangely enough, I found I didn't mind. It was a distraction from thoughts of Alastair's death.

"I should have stopped Alastair. I should have been the one to turn Corinth. You shouldn't have prevented me from doing it," I growled, and then swallowed hard against the tide of rising emotions. *Suppress it. Push it back down. If it starts, it will never stop …*

"You can be angry with me," he said softly. "But you have to let him go, Miss Collins."

"*Never*," I snarled vehemently, my eyes flashing dangerously.

His knee brushed against my thigh, and I shifted uncomfortably, tilting my head to the side to get a better look at him. For a second, all I could do was stare back at him, unblinking. There was something in those dark eyes of his, a flash of sorrow and something else I couldn't quite put my finger on. Regret, maybe.

His eyebrows drew together as he said, "Corinth is alive. He needs your help. Alastair did his part. Now do yours." The cold indifference was back in his voice again.

My eyes drifted back to the bloodied watch still in my

palm. With grim satisfaction, I realized that the metal had cut into my hand. My fingers looked just as stained as the watch did. I needed the physical pain to focus on—to bring me back to reality. Damn, I really didn't want to be here. I wanted to be anywhere but here.

"I'm sorry …" He sounded remorseful and apologetic at the same time, but then his eyes flickered and turned a startling shade of blue—and he struck, his face inches from my own as he tried to pull me in with his *Sight*. Compulsion.

His mental invasion was like treading dark water and feeling the brush of something cold against the side of my leg as it swam by. I sucked in a sharp breath and pushed back, fighting him with every ounce of strength I had, but having just been tortured by Caesar and Sarah, and having not eaten in who knew how long, I was drained beyond imagining.

I practically heard his teeth cracking from the amount of effort he was putting into his influence over me as he ordered, "*Let him go, Larna.*"

And then I was shaking violently, and I did. My mind was too scattered, and I couldn't concentrate enough to fight him any longer. Maybe I didn't want to. Maybe I'd have him wipe my entire mind of all of this.

Alastair.

One second, I was holding him in my arms and the next—he was just gone. They had taken him away from me.

My heart plummeted. *Nooooo!*

"I'll never forgive you," I snarled, and started to get up to rip him limb from limb and then go find Alastair, but Gabriel held his hands out quickly to show me something.

I froze when I saw what was in his grip: *Corinth's blade.*

Gabriel caught my eye briefly before he returned his gaze to the dagger still in his hands. "You have to help Corinth now, or you'll have two people to grieve for today. He almost took out the entire medical wing with it. I'm surprised you didn't hear it from here. They had to take it away from him. It was quite the fight. The doctors gave him a cocktail of drugs to calm him down. It's working … for now … but Corinth will burn through them with his change. He won't let anyone near him. They need you there to talk him down. Corinth is becoming a vampire."

It was as if someone had dumped an entire bucket of ice water on my head. Corinth needed it. He needed me. I remembered Alastair's last words: *Get Sarah.* If I couldn't pull myself together now, I wouldn't be able to do either.

An excruciating ache swelled up inside me. Alastair had turned Corinth. With the help of one of the most powerful vampires on the planet … *Why did it have to be Gabriel Stanton?*

I was pretty sure Alastair had never turned anyone else in the entire time he'd been alive. I knew his opinion on being a vampire. He had hated it. Corinth must have been special to him in order for him to break his own cardinal rule of never turning anyone. I mean, I didn't think Alastair had ever turned anyone, but that was my own assumption—I'd never thought to ask, until it was too late. There was so much I'd never know about Alastair.

My stomach twisted into knots as Gabriel turned the weapon over in his hands, studying it in reverent silence.

After a moment, he laughed softly to himself and shook his head. "Ironic, isn't it?" When I didn't answer, he sighed loudly and, in a flash of movement, clamped his fingers around my wrist. I tried to tear out of his grasp, but he was incredibly strong, and I still felt so weak, like I might fly apart and drift away in the wind if he pulled any harder. He placed the hilt of the blade in my free hand, the one not clutching Alastair's watch. "Anger is neat and clean. Anger you can *use*. What Sarah did to Corinth was a brutal message. I should know—it's right out of my playbook. Now get off your ass and help your friend."

My *Sight* burst back to life, as brilliant as a solar flare. I didn't even remember reaching for it. This time it just happened.

I hated Gabriel for making me watch Alastair end his own life.

I hated him for taking him away from me.

I didn't want to feel loss any longer. I couldn't take it. It was eating me alive. Gabriel's gaze locked on mine. His eyes were dark and fathomless. He seemed pleased he'd actually gotten a reaction out of me. He was right. Anger was neat and clean. Anger was far better than grief. I hated him for being the one person who could get me to move. He should have been the one to die, instead of Alastair.

When he noticed some life returning to me, he stood up and then reached a hand out. I reluctantly took it. As soon as I got to my feet, I swayed. The world was spinning. He put a firm but surprisingly gentle hand under my arm to steady me.

"I still don't trust you," I told him, eyeing his hand on my arm.

"I'd be disappointed if you did."

Suddenly all I wanted to do was be with Corinth. I should have been with him already.

Gabriel was still beside me. I let him guide me through Sozo's extravagant office, his hand not quite touching my lower back as we marched out past the charred wreckage of the double doors, out through the war-torn hallways that had been cleared of bodies. I swallowed hard. These poor people.

As we walked, Gabriel spoke beside me, catching me up on current events, but I could barely concentrate on anything he had to say as another swell of grief came flooding in.

"Corinth doesn't know he's been turned yet. It should have taken him a lot longer to get through the change. Something's wrong with him. He's been in and out of consciousness, asking for you"—he nodded at the blade in my grip—"and that. He'll need someone to walk him through the transition. You know what will happen if you don't … feral violence and all. An untamed vampire on the loose is not exactly ideal for any of us, especially since we don't know what he is capable of."

I tucked Alastair's pocket watch away, along with all my feelings of loss and regret, and then slipped the blade through the cinched belt at my waist. The white-hot anger I'd hold on to—I needed that in order to get Sarah and Caesar.

As soon as I walked into the medical ward, two guards stopped me. The man had copper-colored skin and a bushel of curly brown hair on the top of his head, and the other guard was a dark-skinned lady with long braids. I recognized her immediately. She'd been the one to let me pass by so that I could talk Corinth down back in the meeting hall when we'd first arrived—after he'd gone all *Mortal Kombat* as soon as he'd seen Gabriel.

She put an arm on my shoulder, halting me from continuing past her. I turned around to gesture at Gabriel, annoyed, but he was no longer behind me.

The woman's gaze lingered on Corinth's dagger, shoved through my belt at the hip. "He almost took out the entire wing with that thing. You prevented that monster from killing more of our people, but you lot were also the cause of all this … " She pressed her lips into a thin line. When she spoke again, I heard her trace of an accent. Scottish, I thought. "I can't let you give that blade back to him, not in his current state of mind."

I nodded reluctantly. "Fine. But you're not taking it from me."

She seemed to relax a little once she thought I was going to cooperate. I didn't blame her for being on edge. She'd probably lost friends. This was our fault. If we hadn't been here under their protection, they might not have been attacked in the first place. Of course, Caesar and Sarah were bound to do more harm than good in the end. It might have happened no matter what we had done.

"He is being restrained for our and his own safety," she added.

Anger swirled inside my chest like a storm. "Get out

of my way. *Now*," I commanded. For a moment, all I could see was the maddeningly blue haze of my *Sight* as it surged back up, taking over. I felt the tips of my incisors start to lengthen. She pulled her hand off my shoulder.

He doesn't like needles. He's freaking out. This is all my fault. I should have been here to calm him down. I'll make sure he doesn't hurt anyone. He's not the enemy. I promise.

All the things I should have said but didn't. Instead, I clenched my fists and took a menacing step toward them both, ready for a fight. "If you don't want me to redecorate your walls in your own blood, then I suggest you move out of my way."

After a quick check with her partner, they both let me pass without further comment or delay, and as I started past her, she said, "Is it true—the rumor?"

"What rumor?" I asked, hesitating.

"We all thought it nonsense … until I saw what he could do. He shot bolts of lightning out of his hands—like that angel Caesar. The kid's eyes … back in the hall … they weren't even eyes at all." She shuddered. "They were made of *lightning*. Is he angel *and* vampire?"

Word had already gotten out. I knew it didn't take a genius to figure out there was something different about Corinth. He'd put his ability on display the minute we'd all gotten here.

I glanced around, taking note of all the medical staff scurrying about and the other guard standing next to the door, staring at me with mouth gaping. Any one of them could be spies working for Angela. The Grigori.

I still had trust issues. Of course, it wasn't like the cat wasn't already out of the bag … We couldn't really hide

Corinth's condition. Did Gabriel know what Corinth was? Surely he had put two and two together by now.

"He's my best friend and he needs me … That's all you need to know."

She put a hand up to her mouth as I moved past her.

It wasn't hard to find Corinth. I just followed the path of scorch marks emblazoned like black arrows along the linoleum floors and walls. The overwhelming odor of burning plastic assailed me as soon as I stopped before the small cordoned-off area around him. There was a burned-to-a-crisp table across the room. All of the now-empty gurneys had been vacated, their white sheets still rumpled.

Curtains were partially closed around his tiny hospital bed, giving Corinth only a small amount of privacy. It looked like a bomb had gone off around him, leaving him completely unscathed—he was at ground zero.

I assumed it had been standing room only due to the Grigori's attack. There were humans who lived here too. Now, though, he was the only patient in this part of the wing.

My breath caught as soon as I saw him.

Corinth looked halfway decent for having been in such a bad condition over an hour ago. Thanks to Gabriel's omnipotent blood, that is. He should have been in the fetal position, burning through the process of being turned, but instead, he was semiconscious with an IV pumping him full of painkillers, fluids, and who knew what else. His usual good-natured smile had been replaced by a haunted, vacant look.

I didn't think Corinth would survive—having to go

through being turned on top of everything else was a pain I wouldn't wish on anyone.

Alastair had saved Corinth's life. His death hadn't been for nothing. *Alastair.* A mental image of his blond hair and blue eyes popped up, and my knees almost buckled out from under me.

I shoved the vision of him back down. *Get it together, Collins.*

Corinth was shirtless. He had on blue pajama pants, and a heating blanket was wrapped around his legs to promote blood flow. His purple lips quivered, and his dark hair hung lank across his forehead. I was glad for the bandages covering his entire torso. It had been such a brutal attack—Sarah stabbing him so many times. The jagged cuts trailing the entire right side of his cheek, where that vamp on the cleaning crew had clawed his face, had already faded to three tiny pink lines. I had thought his wounds would scar, but they were going to heal right along with the rest of his other heinous injuries.

I breathed a deep sigh of relief until a sudden image of Caesar and Sarah callously grinning down at me flashed across the backs of my eyelids.

A jolt of panic tore through me, making my heart stutter-stop painfully in my chest. I broke out in a cold sweat just thinking about it. I hadn't even had time to change out of my ruined clothes or take my broken vambrace off. At least I had Alastair's jacket to give me a small measure of comfort. I pulled it tighter around my shoulders.

The frazzled medical staff hovered near Corinth's bed, just out of arm's reach but still close enough so that they could read the vitals on the monitors. When they saw me approaching, they parted like the Red Sea, as if glad I was there to help.

His eyes were glazed over, and his hands were stretched out by his sides. Before I could think better of it, I launched myself at him and pulled him into a tight hug. He didn't return my embrace. I heard his sharp intake of breath and immediately drew back, meeting his gaze with concern.

"Hey, Collins," he said, half-drowsy. "You know, if you wanted to tie me up, all you had to do was ask." His gaze traveled down, and I followed his line of sight to see the IV inserted in the vein on his right hand, and then the restraints fastened securely on each of his wrists—white Velcro straps that looked triple reinforced. I'd forgotten they'd told me they'd had to restrain him.

A relieved laugh bubbled out of me—joking was a good thing—but then a fierce desire to protect him rose up inside me at seeing him tied down like that, especially since one of their so-called doctors had stabbed him repeatedly. *Sarah.*

I fumbled with the straps on his wrists. "I'm *so* sorry, Corinth. I should have been here as soon as you woke up."

He was still in an incredible amount of pain: his eyebrows were knitted together, and his face looked pinched and strained. He wound his fingers through mine. I couldn't stand seeing all that regret and anger crossing his features. He'd been holding everything in until he saw me, I thought. I felt the same overpowering sense of empathy surge up inside me.

"I thought you were dead," he croaked. "No one

would tell me where you were, and then that douche nozzle Stanton came parading in here. They wouldn't let me go." He tried to lift his arms, but the leather around his wrists snapped in protest. "I tried to stop him from taking my blade. I thought they were going to steal my blood … *again* … and then Gabriel took it …" There was a raw edge of hysteria in his voice now.

I laid a hand on his arm, trying to calm him down. "I've got your blade. Everything is okay."

Corinth slumped back against the propped-up pillows, seemingly relieved, and as soon as I'd finished undoing the fastenings at his wrists, he reached up to rub a hand across his face.

We became silent for a contemplative minute, both of us trying to take everything in, I thought.

"Sarah and Caesar … they killed Sozo's guards, and Benny, the old guy, is—*was* a Watcher … He tried to save my life." As soon as he attempted to sit up, I put a hand on his chest, stopping him. He fell back again, his breath sawing out of his mouth from the apparent pain he was in. "What is wrong with me?" he asked weakly. His honey-colored eyes found mine, and then he was studying me more closely. Finally he murmured, "'What's wrong with *you?* is what I should have asked from the beginning." He eyed me up and down, noticing my torn and bloody clothes underneath the jacket. "Is that Al's jacket?"

I collapsed onto the teeny gurney he lay on and curled up against him, feeling pale and sick with dread and worry. The impending sense of doom came back with a vengeance. A feeling that I knew wouldn't leave me anytime soon.

"Larna, what's going on? Everything's not okay, is it?

Where's Al?"

I didn't know how to tell him about Alastair … I couldn't even admit what had happened to myself, much less say it out loud. And then his death slammed into me all over again. *He's gone.*

"You can tell me anything—you know that, right?" he urged.

I put my face in my hands, but when he didn't say anything, I eventually shared a quick glance back at him, suddenly terrified of how he was going to react. Maybe I shouldn't have freed him of his restraints just yet. He could blow this whole place up by the looks of it. He didn't know he was transitioning. The drugs were helping him handle the pain of the process, but he should have been feeling worse … and yet—

"What do you remember?" I asked finally.

"Angela … she … our *meeting* …" He emphasized the word *meeting* as he set his jaw. "It was a setup. Sarah drugged me. They—this angel, Turiel, he disintegrated Dave. Sarah told me she wanted to get back at Al for killing … Wrentmore—that was his name, right? Sarah was working with the Grigori, apparently. When I came to, she … she stabbed me. I remember you lying in a heap in the corner of Sozo's office." He jerked involuntarily beside me, and then there was a strange sizzle of electricity coming off his fists as he clenched them tight. "Caesar told Sarah to finish the job—" He took in a gasping breath before saying, "I tried to stop them … but she stabbed me again and then … *Lights out.* Tell me you killed those bastards."

I shook my head. "Not for lack of trying, but they got

away."

He was stronger now, despite his weakened state. I could feel the corded muscles in his arms bunching as he tensed up beside me.

I sagged back against him, realizing just how much I needed to hear his heart beating, to feel the blood pumping through his veins—to convince myself that he really was alive. My best friend was still with me.

His brows creased, meeting in the middle. "The cuts on my face … they're almost gone. Sarah stole my blood, and as soon as I woke up here and saw Gabe standing over me … I … I just flipped out. He had my blade … I tried to take him out …" His eyes flicked to the IV still inserted securely in the back of his hand. Before I could stop him, he ripped the needle out, wincing as blood bloomed bright against his pale skin. "When you see people do that in the movies, it doesn't look like it hurts … but it does in fact hurt."

I grimaced. "Those were painkillers. They're not trying to hurt you or steal your blood, I promise."

He chewed on his bottom lip in thought, clearly still agitated by the needle. His eyes drifted to the blood on his hand. The wound was already healing, but he didn't seem to notice. He had a faraway look on his face. I thought for sure he was going to ask me why he was healing, but instead, he only said, "Where's my blade?"

I patted my belt and his eyes zipped down to my side.

He put a hand out for it, but I shook my head. "You almost took down the entire building with it. Let me keep it safe for now. I'm not going anywhere."

I knew I needed to teach him about what to expect

when becoming a vampire, but I couldn't seem to go there just yet. I wanted more time with him before everything changed—before both our worlds came crashing down around us.

I had this sudden memory of him when he used to sneak over to my house in the fifth grade and crawl under the covers with me. We'd read together into the wee hours of the morning. Lying next to him now made me feel dizzy with the recollection of it. I wished we could go back to that simple time again. I wouldn't feel the pain of losing Alastair.

We were quiet for a moment until I finally said, "What went wrong with the Grigori?"

I felt him stiffen beside me, but eventually, he whispered, "Angela told me the dagger is a devastating weapon. I couldn't beat her, Larna. She was too strong." He looked down again at his hand. "This … isn't … possible. How is this possible? I can feel everything. It's so clear—like I just used anti-*Sight*, but this isn't going away. I can hear everything. Taste the air, even. And that ticking … it … it's so loud. Where's it coming from?" He gave me a sidelong glance, his eyes raking over my pocket. "It's coming from your pants … Is this a side effect from the drugs?"

Corinth had been half-dead when he'd been turned. I'd felt the same when I'd transitioned, except when Gabriel had turned me, he'd made sure I knew what was happening. He didn't know what was happening to him. I could see the gears spinning in his head as he tried to piece it all together.

I placed a hand on top of his, and his fingers encircled

my wrist. A pop of static sparked off his skin and jumped onto mine.

The corners of Corinth's mouth tightened as he blinked down in confusion at his almost-mended body. "Did Dave do this? I know you're keeping something from me, but there's also a part of me that doesn't want to know what that is."

"You were dying … Alastair … *he* …" My voice cracked. "He took matters into his own hands." Slowly I extricated the timepiece from my pocket, holding it out to him. "It's not the drugs," I said softly. "It's *you.*"

Corinth took the timepiece from me. It was still stained with his and Alastair's blood. His pupils blew all the way out, making his irises look darker and strangely enthralling, hypnotic. "Why is there blood on this?"

I could see the moment it clicked into place for him, because his face crumpled as if he were in extreme mental anguish.

"You were dying and we were out of options." I put my head in my hands. "The only way to save you was to turn you."

"That's not possible. What you're saying doesn't make sense … I can't be turned. My blood is toxic—"

"That's why it took two vampires to turn you … Alastair *and* Gabriel."

I glanced back at Corinth. His mouth parted slightly, and he jerked upright so suddenly he almost fell off the bed, his face going white as a ghost's. He ran a hand along the side of his neck in stunned disbelief. "*No … it's not possible.*"

"You're transitioning. It's why your senses are so

heightened. Look at your hand." I pointed to his hand where he'd ripped the needle out. He glanced down slowly and wiped the blood away. There was no trace of the cut left.

He bent over the side railing, away from me, clutching a hand to his abdomen. "I feel sick." His eyes lit back on Alastair's pocket watch, still lying on his lap. Slowly he unwound the blanket from around his feet and, with surprising strength, pulled me closer. He was burning up with fever. "*Al* … no. No. No. Not Al." Corinth's voice was shaking now, but not in sorrow—in rage. "I would have told him no … If I'd had a choice, Larna, I would have said *no*. Why did you let *Gabriel* … do this to me?"

I couldn't take the accusatory glare from him any longer. I yanked myself out of his embrace to stare at the deep scorch marks on the tiled floor. They flared out, peculiarly strange and ethereal looking—like charcoal wings painted on a mural. Perhaps an omen of things to come.

"I tried to stop him," I breathed. "I tried to do it myself …" Another wave of guilt swelled up, threatening to tug me under like a rip-tide. "Alastair wouldn't let me. He … he knew I was going to try to save you, and he prevented me from doing it."

I couldn't voice my next thought: *If I had been successful, Alastair would be here right now and I wouldn't.* My heart shattered to pieces all over again, which I didn't think was even possible.

"No one gave me a choice," he repeated, his voice rising. "You knew I didn't want this, right?" As if he was just starting to believe it, he said, "*No, no, no ... not for me.* Al's not gone. He can't be."

There was a sudden pressure in the room and a metallic zing in the air, like how it feels right before a lightning storm. I glanced down to see his fingers crackling with purple sparks. My hair started to lift from the top of my head.

I placed a hand on his bare chest and gently pushed him back down. "You have to calm down, Taylor."

He pressed his palms against his eyes and the sparks suddenly dissipated. "That self-sacrificing do-gooder. Man, this hurts worse than being—"

Then he was leaning over the bed railing again, putting a fist to his stomach as if he could quell the sudden onslaught of pain. I knew the change was hitting him hard now that the drugs were no longer in his system. And he was in agony over what Alastair had done to him—*for* him. I could see it in the way his eyes filled with tears.

"Is it supposed to feel like my gut is collapsing in on itself? You went through this?"

"I think I compared it to the movie *Jaws*," I said. Moving with the speed I'd been graced with, I grabbed a plastic cup from across the room right as he sat back up. I had filled it with my blood and had it in his outstretched hand by the time he knew what was going on. "You need to drink. Now."

He screwed his face up in revulsion. "I do *not* want that."

"I knew something was wrong with you. Corinth, by now my blood should smell like a little slice of coffee-filled heaven to you."

"What if I don't drink it?" He ran a shaky hand through dark, sweaty locks. "Please tell me this is just a really bad nightmare and that I'm going to wake up soon—"

"We don't have time for this."

A familiar voice spoke up from the entry to the hallway I'd just come from, interrupting Corinth.

Our heads snapped up at the same time. Gabriel Stanton was standing at the end of the bed we lay on, the curtains pulled all the way back. There had been no one there a moment before. He had his arms crossed resolutely over his chest, and his lip was curled up on one side of his mouth as if he'd witnessed our emotional reunion and was sickened by it.

I had forgotten all about him as soon as I'd seen the state Corinth was in.

"Give me my blade, Larna," Corinth growled.

Gabriel's smirk widened, his scar stretching across the left side of his cheek. He was an imposing figure even when he smiled. "Play nice, Corinth. You're one of us now. Ascended being and all, you know."

I stuck a hand out before they could go at each other. I wasn't afraid of what Gabriel would do to Corinth; it was the other way around. I'd seen the damage he'd already caused. Who knew how much he'd been changed by the turn, how powerful he'd become—half angel, half vamp? It meant he could have any number of other reactions to being turned.

He needed blood, stat. There was a reason why we couldn't drink his blood, and a reason why his dagger harmed us in the way it did. His powers were in some ways the opposite of our abilities. Dave had admitted as much.

"I'm not *one* of *you*," Corinth said in a whisper-soft voice, and then his eyes lit up with preternatural energy, sapphire-colored sparks shooting out of empty eye sockets—a sign of his newly formed *Sight*, and something else entirely. Something terrifyingly powerful.

A fusion of blue swirling lightning and phosphorescent flames were where his eyes should have been. It looked even more frightening than vampire *Sight*.

"No-o-o-o ... *not now* ..." Corinth reached a hand up to his face and then doubled over and retched, but there was nothing in his stomach to heave up.

Gabriel pointed to his own eyes, nodding at Corinth. "Fascinating. Your eyes—I've never seen anything like that before. I mean, not from one of our kind, anyway."

His voice seemed to come from terribly far away, because all I could think about was *What did we do?*

Chapter 2

Larna

I PLACED A HAND on Corinth's back, glancing at the full cup still in his hand. "Corinth—you could hurt a lot of people if you don't get a handle on this right now. You have to drink. The consequences will be worse if you don't. You could become uncontrollable. A slave to your thirst." My eyes flitted to Gabriel to prove my point—speaking of bloodthirsty.

Corinth went stiff all over and then sat up ramrod straight. I could see the struggle in his eyes as they ticked back and forth, completely lost in his own thoughts. "I don't think I can do this. Do I have any other choice?"

"No. And you *can* do this," I insisted. "You're one of the strongest people I know. Don't make Alastair's sacrifice all for nothing."

I sat back down on the bed beside him, gently taking his hand in mine.

Gabriel noisily cleared his throat. "Seriously, this is how you two handle things?"

Corinth rolled his eyes. "This figures. I *would* be the

only vamp who hates the sight of blood." Then without another word, he downed the contents of the cup in one gulp. He peeled the bandage off his chest. We watched as the last of his puncture wounds vanished, and the three faint pink fingernail marks on his cheek disappeared completely, as if he'd never been hurt in the first place.

I felt myself start to relax, realizing how anxious I had been about this part of his turn, and how his body would handle it. With him being part angel, we had entered the realm of the unknown.

"That was ghastly—" Corinth started to say, but stopped himself short, his face turning a shade of green that reminded me of the color of lizard scales.

He moved with surprising speed to a small metal sink in the corner of the medical wing and then unceremoniously threw up, emptying out the contents of his stomach. When he recovered somewhat, he wiped a hand across his mouth and met my concerned gaze. "There's something seriously wrong with me, isn't there?"

The trouble is we think we have time.

I'm not sure where I'd heard that saying before, but time runs out no matter how much you rally, fight, and plead against it. I knew it was running out for Corinth too, as soon as he upchucked all over the place after drinking my blood. We were messing with things that we didn't understand—turning Corinth without knowing what it would do to him in the process.

Gabriel sauntered closer, stopping just shy of the sink where Corinth stood. Silent. Gabriel only stared at him as if he were trying to solve a complicated puzzle.

I put a soothing hand on Corinth's back as he raised a fist in warning to Gabriel, but before they could go at it, Sozo marched into the medical wing, the double doors whooshing open, his dark robe fluttering around his legs as he stopped in front of us.

He was wearing all black except for two very bright, pearlescent stripes shining at both of his shoulders. Mourning robes, I guessed. Behind him trailed his staff and several stern-looking bodyguards—they had exchanged their normal white attire for black too. He looked out of sorts, as we all probably did.

Sozo was more than a little curious about Corinth's new condition. This kind of curiosity could leak back to the Grigori—everyone here knew Corinth was part vampire now, but not everyone knew about him being part angel. How long would it take before it got back to the Grigori or Angela that he was still alive? I just didn't know who to trust anymore.

Without pretense he said, "I am sorry it took me this long to come and see you. We are still recovering, as you can imagine. On behalf of my people, I apologize for our part in what happened to you, Corinth." He looked away for a moment. "And to Alastair Iszler." I was surprised to hear how sincere he sounded as he continued. "This is as much of a shock to me as it is to you—"

"Doubtful," Corinth interjected, rubbing a hand across his mouth. He still looked green around the edges, but at least some coloring had flooded back into his cheeks and the tips of his ears, although it only served to make him look blotchy and feverish.

A flicker of something I likened to annoyance crossed Sozo's face. "Alastair fought bravely to help rescue our people. As did you. I was told he tried to get as many to safety as possible. In such a short amount of time, he managed to make a huge impact. *His* was the ultimate sacrifice. I would like to have a memorial for him, if you are willing to speak on his behalf."

A tiny explosion went off in my head at hearing the word *memorial.* I knew Sozo was only trying to help, but I couldn't hear the rest of what he was saying. The ground shot up to greet me before I knew what was happening, but before I collapsed, someone's hand shot out of nowhere to help steady me.

I glanced down to the fingers wrapped around my forearm—and then I took in a deep breath, managing to focus on the face of the one whose hand was still latched on to my arm. Gabriel. He was staring at me with something like pity in his eyes.

Memorial for Alastair. He's gone.

I brushed his hand away as Sozo said, "Ms. Collins, are you all right?"

For an unsettling second, the ache of loss was so overwhelming it felt like Caesar was gripping my heart all over again and electrifying it into a pile of grisly embers.

Corinth was beside me. He put a strong arm around my waist and gave Gabriel a "Go to hell" sort of look. "If you could … just … give us some more time to recover … It's just … I'm not feeling well—and Larna is … grief-stricken, as you can imagine."

Sozo laced his fingers together, and when he spoke, I could hear the edge in his voice, as sharp as a knife. "Of course. Take whatever time you need. But please know we lost twelve souls in the attack by Caesar. I am devastated—and livid. This kind of violence has never happened to us before. That's why time is something we can't afford to waste."

There was something hidden in Sozo's furtive glances at Corinth. According to Corinth, the Grigori, a group of rogue angels who had fallen long ago, wanted to control humans and kill all Nephilim. They were against the Watchers—Dave's so-called group of avenging angels. But what were Sozo's clan's intentions?

"Gabriel told me what happened. You are one of us now—*vampire*. We have been infiltrated, and our kind killed … We need to know how best to prepare," Sozo explained.

"I promise I will tell you what I know, but we just need some time to sort things out," Corinth said.

Sozo nodded. "I'll give you time to grieve and put things in order."

Chapter 3

Corinth

Al is dead because of me.

I am no longer human.

I shouldn't be alive. Al should.

Panic started to claw at me once again. My stomach heaved, letting me know how displeased it was with the sudden need for blood in order to survive. I felt fractured, like I'd been cut up into a million tiny pieces and then haphazardly glued back together again—by Gabriel Stanton. If this was what an "ascended being" felt like, he could keep it. It was bad enough that I was the last surviving Nephilim; now I was also vampire.

I found the myriad of beeps and dings from hospital equipment disorienting. The medical staff skirted around us, keeping a wary and watchful eye on me. I thought they might be mad that Larna had released me from my restraints.

I sat up, gasping, scrambling wildly at the bed railing. I pulled my hand up to feel the two sharp points in my mouth, and gagged.

A hand went to my shoulder, guiding me back down. "Easy."

Those dark hazel eyes staring down at me were gentle. Caring. Kind. Larna had my hand in hers. "I know it hurts. I know it seems like more than you can handle. It's not, Taylor. You can do this. I'm here with you." She gave my hand a gentle squeeze. "Each minute. Each hour. It'll get better. Just breathe."

I let the rumble of her voice lull me back into a state of semi consciousness. All I had to do was lie here, I reminded myself. Eventually, I tore my mind away from the pain of turning, to think about Al. That was an even worse pain. *Damn.*

There had to be a way to bring him back.

If angels were real, anything was possible. I refused to believe he was just … gone. Because of me. I thought back to what he had told me when I'd just found out I was Nephilim: *When one of us can't carry the load anymore, the other one takes it up. That's what family does for each other.* My chest constricted, partly in anger and partly in torment. He'd taken up the load for his family all right. For all of us.

Now it was my turn to repay the favor.

Larna said very little after she'd told me Al was dead. She looked worse than I felt. I wished there was something I could do to make it all better for her. She lay so close I could feel the pounding of her pulse through the thin material of her T-shirt. I didn't know if this was because I was vampire or because she really had lost a part of herself when Al had died, but she felt so small and fragile curled up next to me.

Before, my body had radiated heat like the sun. Now I only felt cold. I wasn't sure if it was due in part to my new hypersensitivity or to shock, or if this was just how vampires felt all the time. Everything had changed in the blink of an eye.

My mind drifted, taking me back to where I didn't want it to go: *Sarah and Caesar.* They had gotten away. Dave was gone—probably dead. Angela was out there somewhere, ready to start her plan for world domination.

I shivered, thinking about the last time she had burrowed inside my skull, her words piercing my head like ice picks: *The blade holds enormous value—imbued with seven angels' power—it is not meant for half-breed, mortal hands … I can't allow you to use this weapon against us.*

At least there was one good thing that had come out of all this: the Grigori thought I was dead. If they found out I was alive, my mind would be open season once again. Angela had said accessing it would be as easy as opening up a bottle of water.

Icy fingers of dread crawled up my spine at the thought of not having Dave's protection to rely on any longer. I'd have to deal with that when the time came.

Idly I thought about where Gabe could be right now. *He's been all up in our business, and now he just disappears again?* I bet he hated witnessing anyone share emotions—empathy.

Larna must have felt me tense up beside her, because she squeezed my hand again, letting me know she was still with me. It was nice just having her by my side. She was my guiding light.

After a while, I slipped into a troubled state of sleep, my body racked with tremors, my head feeling like it might split open at any second. *Vampirism. The gift that keeps on giving.*

Chapter 4

Larna

CORINTH HAD TRANSITIONED IN only a few short hours—where it had taken me a few days. Everything affected him differently now, because of the angel blood running through his veins, I assumed. It wasn't like we had an expert on the subject to tell us how he would react to any of this. Gabriel was the closest thing we had, and that was not a heartening thought.

At least I'd managed to have a quick shower and change of clothes. I zipped up Alastair's jacket, and the smell of leather and his old-man deodorant wafted up to greet me. A flash of those sparkling blue eyes hit me, and I almost doubled over from the pain of missing him.

The sense of looming doom would never go away. It was all-consuming. Time didn't heal all wounds—some it only made worse.

I found myself staring miserably at a copy of an abandoned term paper titled "Interpretations of Different Ways to Communicate through the Act of Mind Control and Manipulation." The cover page said it was written by a Copernicus Holyfield. I wondered if Copernicus had been one of the casualties of the Grigori.

With the sudden and unexpected violence recently, they had suspended all classes for the time being. The paper reminded me of how brilliant and disconnected some of these people were here. To study for your entire life but never put forth that knowledge seemed pointless, in my opinion. Most of these people lived in a well-protected bubble—now, though, that well-protected bubble had burst, and there was talk of war. With it came talk of dissension among the ranks. Who could be trusted if such a high-ranking citizen like Caesar had been involved?

I flipped the page over, thinking about Alastair's last request. *Get Sarah.*

Corinth plopped down across from me, adjusting his blade, sheathed at his hip. He looked better than he had before, but not much. I wondered what he was thinking.

"First things first ... how do we bring Al back?" he said, answering my unasked question.

I felt myself blanch. That sinking feeling in the pit of my stomach returned tenfold. Corinth hadn't witnessed the life drain out of Alastair. He hadn't witnessed him take his last breath, or seen his bright blue eyes dim forevermore. Hope wasn't something I could cling to anymore. Alastair was dead, and there wasn't anything anyone could do about it. Just like my dad. Just like the rest of the lives we'd lost. All of a sudden, I found myself starting to get mad.

"Before you say anything ... I know there has to be a way. I refuse to believe he's just *gone* ... Angels have the ability to heal—the rest of the Watchers. Maybe it's time we seek them out … They can help."

Gabriel grabbed a seat across from us, and I rubbed a hand over my eyes. *This guy is worse than a plague.*

When he spoke, he didn't sound as superior or self-righteous as he once had. "Alastair *is* gone. The sooner you come to terms with that, the sooner we can resolve your situation and go after the cure."

"Why are you here again?" Corinth asked. "Because I distinctly remember *not* inviting you."

Gabriel arched a dark eyebrow at him. "Because when it comes to an opinion, mine is the only one that matters."

"You know what they say about opinions, don't you?" Corinth hissed.

I interjected quickly, speaking over them. "This isn't helping. First and foremost, we need to figure out what's wrong with you, Corinth, and *fast.*"

"It's obvious what's wrong with him—" Gabriel started to say, but I stopped him with a look.

Corinth rolled his eyes. "O wise one … please share your ancient, albeit *obnoxious*, knowledge with us."

"Your body is rejecting the turn," he explained. "Even though you transformed into an ascended being in a record amount of time, you're having the same reaction we do when we drink your blood, *Nephilim*. I would guess at your current rate of deterioration, you have a month left to live."

Corinth's jaw dropped open. "What's this about a month left to live?" he said warily. "Wait … hold on a sec. How did you know I'm a Nephilim? The only people who knew that were Larna, Al, and Dave." He glanced at me, and I shook my head, indicating I hadn't told Gabriel his not-so-closely guarded secret.

Gabriel shrugged as if it was evidently apparent. "Come now. Did you really think the show you put on back in the meeting hall would go unnoticed? You have the power to fight off compulsion. Lightning shoots out of your fingertips. Besides the fact that everyone around here is talking about it … I've known about you for a very long time. That includes your *entire* family's genealogy and history. I've been waiting for you to play catch-up for years. It's been fun," he added dryly.

"*Of course,*" I breathed. "The Bible. I noticed it on your desk back at your estate. You were studying it … to find out all you could about angels. You knew all this time."

Gabriel gave me an impressed nod, his dark eyes sparkling. "You were paying attention. I've said it all along: we're all on the same side."

Corinth rubbed a hand across his jaw in agitation. "Why not share this important bit of information with me *earlier?*"

"I never share information unless I absolutely have to. You're the key to a cure, and I—*we*—need that cure," Gabriel said in a measured tone.

Corinth leaned across the table toward Gabriel, his fingers interlaced and knuckles going bone white. "Why do you want it so badly?"

"I told you a long time ago: we're on the same side," Gabriel repeated. "That's all you need to know."

"Yeah … sure … I'm so tired of your evasiveness." Corinth's eyes flared up brilliantly in the dim lighting of the conference room. "I think it's time I test out my new vamp abilities and show you the Nephilim part of me. I bet I could give you a run for your money on compulsion, *Gabe* … With me and Larna working together, we could subdue you pretty quickly."

I cocked my head to the side, considering. "That's not a bad idea."

Gabriel picked at a piece of lint on the sleeve of his jacket. I knew that hidden underneath those sleeves were his vambraces, housing razor-thin blades. "It depends on how messy you want this to get—"

"Dave is gone," I said quickly. "Angela is in the wind, and we're no closer to finding a cure than before. If Corinth can't drink blood, he dies, right? The very thing he needs to survive is also the very thing that's killing him—so you say, Stanton. Why should we trust anything out of your mouth? You're a liar and a murderer."

"I may not reveal everything all at once, but I'm not lying. You're just not listening. Corinth is rejecting our blood because he has angel blood running through his veins. His body can't process it in the way we do. My best guess is that his body *will* eventually shut down. He was able to heal after drinking your blood, Miss Collins, which is a good sign." He paused, thinking, and after a second said, "But maybe *my* blood, which is clearly more potent, can extend his life for a little while longer." He waved a flippant hand in the air. "Of course, that would come with a price tag."

"Wow!" Corinth scoffed. "You're brilliance and level of greed never fails to astound me. I would *never* have guessed that you'd want something in return … So, what's this price—?"

The room exploded in cobalt light and a crash of thunder. Lightning arched out of the fixtures, dancing from one electrical socket to the next, sparks shooting out of them in all directions. The electricity flickered off and on as a ball of energy formed and expanded outward in the middle of the room—the same kind of energy that occurred when angels transported themselves from one place to another.

I jumped to my feet, my heart rate skyrocketing as I leaped in front of Corinth, but he was already reacting just as swiftly. I'd almost forgotten about his vamp super speed now. In a quicksilver flash of light, his dagger was up and in his outstretched hand, impressively fast.

And as if the flood of power was too much for him, he reached out to steady himself on the edge of the table, his breathing labored. I didn't think he had become accustomed to his preternatural senses just yet. Still, light crackled and fizzled across the tip of the blade in his hand. He looked like the sort not to mess with.

The fireworks show increased and then quickly dissipated, and then the giant sphere broke apart in an explosive *POP*. Out of the vanishing light, a form dropped down, crouching in front of us.

Only when he stood to his full height was I able to get a good look at who it was. And when I did, my mouth fell open in astonishment.

Dave.

We stood our ground, frozen by indecision. I thought we were all waiting for the same thing: to see who was going to make the first move.

Corinth started toward him, but I threw an arm out,

barring him from going any further. "We don't know if we can trust him."

Dave wore his usual linen suit, just like all the other times I'd seen him, but his hat was missing. There was no trace of stains or blood on his clothing. Actually, for having been blown to bits and ash, he looked good. I could sense something was off about him though. His eyes, which had been so full of life—of galaxies and stars and supernovas—were now dull, a normal shade of dark brown for an angel, I mused.

He bent over at the waist, panting as if he'd just sprinted a mile. "Took me longer to get back … Turiel disintegrated my favorite hat …"

Corinth pushed past us, his dagger still in hand. "Thank God you're alive. Did you get it? The cure from Angela?"

I eased back a step, relaxing a fraction as Gabriel turned toward me, assessing the situation. I gave Gabriel a quick nod to let him know to stand down. Surprisingly, he listened, retracting the blades back into the hidden sheaths at his wrists. *Will wonders never cease?*

Corinth moved around me, putting himself within arm's reach of Dave.

Dave's eyes flicked over Corinth. "Something's wrong with you." He gave each of us the once-over until finally his eyes homed in on Gabriel and stayed there. After a moment longer, his pupils narrowed down to two tiny pinpricks, and he said, "*Vampire … you are responsible for this?*"

One side of Gabriel's mouth quirked up at the corner as Corinth inched closer to Dave, stretching a hand out toward him. "The cure, Dave. Did you get it?"

After a moment, Dave ran a hand along his face and sagged back down to collapse into a chair at the table. "No. Angela was too strong. She was … ready. I'm sorry I let you down. I was so focused on getting the cure that when Turiel attacked, he was able to gain the upper hand."

The seriousness of Corinth's situation settled back onto my shoulders. I was suddenly so very tired, and it was all I could do to keep my head upright. *Keep it together, Collins. For Alastair—he would tell you to keep it together. Stay strong.*

Corinth blew out a frustrated breath. "I thought they'd killed you."

"I told you they couldn't kill me during an armistice," Dave clarified. "But they *were* able to send me scattering in the wind. It took my metaphysical body time to stitch itself back together again … By the time I got back, it was already too late." He turned to Gabriel, his fists suddenly glowing like twin balls of blue flame. "Now explain yourself, *vampire*, before I wipe that smirk off your face."

Corinth piped up first before Gabriel could say anything. "As much as I want to see you wipe that smirk off his face, it wasn't entirely Gabe's fault. Angela wanted Caesar to take me out while she distracted you … When I was stuck in the dream state with you and her, I was already dying in real life. The only way they knew how to save me was to turn me. They took a chance, thinking I might be able to heal myself from within … and voilà, here I am. A vampire."

Dave planted a hand on the side of his cheek. "You

can't simply *turn* an angel. If a vampire were to drink our blood, they would die on the spot. There are major consequences. This *vampire* might as well have signed your death certificate—"

"Ascended being," Gabriel interjected.

"He's not full-blooded." Dave's eyes snapped to meet mine questioningly as I added, "He's only half angel, right? Doesn't that make a difference somehow? If he's part human, I mean, that's the part that was changed, that enabled him to transition."

Dave nodded, seemingly lost in thought. "It's probably the only reason Corinth isn't dead right now. Angela only ever experimented on angels. Whenever she came across a Nephilim, she would kill them without hesitation . . . so you"—Dave's eyes went round as he gazed at Corinth before coming to some sort of conclusion—"are something none of us has ever seen before. Something extraordinary."

"Benny," Corinth began, "was a Watcher, right? One of you? He tried to save my life, but there's something I don't understand. How was he able to pass himself off as a vampire for so long, among other vampires, I mean, without being discovered?"

"Angela specifically engineered vampirism to be a step down in the evolutionary chain. But she needed vampires to be stronger than mere mortals. That's why the virus has similar attributes to our own genetic makeup, because she used her own blood to create it. Her goal was control and manipulation. She didn't want a vampire to come back and bite her ... Sorry, no pun intended. It's why our powers affect vampires so negatively, why our blood is toxic to them, and why we can't be compelled—" Dave cleared his throat "—or turned. We can change our appearance when it suits us, make you think what you're seeing is real. Where do you think compulsion comes from?"

Dave smiled, and I saw two pointy teeth slide out of his gums. *Fangs.* I shot forward on instinct. Corinth almost fell off the edge of the table he'd perched on, his eyes stretching wide.

Stanton sat up, suddenly interested, but Dave only continued to smile, and then the fangs vanished. A trick of the eyes.

Whatever the case, it was a scary revelation indeed. He'd made us all think we'd seen fangs when there were none really there.

"That's a neat trick," Gabriel murmured.

He did seem impressed, I noted.

Dave took a seat beside Corinth, who was still propped up against the edge of the table, half sitting, half standing, and he gave Gabriel another quick glance in disgust before saying, "I am not sure I am comfortable talking in front of this *vampire*—"

"*Ascended being*," Gabriel corrected for the second time.

"Go ahead," Corinth said, sounding resigned. "He's bound to find out anyway . . . and apparently, he already knows everything else about me. At least if he leaks it to anyone, we'll know it came straight from him, and then we'll deal with it accordingly." Corinth's blade sparked brightly in his hand, the light glinting dangerously off the sharp tip.

Dave inclined his head. "In order to imbue the blade

with our power, it meant losing some of our own. Some of us reacted differently to losing so much of ourselves in the process. In Benny's case, he had already lost a child—his only son—by the Grigori's hands. Benny never fully recovered from it. His mind went, right along with his power. Every once in a while, he'd have a moment of lucidity, but we felt it best he come stay here, to keep an ear to the ground and be ... somewhat comfortable." Dave's voice cracked. He seemed like he really was broken up about his death. I wondered how well they had known each other. Very well by the looks of it.

Gabriel threw his legs back up onto the table and folded his hands in his lap. "For once, this was not all *my* doing."

"You played your part, *vampire*," Dave snarled. "This goes well beyond anything that I've ever dealt with. There has never been a vampire–Nephilim hybrid before. Corinth will not survive. The Nephilim part of him is warring with the virus inside him. I can sense it."

Gabriel's eyes flashed dangerously at the word *vampire*.

"Ah," Dave whispered, realization dawning on him. "Alastair—he helped to turn Corinth, didn't he? That's why he's not here." He glanced between each of us. "He is dead."

My heart lodged itself in my throat, and I nodded, staring numbly down at my hands. Unable to keep the pleading out of my voice, I said, "You were able to heal Corinth before, right? Dave, tell me you can ... fix him. Cure Corinth again."

"To hell with me," Corinth snapped, raking a hand

through his hair and mussing it up. "Al saved my life … or at least gave me a fighting chance. *You* left me alone, Dave. *You* said you'd protect me, and you didn't. As far as I'm concerned, my condition is partly your fault." Corinth lowered his voice, and I could hear the anguish in it when he spoke again. "There has to be something you can do to bring Al back. Please. Please tell me he didn't waste his life just so he could prolong mine for a short time."

Dave dropped his gaze to the floor, clearly upset, but there was another reason why he avoided our gazes—*dread.*

An empty sort of detachment washed back over me. I was going to lose someone else I loved, and there was nothing I could do about it. I bit the inside of my cheek, hoping physical pain would take away some small margin of mental suffering. I didn't think I could lose Corinth too.

Dave's eyes swung back and forth like a pendulum, as if he were deep in thought. I didn't want to push him—maybe, just maybe, I could cling to some small shred of hope. Feelings like these were dangerous.

Finally, after what seemed like an eternity, he said, "Where's Alastair's body?"

I stiffened, and every single nerve in my body felt like it was on fire as I wheezed, "Why?"

Gabriel sighed, clearly incensed. "Alastair is *dead.* Why does it matter where his body is? You people madden me. We need to figure out our next—"

Dave met my anxious gaze, and my breath caught at the way he was looking at me. He said, "Because there might be a way to bring him back."

Chapter 5

Larna

THE MORGUE WAS EXACTLY how I expected it to be—cold, sterile, and full of cadavers. There were twelve lost souls all lined up, with white sheets covering each body. Alastair was right smack in the middle of the bunch. Benny was one of the corpses too, the one on the far end.

A horrible coldness crept over me.

I couldn't handle seeing Alastair's lifeless body again—not after holding him in my arms as he lay dying. It was worse than torture.

Apparently, Alastair was in line for cremation. I wondered when they were planning on starting. That was what they did with the bodies here. They burned them. There was a giant furnace along the far wall.

Corinth looked at me out of the corner of his eye, his sharp features contracting slightly with the pain of empathy. I knew he felt the same thing I did, that Alastair shouldn't be in this cold and desolate place. Not alone. I could feel him growing more and more livid by the second.

Even though he whispered, Corinth's voice seemed

to carry deafeningly in the quietude of the room. "You don't need to be here for this, Larna."

My heart gave a sudden lurch as I thought about Alastair all by himself down here. I'd been unable to make myself say goodbye one last time. Those baby blues of his had held so much sorrow, joy, and wonder. All of those things had been sucked right out of him. It was enough to suck the soul right out of me too. I felt like an emotionless husk—empty—save for an incredible guilt that wouldn't let up.

"Yes I do," I told him.

I tugged his jacket tighter around my shoulders, trying to let the smell of leather and grease, like gun oil, engulf me—the smell of him. Seeing Alastair stretched out on that cold slab of metal, I realized that no amount of clothing would be able to warm me up.

My eyes just kept going back to his lifeless form.

Corinth bowed his head and closed his eyes, paying his last respects or maybe praying for a miracle. Dave was just as somber as he gazed down on Benny's lifeless form.

Only a thin sheet covered Alastair's body, everything except for the tips of his bare feet. Someone had removed his boots and socks. There was a washbasin at the end of the table, containing what looked like soapy water. Underneath I knew Alastair was still fully clothed in dark-wash jeans and a white T-shirt.

I thought how weird it was that someone had removed his boots and socks and nothing else.

Maybe he'd been picked first for cremation, or maybe they wanted to give me his personal belongings ... I shuddered at the thought. There was something jarring about seeing him look so vulnerable. It showed the fragility in his death.

We all jumped when the iron door to the room cracked open a fraction and a pale, ancient face wedged itself through the gap. Glossy old eyes looked us up and down before a gray-haired woman stepped inside to greet us. She was wearing a tan smock.

"Pardon my interruption." She shuffled toward Alastair and then pulled the small washbasin into her withered hands, soapy water sloshing out and dripping onto the floor at her sandaled feet.

"Excuse me, but what is that for? Why take his shoes and socks off?" I couldn't hide the anger edging into my voice.

The woman's eyes skimmed to Alastair's prone form, and she lowered her head, bowing slightly. "Pedilavium. A custom we do here—done to those who we hold in the highest respect. This young man saved my daughter's life. I was washing and purifying his feet for his journey onward. I was about to begin with the others."

I clamped my eyes shut and gnashed my teeth together, trying to quell the sudden urge to breakdown completely.

Corinth threaded his fingers through mine, and I winced as he squeezed my hand. I didn't think he realized how strong he was now. I also didn't want to tell him that he was hurting me, mainly because I was using the pain as a distraction. Corinth's once-baby-soft skin had long since been calloused from hours and hours of training with his blade. That hadn't healed over when he'd been turned.

I opened my eyes and they slowly slid to his. Corinth

was still silent, his eyes closed. His faith was what held him together. Nothing would ever hold me together—not unless Alastair returned to me whole again.

"Thank you," I finally managed to tell the old woman.

She gave me a small nod. "I will come back later." And without another word, she slipped silently back out the way she'd come in.

Dave reached out to gently close Benny's eyes, speaking in a language I didn't understand. It felt like I was prying into a private moment between old friends.

After a second longer, he moved back over to Alastair and, without preamble, dragged the sheet down past his head.

I sucked in an icy breath, the air in my throat pushing down a scream on its way out. My stomach clenched as I pulled my hand from Corinth's and put it to my mouth. I bit down hard on my knuckles.

Except for the gray pallor of his skin, Alastair could have only been sleeping. His blond hair looked feather soft, swept neatly across his forehead. I wanted to reach out and brush it to the side, the way he always wore it. From chiseled jaw to chest, he was a vision of perfection, like fine porcelain. Italian Renaissance artists couldn't have found a better model to recreate a masterpiece with.

Corinth forced my hand into his once again. This time I was sure it was for his comfort and not my own. There was empathy and pity all rolled into the hard lines of his mouth.

His grip tightened to an agonizing degree. "Al isn't getting off that easy. This *is* going to work. Something good has to come out of all this …" He lowered his voice to a fervent whisper. "*It has to.*"

"I can't heal him like I normally would," Dave explained. "This is going to take a lot more strength and power than I possess. It will put me out of commission"—his gaze swept back over to Corinth—"and you back in danger. Your mind will be left unprotected without me there to prevent invasion."

"I don't care," Corinth said adamantly. "I mean, I care about your well-being, of course, but not the danger it puts me in … As long as it won't hurt you, then we're doing this."

Dave shook his head, but the way he pursed his lips didn't convince me of this fact.

Corinth said, "Can you draw energy from me? Like you did before with Angela?"

"I am going to try," he answered. "Are you sure you have enough strength?"

"Do what you have to do to bring Al back," he insisted. "I'll do everything in my power to help."

"Corinth, Alastair … he wouldn't want you to risk it, not if it's too dangerous." I turned back to Dave. "How are you able to do this? I didn't think vampires could be healed by angels."

"They can't. But Alastair died turning Corinth, which means he still has angel blood in his veins. I can mend Corinth's blood. I've never done this before though … I'm not sure how it will affect Alastair, *if* he comes back."

I could feel my pulse thudding to the point where everything else around me sounded muffled. I knew there had to be a catch. "What does that mean?"

"I mean that he may not even come back as a vampire," Dave said evenly. "I can't heal vampires. If this works, the virus in him will be burned away."

"You mean he might come back—" Corinth started to say.

"*Human*," Dave finished for him.

That word was like a punch to the gut. *Human?* That would teach me to think I had no more tears left to shed. I knew Alastair had wanted to be human again. It was what drove him to protect people in the first place, and why he'd joined my father on his crusade. Why he had never lost his touch with humanity after all those years. He was more human than most humans were.

I swiped a hand under my nose, swallowing past a scratchy throat. "I don't care if he's vampire or human, or an ogre for that matter … just so long as you bring him back to me."

I needed to feel his warm breath against my neck, feel the touch of his fingers on my skin, have him talk about all the movies he'd never seen before—so I could watch them all with him. I was already taking myself to places I shouldn't, thinking about restaurants and visits to museums in faraway places. *Second chances.* Things he'd promised me before he'd died. There was just so much we hadn't been able to do.

Hope could be both devastating and wonderful at the same time.

I snuck a quick glance at Corinth, trying to judge

how he was taking this news. His eyebrows were knitted together like puzzle pieces, and his mouth was slightly open.

Dave realized the impact his words had had on me as soon as he saw me start to cry. His smile could light a million candles. It was the stuff of brilliance.

I could hear the sincerity in his voice when he spoke. "What a terrible waste of life, to always take the easy path, to never know what it is to risk everything for what you love." He paused before saying, "You love Alastair. I can feel it and I can see it in your eyes. Both of you do. Love is easy to read—and it's agony to lose. I would never wish that feeling on anyone." His gaze flitted to Benny on the table before drifting back over to me.

"You can do this? I mean, bring him back?" I whispered, hating how vulnerable I sounded to my own ears. I knew he'd already answered this, but I couldn't help but keep asking it. It felt more like a mantra.

Dave placed a surprisingly gentle hand on my shoulder, looking down at me from his seven-foot vantage point. "With Corinth's help, I believe I can."

I took Dave's hand in mine and squeezed it. At first he seemed startled by the contact, but then he gave me a small sad smile. I felt that he wanted to share something else with me, with both of us, but he only gave my shoulder a gentle pat.

"I don't know what to say. This … means … more to me than you could ever know." More tears slid down my face. I didn't bother wiping them away this time. My eyes automatically settled back on Alastair's face, and my heart wrenched painfully in my chest. "If I have a soul, it belongs to him."

Dave's smile widened, and the crinkles at the corners of his eyes softened as he watched me stare at Alastair. "Oh, you have a soul all right—and it is heavy and golden. Healing doesn't mean the damage never existed. It means the damage no longer controls our lives."

Corinth was normally the hugger, not me, but I couldn't help myself. I flew into Dave's arms, only reaching waist height.

It felt right, though, as I turned to Corinth and pulled him over to me too, hauling them both into a hug. "You sure you can do this?"

"I can," Corinth said firmly, drawing my arms from around his waist to study me.

I glanced away from his penetrating gaze, unable to tell him not to go through with this, ignoring how pale he looked, ignoring the dark shadows ringing his eyes. He was dying and I was the selfish one asking him to try and bring Alastair back. I should have considered Corinth's condition more than I did—someone who was still alive. Dave had said there was nothing he could do for Corinth, but surely doing this wouldn't help his condition any. I was going to have a big 'ol' helping of selfishness for breakfast, lunch, and dinner if he could bring Alastair back. I'd do anything to get him back. Anything.

"*Are* you fine, Mr. Taylor? Because you don't look it."

I turned to see who'd spoken, only to find Gabriel standing in the open doorway behind us. His arms were folded across his chest, and he had this superior smirk on his face. I noticed his ebony-colored suit matched his silk tie. Gabriel's ability to ruin a moment annoyed me. It made his eyes look like never-ending tunnels. I wondered if he was trying to make a statement by wearing all black.

"*Will* you be fine?" he echoed, his breath coming out in a hiss. "Do you think this is a good idea? Dave is the only angel who can help you use your powers to their fullest extent, and if he attempts to bring Alastair back, he'll be out of commission. I heard what he said—"

"Get out," I hissed.

Gabriel ignored me. "Dave is Corinth's only chance at protecting his mind, and you are throwing it away. *And* if Alastair is brought back, he'll be human again. No help to us *whatsoever*. Think this through. I implore you—"

"Jealous?" Corinth asked.

He had already unsheathed his blade. I wasn't even sure how he'd moved that fast, so fast I didn't register it until his dagger was at Gabriel's throat—at the very same time, Gabriel's thin blade kissed Corinth's neck.

"Impressive," Gabriel said coolly as he looked down at the blade at his neck. "But seriously, Corinth. Me, jealous of a dead vampire? You *must* be joking." He laughed softly, but there was no joy in it. Just beneath the surface of that laugh, I thought I caught the hint of irritation. Gabriel really did despise Alastair, which only served to make me angrier.

"It sure sounds that way to me." Corinth's eyes grazed over me briefly. "What are you going to do, Gabe? Kill me? Go ahead and try, and see what happens."

"Careful what you wish for, kid," he cooed menacingly. "I'll split you open like a pig on a spit and go on my merry way without a second glance."

"I'm waiting," Corinth growled, his eyes pulsing with blue light. "Get on with it."

Before they could go at it, a white-hot light engulfed us as Dave's hands burst into eerie blue flames. The air crackled and surged with fire and electricity as he roared, "*Enough!*"

I froze, not daring to move a muscle for fear either one of them might slice the other's throat open. It was a frightening sight to see Dave's hands lit up like a bomb about to detonate. It reminded me of witnessing Caesar's power, and I shuddered.

One side of Gabriel's mouth quirked up as he took Dave in. After what seemed like an extremely long time, he cocked his head to the side and said, "Old habits die hard."

Corinth's eyes disappeared in a strobe-like flash. Inside hollowed-out sockets, I could only see a black abyss. A sliver of fear tore through me as I watched another strobe-like beat reveal dark-brown-flecked irises. In another pulse, they vanished, showing inky darkness once again. If lightning had a heartbeat, this is what it would look like.

Goose bumps pebbled my flesh. Dave was right. Corinth was something different. My stomach did a somersault, turning over. Maybe it had the intended effect on Gabriel too, because he immediately retracted the thin blade back into the armor at his wrist and dropped his hand back down by his side.

Corinth followed suit, taking his time in lowering his dagger, I noted. He struggled to pull in deep breaths of air, his hand curled around his stomach, clearly trying to control some huge flood of power coursing through him.

I bolted forward to help guide Corinth back to where Dave still towered over Alastair's prone form on the table.

"Are you okay?" I asked him, worry lacing my voice.

Corinth placed a hand on my shoulder to keep himself upright. His fingers were so cold I could feel them through the thick layer of Alastair's leather jacket.

"I'm fine," he whispered. "But Gabe doesn't get to stay in here. Not for this." He balled his fists by his sides, and they started to spit electrified sparks at his feet. "If you don't leave ... I'll make you leave."

Gabriel closed his eyes and reached up to pinch the bridge of his nose in defeat. "Don't say I didn't warn you." Without another word, he turned around and marched out of the morgue.

"Go ahead, Dave. If that jagweed tries to stop us ..." Corinth let his voice trail off, leaving it open for our interpretation of what would happen if Gabriel did try and stop us.

I glanced to the blade still in Corinth's grip before saying, "Corinth, maybe you shouldn't—"

"Don't even try and talk me out of this, Collins. Al didn't give up on me ... and I'm not giving up on him either. You're not the only one who's upset here. You're not the only one who's lost someone. I lost a brother, and I didn't get a say in the matter. Now I do."

Dave rubbed his hands together as if that settled it. He placed them over Alastair's chest and gradually closed his eyes. After a while, he took in a deep breath and, with eyes still squeezed closed, said, "Corinth, I will need your strength in order to do this. Please, keep hold of your dagger and stay nearby."

Corinth gave a quick nod even though Dave couldn't see him, clenching the blade in his white-knuckled grasp.

I rolled my shoulders back, trying to loosen up some of the tension that had built up. The apprehension was thick in the air. We were both unsure about what was about to happen. I couldn't stand the sight of Alastair so still. It was incredibly difficult to watch.

I thought about all the awful scenarios that could happen if this went wrong. What if Dave brought Alastair back as a mindless zombie? Or maybe he'd have amnesia and wouldn't remember any of us—that one I could live with if it meant he was alive. On the other hand, Alastair might resent all of us for bringing him back. What if he hated me? I could live with that too, I decided.

Then there was the ever-present worry that this wouldn't even work at all. Dave was confident, but if this didn't work, I wasn't sure what I would do. His hands started to glow like lava, and tiny beads of sweat popped up on his forehead. Did angels sweat?

I wondered how long I had been staring at Alastair, because when I heard Corinth speak, I jumped, almost forgetting that he was even beside me.

"Being a vampire … it feels … like I'm out of sync with my own body. I guess *unbalanced* is a good word for it. It's like standing in a pitch-black room, trying to peer into a mirror to see my own reflection. But I know," he said heatedly, "I know, Larna, that when those lights come on, it won't be me staring back at myself in that reflection—it'll be someone else. Someone worse." The hairs on my arms stood on end as he added, "I can feel the presence … there … in the darkness. Watching. Waiting."

I was almost too afraid to take my eyes off Alastair, but the way in which Corinth spoke, so haunted, made me finally tear my attention from him momentarily.

He was staring at the blade in his hands in bafflement. I noticed it was now gleaming the same bluish hue as Dave's hands.

"I'm sorry, Corinth. I didn't even think to ask how you . . . how you're—" I cleared my throat "—handling all of this."

He seemed just as lost as I felt.

"Does it hurt?" I finally asked, hesitating.

He smirked, but I could see the pain hidden behind it. "It's nothing some good old-fashioned dark roast coffee won't cure."

I couldn't help but notice how his hands still shook. Before I could point this out, the lights in the room flickered. I sucked in a stunned breath—

Just like that, Dave disappeared, and a ball of blinding light began to take form in the place he'd just been standing. The light broke apart into a million tiny droplets of golden glitter—radiant. My mouth dropped open when I saw the particles drift down over and onto Alastair's entire body.

After a moment, his skin started to glow from the inside out. The reddish-golden light reminded me of a time I'd played hide-and-seek with my mom. I'd been hiding in a dark closet, with a lit flashlight held against the back of my hand. I'd naively thought it was my own blood shining through my skin.

Even in the harsh fluorescent lighting of the morgue,

Alastair's skin looked the same way—angelic and timeless—as if he had been preserved in amber.

The globe around him and light coming out of his still form intensified to a blinding degree. I threw a hand over my face, spreading my fingers wide so I could continue to watch. When Alastair began to levitate off the table, I let out a tiny gasp. I couldn't bear to blink, even though my eyes filled with water.

In a strangely hypnotic tableau, the thin sheet draped over his body slipped off him and drifted in exaggerated slowness to the floor, reminding me of a rose shedding its last petal. His body looked like soft embers burning in a fire, like he was bathed in sunlight.

A part of me felt that it symbolized transformation. *This is going to work.* My chest heaved up and down in anticipation of him coming back to me.

Except his eyes were still closed. His heart didn't pump blood. No breath left his lips.

Corinth fell to a knee beside the table, both hands clutching his dagger in a death grip, his eyes never leaving Alastair's floating form.

"I can feel a pull on my energy ... Something's ... happening," he wheezed.

The light became brighter, and this time we both had to cover our faces. And just as suddenly as it had started, the show ended.

I expected to see Alastair sitting up, staring back at me with those gorgeous eyes of his, so when my own eyes flew back open to see his slack body resting once again back on the table, my heart plummeted.

One of Alastair's limp arms dangled over the side of

the table, the only sign that he'd actually moved at all. Acid rose in the back of my throat.

There was no trace of Dave anywhere. Or, for that matter, the strangely glowing light that had been emitted from Alastair's body.

I shot a glance at Corinth and caught him gawking down at the blade clasped in his hand. He got back to his feet, gripping the side of the table for support, half closing his eyes from the effort. "*Whoa,*" he breathed.

It didn't work.

Come on, Alastair. Come back to me. I dug my fingernails into my palm. *Bring him back, Dave. Please.*

Corinth was beside me now. I didn't remember seeing him move. We stood shoulder to shoulder, both of us completely shell-shocked. He dropped his blade. It struck the ground with a clang of finality. The color drained out of Corinth's face, and he turned away from me. Seeing that hope leave him hurt more than anything else did about this whole damn situation.

His shoulders shook. Then he was turning around and swiftly wrapping me up in his arms, his hands fisted tightly at my back. He clung to me as if he thought I might drift away from him forever.

Corinth had put all his faith and hope into believing Dave could bring Alastair back. His ragged breath stirred my hair, and his chest rose and fell in time with my own. When I finally realized he was crying, it felt like I was experiencing Alastair's death all over again—

He wasn't coming back.

Chapter 6

Corinth

I STRUGGLED TO DRAW in oxygen, each breath coming in shallower and shallower. "I was so sure … it … was … going to … *work* …" My voice caught as I choked on my own tears and heartache. It was all I could do to stay on my feet, not because I was feeling any worse than I already did but because I couldn't believe Al was really gone. I had been so sure Dave could bring him back. As sure as anything in my entire life. I had felt it happening.

Larna drew back from me, folding her arms across her body as if she were trying to hold herself together. "I can't be in here … it … it hurts too much."

She bolted for the doors, flying through them before I could stop her.

I sank to my knees, screaming at the top of my lungs, in pain and sorrow and torment—

I'd been turned. I was dying. We'd lost Al. What was the point of Al dying only to prolong my life for a little while longer?

Vampire speed was disorienting. I had moved within the span of an eye blink, and a vivid memory of Al's words came crashing back to me as soon as I thought about it: *Two point five seconds*, he had explained, *is all it takes for a vamp to overcome you*. I wasn't even sure how I'd gotten across the room until I'd slammed my blazing fist into the wall, realizing too late that the wall was made of concrete and not plaster.

I heard the crunch long before I felt the pain. I'd annihilated the stone, punching a hole clean through it, crumbling part of the wall to dust and, in the process, shattering what felt like every tiny bone in my hand. A black scorch mark that looked a lot like a jagged bolt of lightning ran up the entire length of the wall.

Concrete and plaster blanketed me in gray powder as I glanced down to my left hand, the one I hadn't broken, to see that I was holding my blade. I had no idea how it'd gotten there. The last thing I remembered was dropping it.

I clutched my injured fist to my stomach, expecting the discomfort to vanish. Instead, a sharp, throbbing pain radiated up my arm all the way to my shoulder and neck.

I watched, in part, feeling disconnected from my body as my knuckles turned purple and swelled. "I can't heal like a vampire either," I muttered, spinning around in a slow circle.

After an excruciatingly long time, my hand stopped aching and the inflammation subsided, replaced by a sudden stabbing sensation right smack behind my eyeballs. This agony went well beyond any migraine I'd ever had before. For a moment, I couldn't figure out why I felt so horrible, until it hit me. These were hunger pains. I mean, the longest I'd ever gone in my human life without eating something was twenty-four hours. I'd been playing *Fortnite* at the time, and afterward I'd eaten two whole boxes of pizza all by myself. But this … this felt like someone had ripped my stomach out, wadded it up like a piece of paper, and then shoved it back down my throat.

I doubled over as Gabriel Stanton's face flashed across my vision. The itch to go running after him was what made me suddenly hate, with every fiber of my being, what he'd turned me into. I hated it more than the blade's influence over me. This feeling stemmed from something born on desire and instinct, and it left me feeling hopeless and desperate and plagued.

Hunt, feed, eat. Kill. I now knew why Gabe had wanted to get his hooks into me for so long. It was all so very clear why he'd turned Larna and then compelled Al. Control was the *only* play in his playbook, and he was extremely good at it. All vampires were. He'd gotten exactly what he'd wanted. And I could also see why the Grigori had chosen vampirism to spread their epidemic. I was just another one of the infected to join their rank, and it was addicting, this feeling of needing to eat. To bond. To stalk. Gabe had used his blood to turn me.

I let out a frustrated sigh, wiping off the trails of salt and tears from my cheeks. Ever so slowly I found myself gravitating toward Al's motionless form.

He looked peaceful, like he could just be taking a nap. I imagined him hopping off the table like a ninja, bare feet and all, to surprise me. "Just kidding!" he'd declare. When I couldn't stand willing Al to wake up any longer, I turned my attention back to Benny. He was resting on a table at the end of the long row of departed. Benny didn't look as peaceful in death as Al did. His eyes had been open before Dave had closed them though. I remembered how he'd looked at me, as if he were silently pleading for my help. He was dead because he'd tried to save my life. My eyes raked over all the other covered bodies, and I shivered.

My fault. My fault. My fault.

No. Screw this.

I would not give up on Al or Dave.

Not now or ever.

I held a flat palm against Al's chest before I even knew what I was doing. His skin was cold, matching the temperature of the room. Distantly I was aware that my injured hand had already mended itself. My bones were no longer broken. My skin was no longer bruised or inflamed.

Up close, Al's skin, however, had a bluish-gray tinge to it. I held my blade a few inches above his chest, almost on instinct, as if someone were directing me to do it. Maybe Dave. Maybe something else entirely.

I closed my eyes, concentrating on the invisible vibrations in the air around me, just like Dave had taught me to do. I focused on how it felt when I willed my blade to appear in my hand. There was still a coppery zing to the air, the telltale sign of an angel having recently used their gift—a mixture of ozone and plastic burning. Dave was gone, but somehow I could still feel his presence nearby. All I had to do was figure out how to channel his energy, along with some of mine, down into Al and repair my blood still inside his system. It made sense to me on a level I didn't quite understand.

The last time I'd tried to siphon energy from

someone, it was from Caesar. I wondered whether I could have used his own powers against him if Sarah hadn't stopped me.

My fingers tingled with the all-too-familiar jolt of supernatural currents coursing through me. Electrical energy swiftly surged up, flooding my body, snaking through my bloodstream, shooting down to the tips of my toes. It was warmth. Life. Strength.

A trickle of sweat slid down my back right as a searing ache flared up in my belly once again. I ignored the pain, pulling at the ripples in the ozone-rich atmosphere, like pulling on a loose thread. I opened my eyes to see a ribbon of cerulean lightning pouring out of my fingertips, spilling onto the sharpened edges of the blade.

I gently laid the dagger on Al's chest. The static arced, sizzled, and flared across his body, and so I drove all that energy down into his core—to his heart—focusing on the sound of my own blood thumping deafeningly in my ears. I imagined my blood was his blood. His heart was my heart. It was beating strongly. I imagined his pulse quickening in tune with my own, imagined my blood thick in his veins. His heart was a muscle. A machine that could be fixed. Restarting it would be like replacing an old battery with a new one.

I felt the connection instantly and threw my head back, weaving the threads of energy through my fingertips, noticing with a vague recollection that it looked like mineral oil in a heated lava lamp.

I set my blade on the tabletop, beside Al's head, and placed one hand on top of the other, lacing my fingers together. His blond hair started to stand on end, and a pungent odor of wet weather after a thunderstorm permeated the room.

I transferred my will, along with everything else I had left in me, to begin performing CPR on him. My hands glowed with each burst of light that sank down into his torso, briefly illuminating an intricate pattern of veins, ligaments, and arteries—making his insides look like the topography of a map.

A sharp stitch knifed its way through my side, but I kept going, pumping his chest up and down, willing his heart to start up once again. There was something cathartic about losing myself in the task. This was all that mattered. Bringing him back.

I can start Al's heart. He will *live.*

"You don't get to die," I mumbled under my breath as I worked, panting from the exertion. I heard one of his ribs crack under the amount of pressure I was putting into pumping his chest. "If you had given me an option, I would have … told you … *not* to bring me back … *not* like this. Not *vampire* … not under Gabe's thumb." Tendrils of electricity sank down into his body and then dissipated. "This isn't fair—you looking all peaceful on this table while I'm over here dying." I slammed a fist against his chest, and I wasn't sure if I had done it because I was mad at him for turning me, or if because I wanted to jump-start his heart like a car battery. Probably both. "You don't get to go … out … like this … not because of … *me*," I gasped angrily.

Too exhausted to stay on my feet any longer, I slumped over the steel table, resting my head against Al's limp hand, trying to catch my breath. My head was a swirling mess, and my heart slammed agonizingly against my rib cage. *Stupid beating heart.* I didn't know how long I'd been at it, but it sure felt like forever. My body was on fire.

That was why, when I felt heat radiating off him, I thought I was only imagining it—a side effect of all the power flooding out of me. Then I felt something. A slight fluttering sensation that felt like the beating of hummingbird wings against the side of his wrist.

Only a figment of my imagination.

I thought I also imagined hearing breath leave his lungs in a rush of air that sounded like an *oof.* I had wanted this to work so badly—

"You're not exactly the person I expected to wake up in the arms of."

The voice was hoarse and weak and blessedly familiar. Hearing it now, in the abnormal stillness of the room, jarred me to my core.

My head snapped up to see blue, sparkling eyes quizzically staring back at me.

"I mean, I like you, Corinth, but not like that."

I staggered back, clutching my chest, shaken. My heart gave a lurch at the sight of him—*alive.* Actually, it almost gave out on me. I folded like a stack of cards, hitting the ground on my rump, hard, my mouth hanging open. I mean, I'd thought it *might* work, but I'd had no idea.

All I could do was stare dumbly up at him as I watched him swing his legs over the side of the table, eyeing his bare feet, wiggling his toes.

Color had flooded back into his cheeks. He looked

like he was glowing with the renewed flush of skin tone, the blue tinge having completely vanished. I didn't think I'd ever seen his eyes that color of blue before—like sapphires.

He is alive! Al is alive!

With a grunt of effort, he sat up and held a hand out toward me—*to help me up*!

I laughed. The dude had just been dead, and now he wanted to lend me a hand. The laughter came only because I had no other way of expelling all of the pent-up emotions inside me. It was either that or cry—and I wasn't crying in front of Al, even if they would be sweet tears of relief.

And then my belly laugh turned into a deep, rattling cough.

He was staring at me with an eyebrow raise of concern, as if I'd really lost my mind this time, but he didn't say anything. Probably he was just as astounded as I was.

As soon as I was able to catch my breath, I said, "How do you feel? You don't suddenly have a craving for brains, do you?"

For a good long while, he only studied his hands, flipping them over and over again, as if he thought they were a separate entity from his body, as if he didn't recognize them at all. His eyes raked over the table and down to the sheet on the ground, and then he slowly took in our surroundings, his troubled gaze sweeping the room full of cadavers.

Finally he whispered, "Oddly enough—*human*." He put a hand to his chest. "It feels like an elephant has been tap-dancing on my lungs. This isn't *possible*. Is it? Where's Larna?" His gaze bounced from covered body to covered body. "She's not under one of those—"

"No," I said quickly, "she's not."

Al had a relieved look on his face until he caught sight of Benny, and his face fell. And then his eyes were darting back down to his bare feet and then slowly to the tabletop he'd just been lying on. Then he caught sight of the ruined wall with the jagged burn marks and giant hole I'd caused in my anger.

"Did you did that?" He looked rattled, his face paling considerably. "How long have I been out? Corinth, why are we … in the morgue? *Was I dead?* Did you get the cure? Did you do this to me? Benny … he was one of Caesar's victims?" He swallowed heavily, his now-lively blue eyes stretching wide.

Despite all the questions, he was handling everything quite well, I thought.

A deep exhaustion worked its way through me, leaving me bone tired. Most of it was relief—relief that he was alive again, and relief that he seemed like himself so far, and that his memories were indeed intact.

I sheathed my blade back at my thigh and collapsed against the empty table behind me, using my elbows for support. "Welcome back to the land of the living, Izzy. Dave, he brought you back. I mean, I might have played a small part." More to myself than to him, I whispered, "Don't tell me you're blown away by coming back from the dead? First you're dead and now you're not. You used to be a vamp and now you're human … I used to be a Nephilim; now I'm a vamp. A lot of strange things happen to us."

I couldn't stop my hands from shaking, but I did do a good job of hiding it. Maybe I'd hit my nine-lives quota after Sarah had stabbed me—forty-five times.

A sharp stitch knifed through my abdomen and then worked its heinous way up into my chest, and the migraine returned full force. I gasped at this sudden onslaught of torment, doubling over.

Al reached out to place a hand on my back. "Something tells me I look better than you do, and that's saying something, especially because I was recently among this lot." He gestured around us. "You're right, we've been witnesses to a lot of strange things since you've possessed that blade … but *this* … *this* is … astounding. Corinth, bringing someone back from the dead is …"

"Miraculous?" I finished for him.

He nodded. "A simple thank-you sounds so terribly inadequate right now."

"It was Dave," I insisted, and I wasn't sure who I was trying to convince more of this fact, myself or him. What he must be going through right now … I could see all of the different emotions flickering across his face as if he were still in disbelief about being alive. Being human.

"Where is he, then?" Al asked, glancing around. "Dave. And why isn't Larna here? Is she okay?"

I pursed my lips, thinking about how to begin. "Dave is … he's gone, as per his usual disappearing act. Every time he comes back, I think I'm going to get some answers from him, and then he vanishes again … uh, *into* your body, I might add. And Larna is devastated, but she'll be much better when she sees you," I breathed. "Good luck with that conversation, by the way."

Al let out a deep breath and patted his chest as if he could physically feel for another presence inside him. "Should I be worried? I don't feel any different, I mean, besides the human part." He glanced around the room. "So … I assume Stanton finished the job of turning you. It worked. Please tell me it killed him in the process."

I ran a hand through my sweaty, wild locks. "Uh, I don't know what I am … and about that, thanks a lot," I added bitterly. "He finished turning me all right—and now he's been hanging around us like an unwanted ghoul. I can't get rid of the guy. We'll need to perform an exorcism stat."

"Let me deal with Gabriel … but, Corinth, are you sure you're okay? You look terrible."

"I'm not the one who's human now," I said, evading his question. "How does it … feel? Does it feel like you're going through puberty all over again?"

One of his eyebrows quirked up as if to say "Where should I begin?" After a brief pause, he said, "I … I don't know how to process this. I just need a minute … or a lifetime. Actually, it's *been* a lifetime since I've been human." He rubbed a thumb across his forehead before saying, "I had pneumonia when I was a kid in Germany. The village healer said I wouldn't make it—the infection had worked its way down into my lungs. I used to be a runt, believe it or not, and I had this wet, rattling cough that wouldn't let up for weeks. I still remember how my body felt: boiling with fever, and I couldn't stop shaking. I felt clammy all over, but I didn't sweat. I felt as fragile as glass. It's akin to how I feel now. I mean, vamps don't really eat anything for nutritional value, besides their healthy dose of iron. We … they … eat only to keep up appearances, to pass themselves off as human, because that's what makes us … uh, *them* feel human. But right now, all I want is a warm, solid meal and a bed. My senses aren't dulled as much as I thought they would be, and I'm pretty sure I'm going to miss having night vision. It just feels … different, and oddly quiet inside my head. The presence—my *Sight*—it's gone." I caught the ache in his voice, as if he missed it. "I've lived with a dark appetite for so long I forgot what it feels like to not have it. It's nice. Simple. Quiet."

I didn't know what I was—a melting pot of good and evil, vampire *and* Nephilim. No longer human, that was for sure. But I did know one thing: I could feel my *Sight* stirring restlessly in my chest, just like he'd described, and I could feel the pain of needing fresh blood, but it was better for me to keep it tamped down and under control. Contained. I wasn't sure how any newly turned vamp got used to this.

I caught him staring at me again with his eyebrows raised. He reached up to touch his hairline. It was important that he not look at me as if I was some kind of superior being.

"You still had my blood in your system after you tried to turn me," I said, trying to explain his awe-filled look away. "Dave figured that he might be able to heal my blood still in your veins, thereby eradicating the vampire virus, or whatever you want to call it, inside you." I shrugged. "He's a riot at parties, but life insurance companies hate him."

Al pushed his shoulders back and straightened to his

full height. Without his shoes on, he was still a few inches shorter than I was.

He put a hand on my shoulder and said, "I need to talk to Larna. Where are my boots?"

Chapter 7

Larna

BEING DOWN IN THAT cold mortuary had sapped me of all my body heat and strength. Seeing Alastair lying on that table had made the hole in my heart stretch wider, gaping open like an exposed nerve. I couldn't stop shaking. I lay hunkered under a pile of covers in his bed, wearing his leather jacket. The impression in the mattress was still there. I could feel his presence in the room, still smell his old-man deodorant lingering from the attached bathroom. I imagined him whistling softly to himself, and I also imagined that radiant smile of his shining back at me.

I knew I didn't have time to lie around—I needed to press Gabriel for answers about getting the cure for Corinth—but it was all I could do to lift my head at the moment. *He is gone for good.* The ache in the pit of my stomach was a constant reminder of how much I'd lost. I'd been so sure Dave could bring him back. That's the problem with hope: before you know it, it twists its ugly hooks inside you like an infection.

The weight of knowing he would never return was soul crushing. I should have told Dave not to try to bring

him back. Dave was gone and he couldn't help Corinth—
and neither could I.

I heard the soft whoosh of the connecting door to
Alastair's room open. No one else had access to it except
Corinth. I assumed he was coming in to check on me. I
didn't have the energy to tell him to leave, and yet I
couldn't seem to make myself move either. My limbs felt
impossibly heavy. I tried to hold back the sting of tears as
the image of Alastair's bare feet flashed across the backs of
my eyelids. *No. I will not go down that rabbit hole again.*

I felt the presence of someone standing at the foot of
the bed. Every single hair on the back of my neck stood
on end. It wasn't Corinth. Corinth smelled like soap and
hair gel and earthy, simple tones. This person smelled like
. . .

Alastair.

I threw the covers back.

He was there, standing at the end of the bed in his
white T-shirt and blue jeans. What he'd been wearing at
the time of his death.

His bright blue eyes blinked back at me, full of light
and life again. Exactly how I remembered them, but
different.

I gasped and then dug my nails into my palms. *Is this
real?* My heart slammed agonizingly in my chest. It was a
hallucination. It had to be. It didn't surprise me. I was
exhausted and a wreck and hungry. I squeezed my eyes
shut. I really had lost it. *You're only imagining him standing
there.*

I opened them again.

He was still there, albeit with a half grin of apology

on his face, and the tips of his cheeks flushing bright red.

He appeared just as flustered as I felt. Real. Really real. I bolted upright. I didn't realize I had backed up until my head hit the accented metal-frame headboard, hard. Stars shot across my vision. The sound of my own breathing was loud and ragged in my own ears. My vision tunneled around the edges as my brain fought to catch up.

"That jacket looks way better on you than it ever did on me," he said in a breathy whisper.

He was alive. This was him. I could see the vein jumping out on his neck, beating out a steady rhythm.

I reached a hand out toward him. I needed to feel him—to know he was real. My voice had left me eons ago though.

He crawled onto the end of the bed, inching closer to my outstretched hand. I had a mental image of the first time he'd carried me back to my room at The Swan after I'd been attacked by a vampire. He had that same look in his eyes now as he had back then. The look that said he needed to be cautious about approaching a wild animal. I licked my dry lips, too stunned to talk. I had been just as scared then as I was now. This was a different kind of scared though. I was afraid he might disappear. This might still be a mirage.

He stopped about a foot away, within an arm's reach really, sitting up on his knees. He could have been across the ocean as far as I was concerned.

Gently he reached up and took my hand in his. The tips of his fingers grazed the inside of my wrist, and I shivered. A jolt of energy ran up my arm and catapulted my heart into my throat. His skin felt molten compared to what it had looked like in the morgue. I could feel the flow of fresh blood pumping through his veins. He waited patiently for me to catch up, a small smile playing on his lips at the same time.

Oxygen had always seemed easy to come by until now.

I breathed his name. "*Alastair ...*"

He pulled my hand up to place it over his now-beating heart. "It's me." His pulse thumped rhythmically against the tips of my fingers. Strong. Steady. *Alive.* My own heartbeat started to match his, speeding up and pumping like a locomotive.

Lightly, he brushed his head against my cheek, along my jawline. Goose bumps pebbled my flesh. I wondered if I looked as shocked as I felt. I blinked.

He wound his fingers through my hair and tilted my head back. My heart lurched at the sight of him. I wanted to soak him in, down to every last damn crease, line, and dimple on his face. I put my hands against his chest, letting the strong, steady beat lull me into a safe place. *He's alive.* The longing and desire always seemed to steal my breath away. But this feeling had intensified. I loved him with all my heart, and I felt more like myself than I had in a long time. It was a nervous, giddy feeling.

And suddenly I couldn't get enough of him.

Alastair curled a hand around the back of my neck, pulling me closer so that our foreheads touched, just like he'd done right before he'd attempted to turn Corinth. Before he'd left me.

"It's really me," he repeated.

It was all I needed to hear.

He was sitting up on his knees, so when I threw myself on top of him, bowling both of us backward in a messy tangle of arms and legs and body heat, he wheezed, "*Ouch* … human now."

I sat up quickly, sucking in a steadying breath. *Human.* The shock of that word was sobering, like ice water injected directly into my veins. "Dave … brought you back … It *worked.*"

Alastair sat up with me and put his hands on my forearms, nodding. "Not just Dave—*Corinth*. He brought me back." He ran a hand along his jaw in thought, and suddenly I could see the worry lines etched into his forehead. "Corinth … he doesn't look good, Larna. The change—it didn't take, did it?"

I bit my lower lip before saying, "No. He is rejecting the turn. But if we can find the cure … he still has a chance." I mirrored Alastair's concern as I said, "That courageous, self-sacrificing *Nephilim* … where is he?"

"He wanted to give us some alone time." Alastair glanced down, his face reddening slightly. It highlighted his features, giving the tips of his cheeks a ruddy glow in the soft light of the room. "He knew we needed it. That I needed *you.*"

There was a desire in his voice that made me swallow against a dry throat. I wasn't used to seeing him blush—not in this way. It showed a vulnerability that I'd never seen in him before. I don't know why I was so nervous around him all of a sudden. It was as if we were meeting for the first time all over again.

He had always been able to throw up an inscrutable mask whenever he needed it. It had been so hard to chip away. Now, though, I knew what he was thinking. His pupils were blown out—as dark as I'd ever seen them, ringed only by a thin circle of indigo. I wondered if this was something that had changed in him because he was human now. So enamored, I reached a hand out to run it gently along his cheek, still not sure he was here with me. He shuddered and closed his eyes. *He is here.*

I planted my palms against my eyes. He had asked Gabriel to hold me while I watched him save Corinth's life and take his own. I was still angry with him for leaving me the way he had. It wasn't exactly an easy thing to shake. I tried to tamp those feelings back down. He was alive and next to me. That was all that mattered. His heart was beating.

After a minute, Alastair tugged my hands away from my face.

He was staring at me with those wide blue eyes. "What are you thinking?"

"I just need a second to take this all in. I …" I halted, thinking about what to tell him. There had been so much that had happened to me this year, but my boyfriend coming back from the dead took the cake. "Can you lie here with me for a while? I just need to listen to your heartbeat—and nothing else."

He smiled that white, dazzling smile of his, and then he hauled me to him without a second thought. I let him guide me back down to the bed, our bodies entwined together. Warm and solid and comfortable. I laid my head against him. He wrapped his arms around me, snug, and drew my hand down across his chest. I could feel the hard line of muscle. All that separated my skin from his was a thin layer of material.

There was something seductive in his movements. My breath caught. The familiar ache of desire ran through me. I loved him fiercely before, but something felt different between us now. Altered. Torn down and then put back together again to reemerge stronger. We'd both been tested by something greater than anything we'd ever experienced before. I felt it in him too. Maybe he was thinking the same thing. He weaved his fingers through my short hair. I felt his chest moving up and down. His heart was beating steadily away beneath my fingertips. A metronome. The body's best musical timekeeper.

With the slightest flick, the tune can change. Or be snuffed out completely.

Finally, when I believed he wasn't going anywhere, I let myself drift toward sleep's embrace, listening to the soft, rhythmical ticking, feeling the gentle flow of his blood pumping through his veins. And for one glorious moment, the thud of my own pulse melded with his, and everything seemed right in the world.

I whispered, "Right now, in this moment, reality is way better than my dreams."

Chapter 8

Corinth

WHEN PEOPLE HEAR ABOUT a miracle, some try to refute it or explain it away—there's a rational explanation for everything. I was guilty of it, and I had faith. Maybe it's the stories about people having near-death experiences—when some people are brought back from the brink of death, they say they've seen God. But have they really?

There has to be an answer for everything, but there's also something special about not having one.

Maybe it just boils down to the unknown. People fear what they don't know.

In Al's case, there was no explaining his coming back. What Dave had done was miraculous and everyone knew it. There had been too many witnesses to Al's death for anyone to contest he'd ever been dead in the first place. It was why the entire clan was abuzz with activity, gossip, and speculation.

When I'd arrived, I was the freak who everyone had gawked at—to be fair, they still looked at me like that— but Al was now the one dealing with the brunt of their attention. It was big news: once a vampire and now a human. The unthinkable had happened. Word had already gotten around about him being human—they could smell it on him. Vampires sought each other's blood for that extra bit of strength, youth, and vitality. Even though human blood wasn't something vampires were normally attracted to, to me, Al smelled different. Not quite human. But I was no ordinary vampire either.

From the look of Al now, he couldn't care less what other people thought about him as he shoveled another bite of cherry pie into his face hole. He had new taste buds to go with his new lease on life.

We had settled for the cafeteria, and clearly, it was a mistake. It was full of people and vampires alike. They were all watching us with open hostility mixed with fear and a whole lot of curiosity.

So far no one had approached us, but it was only a matter of time. They were mad we'd upset the delicate balance of their way of life here. For a second time. War was coming, and the vamps blamed us for it. I made the mistake of making eye contact with an old man across the way. He was sitting alone, mumbling to himself, and the image of Benny's lifeless face left me feeling winded once again. I went cold all over thinking about his death. Innocent blood was on my hands. And speaking of blood, I recalled the uniform drip, drip, drip of my life force pooling underneath the cot as I had bled out. I swallowed past the frog-sized lump in my throat and turned my attention back to Larna and Al. *Shake it off.*

With mouth still full, Al pointed his fork at me and said, "I have never enjoyed pie more in my entire life." He glanced down at his plate in amazement, eyes round. "Has it always tasted like this? Has crust always tasted this good?" He sighed. "This is unbelievable. The sweet tartness of the cherry and the crust together like that tastes like a little slice of heaven."

I laughed and pointed at his stomach. "Yeah, it's sugar and carbs. You might want to slow down, or you won't be able to fit into that fancy leather jacket of yours anymore."

Al shoved another big bite into his mouth. "*Worth it.*"

"I gotta know, Al. Did you see anything while you were … ya know, gone?" I asked. "On the other side?"

Al leaned back, swallowing his last bite, and, I was pretty sure, he considered licking the plate for good measure. He glanced at Larna out of the corner of his eye. "Nothing. I don't remember anything before I woke up on that table in the morgue. If something happened … uh, elsewhere … *beyond* … I don't remember it." He pressed his lips together before saying, "Now, catch me up on what I missed."

Larna cleared her throat. "Corinth—he has maybe a few weeks before his body shuts down completely. We're on the clock to find the cure—or at least for him, like we did for you. That's why we need to discuss our next course of action. Finding Caesar and Sarah—"

"When are we never on the clock?" Al asked, interrupting. His head swiveled in my direction, and he gave me the evil eye.

The sudden onslaught of complete exhaustion hit me. It was all I could do to keep my eyes open. Actually, I must have closed them for a second, because when I forced them back open again, Larna was staring at me with a frown on her face, those hazel eyes of hers staring a hole right through me.

Al, on the other hand, had pushed his empty plate toward the other empty plates he'd already polished off. He put a hand on his stomach and licked his lips in satisfaction. He looked like Winnie-the-Pooh in human form—I mean, if Winnie had abs. I raised an eyebrow and then took a long, slow sip of my coffee. He was right. Things didn't taste the same when you were supposed to only ingest an iron-enriched diet.

I slammed my cup down, and hot liquid sloshed onto my hands. Al and Larna stopped to stare at my sudden outburst.

"*Great*," I growled. "I don't even like the taste of coffee anymore. The one thing I enjoyed drinking most, and it's been taken away from me. Stop looking at me like I'm going to keel over at any second." I glanced between the both of them. "I'm fine."

"You say that a lot," Larna said, clearly not believing a word out of my mouth. "Did you … uh, try to eat yet? Because Gabriel is supposed to supply you with his blo—"

Al held up a hand. "I said I would handle Stanton. I'll make sure he cooperates."

"Oh, because suddenly you're stronger than a vamp now? Especially one like Gabe. I mean, look at you, Al … I could probably breathe on you and you'd wilt."

Al's eyes flashed dangerously and he cracked his knuckles. I could hear a faint popping noise as he hissed, "Don't ever underestimate me, Taylor."

Al may have been human, but he hadn't lost all of his edge. I cocked an eyebrow in acquiescence.

We were all silent for a moment until he said, "Put Kahlúa in your coffee. It helps with cravings, and it'll help with the blandness too."

I flashed him the most arrogant smirk I could muster under the circumstances. "Oh, how the tables have turned, my friend—and thanks for the advice."

Larna leaned across the table, her elbows digging unforgivingly into the Formica. "How do you feel, Alastair?"

Al raised an eyebrow. "Better, now that I've eaten. And not at all fragile, like the way you're both looking at me suggests."

Larna's eyes caught mine briefly. "The Grigori don't know you're still alive, which is to our advantage. If we can find Sarah and Caesar, I can force the cure out of them."

"But how do we find them?" I interjected. "Sarah and Caesar straight up *Harry Potter*-style apparated out of here—"

"I want to get Sarah back for what she did to Corinth and to Larna, I do," Al said, cutting me off. "But we need to stay focused on what we have right in front of us. It's time we pressed Stanton for answers—by *force* if necessary. He knows more than he's saying."

Larna sat up straighter at the mention of Gabriel. "I realize Gabriel has his ulterior motives, but he's already agreed to help us. I should be the one to talk to him—"

"Absolutely not." Al shook his head adamantly. "Larna, I don't think you understand the gravity of the situation here. Gabriel is not our ally. Nor has he ever been."

"You didn't seem to think so before … when you had him hold me against my will while I was made to watch you kill yourself."

Al had opened his mouth to say something, but immediately clamped it shut, his face going white as salt.

When neither of them said anything, I spoke. "Did I miss something? What happened between you two? Not that I want this to happen, but shouldn't y'all be all lovey-dovey with each other right about now?"

"Never mind," Larna said. "What other option do we have? Alastair is human now." She stopped herself short. "I'm sorry, Alastair. I didn't mean to sou—"

Al responded with some not-so-choice words, but his voice became distorted and fuzzy in my ears. My head was buzzing. I shook it, trying to concentrate on what he was saying. His voice came back into focus, as if I'd tuned in to the right frequency once again.

" … have super-strength and speed, I get that. But I've been around for a very long time, and I have a few tricks up my sleeve that don't involve supernatural abilities. Intelligence for one." He stopped long enough to draw in a quick breath, and as if he'd been rehearsing what he was going to say, he said, "I know aikido, karate, judo, jujitsu, krav maga, and tae kwon do. I boxed at Harvard, and I'm an expert at *Kunst des Fechtens*—German swordsmanship—quarterstaff fighting, archery, and I've fired just about every weapon you can imagine." His storm-ridden blue eyes met Larna's and then mine. "We're still a team, right?"

A sudden stabbing sensation went through my abdomen. I planted a palm against my thigh, panting. So focused on the amount of torment I was in, I didn't even realize the table had gone silent until I looked up to see Al and Larna's worried gazes resting on me.

"You're clearly *fine*," Larna said dryly. "Don't you see, Alastair? This is why we need Gabriel's help. He won't help us if we try to force it out of him, and you know it. Only his blood is strong enough to get Corinth through this ... He volunteered—"

"Really?" Al scoffed. "Let me guess ... for a price? I don't think you understand ..."

And they continued to argue about me and the cure and what we should do next, but it was drowned out by the sound of my own blood pumping through my veins. Two words kept echoing in my skull over and over again: *Gabriel* and *blood*. A part of me hated the idea of drinking blood, but the *other* in me knew I needed it—and fast.

After the pain subsided, I held up a finger and growled, "*Stop*." Once I knew I had their attention again, I whispered, "Two things: Why don't you know kung fu, Al? And, German swordsmanship? Really?" I glanced around at the people still in the cafeteria. It was like looking out at a sea of angry faces. They'd drawn an invisible line down the middle of the room and refused to cross it or get near us. "We need every able *body* we can get our hands on ... even if you're not as skilled in some areas as before." I stifled a laugh when I realized Al was probably considering using his boxing skills on me. "Seriously, I saw what the Grigori can do up close and personal." A tremor worked its way down my spine at the thought of facing Angela again. "We're gonna need help. I may never have fought in a war before, but I know when we need to gather an army. Why don't we start to use Sozo's connections, like he's promised? He owes Al at the very least, and I may have a few favors I can call in with John and his gang."

"I have experienced war before. *Multiple.* And that's the first thing we agree on: gathering an army. Al flashed us his wristwatch. "I'll see if I can get in contact with Vinson, since I have the only working watch, and in the meantime, don't give up on me, okay?"

"Speaking of watches …" Larna fished something out of her pocket and then handed whatever she'd pulled out to Al. When I glanced down to see what it was, I noticed it was his antique pocket watch. He curled his fingers around it before tucking it back into his own pocket with a nod of thanks. Something flickered in his eyes, but I couldn't quite get a read on what he might be thinking.

"What? You're not going to tell me to keep it?" Larna asked.

Al dropped his gaze from hers and said in a whisper-soft voice, "The next thing I give you won't be marred by Sarah's touch."

"I agree with you about that part," she said.

I stood up, and both Larna and Al regarded me expectantly as I explained, "I have a meeting with Sozo—this could be my chance to convince him to join our side. I'll catch up with you two later."

Sozo's office was about as ornate as a Catholic church, from the luxurious leather chair to the intricately carved marble desk and gold Greek pillars in all four corners of the room. But the stained glass window right above his desk captured my attention now. It hadn't been there before all the damage was done to his office. I was sure I would have noticed it. Maybe it was a new addition. After all, Caesar and Sarah, and Benny for that matter, had wreaked a lot of havoc here. They had made a lot of repairs in just one short day.

The place reeked of oak and furniture polish and cleaning solvent. The iron doors had been replaced with a set of wooden ones, with a beautifully hand-carved oak tree in the center of them. I wondered where they kept the wood to make these things—maybe they had a wing for carpentry.

And I was in the middle of trying to figure out what I found so off-putting about the stained glass when it finally hit me: We were three hundred feet below ground. There shouldn't have been natural light behind it. A light bulb lit up the glass, making it appear like daylight was shining through. It was what gave the room its soothing ambiance. The glass itself was beautiful. Someone had taken great care in polishing the brass frame to a high shine. I could see my distorted reflection in it, and I noted I looked a little too waxy and sullen for my liking. Then there was the image itself, which was just as intriguing. It was a picture of a sapling with tiny red berries adorning it, glowing like little rubies. Jutting branches with emerald-colored leaves stretched out from the center, toward the edges. On the left side of the tree was a crescent moon, and on the right, a golden setting sun. It was a dazzling piece of artwork.

I hadn't had time to contemplate everything that had

happened to me over the last forty-eight hours. That was why sitting here, all alone in Sozo's office, had me bouncing restlessly in my seat. This was where I'd been almost stabbed to death.

I loathed being alone, because that's when the images of the past liked to creep back into the forefront of my memory. Sarah and Caesar standing over me. Me bleeding out on that tiny cot, and Sarah giving me a superior smirk as she flashed that scalpel in front of my face—

Having supernatural abilities was both a blessing and a curse. I knew I was no longer by myself. Maybe it was the rustle of fabric or the telltale scent of lemon that clung to his skin, but I knew Sozo had been intentionally quiet upon his approach, maybe testing my newfound abilities. Maybe he wanted to study me without me knowing. Vampirism made me hypersensitive to smell, touch, taste, and sound.

I felt eyes boring into the back of my skull, but I didn't turn around. Instead, I stayed staring at the artificially lit stained glass.

"Ironically, that particular piece has never seen the light of day before."

"Seems like such a shame," I said softly.

"I agree." Sozo moved around to his desk, his black robe shimmering just as brightly as I'd imagined a bejeweled crown on his head might. For a second, I wondered if he did have a crown hidden away somewhere. His dark hair was styled in a sweeping mane past his shoulders. The sharp, angular lines on his face reminded me of a horse's face. Not an ugly, overworked horse, a majestic, well-fed one—kingly, like the one from *Tangled.*

I had younger brothers and a sister. I'd seen enough Disney movies to compare him to an animated horse.

"Thank you for waiting. I had some urgent business. I trust you were able to get ample rest."

"I don't know if it was ample or not, but I appreciate your concern all the same."

Sozo inclined his head. "I would keep the pleasantries going all day if I could, but we have much to discuss. You seem to have a knack for upsetting the balance around here. Bringing someone back to life … that was your doing? And if so, you wouldn't be able to bring back any of my people who lost their lives in the attack, would you?"

He blamed me for the loss of his people. I could hear it in his voice. The worst kind of guilt trip. I couldn't argue with him. He should have turned me over … If Sarah and Caesar had killed me first, they would have left all these people alone, never having used them as a distraction to get at me—*maybe*—although I was pretty sure Larna and Al had been targets on their list too.

I stayed silent for a second, deciding on what to tell him. I'd only been able to bring Al back because he'd had my blood still in his veins when he'd died. I couldn't have brought anyone else back—even with Dave's help.

After a while, I said, "If you're insinuating that I can bring people back from the dead, I can't. That wasn't me. It was Dave."

Sozo let what I'd just said hang in the air for a moment before he quirked an eyebrow, steepled his fingers, and leaned across his desk. "Alastair … he's human … Does this mean there is a cure for vampirism?"

"Al *is* human," I confirmed, "but we haven't found a cure." I didn't want to give him the entire truth, because if word got around that Al had had my blood in his system when he'd died, I might become a target for others looking for the same thing—not that it really mattered: I was already a target. I just didn't want to pile on another reason for people to come after me. "You've been nothing but accommodating since we arrived here—up to and including letting me walk around with this." I glanced down at the dagger sheathed at my belt and then reached for it, slowly so as not to spook him. I was sure he had his guards right on the other side of his office doors. "I just can't quite figure out whose side you fall on. Ever since I arrived here, I've felt like something hasn't added up. Why trust me? You've been trying to promote peace this entire time, and I've been creating chaos. Why not try and take the dagger from me as soon as I arrived?" I extracted my blade from the sheath and set it on top of his desk in front of me.

Sozo's eyes narrowed to two tiny slits. A part of me was all predator now, and I could sense his unease immediately. He remained motionless, seemingly confident that I wouldn't harm him with it. If I gave him trust, maybe he'd do the same for me. I wanted to trust him. It wasn't about politics or strategy, it was about common decency, and that was all I had, because I wasn't good at the former.

Eventually, he said, "Dave came to me. He revealed himself to us before you got here—he is an angel. He gave the council, and me, quite the show, as you can imagine. Dave confided in me about the Watchers and told me about the coming war. He asked for us to join his … *side*."

"So you know what I am, then?" I asked carefully.

He paused briefly before saying, "You are a hero."

Of all the things he could have said, I wasn't expecting that. I swallowed hard. "If that were true, twelve people wouldn't be dead." *But I would be*, I thought. "I am no hero."

"You misunderstand me," he said slowly. "True heroes aren't glamorized. That's foolish romanticism. Heroes don't get the reward; they pay the price. Personally, I would hate to be a hero." He paused and then said, "I know you're Nephilim."

"Well, I guess that's not exactly as closely guarded a secret as I'd thought," I muttered. "I'm also vampire— which means we have something else in common now. Your people are my people."

"It would seem that way, wouldn't it?" Sozo leaned back in his chair, his face inscrutable. "I appreciate your honesty. And because of that, I would like to be more open with you. I've had someone on the inside working with Mr. Stanton. She has been an ally of our cause for quite some time. I am not a proponent of violence, but I do need to know what's going on out there … in the real world."

As if on cue, the large wooden doors creaked open behind me. I swiveled around, peering around the high-backed chair to see Imani striding toward us. She was quite the vision, wearing a tight red silk top tucked into slacks that were a shade darker than her shirt.

Imani garnered the sort of reaction from people that I was trying desperately not to supply her with. I was pretty sure men, women, babies, even Buddhist monks, couldn't resist a double take in her general direction … It was the reason why I shoved all my inappropriate thoughts down to what I liked to refer to as Siberia for my brain.

"What is it with you and the color red?" I asked as she stopped beside me, near the chair next to the one I was sitting in.

She regarded me with a cool raise of an eyebrow. "I think we've had this conversation before."

The way she could snap my attention away from everything else going on in my life, even from the fact that I was dying, was hard to grasp, although, on the other hand, I was a guy, so it really wasn't that impossible to fathom.

"Imani, thank you for joining us," Sozo said, interrupting my rampant thoughts.

She sat gracefully in the matching baroque-style chair next to mine and crossed her legs, folding her hands around one knee, looking as composed as ever.

It was at this point that I realized I'd left my dagger sitting unprotected on Sozo's desk. My eyes flew down to it on pure instinct.

Imani, seeing my reaction, let out a soft laugh. I imagined it sounded like a cross between Tinker Bell and the Big Bad Wolf.

We'd been in this situation before, and she'd bested me.

Today was a different story.

I was interested to see who would get to the dagger first, but to my surprise, she didn't go for it. Instead, she clasped her hands together and threw her head back, dark curls bouncing. I got a whiff of her hair. She smelled as lovely as I imagined, like orchids and oranges.

"You really should be more careful where put your things," she told me dryly.

"Imani did try and kill us back at Gabriel's armory." I plucked the dagger back up into my grip, smoothly sheathing it at my side once again. All the while, I could feel the heat of her stare on me.

"So you were the one who told Gabe that we were going to be here." I met Sozo's unwavering gaze. "You told Imani about our arrival, and then she told him."

Sozo inclined his head. "Yes. She was supposed to bring you here after the warehouse incident. Ultimately she convinced me to let you come here—with your weapon in tow—not Alastair. We needed to see what kind of threat *or* ally you might become. I am truly sorry for underestimating you. It was a decision based solely on the fact that the needs of the many far outweighed the needs of the few. I will never make apologies for doing what I think is right for my people."

My gaze drifted over to Imani, and I felt the beginnings of anger stir inside me. "You were going to kill my friends. We barely got out alive—"

"But you did," she said in a measured tone.

"Does Gabe even know you're working for Sozo?" I asked, and I couldn't keep the fury out of my voice.

She gave me an infuriating smile. "He knows. I came clean to him about everything and asked him to come here to help work out a solution—to join clans."

Sozo spread his arms out in front of him. "We assure you that we don't want you dead. Quite the opposite, in fact. We want your allegiance."

"So what did Imani say to make you change your mind about me?"

The usual smirk on Imani's face vanished, replaced by a flicker of something else—fear.

"Imani is a diviner of truth. A spiritualist, if you will, who has been studying the art of extrasensory perception in order to interpret certain celestial patterns—to uncover future events."

"So, like, you read the stars or something?" I asked. "You're a fortune-teller?"

"Fortune-telling is gimmick and nonsense. My method uses science, math, astronomy, and astronavigation. It takes centuries to grasp."

I held up a hand. "Seriously, you can predict the future? Because there has to be a lottery—"

"No one can predict the future," she hissed between her teeth, shaking her head. "It's an ever-changing, evolving beast—an entity without a body. To have a body would mean it would be whole. But the future will never be whole or complete, because it hasn't happened yet. It does, however, have substance, which makes it possible for me to garner bits and pieces of information in order to predict certain outcomes."

"That sounds just a little far-fetched …" Still, my breathing sped up all the same. Could Imani hold the answer to the many questions I had? Maybe she knew about my Nephilim lineage or about the cure. Maybe we wouldn't need Gabriel or Dave or Angela to get it. Even though I didn't believe the future could be foreseen, I still felt my pulse quicken at the prospect. "Prove it."

"I gain my forecasts in stages—only after researching history and time. Back in Gabriel's warehouse though, I saw something in your eyes … when you were holding the blade. A flash of future events, perhaps. You had cuts on your face and neck." Imani's gaze flew to my hands. She licked her lips before continuing. "It felt so real … and you were at the heart of it all, consumed by fire and lightning and chaos. It was like nothing I'd ever seen before. The weather was torrential. Trees surrounded you on all sides. You were looking at something I couldn't see—but your eyes …" She faltered, and it was the first time I'd seen her truly look concerned for me. "They were dreadful, hollowed out, and flashing with a strange light. It was terrifying."

The trepidation in her voice made goose bumps rise all over my skin. I tried to keep my face a blank mask, but inside, my heart was thrashing away, threatening to evacuate the premises. I started to feel light-headed. I'd had the same vision or dream or nightmare, except I couldn't admit that what I'd actually been standing on wasn't a hill—it was a mountain of devastation, of bones and ash and death. Desolation stretching on for miles and miles around me, and I'd liked it. A tiny voice at the back of my head admitted, *You should have killed me when you had the chance.*

"Do you have a date, or location, or anything else to go on? Otherwise, seeing a vision of me with bloodied hands and face doesn't do me a lot of good. That's par for the course, actually."

"Imani has received no other visions nor gleaned any other information," Sozo interjected.

Imani, who was always confident, refused to meet my gaze, only staring miserably at her fingers twisted together in her lap. "I thought that if I took the blade from you, I might be able to change it—the future. You will be at the center of a great battle, and I was only thinking about preventing that from happening. It looked like the end of the world," she whispered.

I reached a hand out toward her, putting on a fake grin. "Maybe some skin-on-skin contact will help you pick up more information about me. Maybe it will give you another vision. Prophecy sounds cool."

Her eyes met mine, and they were full of fire and spirit. "You think this is a joke?"

"I'm not one to say what can or can't happen, especially with some of the things I've already witnessed. Something tells me most of it will never be explained, but I have to deal in facts here. I won't waste my time on anything else. Visions, predictions ... whatever you want to call them, none of it is going to help unless you're able to tell me when, where, or how—but what *will* help is volunteers." I turned to Sozo, beseeching. "If what she says is true, and this turns into an all-out war, I'm going to need help. I have to find Sarah and Caesar, but we can't do it without you. Sozo, you said you wanted my allegiance. This is how you get it. Lend me your people, and I'll stay here—for as long as you need me to. After this is all over, of course."

Sozo splayed his hands out on the desk and stood, regally tall, his back straight. "I do want your allegiance. But my plan was to prevent a war, not start one. Can I assume you still seek a cure for vampirism?"

"Yes," I said. "I am seeking a cure."

"Then, no. Our way of life has been threatened. To seek out the cure will surely bring war down upon all of our kind. We have had eons of peace. We are happy with how we live. The cure would change everything. We are not willing to go back to being human—even if it can be administered, like a vaccine. That being said, I will not stop you from searching for it." It wasn't a threat, but it sounded like one to me. He held up a finger of caution. "We cannot offer any more assistance to your cause. If Imani chooses to go, I will not stand in her way."

I stood too, and as soon as I did, little pockets of light exploded across my vision, and for a second, everything went black. I grabbed awkwardly at the chair, only just managing to right myself before I hit the ground.

"Are you alright?" Imani asked from beside me. She had gotten to her feet in a flash of movement.

"I'm fine," I said, a little too breathlessly for my liking. Imani and Sozo shared a brief glance at the same time as I said, "So, are you with me, Imani?"

Imani whispered, "I'm regretting this decision already, but yes, I am with you."

Chapter 9

Vinson

VINSON ALWAYS THOUGHT THE caterpillar was much more attractive than the butterfly. In his opinion, beauty was measured in how something survived. Some species of caterpillar invade ant nests, using acoustic mimicry to confuse them, continuously emitting noises similar to those of the queen ant in order to gain protection and food. Caterpillars become so convincing at pretending they're ants that the true ants start believing the caterpillars are superior members of the nest. So superior, in fact, that these ants would kill their own larvae to feed or rescue the butterfly larva in the face of danger. To blend in with a kind other than its own, only to have them take up arms for you … well, *that*, he thought, was true beauty.

It was why Vinson had been somewhat impressed with the kid—that is, up until the two urchins covered in his blood appeared out of thin air. Vinson was not an optimist. He assumed Corinth Taylor was dead. Vinson should have known someone was going to be killed, because he hadn't been around to prevent it.

He wasn't one for back-up, and he certainly didn't

ask for help, but he was no fool either, especially when it came to dealing with beings who possessed strange abilities—the same kinds of abilities that the kid possessed.

Vinson knew evil when he saw it—or in this case, *smelled* it.

The metallic scent still hung in the air. Whatever that being was, he could make himself and another disappear at the drop of a hat. It was unnatural. Vinson felt it was high time to press the locator button on his watch. Not for his own sake—he could take care of himself—but he had a sneaking suspicion Alastair would be only too happy to help put these two creatures out of their misery. Who was he to deny someone else a bit of fun?

Vinson had set up camp about a kilometer from the entrance to the underground clan for a few days. He had been prepared to stay for as long as it took Alastair or Larna to reach out to him, but when the vampire and the demon had appeared in a clap of thunder and lightning, his gut had told him he had to follow them instead.

It had been six hours since Vinson had started trailing them. They were over twenty kilometers from the outskirts of the forest, and the further they moved away from the clan, the more Vinson was convinced that these two would disappear again. He had come to the quick realization that he'd have to make his move before they reached civilization.

Finally … what he'd been waiting for. Action.

Situated right above his two targets, Vinson tried to ignore the gnarled bark digging into his shin as he stretched out across a wide tree branch.

Through the scope on his rifle, he tracked the female vamp's every move. Rust-red blood stained the entire lower half of her blue scrubs and her white sneakers. She looked like someone in the medical field. He wondered idly how she had come to be missing three fingers on her left hand.

The evil-looking, beady-eyed weasel with thinning black hair was wearing what used to be a white toga. His robe was also stained with dried blood—Corinth's blood. Aside from that, he looked like any other ordinary man. Average build, but on the skinny side. Average-colored dark hair, somewhere between black and brown. Average height. Vinson knew better than to let that lull him into being careless.

The sorcerer turned in a slow circle, surveying his surroundings, his nose and forehead wrinkling. These two had been waiting in this spot for a couple of hours now. Something about their stopping here put Vinson on edge—to the point where his skin was crawling.

That had only happened once before … back when he'd first witnessed the kid's soulless eyes alter into all-consuming lightning.

He eased back on the trigger of his rifle and was about to open fire when the man's eyes ticked upward, zeroing in on Vinson.

Vinson sucked in a quick breath. Held it. The demon's eyes were almost worse than the kid's. There was only darkness swelling and churning in his sockets. No eyeballs. In fact, they were so dark and fathomless they threatened to pull him right out of the tree he was perched in. His weapon was an extension of his own arm. Vinson was more than skilled with a rifle. He'd trained with every variety of weapon out there, and he could build any firearm from scratch. In another lifetime, he'd been a gunsmith, swordsmith, woodturner, silversmith, and blacksmith. The scent of oil, wood, and steel had always reminded him of home—when he'd had one, that is. Vinson was used to people being scared of him, not the other way around. He didn't get scared. But something about this creature's eyes, the way they flickered with unholy light, made him take a second too long to react—

He fired, knowing his aim would be true. But instead, Vinson was caught completely off guard when a shimmering ball of light flared up around the demon. His bullet ricocheted off the gleaming surface in a shower of sparks and noise.

He watched, half-annoyed and half-impressed, as the light flickered and then quickly faded out of existence once again. The creature's hands exploded in the same tinge of cobalt energy as the shield, right as he took aim at Vinson, letting loose his ultimate power.

One second, Vinson was in the treetop, and the next, he found himself in a painful heap at its base, branches and leaves and dirt burying half his body in the hard-packed earth.

He shook his head, trying to clear the fuzziness gathering at the edges of his vision as the two figures moved toward him, looking like two dark blots against the green-forested backdrop.

As soon as the man, doubling as a beast, was close enough, Vinson saw two charcoal-colored wings unfurl out of his back. His eyes stretched wide at the sight.

Demon. The wings flickered the most dazzling shade of bronze, reminding him of the hottest embers in a long-burning fire.

The beast spoke. "You think we didn't know you were following us, vampire?"

Vinson was not religious. It had been well over a hundred years since he'd been turned, and in all that time since, he had not given an iota of thought to devotion. Back in his mortal days, he had been a pious Catholic. So when he came up to one knee and found himself in the position of genuflection, on instinct he used two fingers to make the sign of the cross.

He knew a gun would do little to no damage to this demon—one of the reasons he was now glad he carried various other forms of weapons on his person. Some of his weapons included throwing spikes—deadly steel with sharp points at each end. He never liked throwing away a good weapon, but he'd make an exception for this beast. Several exceptions.

When the two of them got within twenty feet he reacted, reaching inside his vest to tug two thin blades free. With a quick flick of his wrist, the thin metal was tearing through the air in a blur right for them both. The projectiles kept going, past their supernatural defenses, one sinking deeply into the winged devil's heart, while the other tore straight through the female's right shoulder, leaving a gaping hole in its wake.

The demon let out a strangled cry that was cut short, and he collapsed.

Vinson jumped to his feet at the same time as the vampire let out a ragged gasp. He was on top of her in less than a second, and they went to the ground in a pile of jutting limbs, rough hands, and pounding fists. He heard something crack, and he wasn't sure if it was his bone snapping or hers—he couldn't feel pain in this moment. He relished the look of surprise on her face though, distinctly aware that the demon was already getting to his feet once again.

Up close and personal, the vivid green of this vampire's eyes swirled together, mixing perfectly with the slate blue of her *Sight*. Vinson didn't trust pretty things. He also didn't like that sadistic grin on her face. It mirrored one of his own, making her look that much more savage. He slammed his fist into her eye, and she rolled to her right, letting out a grunt of pain, scuttling sideways like a crab.

She was a lot stronger than he had expected—and wilder. She threw herself back to her feet in a fraction of the time it took him. As she came at him, Vinson struck out, kicking her square in the chest. The vamp flew backward, flailing arms and legs as she hit a tree behind her, buckling.

Vinson yanked another spike from his vest and let it fly right as she started to get back to her feet again. The spike lodged itself in her rib cage with a satisfying thunk. She opened her mouth, but nothing came out as she scrabbled at the sharp object sticking out of her side.

The hairs on the back of Vinson's neck stood on end and he whirled around, coming face-to-face with blazing hands—hands so bright they burned an image across his retinas, brighter than a flash of lightning.

The demon's eyes matched the blinding white-hot

energy coming out of his hands. A twist of fear wormed its way through Vinson's gut right as a surge of supercharged fire licked at the air and slammed into him—

Vinson's whole body seized up. He couldn't move. He couldn't breathe. His insides felt like burning sludge. He couldn't remember a time when he'd been in worse pain. Still, it was pain. It told him he was alive. Of course, maybe not for long, what with his heart thundering brokenly in his chest. It sped up, and then slowed down, banging agonizingly away before finally grinding to a sudden halt.

He was on the ground with no memory of how he'd gotten there. Sweat slicked his forehead and drenched the back of his vest. His vision faded and folded in around him, and darkness crept in around the edges.

The demon was kneeling over him, leaning in so close Vinson felt his breath hot against his ear. "When will you vampires learn not to go up against an angel?"

Vinson came crashing back to reality through a haze of obscurity and agony and blinding rage. He found himself in a sitting position, propped against a tree, with a rope wound excruciatingly tight around his middle. His legs stretched out in front him, with even more rope wound around his ankles, and the cord was wrapped so taut that it was restricting his breathing. There was a hair's breadth of give in the twine encircling his wrists.

He shook his head, trying to shake off the fog of pain. The vampire and angel—*demon*—were both staring at him as if he were a curious specimen under a microscope. By the way his chest felt, he had had a heart attack.

The demon had somehow stopped his heart just by touching him.

Vinson had to admit, he was surprised he was still alive. They needed him for something. Information, he guessed.

When the vampire saw him wake, the cruel smile on her face grew wider. Her mop of dark hair was curly and disheveled, piled high on top of her head with a single hair tie. There were stray, wispy locks that framed her thin, angular face, making her look feral and wild. With that spray of freckles across the bridge of her nose, she appeared younger to Vinson, seventeen maybe, except he knew there was something horribly deceptive about that assessment. This was an older vampire; he was sure of it.

The demon was a few feet in front of him, crouched down, lazily drawing in the dirt at his feet with one of Vinson's own throwing spikes.

The demon looked positively bored, but he perked up as soon as he heard the female say, "He's awake, Caesar."

Caesar. He would remember that name.

Caesar stood to his feet, slowly wiping his hands off on his stained robe, with Vinson's blade still clutched in his bloodstained fingers.

His eyes focused intently on Vinson, sizing him up, he noted. "I was going to kill you—that is, until I saw this on your wrist." He reached into a hidden pouch on his robe and pulled out Vinson's watch. Frozen on the lit-up display screen was one word: ALASTAIR. Caesar's gaze slid to the vampire's and froze. "I tried to look up the information on it—Alastair's GPS coordinates, address, phone number … but when I laid my hands upon you, it must have broken right along with your heart." He shrugged. "You wouldn't want to share any of that information with me, would you?"

Vinson didn't move or speak.

"I know someone who really wants to see Alastair Iszler again," Caesar continued. "Sarah"—he pointed at the vampire beside him—"wants to greet him again—for old times' sake. They go way back, you see."

The female, Sarah, inched closer, cleaning under her nails on her one good hand with his throwing spike. "Did *he* send you after us?"

Vinson spit on the ground at her feet.

He heard bone snapping long before he felt the pain. Vinson glanced down in ludicrous slowness to see the spike embedded into his sternum, between his first rib and clavicle on the left side of his chest—close enough to his heart to be worrisome. Sarah had thrown the spike in a blur of movement, and he hadn't even seen it happen.

Vinson's lip curled in pain and infuriation as blood oozed out in a slow leak from the wound.

"He's not going to talk." She sounded annoyed, petulant even, as she turned to Caesar and then whirled back around to face Vinson once again. "I'm assuming, *vampire*, that if you know Alastair Iszler, then you know Corinth Taylor too." She waited for Vinson to react. When he didn't, she sighed in exasperation. "I guess we're just going to have to kill you—just like I killed Corinth … I bet he was your friend." She licked her lips. "I *hope* he was your friend. You should know, he died an agonizing death by my hands."

A slow heat crept up Vinson's spine at the realization that he'd been right about the kid being dead. He was going to wipe that smirk off both their faces. For the first time in a long time, he felt something akin to guilt. If he had gone with them down into that dank dungeon, the kid would still be alive—he was sure of it. Vinson lived with anger every day. Guilt was something else. He didn't live with guilt.

Caesar moved leisurely toward Vinson, stopping just shy of his legs, and bent down beside him, his hands lighting up with that ball of deathly energy. Vinson's eyes ticked to those blazing hands as Caesar placed a flat palm against his chest—

"Get away from him. *Now.*"

A clear, hard voice broke the silence, so loud it startled a few blackbirds from their roosts in the same tree he was tied to.

Vinson's eyes snapped up as soon as he heard that voice.

A lone figure stood on the crest of a hill, about twenty yards ahead of them, backlit by the last rays of the setting sun. Just the person these two morons were looking for: Alastair Iszler.

And Alastair looked imposing, holding a short sword in a two-handed grip by his side, a look of complete abhorrence twisting his features as he stared down at Sarah and then Caesar.

Everything went deathly still, chillingly so.

Even the birds and insects could sense the warning

signs of danger before it happened. Vinson's attackers seemed just as stunned by Alastair's presence as Vinson was to see him standing there atop the hill, gazing down upon them with a look on his face that said he needed to settle some scores.

His eyes darted back to Caesar, who was still bent over him. Without losing another moment, Vinson extracted the spike from his chest—along with it came a fountain of blood. In one smooth motion, he cut through the cords wrapped around his torso. His hands and ankles, still securely bound, did nothing for his aim as Vinson launched the blade at Sarah, giving himself a fraction of a second to partially free himself, the spike sinking into the side of her neck at the same time.

Sarah let out a startled shriek in protest, and Caesar spun on his heels, his hands still ablaze, forgetting about Vinson altogether.

Apparently, he only had eyes for Alastair.

A hunger and violent thirst for blood and vengeance coursed through Vinson as he unleashed his *Sight*. His eyes caught fire, igniting into something deadlier, uncontrollable.

This monster had killed Corinth. They were both going to pay.

In the background, Vinson barely made out Alastair's war cry as he bounded down the hill toward them to meet the battle head-on.

About time.

Chapter 10

Vinson

VINSON WAS JUST SITTING up and letting loose another throwing spike when Sarah whipped her head back around at hearing the sharp cracking sound it made as it hurtled straight toward her face.

He had barely finished untying his wrists when she caught the flying projectile and, with alarming quickness, threw it back at him. Vinson noted that for her having just been grievously wounded and having only one good hand, she did this quite efficiently. And he tried his best to throw himself out of the path of the blade, but the rope, still fastened around his feet, prevented him from getting out of the way in time.

The weapon slammed into his side, and what little air there had been in his lungs vacated the premises. He rolled onto his back, too stunned to move. There was no blood this time, only the sound of it rushing in his ears as his brain tried to play catch-up. Vinson still felt the remnant healing of the previous injury in his chest. His heart felt bruised, even.

Sarah had doubled over and was trying to dig the spike out of her neck. At least he had bought himself a few more precious seconds.

Dimly he recalled his fight with Sherry, the vampire who had tried to kill the kid's sister. He had jumped in front of the knife, sacrificing himself in order to stop it from reaching its intended target—the little girl, the kid's sister. He remembered all the lives he'd saved over the course of his lifetime. He'd kept count. It was never enough. None of those lives ever added up to the one life he'd taken: his wife's.

That feeling had almost killed him—this felt the same way.

He reached a hand to his injured side, his fingers slick and swollen as he fumbled with the spike.

Somewhere off in the distance, as if underwater, he could hear each heavy clang of Alastair's sword as it struck Caesar's shield. A vague tolling eerily drifting on the air. Or maybe that sound was coming from his own head.

With great effort, he sat up, ripped through the remaining rope around his feet as a dribble of blood worked its way out of his mouth. He found he didn't have the strength to remove the weapon in his side just yet.

All the while, Alastair was still fighting.

A ghostly blue sphere burst to life, and then rapidly disappeared as Alastair struck out at Caesar again. Each blow seemed precise and deadly. Why the demon's shield only worked on some occasions and not on others, he had no idea.

Alastair collided with the strange glowing light with such force that it sent him rocketing backward through the air toward Vinson.

He landed in a dazed heap at Vinson's feet, his eyes

half-closed and sword gone. Alastair mumbled something unintelligible, his eyes moving rapidly under closed lids, and for an excruciatingly long time, Vinson didn't think Alastair would get back up again.

The wind died down so abruptly that the leaves on the surrounding trees quivered long after everything had fallen silent around them.

Then, as quick as a snake strike, Alastair bolted into a sitting position, yanked the buried blade in Vinson's side free, and hurled it at Caesar—who had been slowly stalking toward them once again.

Vinson gave a grunt of approval mixed with pain as the blur of metal spun toward the angel's face, glinting bright in the sunlight. He stared with gaping mouth as the thin, steel-tipped blade slowed its high-speed pursuit of the angel and then—just stopped.

The spike hovered in the air, vibrating violently an inch away from the angel's face. *Magic. Sorcerer.*

The once-sunny sky changed from a deepening purple to a dull avocado, backlit by surges of blue-white lightning. It flickered and stretched out across the clouds in an ethereal display, and as if that weren't portentous enough, the demon's eyes started to glow scarlet, like laser pointers.

Vinson normally prided himself on his stony indifference, but he couldn't help but share a quick glance with Alastair, who was still beside him. There was a ribbon of blood running down Alastair's chin. Vinson's eyes raked over the shallow cut. A cut that should have healed by now.

He sniffed at the air. *Human. Not human.*

Having recovered, Sarah had already moved to crouch over Alastair's prone form before he could react, holding a razor-sharp scalpel at the hollow space at his throat. Alastair froze, his chin raised and eyes defiant and hard as he met her frosty stare.

"I have to admit, Alastair—" Sarah bared her teeth, running her tongue along the two sharp points "—I didn't expect to see you quite so soon. It is so lovely to see you again. You smell—enticing."

He knew that look well. This was what she had been waiting for, Vinson thought distantly. Revenge. Drain him dry.

"Where's your girlfriend? Larna must be in agony over losing her best friend. Poor Corinth." She chuckled. "He was such a funny, quick-witted thing. Seems like such a shame … his death. But my message had to be clear. I could have killed him quickly, of course, but because of what you did to Wrentmore, I made sure to kill him slowly. I made sure he suffered. *Because of you.* Larna's next—"

A low-throated growl came out of Alastair, and he jerked forward on instinct, his eyes like twin daggers pointed at Sarah, but she pressed the knife harder against his throat, the point digging unforgivingly into his flesh.

Vinson *hated* the fact that his body would not heal fast enough. He wanted nothing more than to butcher these two dogs as ruthlessly and efficiently as possible. By whatever means necessary. His breath was ragged, and his chest shook painfully when he tried to take in air. Feelings were weakness. They served only to get in the way of what had to be done. Cold detachment had always been the way to go … He had never liked working with anyone, *but* she'd murdered the kid. This made Vinson angry.

He waited for another debilitating stab of pain to work its way through his body, and by the time it subsided, something else flared up inside him—something hideous and dangerous.

Vinson heard Alastair suck in a sharp breath, but then he was laughing. Even the knife at his neck didn't seem to bother him, which Vinson thought was pretty bold.

"I never did tell you how Wrentmore died, did I, Sarah?" he growled.

The scalpel bobbed in Sarah's hand as she scraped the blade against his jugular. "*You—how dare you!*" She palmed the knife and gripped Alastair's shoulders, yanking him closer—and was about to rip into his throat with her teeth—

"Sarah, *don't.*" It was Caesar, behind her, his hands still raised, but the fire had gone out of them and also his eyes. He knelt down beside her, placing a firm hand on her arm, and then he pushed her out of the way.

Caesar touched an index finger to Alastair's forehead. Almost immediately, Alastair slumped sideways and his eyelids fluttered closed, a soft moan escaping his parted lips.

Vinson knew that whatever the angel was doing to him wasn't a pleasant experience.

After a full two or three minutes had passed, the angel's eyes flew wide, and he staggered back to his feet, shocked, his face a shade paler than it had been before he'd touched Alastair.

Caesar turned back to Sarah, his eyes round.

"Corinth—he's still alive. Alastair is *human*. This one—he turned Corinth into an abomination, a vampire, and now this changes everything. I must tell Angela." He gestured at Alastair. "We have to go, but we'll take this one with us. He's valuable."

Sarah's cold eyes drifted back up to the angel. Vinson could see her thinking through her options as they zipped back and forth. "It … it can't be … How is that possible? He's human? Does this mean they have a cure?"

"You're not going anywhere," Alastair snarled. "Not after what you did, Sarah."

Alastair slapped at Sarah's hand, the one still holding the scalpel to his throat. The blade drew a long thin red line across his neck, but fortunately for Alastair, Sarah hadn't been expecting it, because her weapon didn't do any more serious damage to him as it went flying in the opposite direction.

Alastair was on his feet before she could react.

Vinson went after Caesar, but the demon called forth some whirlwind like portal and disappeared inside it in a clap of thunder and lightning, disorienting Vinson to the point where he listed to the side, as if he was standing on the deck of a ship on rocky seas.

He took a faltering step toward Alastair, but he stuck his hand out, stopping Vinson. "*She's mine.*"

Sarah wiped a hand across her bloodied mouth. "Come and get me then, lover."

They went at each other at the same time, but Sarah possessed the swiftness of a vampire, and when she lunged forward, she struck out at Alastair's extended arm. There was a sharp snap followed by Alastair's bark of pain.

Vinson had to give credit where credit was due: the pain only seemed to fuel Alastair on as he sprang at Sarah, all spinning arms and legs. Each of his attacks rolled seamlessly into the next as, little by little, he forced her back. So furious was Alastair's onslaught, Vinson found he, too, had to take a step back from them both.

Sarah stumbled off-balance and Alastair landed a solid kick to her sternum. He spun around, thrust an elbow up into her face, and then, in quick succession, ejected the hidden blade housed inside the vambrace at his wrist. She lifted her left hand, barely stopping the blade from hacking off her neck. Alastair's fighting skills almost made Sarah his equal. Predicting her next move was far more advantageous than speed.

She had a panicked look on her face as Alastair ducked under one of her wide swings. Seeing an opening, he dove for her and they went down in a tangle of arms and legs.

Vinson could hear the thundering of Alastair's beating heart all the way across the clearing.

Alastair was on top of her, plunging the blade down to carve out her heart. Before he could though, she took hold of his weapon hand in a two-handed grip and ripped the armor off, breaking the blade in the process. Sarah tried to turn the mangled weapon back on him, but Alastair saw it coming at the last second and knocked it out of her hands. It went skidding in the opposite direction, out of their reach.

Watching Alastair fight reminded Vinson of the first lesson he'd learned while in the Imperial Russian Army: attack the arm that attacks you.

Alastair grabbed Sarah's outstretched arm, flipped her onto her belly with animalistic strength, and then wrenched her shoulder back agonizingly, fire sparking to life in his eyes—not vampire *Sight* but something else.

He meant to kill her. Whatever she'd done to him and Corinth and Larna, Alastair had taken it personally.

Good, Vinson thought. *Finish the job.*

It made him wonder where Larna was right now. He knew she would have been here with him had she known where Alastair was … Had something else happened down in that cursed clan?

Suddenly there came a charged energy to the air— just enough warning for Vinson to fling himself to the side right as Caesar reappeared out of a blinding white light, shooting something out of his hands.

The blast hit Vinson like a thunderbolt to his chest. He flew through the air as if he weighed no more than a Russian nesting doll, smashing into the ground and rolling and rolling and rolling, across dirt and rock, little jagged pieces embedding themselves painfully under his skin. He would have kept going too, had a giant boulder not stopped his progress, causing his head to smack against its surface and black spots to shoot across his vision.

In that moment, he realized one thing: he hated angels more than he did vampires.

When his eyesight finally cleared, Vinson found Alastair standing over him, a grimace marring his features, and a hand to the side of his neck. Blood and dirt had worked their way into every crevice on Alastair's face and neck. The open cut on Alastair's head immediately drew

Vinson's eye to it.

Alastair reached a hand out to help Vinson to his feet, wincing at the same time. "They're gone."

Vinson glanced at Alastair's outstretched hand and then slowly made his way to his feet on his own, grunting from the effort.

"You're human," Vinson growled, "and kid is vampire." He shook his head and spit something in Russian, then added, "You got here quick."

"I was already out here looking for you when I saw this." He raised his arm, pulling the sleeve of his jacket up to show Vinson his watch. On it blinked the word VINSON, and then a second later it flashed his coordinates. "I didn't have time to go back for reinforcements. How did you come across Sarah and Caesar?"

"I saw them appear out of some magic fog. I smelled kid's blood and knew something bad had happened. Kid … he is alive?" He squinted down at the leaves carpeting the forest floor at his feet.

Alastair swiped a hand down his face, suddenly looking exhausted. "The kid *is* alive." He stopped abruptly, his face turning the color of cold ash in a fireplace. "Caesar, he saw my memories. Now *they* know he's alive—we have to get back to warn him."

Chapter 11

Larna

GABRIEL KNEW I WAS standing behind him, but he didn't make a move to turn around. I'd never seen him in anything other than a suit, so when I found him wearing workout gear, doing a handstand with his legs crossed, I was taken aback. *Gabriel does yoga?*

We were in a secluded part of B wing, a classroom abandoned long ago, probably because it was so outdated—old wooden desks and dusty black-boards were the only things that hadn't been stripped away.

I was pretty sure I could scream bloody murder in here and no one would hear it. I tried not to think about why he wanted to meet in such a secluded area. If Alastair knew I was here with him by myself, he would not be happy.

There was definitely something seductive about the way he stretched too. It reminded me of when he'd ripped his shirt off to show me his scar, or the first time we'd met, in the elevator at The Swan. I was certain he put me in these positions to catch me off guard. He was exceedingly handsome. Too bad he didn't have the personality to match. People are only as good-looking as their soul—and his was dark and ugly.

Even so, when he twisted around on the mat, I couldn't help but notice his shirt rising up to expose a flash of bronze skin and flat stomach.

His eyes popped open to meet mine—all black irises and pupils.

I sucked in a sharp breath at the way he was looking at me, as if he was infatuated with a shiny new toy. I certainly wasn't built like a model. I was five foot four and curvy—fat turned to muscle—and I was probably the only one who'd ever bested him or turned him down in his entire life. I wondered if this was what made him so enthralled by me.

Gabriel jumped to his feet, as lithe as a cat as he gestured at me. "By the way you look, can I assume Lover Boy is back?"

"Don't ever call him that again," I snarled. "And what do you mean, by the way I look?"

Gabriel grabbed a towel and sauntered toward me, wiping sweat off the back of his neck and forehead. "The pocket watch he gave you—the one you were clutching earlier—isn't ticking anymore, which means you either gave it back to him or you broke it. And you're not wearing his jacket anymore." He shrugged, and his steely, dark-as-night eyes seemed to swallow me whole as he added, "That, and … the light is back in your eyes."

Pretending to notice something, I moved to the other side of the room. I didn't like his scrutiny or his attention to detail.

Alastair had been insistent about going to look for Vinson. He'd told us he would be back after checking on

Corinth's family. We needed Vinson. It had taken a lot of convincing to let Alastair venture off without me though. The only thing that had persuaded me was the fact that the Grigori thought Corinth was dead, which gave us a little bit more breathing room. Plus Alastair could handle himself … even though he was human now. I also needed to talk to Gabriel without interruption. Alastair was not a fan of his, and he had been insistent that he could handle Stanton by himself. *Not gonna happen.*

Careful not to turn my back on Gabriel, I picked at the Celtic knot carved into one of the empty wooden desktops. These symbols were all over the place.

"I'm going to regret this, but what do you mean by *light*?" I asked.

I could feel his smirk on me without even looking at him, and when he spoke, he all but purred. "Light travels faster than anything else in the universe. Reflection, refraction, frequencies, waves, and scattering … studied by the greatest physicists out there, but it is still not completely understood. Light is like love. There is light inside each of us, and when Alastair died, so did your light— I mean, I had you and Corinth pegged as the 'it' couple, and if Alastair hadn't come along, it would have worked out that way. It's why I turned you, because Corinth loves you." As soon as he said *loves*, I made the mistake of catching his eye, and that was all it took to prove to him that he was on the right track. "Yes, I used the present tense."

My legs moved forward of their own volition. Before I knew it, I was standing in front of him, shaking with rage. What gave him the right to voice his opinion about love? He knew nothing about it. He had wreaked so much havoc in my world, but he didn't live in it or understand it.

Before I could respond, Gabriel arched a dark eyebrow and said, "I was never wrong about Corinth loving you, but the fact that you ended up with Alastair … well … that *was* unexpected. And quite honestly, I admit life would be dull if I was right all the time. Tell me, when you saw Alastair rise up from the dead, was it love at first sight all over again? I'm sure it was quite the precious moment between you two."

I felt the fury constricting my chest now. "You don't get to talk to me like that, to be so flippant about my feelings for Alastair *or* his death. What do you know about love? You sure do have a lot of advice and opinions on the subject. It almost makes you sound like you actually care—or loved at one point in time."

"Love is an extraordinary weapon if you know how to wield it properly." Gabriel lowered his tone, speaking in a whisper-soft voice that was beyond hostile and frightening. "Is he *human?*"

I bit the inside of my cheek as icy fingers of dread stroked down my spine. It was the way he'd said it, as if he was a lion about to pounce on a gazelle. I knew why he'd dropped his tone. Alastair was fair game now that he was human. Would he try and turn him just like he'd turned me? Or compel him? A tremor of fear wriggled in my gut at the thought. Alastair could be compelled a whole lot easier now that he was human.

Not on my watch.

I took a deep, calming breath. "Alastair is off-limits.

If you so much as mention the words *turn* or *compulsion* around him, we're going to have a major problem. In fact, if you don't make it your personal mission to protect Alastair, I'll make it my personal mission to ruin you. If anything happens to him, I'm blaming you first. Not to mention Corinth will take it personally if you mess with the person who saved his life."

Gabriel stepped back, crossing his arms imperiously over his chest. The thin material of his workout shirt stretched, revealing an outline of well-defined muscles underneath. He regarded me with a slight click of his tongue as if disappointed. "*I* saved Corinth's life. Don't forget that, and I can also take it away—by not providing him with my blood."

I found myself stepping menacingly into his personal space. "Or I could just take it from your still-warm corpse."

He grinned down at me. I knew it was because we were within a hair's breadth of each other, but I could feel our body heat bouncing between us as the fury rolled off me in waves.

"I'm guessing that without my help, he will die within a week. And, yes, yes … I know you can *try* to compel me, but do you really think you're strong enough for that?" He spread his arms out wide. "Because I do so love a challenge. It's about the only thing I do love."

"You son of a—"

He threw a finger in the air, interrupting me. "I just want to make sure you know where we stand."

"You agreed that you would leave everyone I care about alone if I helped you find the cure. When did that suddenly change?"

"I will give Corinth my blood, take you and your friends off my most wanted list, and offer you resources and protection. It's not a bad deal, Larna. All you have to do is work with me." He reached a tentative hand out toward me but then dropped it back down by his side. "Have dinner with me—just the two of us."

Of all the things he could have asked for, this was what he wanted? To have dinner? There had to be some angle he was playing at. He never did anything except for his own personal gain. But somewhere way down in the pit of my stomach I felt a tug, and that tug was what really bothered me. I would not define it or give it a name.

I felt my eyes flash dangerously. "*Fine.*"

Gabriel, satisfied with our arrangement, said, "Seven p.m. sharp—don't be late."

Chapter 12

Larna

ALASTAIR STOMPED INTO MY room complete with muddy and torn clothes, a red nose, and a haggard expression plastered across his bloodied and dirt-stained face. As soon as I saw the grime on him and his clothes, I flew to his side, concern washing over me. The smell of damp earth and leaves clung to him—that and something else. Fear.

He blinked rapidly at my sudden appearance, glancing warily at my hands already exploring his chest and neck and face for more injuries.

"What happened?" I asked quickly.

He pulled my hands into his, preventing the rest of my examination of him, and breathed, "Where is Corinth?"

I took careful note of the worry lines etched into the sides of his mouth and along his forehead. "He's in his room. You're scaring me, Alastair. What is it?"

He moved to the connecting door to Corinth's room in two long strides, and I followed right on his heels. Alastair was way too worried about Corinth for there not to be something very wrong. As soon as the door slid open and he saw Corinth lying on the bed, unharmed, he let out a deep sigh of relief.

Corinth had already hopped up, moving with a grace and speed that took me by surprise. I still hadn't gotten used to him being vampire. In all his life, Corinth had never been a graceful creature, but the way he moved now made it seem otherwise—as if he'd been born lithe and athletic and lean. Alert.

He was in front of Alastair even before Alastair realized it.

"What's wrong?" Corinth said immediately.

Alastair's eyes traveled to Corinth's outer door and then scanned the shadowy corners of his room. He was definitely on guard. After Alastair was satisfied that Corinth was indeed alone, he said, "They know you're alive."

My skin went cold and prickly all over, and all of the moisture left my mouth, leaving it bone-dry. But before I could have him explain, the door to Corinth's room zipped open.

As soon as I saw who was standing on the other side, I went as rigid as a bowstring. I couldn't stop staring at those exceedingly dark, familiar eyes.

"*Vinson*," I whispered.

It felt like it'd been years since I'd seen him last.

He marched imperiously into the room, complete with blood-soaked trench coat, which would have made me worry more had it not been Vinson. What worried me was the lack of weapons on his person. He didn't have his trusty rifle slung across his back. I assumed they'd let him in on the condition he surrender all of his guns. I knew he probably felt naked without them. His usual helmet-style hair was a tangled mess. I noticed the way his jet-black eyes took in the room, watchful, tense. I sensed that he hated the cold stone and earth pressing down on us from above. I remembered Alastair telling me how he hated closed-in spaces. He looked like a caged animal.

Vinson would not have come here without believing it was of extreme importance.

Corinth spread his arms wide. Before I could stop him from doing something stupid, he had already pulled Vinson into a tight embrace.

Vinson's arms dangled at his sides. He looked uncomfortable and stiff, and I could hear his low snarl of warning from across the room.

I imagined he was about two seconds away from ending Corinth, but Vinson did something that completely took me by surprise—he let the embrace last for one second longer than I thought he would before shoving Corinth off him.

Surprising me even more, I could have sworn I saw the ghost of a smile tucked into one side of Vinson's mouth.

I gave Vinson a nod of greeting. "It's really good to see you."

He met my gaze and returned the nod in kind. There was a softness in his eyes that hadn't been there a moment before. He almost looked pleased to see us too.

Corinth, unfazed by Vinson's brush-off, said, "Man, are you a most welcome sight. But why are you and Al covered in blood? What happened? Is my family okay?"

Vinson's lip curled up in irritation as his gaze settled

back on Alastair. "Your family is safe."

Corinth raked a hand through his dark hair, looking relieved. "Did you catch Vinson up on current events?"

Alastair nodded. "He knows I'm human and that you're … a hybrid."

"*Hybrid* is one word for it, I guess. Al—please tell me the Grigori don't know I'm alive," Corinth said.

Alastair coughed, bringing my attention back to him. There was a small trickle of blood winding down his neck. It was an odd sensation, not seeing him heal from something so minor.

My stomach growled and I immediately looked away, feeling ashamed. I hadn't found the time to eat and I was starving, but vamps weren't usually attracted to the scent of human blood. *What is wrong with me?*

Alastair wrenched the sleeve up on his motorcycle jacket, past his forearm, to show us the bent and broken armor at his wrist. His wrist had a nasty bruise on it. "I showed up just in time to help Vinson. We confronted Caesar and Sarah, and things went a little sideways."

My pulse started to quicken as I shot Corinth a concerned gaze. I was angry with myself for not being with Alastair when he'd confronted them again. He could have died—*again.* I closed my eyes, but the darkness held no comfort for me, so I snapped them back open again, dismayed.

"They disappeared … like they did after Sarah stabbed you and left you for dead. Corinth, I'm—" Alastair ducked his head to avoid eye contact, and when he spoke, I could hear the distress and guilt in his voice. "Caesar got inside my head. I couldn't stop him. He was

… too strong … He saw some of my memories, I think. I could feel him rifling through them—I could see what he saw. They know you're alive, because of me. He knows you're vampire. He said he had to tell Angela, and then they both disappeared. We had the element of surprise and now it's gone. You're in danger and it's my fault …" He slumped down onto Corinth's disheveled bed, his head in his hands.

"Did you at least get something else to go on, so we can track them down again? Anything?" I interjected quickly.

Alastair gave a slight shake of his head.

The color drained out of Corinth's face, but an instant later, some blood washed back into the tips of his cheeks, and his eyes flared up so brilliantly I almost had to shield my face. He looked feverish and wild. The way he balled his hands at his sides made me think he was a second away from doing something extreme. The air thickened and compressed around us. My lungs felt as if someone were squeezing the life out of them.

Corinth's fists ignited in a purple hiss of sizzling energy. It sounded like blistering meat on an open fire as he snarled, "*Tell me you ended those bastards.*"

The amount of static running through the room made a vivid flashback of Caesar stopping my heart resurface. I found myself gasping and clutching at my chest, reliving the nightmare all over again. I took an involuntary step backward, thinking about how I couldn't count the number of times Caesar had stopped my heart, only to start it back up again—enough times to give me issues with electrical energy, apparently.

Alastair was on his feet, putting a hand out in front of him and easing himself closer to Corinth.

Corinth's eyebrows shot up into his hairline once he saw my distress, and he immediately wrung his hands. The energy dispersed in a crackle that sounded a lot like lit sparklers. "Larna, I'm so sorry ... I ... I got it under control, I think."

Then I felt Alastair's warm hand on my back and his breath in my ear, soothing. "Are you okay?"

My eyes landed on Corinth's hands. "Yeah ... I'm okay," I lied.

"I would never hurt you," Corinth murmured, trying to sound convincing.

I nodded, swallowing hard. I couldn't seem to find the words to tell him that it wasn't his fault. I hated Sarah and Caesar for what they had done. "I ... I just ... kept remembering my last encounter with Caesar and Sarah ... what they did to Corinth ... to Alastair ..." I let the sentence trail off and cleared my throat. "Catch them up on your meeting with Sozo."

Corinth said, "Sozo won't supply us with any of his people—they like their way of life here and don't want a cure. Indifference is the name of the game. Imani has agreed to help—"

Vinson gave a guttural growl of disapproval at hearing the name Imani. He was such a ghost that I hadn't even seen him post up in the corner of the room until now. I knew how much he hated her for stabbing him with her heel back when she'd tried to kill him at Gabriel's warehouse.

I watched him glide across the room to the attached

kitchenette in search of what I assumed would be his drink of choice: vodka. I didn't blame him: a lot had happened since he'd been gone.

I took out my pocketknife—the one Alastair had given me—and slowly opened and closed it, trying to think through our next move. After what seemed like a horribly long time of not coming up with anything, I sank down onto the bed, feeling defeated.

We were quiet for a good few more minutes until Corinth spoke up. "It's okay, Al. Danger follows me around like a lost Godzilla. They were bound to find out sooner rather than later." Corinth was staring at Alastair, but it was as if he was looking right through him, recalling a distant memory, or maybe a not-so-distant one. When he spoke again though, there was a hardened edge in his tone. "I'm going to make them pay for what they did. All of it."

I knew how traumatizing it must have been for him. As soon as I'd seen him in the hospital wing after he'd been turned, well, it was more than devastating. It was horrific. I wasn't going to lose that sinking feeling in the pit of my stomach anytime soon. He'd looked so haunted and lost.

How did you recover from something like that? Alastair had lost his life over it. His oceanic eyes had turned so dim … Alastair's dying words came back to me in a rush: *Get Sarah.* I sucked in a sharp breath and held it until I started to feel light-headed. The image of his life slowly draining out of him wouldn't leave me. I shuddered, recalling the way his heart had finally stopped beating as I held him in my arms.

My eyes wandered to the cut on Alastair's forehead and neck again. I couldn't handle losing him again. Not ever again.

Corinth and Alastair continued to talk, but their words were drowned out as a dark haze settled over me. I tried to listen to what they were saying, but I was in a place that felt cold and lonely and taxing. The sound of Corinth's blood as it hit the stone floor came rushing back to me ...

Someone shook me, hard.

I snapped out of it to find Alastair staring down at me, his concerned hand on my shoulder. He was giving me one of those searching glares. "Larna—when was the last time you slept or ate?"

I blinked several times, trying to clear my head. "You're the one who needs medical attention. Let's get those injuries looked at."

Alastair pulled me to my feet. "Uh, absolutely not. Let's get you taken care of first."

Alastair grabbed my hand to lead me back to my room. I still had supplies left in the medical kit that Caesar had provided me with. I shivered again at the thought of how Caesar had played everyone like a fiddle.

"Please tell me you didn't talk to Stanton," he said hesitantly, "because something sure tells me you did."

I sensed he didn't want to know the answer. And then I remembered my agreement to have dinner with Gabriel Stanton tonight.

All I said was, "He's willing to play ball ... for now."

Alastair raised an eyebrow, studying me closely, his eyes never leaving mine. "I'm worried about you. You're not taking care of yourself. You're frazzled. You look worn-down—"

"Thanks a lot," I muttered.

Alastair shrugged. "You're going to see a madman alone, Larna … Stanton has an angle—and I'm going to figure out what it is."

"You think Gabriel's behind everything? That he's working with the Grigori?" I disappeared and then returned all in the second before he answered, holding the first aid kit in hand. I laid it on the bed and pulled the lid open, eyeing the contents.

At the edge of my peripheral vision, I could see Alastair's concerned gaze still fixated on me. Finally he said gruffly, "I'm going to get you some fuel before you pass out on me. Lie down—doctor's orders. My head will be fine for a little while longer."

I sighed, exasperated. "Your neck is what I'm more concerned about. And I promise I'll take care of myself later, but if you go out there walking around like this right now, there might be a problem. Please, Alastair, let me get you cleaned up first."

He shrugged out of his leather jacket without another word of argument, tossed it onto the bed, and then rolled up the sleeves on his cream thermal. I saw the glint of metal and flash of skin as he unbuckled and removed the broken vambrace at his injured arm. He held it up. "Thanks for loaning me this, by the way. It's a damn good thing Vinson pressed his panic button—"

My head snapped up at hearing that. "Vinson pressed

the button? If he needed backup, it must have been serious."

He nodded. "It was. And it was a good thing he pressed it too, or I would probably still be out there wandering around. He was over fifteen kilometers away by the time I found him. I'm sorry I broke one of your father's blades."

"I would much rather you be okay than weaponry. Now sit down," I instructed. "Besides, I still have one left."

He gave me a lazy smile before perching on the end of the bed and leaning back onto his elbows. My heart jumped in my chest at the sight of him looking so … relaxed.

I pulled a moist towelette out of a sealed package and leaned over him, gently wiping his face off and examining his neck. It wasn't as bad as I'd thought it was—no stitches needed, thankfully. He tilted his face up to look at me, all flashing white teeth. I felt the instant tug of attraction. He really was striking, and he knew it. I wanted to push a lock of his wind-swept hair out of his eyes, but I refrained.

"How do you feel? Now that you're human again, I mean."

He was silent for a moment as if considering what he wanted to say. "Being human has its disadvantages. Everything creaks. Elbows, knees, wrists. Also, it's cold out there. I didn't realize how *cold* the cold actually was until my teeth started chattering. It's been a long time since I've had sensations like these. It's *strange* … I'm hyperaware of everything now, and my temperament … it seems different. More exposed. *Raw*, I suppose, is a good word for it. Humans … they feel everything, and I mean *every* little thing."

"You say that as if it's all bad." My hand stilled on his bloodied cheek. "Is there anything good?"

I couldn't bring myself to look at him. I wasn't sure how long I stared at the big letter *A* in the word *Aid* until I felt a hand on my shoulder. Alastair was on his feet, invading my personal space. I could smell everything on him. The dried blood. The dirt in his hair. Sweat. Before I knew it, he was backing me up into the desk opposite the bed, his chest pushed up against mine so close that I could feel his rapidly beating heart. He wrapped his hands around my waist and pulled me closer, inhaling the scent of my hair right at my neckline. His skin and nose and breath on my skin were like fire. It left me breathless for a moment.

He stopped suddenly when I didn't move to wrap my arms around him. "Larna, you're trembling. What's wrong? Is it me?" He put a hand on his neck. "Is it the blood? Because I didn't think you'd have a problem—"

I sighed. "Boy, this feels so awkward … and complicated. Our lives are weird." I ran a hand through my short hair, feeling frustrated about everything. I didn't know how to have this conversation with him. "Your blood, Alastair, it smells human, but not … *different*."

"Different how?" he asked slowly.

"Richer." I lifted my shoulders. "I don't know. I can't pinpoint it. I think maybe it's me though, and not you. Maybe Caesar messed me up when he repeatedly stopped my heart." Alastair's eyebrows drew together in concern as I continued. "We've all had a lot to deal with … but there's something else too, something that's been weighing on me that I have to get off my chest first. Alastair, the thought of losing you again … It's too much."

"You're going to have to start trusting that I can take care of myself—"

"*You died, Alastair!*"

Once the floodgates had opened, I found it hard to pull back or pull any punches. I needed to make him carry some of the burden I'd carried around with me since he'd died.

Correction—still carried with me.

I couldn't help it. Everything inside me was roiling like a tidal wave.

"I felt your pulse stop, Alastair. I watched your eyes cloud over. You were lifeless in my arms. I held on to you until you were completely gone, and then, even after you were dead … I still held on to you. Gabriel had to force me to let you go … he used compulsion to do it. I don't even have the memory of them carrying you away from me." Tears stung my eyes and rolled down my face before I could stop them. I tasted salt at the back of my throat. I backed away from him, hugging myself. "You made *Gabriel*—the sociopath who turned me and killed my father—hold me while you killed yourself in front of me. I love you, Alastair, I do, but I am so incredibly pissed at you. Do you have any idea what that's like?"

He staggered back as if I'd slapped him, realization dawning on him. "*Larna …*" And there were no words. I could see it on his face: the sorrow, regret, and overwhelming pain and pity welling in his eyes. "What you had to endure …"

He placed a hand to his head, slumping back down to the bed, too overcome for a moment to speak. "I'm sorry." His voice sounded raspy, filled with heartache and anguish. "What I did to you … I'm *so* sorry." I could see how much effort it took for him to hold everything in—it was hitting him now too. *Finally.* Moisture built up at the corners of his eyes and spilled over. "You can't possibly think any of this is easy for me either. You would have turned Corinth instead of me. I couldn't let that happen. But I won't apologize for saving your or Corinth's life—"

"I could have compelled Gabriel to do it."

"I couldn't take that chance," he whispered determinedly. "Stanton hates me with a capital *H*. He's always wanted me out of the picture, so I figured it was the one thing I could ask him to do, and he would listen."

"Yeah, well … *he did*."

Alastair was on his feet and pulling me into his arms. My stomach turned over as I remembered how it felt to be in Gabriel's iron grip again.

I pushed him away, and a flash of hurt crossed his face, but he grabbed my forearm, refusing to back down this time. Tears left tracks down his soot-stained face. It was the first time I'd seen him cry. It meant something to me, seeing him so exposed. I think it cost him something too, so I let him pull me against his chest.

All I could do was stare at the shape of his collarbone at my eye level. He put a hand to the back of my head, and I listened to the sound of his strong, steady heartbeat. We both were crying now.

After a while, I felt him shift on the balls of his feet as

he whispered through clenched teeth, "Did Gabriel do … anything …?" He faltered for a second before adding, "That would make me want to stomp the last living breath out of him?"

I rubbed a hand under my nose. "No," I whispered. "If anything, it was the opposite. And that's what makes me so damn mad. It was as if he cared about me. I could feel it."

Alastair dropped his arms from around me and he pulled back to search my eyes. "That makes everything so much worse, doesn't it? You want to hate him … but … you don't."

And for Alastair to get what I was trying to tell him meant everything to me. This was why I loved him so much.

"It was as if he'd changed his mind about you—your death. Maybe it affected him in some small way—I don't know."

"You'll never convince me that he's a stand-up guy," Alastair muttered, his lip curling in disdain. "Larna, what can I do to make this better?"

"I don't ever want to keep anything from you—ever again. Just like I don't want you to keep anything from me. No more secrets between us. You're not exactly an open book when it comes to sharing your feelings and thoughts, Alastair." I turned back, rummaging through the kit so I could find the alcohol swabs. "I have an idea, and I know you're not going to like it, but I need you to hear me out on this, because trust is a two-way street."

"I'm listening," he said resolutely.

Chapter 13

Larna

AT 7:10 P.M., THE DOOR to Gabriel's room glided open of its own accord. My eyes darted left to right as I stepped inside, scanning the shadows for any signs of danger. Once I was sure there was none, I proceeded all the way into his room.

I saw the small table near his bed. On it was a white tablecloth, a white candle, a single white rose with two empty champagne glasses, and a paring knife. Gabriel sat on the side of the table facing the door, waiting for me, watching. The candle flickered, shrouding half his face in shadow as he gestured to the empty seat across from him.

Why does he have to have mood lighting?

I noticed how pale his scar looked. It was jagged and raised, and it ran down the entire left side of his cheek. I had this incredible urge to turn back around and run out the door. If I didn't know what was at stake, I might have. He was wearing a collared button-down shirt with the sleeves rolled up to his elbows. It was the color of his soul—black—but his tie was as crisp and white as the petals on the rose. *How sweet, he matches.*

He got up as soon as I got closer, and then

courteously pulled my chair out for me. I joined him, sitting down, tense and on edge. His hand brushed my shoulder as he scooted the chair back in.

"You can cut out the theatrics and candlelight. I want to make something very clear right now, Stanton," I snapped. "This is strictly business. Is that understood?"

He adjusted his tie and sat back down, flashing me what I took to be a challenging grin. "Did you tell Alastair you were having dinner with me tonight?"

I leaned forward across the table so the light from the candle illuminated my face. "Shall we get on with this charade? Or are you going to waste time talking about Alastair?"

He put a well-manicured hand on the stem of the rose. It was fresh and it smelled of earth. I wondered where he'd gotten it from. I remembered the roses planted all over his manor. Maybe it was a subtle reminder of the rose Alastair had given me all those months ago, right before we'd escaped together.

I didn't like it.

I glanced around. "Where's the food?"

Gabriel laughed softly in amusement, and then he reached over to one of the empty glasses. Before I knew it, he'd plucked up the paring knife in his other hand and, in one quick motion, slit the inside of his forearm. Then ever so delicately he held the champagne glass to the wound. I watched, admittedly both mortified and enthralled as his blood filled the flute halfway to the top. My stomach rumbled.

There was something enticing about the smell of *his* blood. It filled the room with an overwhelming metallic scent. I resisted the urge to lick my lips in anticipation. My pulse pounded behind my eyeballs. I had already eaten after speaking with Alastair earlier, but my olfactory system seemed to contradict that fact.

"A toast to our agreed partnership and a sign of my trust. I expect the same from you. In exactly the same way. Yes, I know, this is a bit barbaric—but it is a sign of trust, so you know it comes directly from my veins. Fresh. This is the old way. It's how clans were started—and some still are."

Why did I come here again?

Gabriel grabbed a napkin to place against his arm while he let the cut heal. After a moment, he slid the half-full glass across the table toward me as if he'd just sliced up a block of cheese and offered it up as an appetizer.

Gabriel nodded his head at the other empty flute. "Your turn."

"No way." I stood, pushing the chair out harder than I'd intended to. It toppled over behind me. "You said this was dinner."

"This *is* dinner."

I plucked up the glass he'd filled, intending to give it to Corinth. As soon as I got to the door and extended my hand out to touch it, I planted my palm against a hard chest instead. Gabriel's chest. He had moved so fast. I pulled my hand back as if I'd been burned, now face-to-face with him.

He made it a point to tower over me, blocking my exit, his eyes sparking with interest and something else. "This is a peace offering. I'm not doing this because I like you or am trying to make a move. My blood is worth more than any other ascended being's out there—even Corinth's—and we all know how valuable that has been as of late. I may be the oldest living ascended being. I *need* you to know the price of my gift to him. To know what it tastes like."

"I already had a taste of your blood … and I don't want it. Not now or ever."

"Alastair will be left unprotected—him being human and all …" He let the sentence trail off, knowing that it was the one thing that could stop me.

I was fuming now as I stepped closer to him. "So this is your play? Threats? Nothing has changed?"

"I never said anything had changed," he said, coolly gazing down at me. "I am only trying to offer my protection. You know how dangerous it is for a human to run around with *our* kind. All I ask is that you hear me out." He gestured to the table again and then to the glass in my hand. "If you intend to give that to Corinth, be assured there's more where that came from. Please, drink with me and I'll explain."

I flew back, grabbed the knife quickly enough to cause Gabriel to flinch, and ran the sharp blade across the inside of my forearm, in much the same way he'd done. As soon as blood bloomed up bright from the gash, I began to fill the flute halfway to the top, careful not to make eye contact with him.

Once I was done, I picked up the napkin provided and slid the glass across the table to the side he'd been sitting at. He edged his way around me and sat back down, satisfied.

I remained standing while the cut finished healing on

my arm. "This is what you want, fine. But it will be the last time you ever taste my blood."

There was something piercing its way through my stomach that said otherwise though. I *did* want it, very badly, but I kept evidence of it off my face, hating myself for being weak. *What is wrong with me? Where is my self-control? First Alastair and now Gabriel.*

I tilted the glass to my lips. "Bottoms up."

He held his drink up and then lifted it to his mouth at the same time as me. I was going to say something snarky, but my words died on my tongue as soon as I drank.

Heat flooded my face. I consumed every last drop in a matter of seconds. What was in the glass wasn't enough. The crystal, clutched so tightly in between my fingers, seemed to dissolve. The sound of my pulse rushing past my eardrums was deafening. I looked down to see that I'd reduced the glass in my hand to diamond dust.

Gabriel's blood was an elixir of life.

The fountain of youth. *Euphoria.*

Something far greater than anything I'd ever had before.

The room spun, and I found myself blinking slowly down at him from his seated position at the table. He didn't make a move to get up; he only watched me with keen interest. His features were all sharp angles and blocks, his cheekbones contoured by the soft candlelight flickering on the tabletop. It looked like he belonged in an impressionist painting.

I remembered Gabriel telling me in the elevator at The Swan how he'd gotten his scar from an accident a long time ago. Suddenly I found myself more than a little curious as to what had truly happened to him—it had to have been horrific.

One minute I was standing on the opposite side of the table, and the next, I found myself standing over him. He stayed extremely still as I reached out and touched his chin. I didn't know what made me do it, but my fingers went to his scar. He flinched away from me before I could touch it, his eyes flashing with something unfamiliar, and then it was gone.

He got up from the table, standing to his full height. By the way he was looking at me with lips parted, I was sure no one had ever touched him in this way before. I wondered how long it had been since anyone had touched him—without wanting to kill him, I mean.

Was his blood spiked? I saw it come directly out of his veins.

I don't know what propelled me to do it, but I reached out toward him again. He froze, his eyes following my hand, and my fingers brushed the scar on his left cheek. If I'd been in my right mind, I never would have done it.

At first, shock registered in his eyes, but ever so gradually they softened.

He was tall. Taller than Alastair. I ran my fingers along the raised edges. His skin felt cool. One side of his mouth quirked up under my fingertips. Chin and cheek bones—all really big blocks.

Really big blocks.

The world tilted and darkened around the edges of my vision and then lights out.

"I never took you for a snorer."

I was lying face-down on a bed. A pile of pillows surrounded me as if sometime during the night I'd suddenly become one of them. These were the fluffy, feathery variety.

For the briefest of seconds, I thought Alastair was the one who'd spoken. It was why I let out a bone-rattling yawn and stretched contentedly. What a dream. I hadn't had this much uninterrupted sleep since I'd become a vampire.

Actually, it reminded me a lot of waking up on a Saturday morning with nothing else to do but hang out with Corinth all day and watch cartoons. *Those were the days.* Sometimes the best plans in the world were no plans at all.

But when I popped up to look around, I realized I couldn't be further from the truth.

Alastair wasn't here.

I wasn't in my room.

I wasn't in Corinth's room.

Instead, a pair of dark and brooding eyes behind a furrowed brow met mine. Eyes that ticked up to the top of my head just briefly enough for me to realize my hair was probably standing on end, courtesy of having a pixie-style haircut.

It was one of those awkward moments where I couldn't continue to look at Gabriel Stanton any longer, out of sheer embarrassment.

I patted my hair back down, annoyed with myself.

"Your blood … it was … *potent.*"

What I wanted to say was *rejuvenating*, like I'd just bathed in a tub filled with chocolate mint at a resort spa for a few years—as crisp and clean as the sheets I'd slept on—but I didn't.

The realization that Gabriel had put me to bed hit me, and even though I was fully dressed in what I'd been wearing when I'd entered his room, I still pulled the sheet back up to my chin, horrified.

"I didn't think Alastair would have been too happy with me carrying you to your room last night, so I let you take the bed." Gabriel's lips quirked up on one side, and a vivid memory of last night's events unfolded again in terrifying detail. *Everything.* A slow tremor worked its way up my spine at the remembrance of me touching his scar. I hadn't been in my right mind, but still …

"Don't worry, Miss Collins. I was a perfect gentleman. I only took your shoes off."

My cheeks flushed scarlet, but then a sudden jolt of panic tore through me. What if he'd tried to compel me? I didn't have any blank spots in my memory. Unfortunately, I couldn't blame my inappropriate reactions on compulsion. I cursed myself for not being more cautious around him. What if this had been his plan the entire time? What had I been thinking? I'd walked right into a—

He must have seen the panic on my face, because he said, "Relax. I didn't compel you … if that's what you are thinking. There is no need for that. You already agreed to help me. You can always trust me to tell you the truth— maybe not all of it, but I won't lie to you."

I got up from the bed, and the pile of pillows fell to the floor at my feet.

Gabriel glanced to the mound, and he smiled, transforming his face into something a lot more pleasant looking.

"You kept asking me for more pillows."

The humor in his voice gave me pause—that and the fact that he'd actually done as I'd requested. A part of me wondered why he would do something so ordinary and thoughtful—it was so out of character for him. Like when he'd put Alastair's jacket around my shoulders at the time when I had needed comfort the most. It was disconcerting.

The slow creep of blood hit my cheeks once again. I turned away, looking for my boots. Funny how I'd wanted to appear intimidating last night—quite the opposite this morning, apparently, as I noticed the hole in my sock over my left pinky toe. I slipped my shoes back on, avoiding his gaze in my direction, trying to let my flushed skin return to its normal hue.

I lowered my voice. "That … wasn't a normal reaction to drinking your blood, was it?"

Gabriel stood from the seat he'd been in last night: the rose, candle, and champagne flutes had all been cleaned up. In their place was a fresh pot of tea and a grapefruit the size of my head.

I watched in silence as he folded up a piece of paper and crammed it into his pocket. "I'm just beginning to realize that there's nothing normal about you, Miss Collins."

Chapter 14

Corinth

AL'S JAW TIGHTENED, AND I couldn't help but notice how hard he was opening and closing his fists. So hard, in fact, that his knuckles had started to turn a translucent bone white.

"Whoa, calm down, Al. Your eyeballs are going to pop out of your head if you keep doing that," I told him.

When Larna finally came marching back into her room after being MIA all night, both Al and I gave her the once-over. She handed me a full cup with a lid on it, but I immediately knew what was inside without having to look. A stab of hunger worked its way through my gut. My stomach felt like I'd swallowed razors. The confusion about whether or not I wanted to drink what was inside the cup was maddening.

"We were just about to send out the search party." I pointed to her head. "Nice hair, by the way."

She cleared her throat and then combed her fingers through the tangled locks. Her lack of eye contact gave me pause. But when she didn't say anything or explain her whereabouts, I changed the subject, figuring she had been trying to wheedle the blood out of good old Gabe ... *For the better part of the night,* said a voice at the back of my mind.

Which meant … well, I didn't know what it meant.

Larns hated Stanton more than any of us did. Everything I sensed about her, including her disheveled appearance and attitude, pointed in the opposite direction though. The more I studied her, the more I noticed something had changed about her appearance. Maybe it was my sixth sense, or what I liked to call: vampire extrasensory perception. VEP. At least there was one good thing about vampirism.

I could sense a vibrant vitality and youthfulness about her that hadn't been there before, as if she'd come back refreshed and … *oh … oh …* I *did* know what that meant.

Fortunately, Al clearly didn't have VEP anymore, because he didn't catch the faint whiff of Gabriel's expensive cologne clinging to her like a recent memory. I wondered if she'd just sampled some of his *generous* donation. That would be the better explanation.

I gave her a questioning eyebrow raise, but she refused to meet my accusatory glare. I knew Gabe wasn't exactly public enemy number one right now—he'd been downgraded to public enemy number two—but something didn't smell right, literally.

Grrrrraaawwwwwhhhhhhh …

My eyes flicked to the Styrofoam cup in my hand again. I felt that if I drank it, I'd be selling my soul to the Devil. Nope. Not going to cave.

Grrrrrrrraaaaarrrrhhhhhhwwww …

The second rumble was louder, and this time it actually felt like my stomach was a sentient being or a black hole eating itself with reckless abandon. There'd be nothing left of me if I didn't get sustenance soon.

The Devil wasn't so bad, right? *Just one sip.*

I slid the lid off. The overwhelming smell of copper hit me, and I almost gagged.

I hated what I'd become.

Mostly, I hated the fact that I didn't fit in. I hadn't been a normal human. I wasn't a normal vampire. And undoubtedly, I wasn't a normal Nephilim, either. Story of my life. Maybe I could barter for my soul at a later date in time.

"Oh, for the love of all that's holy, just drink it," Al said with an eye roll.

I shot him an annoyed glower from across the room. "Says the human who doesn't drink blood anymore."

There was only one way to do this: quickly. So I tipped my head back, pinched my nose and drank. The still-warm liquid slid down my throat with all the delightful consistency of a slug. As soon as it hit my stomach, I felt as if someone had pulled me straight out of a blizzard and sat me down in front of a blazing fire.

I hadn't realized how badly I'd felt until this very moment. Invisible fingertips skated across my forehead, leaving a trail of heat in their wake. I felt detached, yet oddly in harmony with my body. For one fleeting second, everything was right again. Better than right. I didn't feel fatigued or hungry or feverish. I felt strong and powerful. The overwhelming fear of Angela coming for me in my dreams at any second took a back seat to bliss.

All hail Gabe's blood.

Then, just like that, my moment of reprieve vanished,

leaving behind a bone-chilling cold. My skin prickled, and then suddenly I was shivering all over. Tiny bursts of electricity popped and arced like a million firecrackers over my skin.

I glanced up quickly, frightened, and I caught Al staring at me with an open mouth.

It felt like it did back in the meeting hall when he'd tried to stop me from going after Gabe. A defense mechanism—or a barrier of energy sparking to life around me like a shield. The Nephilim part of me did not like vampire blood, apparently.

Larna stepped toward me, but I held a hand out, stopping her right as I doubled over. "Don't touch me" is what I tried to tell her, but all that would come out was a strained exhalation of air. It felt like all the wind had been forced out of my lungs. A sudden image of Sarah flashed across my mind, leaving me feeling raw and as exposed as a nerve.

I fell onto the bed, slamming back against the headboard as a spasm of debilitating pain washed over me. My fingers curled into the comforter, squeezing. The buzzing snap of electricity was deafening in the small room.

Don't throw up. You're not dying. Oh, wait, yes, you are . . .

Had someone poisoned me? The pressure behind my ears built up until I was positive I was going to explode. Larns would find little bits of my brain all over the room—

My eyes zipped down. I could just make out the blue-white sparks popping off my fingers and skin.

Larna's face hovered over mine as it blurred in and out

of focus—thankfully, she didn't touch me. I am sure she sensed the amount of danger everyone in the room was in.

"Hey, Ringer, you still with me?" I heard her say. Her voice sounded far away and strained. So far away. "You're okay, *Corinth* … Come back to me. You *can* control it … Come back to me …"

But how can she know that? What if I can't?

A thick wave of black smoke rose up around me in a gust of preternatural wind, whipping around the room, tossing papers and books everywhere like a poltergeist. Everyone's hair stood on end.

And when I thought nothing would pull me out of this, I heard a voice rise above the rest. Speaking another language. Russian.

A dark face swam in front of mine, all thick black brows like caterpillars. "Fear's eyes are large," Vinson said.

I curled in on myself, moaning, "*Make it stop.*"

A tentative hand touched my shoulder, and I rolled back over to see Vinson staring impassively down at me. It was enough to pull me out of my stupor and to stop the electrical currents coursing through me. He'd touched me without getting blown to bits. That was something. The gale force winds and smoke died down. The books pelted to the ground like over-sized hail.

"Some believe you must overcome fear," Vinson started. "A true warrior knows they can't. If you do not bring forth what is within you, it will only serve to destroy you. Control your inner demons, *vampire*. It's what I do every single day."

There was something in his voice—a focused calm— that brought me back from the brink of destruction. He was right. I'd been so concerned about keeping everything bottled up it was eating me alive.

Vinson caring what happened to me was more of a shock than the pain was.

He scowled down at me, a hint of approval in his eyes once he saw I was coming out of it.

"Vin … thank you. I … I don't know what I would have done if …" I shuddered, remembering Imani's words about her vision, and the impending war. *Do I believe her?* I hadn't told anyone else about that yet, mainly because I didn't believe it would happen. It couldn't.

Larna placed a hand on my forehead and then pulled it back, sucking in a shocked breath. "You're freezing."

I was cold. Brutally cold. I felt like I'd been left inside one of those cryotherapy spas overnight. I couldn't stop my hands from shaking.

"I'm o-o-o-kay," I said, teeth rattling.

"Cleary, that is *not* the case," Al said, sounding concerned. "I thought Stanton's blood was supposed to help him … Maybe sleep will make a difference?"

I was going to tell Al I was fine—except I had finally come to the realization that maybe sleep was exactly what I *did* need. But not in the way he meant it. It was time I tracked Caesar and Sarah down. Icy fire licked at my insides as I thought about everyone they'd hurt: Dave, Larna, Al, me, Vinson. I needed to get ahead of this.

The Grigori had killed all Nephilim. It was only a matter of time before they came looking for me again, anyway. Why not take the fight to them?

The next time sleep came for me, I would welcome it with open arms.

Chapter 15

Corinth

I STILL FELT THE remnants of Gabe's blood zinging through my veins. My reaction to drinking it had been … something else. My life had changed forever. The way my body refused to adapt was proof of that. A part of me was desperate to find my assailants. The other part was terrified of what I would do with them when I did. *Let them find me.*

Lying awake in my bed, I thought about how I could transport myself from point A to point B by only using my mind. Then the same worry hit me again: I was dying. I could feel it happening. I knew there was no stopping it unless I enacted a cure for vampirism.

My thoughts drifted from Sarah to Caesar—well, mainly Sarah. The physical scars of what she'd done to me had vanished, but the mental scars hadn't. If Caesar knew about me still being alive, why hadn't he acted on it yet? I knew it was only a matter of time before Angela invaded my dreams, just like Dave had been able to.

Without his protection—my mind was open season.

A tingling sensation started at the back of my neck and worked its way down my spine, connecting with the blade still strapped at my thigh.

I squeezed my eyes shut, concentrating harder. Where are you, Sarah? I imagined those exceedingly bright green eyes of hers and held on to that image. A picture of her floated to the forefront of my vision as I recalled her carrying an armload of books—those hands. *Hands … hands … hands … hands …* bloodied and holding a scalpel …

And it must have been the right combination to unlock interstellar travel, because that was when it happened.

I spiraled. Literally.

My stomach lodged itself in my throat, cutting off my surprised cry as thunder erupted deafeningly around the room and a gaping gray mass opened up underneath me, in the exact same spot the bed should have been in, swirling round and round like a funnel cloud—

Larna and Al burst into my room, and I threw a hand out toward them right as the storm swallowed me up whole. I imagined it might have looked like the gaping mouth of a whale.

Inside the tempest, an infinite chasm of light, sound, and gravity surrounded me. Infinite, because I thought my trip down the rabbit hole would never end. Gravity, because the pull of an unbreakable force was yanking me along like a puppet on strings, and light, because it blinded me into submission.

I could've sworn I heard the unmistakable sound of drums beating, until I realized it was only the sound of my own heartbeat.

Equilibrium came rushing back to me in spades, and

my vision tunneled for a second or two as the remaining buzz and hum of energy poured out of me and I landed on my feet. This must have been what it felt like to career through space without a rocket or a spacesuit—discombobulating. When the world stopped titling and I felt solid ground underneath me, I knew I'd arrived at my final destination. Thankfully, all my body parts were still attached. I threw a hand over the hilt of my blade, and took in a gulp of air in relief. Still there.

I had been underground in the clan one second, and the next, well … my eyes were clenched so tightly closed I had no idea where I was. There was a noticeable drop in temperature though. I wasn't underground or on another planet—VEP told me so. The faint scent of fresh cedar and pine assailed me. I took in a deep breath. It had seemed like such a long time since I'd smelled fresh, cold air. Instantly I knew I'd portaled myself here.

I cracked my eyes open.

What the hell …?

Larna's cabin. The flannel jacket hanging from the coat hook used to belong to Jack. I recognized it immediately. *This is* such *a game changer.*

A door slammed somewhere—the front door—and I jumped.

I could distinctly make out two sets of boots stomping their way inside. Maybe Paul. Maybe someone else with him. There could be any number of rational explanations for someone else to be here. Maybe he had company over—but as soon as I thought it, I dismissed it. Paul wasn't the company sort, he was the loner sort, especially since this place was supposed to remain secret.

I had transported myself here for a reason. The hairs on my arms began to rise. Whoever was here hadn't heard my arrival yet. At least they didn't seem to show signs of noticing my presence. I crept closer toward the living-room door, trying to make as little noise as possible.

Someone spoke. I froze in place just on the other side of the closed door.

That voice I recognized, and it made my whole body go rigid all over.

How did they find the cabin? And then it came to me. Al. Caesar had accessed his memories. They knew about the cabin. *Shit.* I hoped Paul wasn't here. I expelled a shaky breath, not believing that that would be the case. We weren't that lucky.

"You *said* I'd get to have my way with him," Sarah whined. "You *said* this would all be over soon. You *said* we were going to take Iszler back at the—"

She emphasized the word *said* exactly how I imagined Veruca Salt might in *Charlie and the Chocolate Factory*. I didn't know how I'd ever found her attractive in the first place. Acid hit the back of my throat. I *hated* that voice beyond any others. Apparently, I loathed it so much that I'd been able to transport myself right to it. I wondered if I could teleport myself at will now, just like Caesar and Dave.

All other rational thought went out the window as three words ran rampant in my head: *Retribution. Revenge. Payback.*

"Sarah," Caesar said, interrupting my thoughts. "You know I can't take more than one person at a time with me when I travel through lightning. I would have had to leave you behind in order to grab Alastair … and he is *not* the priority here."

I heard the clomp of boots pacing the length of the floor as Sarah snarled, "He's *my* priority."

"This is about more than just vengeance. If the plan goes accordingly, you can kill Alastair Iszler as slowly as I'm sure you've already played out in that twisted little frizzy-haired head of yours. But now that we know Corinth is alive, we have to act fast." At that my pulse started to quicken. "Alastair … well, he's only a consolation prize."

"I don't want Alastair dead yet," she snapped. "I want him to suffer. This is why we chose *this* cabin … I get that you want Corinth. Fine, *whatever*. You can have him. Alastair is susceptible to compulsion now that he's human. All I have to do is make him kill his love … slowly and intimately … and then I'll make him live with what he's done for the rest of his life …" She laughed again, clearly delighted.

The hairs on the back of my neck stood on end. *What a sick, twisted nut-job.*

I heard a faint muffled response from somewhere in the room. I cocked an ear, listening more intently. There was the sound of a chair scraping back and forth against hardwood flooring. A third person in the room. I got a whiff of friction burn from rope rubbing together—*VEP is awesome.* Someone was definitely bound and gagged. Then there was the glaring smell of stale cigarette smoke, but that was everywhere.

I knew what that meant. *No, no, no …* they'd kill Paul in a heartbeat. I bit the inside of my cheek, leaning against the hallway end table for support. *Please, legs, don't give out on me now.*

I missed the rest of Caesar's words before catching, " … in exchange for Corinth and Alastair. I want Corinth, and you want Alastair—*alive* for the time being. You said he has a bleeding heart. Well, so does the Nephilim. They won't be able to say no when their friend's life is on the line. And once Alastair is yours, you can rip that bleeding heart out of his chest, or make him rip Larna's heart out first," he added hastily, "and then his own."

Sarah gave an amused chortle that sent a shiver down my spine. "Where Alastair is … Larna will follow."

There weren't many people I despised in this life, but Sarah definitely was one of them. I'd put my trust in her—*liked* her, even—more than I cared to admit. And she'd thanked me by stabbing me. At least Gabe had an agenda. Sarah was just plain ruthless and unpredictable—the worst combination.

I thought about what they'd just said. It sounded a lot like they were working against Angela or maybe had their own side scheme going on. If Angela knew I was still alive, I was sure she would have tried to come for me by now. They were keeping my emergence to themselves, and that was a very good thing.

One problem at a time though. I tried to think through my options. I wasn't exactly sure how to transport myself away from here—and I wasn't leaving Paul alone, not with those two. I did have the element of surprise. If it meant saving Paul's life, I didn't care what happened to me.

"All I need is your undivided attention on our work at hand. You have his blood," Caesar continued. "Do you remember what you told me? You need Corinth alive—so you can experiment on him for your cancer research. Now that he's a vampire–Nephilim hybrid, we can create a new virus. We can be the first to unleash it upon the world. The possibilities are endless. Angela will be forced to listen to me. *I* will be the one with the cure, instead of her. The rest of the Grigori will side with me. You said this would be a cinch … *Cinch* was your word, Sarah, not mine. You told me Corinth would make for a perfect lab rat."

Sarah sighed. "*Pet* is more like it."

A wild notion of me bursting into the room, blade drawn in one final act of glorious battle, struck me so suddenly I rocked back from the closed door. The sole of my shoe scraped across the hardwood with a faint squeak. I squeezed my eyes shut, waiting for the fallout.

"Shh," Sarah said suddenly. "Did you hear that?"

Caesar said, "Hear what?"

They went quiet for a second, and then she said, "Nothing. Never mind."

I was not going to be a lab rat. *Never.* They would have to kill me first. It would be worth it, just to see the dim-witted looks on their faces as they realized I was right around the corner.

Caesar said, "I'll make a trade with Angela … for the Nephilim's life. I mean, right after I create the virus and get what I need out of him. It shouldn't take too long—"

"No," Sarah barked. "I already tried killing him once, and it didn't take. That wasn't my fault. I did what Angela asked of me. That's all on you, *Grigori.* Let's have a little fun this time. You said he would be mine to do with as I please … You *said* so … Besides, I have no qualms about experimenting on him when I know he's not even human anymore."

I let that sink in for a minute, trying to ignore the sting of those words. Even coming from a psychopath they still hurt. Was there any humanity left in me?

I heard someone wave a dismissive hand in the air, probably Caesar. "Again, the possibilities are endless when it comes to having him in my—*our* pockets. He's worth way more alive now than he is dead. Angela won't be happy I went behind her back, but it won't matter in the long run. I'll be the one holding all the cards. She respects resourcefulness. She'll forgive me. I'll be on top."

I almost snorted out loud at that. *Has he* met *Angela?*

Thunderblade hummed at my side, insistent. *Unsheathe me. Cleave them in two. Destroy them.*

What would Vinson do?

He'd tell me "not to be hero cowboy" in his thick Russian accent. And then he'd say, "Go gather intel and report safely back to group"—*if* I could get back at all. Funny thing was, I knew Vinson would do the opposite— go in guns blazing.

That was a much better idea.

I inched closer to the door, and a floorboard let out the smallest of groans. This cabin had the kind of large wooden planks that could survive an apocalypse, but they were susceptible to the slightest movement … even of one as light-footed as Legolas.

Drawing in a deep breath, my hand on the hilt of my dagger, quick as instinct could take form—

"*Come out, come out, wherever you are.*"

My heart hammered out its appropriate response at

hearing Sarah's voice right on the other side of the door I was standing behind.

She put a flat palm against the door. I heard her take in several deep breaths before she said, "I know you're there, Corinth. I can smell your *fear*. It smells delightful—and so do you."

I didn't realize how many complex layers of anger could rush through me in two seconds flat. Only a thin layer of wood separated us now.

"We were going to pay you a visit," Sarah said, her voice rising, "but it seems there's no need now. Using your powers to transport yourself here, I see. Learning new tricks like a good little angel?"

I shouldered through the door, and it swung wide, knocking her back several feet as I exploded into the room. My *Sight* overpowered everything else inside me. The blade was in my hand as fiery blue sparks shot out of the tip, pointed in Sarah's direction.

I took everything in. From the pool table in the corner of the room to the small sofa, two lawn chairs propped up against a wooden coffee table. Paul bound tightly to a chair with duct tape over his mouth. A dribble of fresh blood leaked out of one corner where he'd been struck recently. Lastly, my eyes fell on Caesar, who was standing behind Paul, holding a serrated knife to his throat.

I had to hand it to Paul: he was one cool dude. The only thing that told me he was worried was the slight twitch of his handlebar mustache. I met his eyes briefly before giving him a reassuring nod that I hoped conveyed, "I'll get you out of this."

My eyes found Sarah's again, and she held my gaze,

unafraid. Rage rose inside me at seeing her again. Her green irises were just as vibrant as I remembered—the color of kiwi. For a moment, I felt trapped inside them.

She took in every inch of me and I took her in too. Her hair was a curly mess, as if she'd been running her hands through it many times over. Those bloodied blue scrubs she'd been wearing when she'd stabbed me had been replaced with skinny jeans and a beige knit cardigan. She looked like she was ready to go do something active— like paddle-boarding or bowling with her boyfriend.

"I've been doing a lot of thinking lately," I drawled. "I think we should separate—as in, separate your head from your body."

It wasn't my best line, but it would do in a pinch.

Sarah's cheeks lit up, rosy and bright, illuminating the butterfly pattern of freckles across her nose and cheeks. There had been a time when I thought that was one of her best attributes. All I could see now was the hidden malice boiling just below the surface, waiting to be let loose.

A ghoulish grin broke across her face. "First Alastair, and now you, Corinth. I admit, I am exceedingly *ecstatic* that you survived round one. Shall we try for round two, then?"

I looked at Caesar again. He had a curious spark in his eyes, as if he wanted to see this play out. I broke eye contact with him, my gaze sliding over to Paul briefly.

"I'll get you out of this," I told him.

I raised my dagger high in the air. Outside, through a gap in the curtains, lightning turned the night sky to molten fire—it looked like a volcano erupting. An unbridled frenzy wrapped its sinister hands around my throat as the bolt zigzagged its way down and then froze midstrike. Colors erupted and exploded outward in a purple blaze of light—

And then it was tearing its way through the roof like a wild animal.

Thunder rolled in right behind it, hitting the cabin so hard the windows shook in their frames. Howls of pursuit. *Hellhound.* The energy bounced off walls, shattered light bulbs, broke windows, and destroyed furniture on its destructive path to my outstretched hand.

Whatever darkness had lain dormant inside me was now alive and kicking. And it craved blood.

I funneled all of it into the blade as it slammed into me, shockingly cold—crisp. The sensation sent a shiver of pleasure through me as it carved its way through my bloodstream. This was energy beyond anything I'd ever experienced before.

When the current shot out of my fingertips, only then did I let out an earsplitting howl. I wasn't sure what it was filled more with—agony or power.

Every single light in the cabin winked out at the same time. Even with vampire *Sight*, I found it hard to discern shapes and forms in the pitch black. Space wasn't even this bleak.

My dagger lit up gloriously as if it had absorbed all of the light in the room. It blinded everyone, throwing black-and-white shadows harshly against the walls behind them. After this, I wasn't so sure they *would* have shadows.

I pointed the burning blade at Sarah.

"*I wouldn't,*" Caesar shouted, "*if I were you.*" He dug the knife into the side of Paul's neck and a dribble of blood ran down his shirt collar. He inclined his head at Paul. "This human's life in exchange for yours and Alastair's."

I barely stopped myself from taking all of us out in a blaze of glory. Barely. A trickle of sweat rolled into my eyes. It took everything I had to keep all that churning power inside me contained.

Some small part of me knew I should stay calm, that I needed to think things through—Paul was caught in the cross fire for one thing—but that part of my brain kept replaying the torture of being repeatedly stabbed with a scalpel over and over again. I didn't care what kind of collateral damage I inflicted, even if I took an innocent life with me.

Sarah was going to die today no matter what the cost.

Rough hands seized my shoulders, yanking me backward off my feet. Whoever had grabbed me was supernaturally strong.

A gaping tunnel of wind and thunder opened up, monstrously huge, as I tried to fight whoever had grabbed me. It felt like an invisible force was holding me captive. Just like when Angela had stopped me from moving in my dream.

No, no, no! I have to kill Sarah!

Right before I was ripped from this plane of existence, I heard Caesar's voice echoing in my head, as sharp as a razor slice: *You have twelve hours!*

Suddenly, I was moving away at such incredible speed, it left my entire body feeling like it had whiplash.

I thought I was going to suffocate.

My breath didn't return to me until I slammed face up onto the gigantic iron table in the meeting hall back at clan Eleutheros.

The light I'd sucked out of the cabin was now blazing off me in waves. I wondered if it was like staring directly into the sun.

My blade flew out of my hand. I heard the distant clatter of it hitting polished marble. My back arched up off the table in a spasm as all that pent-up lightning flooded out of me, ricocheting around the hall and sending people scrambling to get out of the way. I heard their screams and shouts as they tried to escape the path of the deadly lightning.

In a last-ditch effort, I raised a hand to the domed ceiling and commanded it to disperse. It obeyed, vanishing in a deafening *CRACK* that resounded around the room.

I closed my eyes, praying no one had gotten hurt in the aftermath.

Today's main course—*me*—served up like a turkey with a side of mashed potatoes. I mean, the situation could have been better had the meeting hall not been filled with people, standing room only.

Oh, how I love being the center of attention.

When I finally opened my eyes, I found Sozo staring down at me in surprise. He had arrived at my side at some point, his eyebrows shooting comically up into his dark hairline.

When my heart returned to somewhat of a slow gallop, I managed to roll over onto my side, gasping, "*And for my next trick …*"

For my next trick, I proceeded to get sick in front of a thousand stunned onlookers.

Chapter 16

Corinth

NO ONE HAD BEEN hurt in the meeting hall, thankfully, but I'd made quite the mess. I'd been rushed to the hospital wing for the second time in twenty-four hours. You'd think being vampire I'd be able to avoid such places. I'd grown so ill that I hadn't even been able to answer anyone's questions. I would have told them not to bother taking me to the infirmary, but they didn't know what to do with me, and my system had been overloaded.

As soon as I was able, I'd scrambled out of the tiny hospital gurney, grabbed a cloak and robe that had been provided for me—and ran past the guards before they could stop me. I was ashamed to admit that the robe was surprisingly comfortable, but I drew the line at wearing sandals. Good thing my Chucks went with just about any outfit, or I'd really look silly.

Tucking my blade into the deep pockets of my cloak, I lurched through a set of motion sensor doors out into the hallway, still feeling only slightly embarrassed that I'd puked all over Sozo's extravagant iron table.

A quick glance in a mirror I passed showed me how

awful I looked, but none of that mattered right now. I had to find Larna and Al. We had to get to the cabin as soon as possible.

As it turned out, I didn't have to go far to find them, because as soon as I rounded the corner, Al collided with me, bouncing off my chest like a rubber ball. They were already on their way to me, having heard about what had happened, I assumed.

He landed on his backside on the smooth, polished stonework with a grimace. I stuck my hand out to help him up as he brushed himself off.

He gave me a questioning eyebrow raise. "What's with the outfit?"

"No time for our usual verbal judo," I told him. "We have to get back to Larna's cabin. *Right now.* Paul's in danger."

Larna rushed around the same corner, interrupting Al before he could respond. Vinson was right on her heels, followed lastly by Gabe and Imani, who both looked extremely uncomfortable being with them.

Apparently, Larna and Al had convinced Vinson not to kill Gabe just yet—which was a miracle in and of itself. I noted Gabe had shouldered his way past Vinson to stand beside Larna. His appearance irritated me. There was something going on between those two that I did not like.

"Where did you go?" she cried, her eyes landing on my outfit and raking over me. "All we saw was you vanishing in a clap of thunder and vapor and lightning. I thought the worst … We heard what happened in the meeting hall." She put a supportive hand on my arm, her lips parting slightly with worry. "Corinth … you don't look well."

I couldn't keep my voice from shaking. "Weird things happened. Very weird things. I think Gabe's blood triggered an episode or something."

Everyone turned to look at Gabe, and he shrugged in conceit as I said, "I managed to transport myself right to Sarah and Caesar. They were at your cabin, Larna. I just got so angry, I wanted to end her, and then I found myself hurtling away without a choice in the matter." My eyes found Al's. "Caesar must have gotten the location from inside your head. I heard them plotting. They want Al and me to turn ourselves over. They have Paul."

Larna's grip on my arm tightened. She gave Al a quick glance before looking back at me.

"You seriously transported yourself? Like a real *angel*?" Al interjected, sounding amazed.

When I didn't say anything, Larna stepped away from me to curl an arm around her stomach. This must have been where the saying "sick with worry" came from. "Corinth—"

"You're not sidelining me, Larns." I straightened to my full height and threw my shoulders back. A tiny voice at the back of my head said, *You should be sidelined.* I had almost killed us back there—Paul included. If someone hadn't intervened, I might have. "I overheard Caesar saying something about only being able to transport one person at a time through lightning. I think maybe someone was helping me ... I felt another presence, and then they were hauling me out of there and back here."

Larna spoke up quickly before anyone else could. "You think ... it might have been Dave?"

I chewed on the inside of my cheek in thought and

then nodded. It was a possibility. I couldn't help but feel the heat of Al's gaze as it bounced from Larna and then to me.

"Guilt doesn't look good on you, Al," I said finally.

"This is my fault," he whispered. "Sarah won't stop until she gets what she wants—*me*. I have to turn myself over—"

"As much as I want to see Lover Boy over here give himself up for the greater good again," Gabe said coolly, interrupting, "how long did they give you?"

I shot him a look that could curdle milk but answered anyway. "Twelve hours."

Gabe's black eyes glittered like twin stars. I could see his mind already playing out all fifty million ways in which he could use me to his advantage. "Can you do it again? Teleport to any place you want?"

"That depends," I said. "Why?"

I expected him to argue, to tell us to let Paul die, but instead, he did the opposite, surprising the hell out of me.

"Because I have a plan, and I can get us there in five hours."

Chapter 17

Larna

THE COLD SLICED THROUGH us as the wind funneled its way through the cracks in the helicopter doors. The one and only good thing about having Gabriel Stanton around was the fact that he was a billionaire—and, I begrudgingly admitted, he was a brilliant strategist.

He had access to aircrafts—as in, more than one—and this one just so happened to be in stealth mode, heavily modified for quieter operations. Probably the same one that had gone after Corinth at Gabriel's armory when we'd been attacked. Never in a million years had I thought we would ever accept help from the likes of him—but here we were.

We had packed up what we needed and changed into black fatigues, provided by Gabriel, of course. Things were happening quickly now. The sleek black chopper had been waiting on us as soon as we'd come out of the clearing from the clan. Ducking under the rotating blades, Gabriel yelled something inaudible to his pilot.

When it was clear, he waved us all over, and we swiftly climbed aboard, leaving Eleutheros behind for the time being. The pilot hadn't even waited for us to get settled before he took off.

I hurriedly grabbed a seat at the back of the ten-person chopper, next to Corinth, noticing for the first time how sunlight affected him.

He hadn't felt the light of day since he'd been turned, so when the natural light hit him at eye level, he winced, placing a hand in front of his eyes as if he had a gnarly hangover. The surging storm clouds swallowed the sun back up, and I watched the tension slowly drain back out of his body. He hadn't always been one for the outdoors, but now that he knew the sun was an irritant, I thought he was troubled by it.

There was one person who seemed to enjoy the weather more than the rest of us though. When the rays did manage to poke their way out of dark cloud cover once again, I saw Alastair tilt his head back and close his eyes, soaking it all in.

I wondered what he was thinking. Maybe he wasn't thinking. Maybe he was just relishing the moment. He looked content, whatever the case. Suddenly all I wanted to do was to run my hands through his hair and kiss him. I imagined he hadn't *truly* enjoyed the company of the sun for over two centuries, not really. I mean, vampires could go out during the daylight just like anyone else, but it felt like a painful skin rash, or like having an allergy to something you knew you had to avoid for the rest of your life.

The only noise other than the beating of wind against the propellers was the snap, crack, and click of rifles, magazines, and ammo being loaded, rechecked, and stowed.

Gabriel sat at the far end of the cabin. He was the only one wearing an expensive suit. He looked somber as ever, mainly, I thought because he didn't play well with others. It was fine by me.

Imani had chosen to join our merry band of travelers, but I noticed she kept a wary eye on Vinson. He wasn't forgiving the fact that she had stuck her heel into his thigh. Vinson didn't forget. His eyes kept snapping over to her, his scowl deepening. He was holding on to one of the support bars with one hand, stuffing the rest of his gear into a duffel with the other. I wondered idly when they would have it out. Hopefully, not until *after* we got Paul back.

Another wave of guilt and fear swirled in my chest at thinking about Paul. He was a kind, loyal, and committed friend and ally. I had a flashback of him taking me to see my dad for the first time in six years. He'd helped us get out of jam after jam after jam—never complaining.

The guy was a saint among men, and one of the nicest human beings I'd ever known. And, I was ashamed to admit, I hadn't gotten a chance to tell him how much he meant to me. He reminded me of my father—so much so that my heart began to ache from the pain of missing him all over again. Paul had a quiet resilience that I respected. It was what I liked most about him.

If anything happens to him …

On the pretense of stretching my legs, I got up and made my way to the back of the cabin, feeling restless. My breath was leaving me in the form of ragged gasps— anxiety attack. I tried to slow my breathing, tried to concentrate on the plan we'd come up with, going over it step-by-step in my head, until I was able to somewhat recover.

"Careful," Gabriel said, nodding toward Alastair. "Your boyfriend might get jealous with you back here with me."

I couldn't help but glance at Alastair. His overly bright blue eyes were focused on something in front of him, his arms crossed resolutely over his chest. He looked like he didn't have a care in the world, but I knew otherwise. He set his jaw, and I could see a muscle tick as he clenched it tight. Even though he was human, he looked just as intimidating as ever, wearing a bulletproof vest that had pockets for its pockets. In each one, I knew he had a different weapon. He was also wearing vambraces on each wrist, thanks to Gabriel's weapons stash.

My eyes flitted back to Gabriel. "Why are you helping us? What's in it for you?"

"Like I said, I made you a promise to keep your friends safe if you worked with me. Since actions speak louder than words …" He shrugged. "Besides, I am positively overjoyed at the fact that you'll owe me one after this. I just wish you'd let me bring my people along … They're much more skilled at fighting."

"Ah, there it is—that self-righteous narcissism."

Gabriel spread his arms wide. "I have never pretended to be something else."

I wasn't so sure about that. I could sense something subtly different about him. When he didn't think I was looking, I'd catch him staring at me with a strange glint in his eyes. He only did it when he thought I wasn't looking though.

The helicopter seesawed up and down. I stumbled back, throwing an arm up and grasping at empty air. I was normally steady on my feet—on the ground. But being up in the air was a different story. We hit another rocky bump, and I staggered back, losing my footing—

And fell backward right into a hard chest. Gabriel wrapped his arms around my waist, holding me securely in place before I could fall. A quick flashback of him preventing me from helping Alastair struck. I took in a startled breath and tried to pull out of his grasp, my cheeks lighting up red in the dark, but we hit another air pocket, and I stayed put for way longer than I wanted to.

Up and down. Up and down. Up and down.

It got so choppy my stomach somersaulted. Finally, after what seemed like an extraordinary amount of time had passed, I extricated myself from his arms. Careful not to look at him, I made my ungraceful way back over to sit beside Alastair.

He whispered, "Laying it on a little thick, don't you think?"

I frowned. "Just doing what you taught me to do."

"You do realize the only reason I'm not ripping his throat out right now is because we need him, but if he touches you again, fair warning—*I will*."

Alastair's fingers brushed mine as I said, "Duly noted."

His eyes landed on Gabriel again. "You sure you want to go ahead with this plan of yours?"

I pulled a bottle of water out of my bag on the seat beside me and drank, swishing the liquid around in my mouth, trying to bring moisture back to it.

"Mine or yours? 'Cause I don't like either," I admitted.

Alastair tugged my hand into his and then gently kissed my knuckles. He leaned in closer to whisper in my ear, making it appear as if he were just going to kiss me on the cheek. "Making Stanton think you're—" he cleared his throat "—on his side in order to gather intel on the cure is ... *risky.*"

"I know," I murmured. "But if you've got a better idea on how to get this information out of him—other than me trying to compel him—I'm open."

He closed his eyes and nodded.

An instinctive impulse drew my eye back to Gabriel, one that bothered me more than I cared to admit. His dark, wavy hair barely touched the top of his collar. Not a hair out of place on his head. I wasn't buying his story about me owing him one. *What is in it for him?* As soon as we'd loaded up, he'd told me point-blank he wouldn't be going with us.

His words: "I don't get my hands dirty. If you should get your friend out alive, I will make sure he is transported to safety, and then I will come back for you."

I couldn't help but wonder who he meant by *you.*

Gabriel's onyx-colored eyes slid to mine as if he knew I was staring at him. There was a tiny grin tucked into the corner of his mouth.

I quickly averted my gaze.

Vinson clambered over to sit opposite Corinth, beside Alastair. Corinth had a strained expression on his face. I knew he didn't like flying, which was mildly amusing, because he was half angel.

"You look nervous," I shouted over the sound of the wind lashing out at us like an invisible kraken in the sky. "You sure you're up for this?"

Corinth's face turned a shade greener each time the helicopter dipped. It was all I could do to hang on. Another swell upended Imani, seated next to Corinth. She flew into his lap and his face went scarlet as she gave him a wink and slowly righted herself.

"It's not natural—*flying*," Corinth said through gritted teeth. "And yes, I'm up for this. We're saving Paul."

Vinson leaned over to him. "This is Sikorsky UH-60 Black Hawk. Very good machine. Pilot is okay flyer or turbulence would have pushed blades into tail boom by now. Paul can take care of himself. He has tough skin—like Russian. Once we are out of weather, we make our move."

"That's good to know," Corinth snapped. "Seriously, are we all good with your plan, Tac Leader?" he said, turning back to face Vinson.

Vinson mashed his lips together in disapproval at the reference.

I arched an eyebrow at Corinth. "Tac leader?"

"Yeah, you know, as in, tactical leader. This is partly Vinson's plan, which makes him team leader, right? It's not going to be Gabe, that's for sure. I'm going to call Vin TL for short, which is also short for 'tough love.'"

Vinson growled.

Corinth said, "Come on, *TL*, you know you like it."

Imani met my gaze and then pulled a face. "Is he always like this?"

I grabbed the oh-shit handle above my head to hold on as another bout of wind rocked the chopper. "You have no idea."

I still didn't know what to think of Imani. Corinth had told me about her real motives. I saw the way she looked at Corinth though—with fondness. I wasn't sure if Corinth saw it or not. He was a little preoccupied with his thirst for retribution and the fact he that was dying and all.

I had no reason to trust her, and I didn't—not yet, anyway—but her being here was a step in the right direction. I begrudgingly admitted to myself that she had saved his life.

I turned my attention back to Corinth. His teleporting experience did nothing to help ease my growing anxiety. He looked so pale, and he wasn't nearly as hot as I remembered—temperature-wise, I meant. His body used to run as hot as the sun. Now his skin felt ice-cold to the touch.

Even though my brain was still going a mile a minute, I felt a bone-weary fatigue sweep over me. I thought it was a deep mental exhaustion. I rubbed my eyes, feeling the full weight of everything that had happened over the last few days. *Alastair is human. Corinth is vampire. The two people I hate most in this world have abducted Paul.*

Alastair reached a hand up and gently guided my head down to his shoulder. I had already closed my eyes by the time he whispered, "I'll wake you when it's time."

Chapter 18

Corinth

WHOOMP, WHOOMP, WHOOMP.

The helicopter shook as it hit another rough patch. I hated flying. *You can do this.* It was just a matter of willpower. I pressed my palms into my eyes until I saw black spots.

Vin had materialized out of nowhere; I knew it was him without even looking. He was the only one who had no telltale sign of breathing. Silence was his tell. Removing my hands from my eyes, I let my sight adjust back to normal and then gave him a sideways glance.

"We are nearing drop location," he said in his thick Russian accent. "Weather will clear for few minutes."

I stood up, crouching so that my head didn't hit the ceiling of the cramped cabin. When Al saw me get up, he followed suit, gently extracting himself from Larna's slumbering form. On any other occasion, I would have questioned how she could sleep during a stressful time such as this, but I knew Larna hadn't been getting in the amount of rest she needed as of late, even with her being vampire. She had been through a lot, and her body was paying the price—there were some things you just couldn't get over, like the fact that her boyfriend had died right in front of her eyes. Or maybe it was me slowly dying she was worried about … or Paul, or having been electrocuted by Caesar—the list could go on and on, I mused.

He shook her awake, and her eyes popped open, meeting mine.

I gave her and Al a quick nod to let them know it was time.

"You think you can do this?" Al asked me.

I threw on a pair of expensive-looking rappelling gloves Gabe had provided me with—the kind with double leather on the palms—and then adjusted the blade at my thigh for the umpteenth time.

"We're about to find out."

Vinson didn't just look mean; he was the definition of it, and even though he didn't so much as crack a smile, I could tell he was excited at the prospect of rappelling out of an aircraft. This was his dream siege. Luckily, the weather had calmed down just enough to make this happen.

Larna was up now, strapping on her own gear, looking as fierce as I'd ever seen her. Her jaw was clenched as she pulled on a ski mask and then a helmet. Our ragtag group was no longer ragtag—it was semi organized and full-on intimidating. A lot of money and the right equipment went a long way.

Larna caught me staring. Her eyes flickered to mine. She glanced down and, as if deciding something, elbowed her way over to where I stood.

Imani had conveniently switched places to position

herself next to Gabriel, and they were whispering conspiratorially to each other.

I tried to ignore my growing apprehension as I turned my attention to Larna. Even though the ski mask hid the look on her face, I could hear the assertive cadence in her words. It was oddly reassuring. "Paul is *not* going to die today. I am *not* letting you or Alastair trade yourselves. You *will* beat them. You two have a tendency to go off script when it comes to our plans. Stick to the script. Got it? No one is playing the self-sacrificing hero today. We're in this together. I'll be right behind you."

I held my arms open and then yanked her into a brusque hug, then inclined my head at Vin, who was looking just as vicious and threatening in his ski mask as Larna and Imani did. In my head, it sounded weak, but when I spoke, I surprised myself with my confidence. "It's Vin's plan. Don't worry, it'll work. Imani will be with you, Larna. We'll be inside when you get there, hopefully, successfully stalling. Remember, Paul will most likely be tied to a chair in the center of the living room—in the exact spot I saw him in. Caesar will be behind him with the knife. Swing in and grab Paul and then get out … The *Payload* will distract Sarah."

"Will you quit calling yourself the"—Larna used air quotes—"*Payload*."

I shrugged, giving her my lopsided grin in response.

"We don't even know this is going to work—"

"FIFTEEN MINUTES!" the pilot roared. The deafening rumble of the rotors fighting the impending storm was a sign that we were cutting it close.

Al checked the armor at his wrists and then the

holsters holding both his guns at his thighs. Once he was satisfied, he nodded to let me know he was ready. I worked on clearing my head, ignoring a sudden unsettling surge as the chopper swung side to side in another gust of wind. Even though I wore gloves, my fingers were numb from the cold.

Al put a hand on my shoulder and I closed my eyes. I could do this. All I had to do was get angry, which wasn't hard. I thought about Caesar holding the knife to Paul's throat. I had been hyperaware of each serration of the blade. The blood dribbling down Paul's neck.

I felt the heat swirling in my chest and channeled the flood of power, letting the energy wash over me. *Take me to Paul. Paul. Paul. Paul.*

The air thickened, shifted, and churned around us. A moment later, a spiraling gray tunnel opened up behind both Al and me, stretching wide. Without a second thought, I tugged him backward with me. As we fell into the swirling mass, the last thing I saw before we disappeared was Vinson snapping his line into the rappelling hook.

And then we were racing through that bizarre *other* place—the both of us, thankfully. With my eyes open this time, I was barely able to make out the edges of the passage hurtling us onward. It was loud—louder than a tornado with the chopper and looming storm.

Al's grip tightened on my arm, letting me know he was still with me. This time our arrival happened much faster than the last time I'd tried this. Even though I was starting to get the hang of teleportation, our landing wasn't as graceful as I would have liked.

I heard Al gasp in surprise as we burst out of the vortex, landing unsteadily on our feet in the middle of the cabin. And of course, I'd managed to dump us right smack in front of them.

Everything hit me at once. The smell of forest. Blood. Burned wood. Paul tied to a chair with dark shadows under his eyes. Bits of glass crunched under our feet, from the mess I'd made the last time I was here.

I caught movement out of the corner of my eye. Caesar and Sarah were staring at us both with grotesque grins cracking their ugly faces.

Something sharp and metallic flashed in Sarah's good hand and a stab of icy fear sliced through me. My heart tried to beat its way out of my chest, and sweat beaded my forehead at the sight of the scalpel clutched between her fingers.

They had been waiting for us to arrive. Caesar was beside Sarah, who was now holding her signature weapon of choice to Paul's throat.

Sarah waved at us. "Well, hello there, boys. Shall we get this party started?"

Chapter 19

Corinth

OONLIGHT SPILLED IN THROUGH the cabin's windows. The weather felt as ominous as our situation did. I knew the storm clouds rolling in would hide the wan light from view soon, but for now, it hit the sharp edge of the blade Sarah had pressed to Paul's jugular. I shuddered, thinking about how I'd been on the other side of that weapon not too long ago.

Paul's skin looked waxy. His five-o'clock shadow and now-lackluster mustache told me he'd been tied up for the entire six and a half hours I'd been gone—probably longer. But his eyes were hard and defiant, even with the point of the blade cutting into his skin. I could see why Larna's father had liked him so much. It made me like him that much more too. I remembered him spouting off Jack Kerouac right before we'd left. He'd always been the silent ship in the storm.

I met his eyes briefly. There was a flicker of fear in them. Remorse swelled up at the thought of me almost killing him.

I realized how dark it must be for Al in here, now that he was human. Fortunately, there was still enough natural light for him to see by, because he whistled softly to himself, looking around the room. Glass crunched as he shifted on the balls of his feet. "What the hell happened in here?"

I shrugged in confession.

Caesar tilted his head toward us. "Corinth, toss me the blade. Kick your weapons over here too, *human*."

A shadow passed over the room as rain started pelting the windows with a whip like ferocity. Water leaked in through the giant hole in the roof I'd created the last time I was in here. I hoped Larna and Vin had made it out in time. This weather was not good.

All that raw energy inside me surged up again, threatening to pull me under. It wasn't hard for me to tap into it. I put my gloved hands out in front of me, reaching for the blade strapped at my thigh. "I realize this might be counterproductive, but don't do anything stupid, Caesar."

Al kicked over the two pistols from his holsters, his face a stony mask of defiance.

Sarah raised an amused eyebrow at seeing his obedience. "Don't forget those hidden blades at your wrists. I learned my lesson the hard way." Her voice dropped menacingly. "Speaking of, where's your lover? Hmm. I know she has to be lurking in the shadows nearby … I owe her for this." She held up her left hand, showing us the two remaining digits. It looked like she was holding up a peace sign.

"*Peace.*" I couldn't help it. I barked out a throaty laugh.

Her eyes narrowed as they homed in on me like lasers. "You won't be laughing when I carve into Larna's heart with this scalpel," she vowed. "She stole something precious from me, and I mean to do the same to her. Better yet, why don't you come over here, Alastair, and I'll compel you to do it for me." She gestured at him. "The blades. Now."

Sarah shouldn't have mentioned Larna. Al rolled his sleeves up all the way to his elbows, revealing the leather armor at each wrist. It was as threatening a gesture as any I'd ever seen. He unbuckled them slowly, doing as she'd asked, sliding them across the ground.

Out of the blue, Al spoke softly and only to Sarah. "Wrentmore died a most horrible and painful death. I made sure of it. Would you like to know how?"

The way he said it, with such a frightening quality to his voice, startled even me. My mouth fell open. I actually *did* want to know how he had killed Wrentmore. Our plan was to stall …

Sarah froze, and I could see her struggling to keep it together as her face turned a bright red. "You … how dare you … be so insolent …" She pointed the scalpel at him but seemed to be at a sudden loss for words, her mouth opening and closing.

"I ripped him limb from limb. And when I say limb from limb, I mean it in the most literal sense. Body parts were everywhere. A leg in a tree. A hand in a shrub."

I turned to regard Al, my eyes stretching wide as he said, "Fingers scattered in the grass. I tore his fangs out and stomped them to dust at my feet." He laughed, and it was chilling.

Human Al was just as intimidating as vampire Al. I'd never heard him sound so callous before. I sensed bloodlust thick in the air—like a wolf catching its prey's scent right before taking it down. To pull another vamp's fangs out and stomp them to dust revealed to me just how much he had hated Wrentmore.

This was not the Al I knew. It made me wonder about the type of person he used to be. Evil. Vengeful. Mean. To me, Al had always had his head screwed on right, but to hear him admit something so sinister and cold was more than a little unsettling.

Sarah wanted blood on her hands tonight, but I wanted to make sure it wasn't any of ours. All I needed to do was get Paul outside, to the waiting helicopter, and Gabriel would take care of the rest. With the blade still in my grasp, and all that power coursing through my veins, I wanted nothing more than to go to town on Sarah and Caesar, but I didn't want to get Paul killed in the process. I'd almost taken him out the last time I was here. I had to be careful.

If Al continued down this destructive path, that might not happen.

Caesar must have sensed the danger too, because he said, "Sarah ... he is *baiting* you. I said, give me your blade, Corinth," he insisted.

I held it up for him to see, and sparks shot off the sharp edge. "Let Paul go, and I'll slide it over to you."

Caesar clucked his tongue in annoyance and then motioned at me again. "Give it to me, or Paul dies right here and now."

He gave Sarah a nod. With great reluctance, she tore her gaze away from Al so she could mash the tip of her scalpel against Paul's throat again. Blood dribbled down his neck in a long crimson stream.

I pressed my lips together at seeing Paul flinch. "Wait. *Wait*," I snarled. "I'm doing it. I'll do it—don't hurt him."

Oh, how I am going to make them pay.

I kicked my blade over to Caesar, who immediately plucked it up into his grasp, and as soon as he did, he let out a cry of pain as a charge of electricity zapped him on his hand. He almost dropped it, but then his brown eyes danced in delight as he clenched his fists around it in triumph.

"You got what you wanted. Now let him go," Al said. "We're cooperating."

The clap of thunder and blaze of light bursting into existence behind me spurred me into action, only I was a blink of an eye too late—

Strong hands wrapped around my throat, dragging me backward at the same time as another figure grabbed Al from behind. Whoever had seized hold of me was tall— *Grigori* tall—and preternaturally resilient.

My heart thundered erratically in my chest as I tried to fight off the person who had suddenly appeared behind me. It felt like I was hitting a brick wall. I fought back on pure instinct and adrenaline, but as quickly as it had started, the fight drained out of me. We were outnumbered, and Paul was still at Sarah's mercy. We weren't going anywhere.

Al must have come to the same conclusion, because he didn't struggle like I did. He only gave me a quick shake of his head.

My attacker's hands loosened around my neck just long enough for me to drag in a precious breath of air.

"Glad you could join us, Turiel," Caesar said.

My blood ran cold at hearing that name again. I knew without looking that Turiel was the one wringing my neck. He had it in for me. Turiel had tried to take Dave out. He was Angela's number two.

I risked a quick glance at the person standing behind Al. He was just as tall as Turiel, but he had bronze-colored skin and a headful of dark, curly hair, almost Turiel's opposite.

Sarah twirled the scalpel in her good hand, making a beeline directly for Al. "What was that you were saying about killing Wrentmore?"

"I was just telling you how much I enjoyed it," Al confessed. He sounded like he was in a lot of pain. Out of the corner of my eye, I could see the Grigori behind him, twisting his wrist up at an odd angle.

"Well, I guess once I compel you to choke the life out of Larna, it might just make us even." Sarah stopped inches from Al. Her normally green eyes lit up, glittering blue with her *Sight*. "I mean, I want to watch you do it, because by the time I'm done with you, you'll even enjoy it."

He smiled coldly at her.

"What's the matter, Alastair? Cat suddenly got your tongue?" She grabbed his chin with her injured hand and pulled his face close to hers, eyes flashing.

I realized a moment too late what she was going to do—compel him. I couldn't let that happen.

"*No!*" I shouted at the same time as I ripped out of Turiel's grasp. My eyes locked on Caesar. He was holding my blade. It was burning ghostly blue now.

I held my hand out and beckoned it. The dagger winked out of Caesar's grip in a flash of light and reappeared in my grasp in an instant. Caesar's eyes went round right as a wall of flame and fire lit up the night sky outside, and our backup came crashing through the window closest to Sarah.

It happened so swiftly that the concussive aftershock surprised even me, and I knew what was coming.

Glass, wind, and rain drove its way inside the trashed living room. It sounded like a stealth bomber landing beside me as smoke shot out of a canister next to my foot. Multiple forms materialized out of the smoke and haze and confusion.

I threw my full weight against Turiel, ramming the back of my head into his nose. He grunted as I ducked back into the melee.

He was in hot pursuit behind me; I could feel him right on my heels. At the last second, I drop-rolled out of the way of a closed fist, and, using my heel as a hook, kicked up, just like Al had taught me to do, striking him right in the jewels. He went down hard. Apparently, that move still worked on angels.

I staggered back to my feet, slipping on glass and debris in the process, and went after Paul as I caught snippets of everyone fighting around me. Darkly clad bodies pressed close, punching and kicking at each other in a frenzy. Sarah was ripping Larna's mask off and slashing out at Larna with her scalpel, her eyes glowing azure in the smoke-filled room.

I twisted around to go help but stopped as soon as I caught sight of Paul near the door. He had somehow managed to jump-scoot his way, still tied to the chair, over to it.

I exploded into action, going after him, my arms and legs pumping—

Turiel wrapped a massive arm around my throat, and instinct took over. I pivoted, lowered my center of gravity, taking him to the ground with me, and drove him over my back. He landed flat on his back in a stunned heap. I came down to a knee and struck him in the face—two times, in rapid succession—and heard the deep crack of bone breaking. Something inside me broke right along with his face. My glowing fists slid off bone and sinew, and scraped his teeth as I struck him over and over again. A primal scream tore out of my throat. I kept hitting him even when he'd stopped moving. Even when my fingers were slick with blood. Even when my gloves were shredded. Even when my hair was damp and lashing me in the face. Even when my hands were raw. I didn't want to stop though. I couldn't breathe. All I could think about was how much I wanted to beat him to a bloody pulp.

A voice at the back of my head questioned the fact that he was bleeding—angels didn't bleed, did they?

The only thing that brought me out of my rage was a devastating flash of lightning that came from inside the cabin, filling the room with the smell of something acidic, like wires and plastic and hair burning.

My head snapped up, and I caught the tail end of Caesar's brutal attack on Larna.

The bolt he'd thrown struck her right in the chest. It was as potent and raw as anything I'd ever produced. From across the room, the force of it rattled my teeth.

It had happened in an instant, but for me, everything ground to a halt as that one awful moment stretched on forever. My heart skipped a beat as I watched Larna's hands fly out in front of her body. She folded in on herself to the point where she was almost touching her toes. All stuffing and no bone. It was horrific and violent. The blast flung her up and through the already-smashed-out window. And just like that, she was gone—tumbling out into the tumultuous storm. A devastating blow.

The moment I heard her cry cut short, my heart plunged, and something inside me fractured all over again. I had witnessed her last moments on earth. She was dead.

My eyes lit up with vampire *Sight*. My fangs were sharp against my bottom lip, and I felt something else— something wicked—as I went after Caesar. I threw my hands together, summoning lightning faster than any unit of time could measure. It came to me in a clap of thunder straight out of heaven. The deadly current shot out of my hands, heading straight for Caesar.

It would have been a perfect shot had it not rebounded off the shield he'd conjured at the last second. The bolt backfired and hit me square in my chest. I was pretty sure my soul left my body. The concussive shock wave drove down through me, shattering my spine, ripping through my chest, and stopping my heart. I rolled to a stop, fetching up against the side of the pool table in the corner of the room. I realized a little too late that I was part vampire, and vampires reacted negatively to angel energy—plus I thought my power was greater than other angels'.

I glanced up in a daze, my hands splayed out by my sides, paralyzed. A wave of debilitating pain rolled through me so intense I forgot to breathe.

I was distantly aware of Vin and Al trying to take

down the other Grigori, the one who had come with Turiel. Al had somehow gotten his blades back and was slashing with a ferocity and swiftness that surprised me.

I could see Imani's dark red lips through the hole in her ski mask as she went after Turiel. He had managed to recover enough to get back on his feet, wiping a hand across his bloodied face. There was a flash of blinding light as he called up lightning. It pulsated eerily in his hand, undulating and moving like a living organism as he weaved his fingers around it, manipulating it like molding clay.

Then Turiel was hurling that globe right at her. I wished I could warn her, but I couldn't move from the waist down. My lungs were on fire. Every single part of me was on fire.

Imani barely dodged out of the way at the last second—part of her vest was still burning—as she yanked a small cylindrical device from her belt and chunked it at Turiel. The light on the grenade started blinking red. A second later it exploded at his feet.

I threw a hand up to shield my face right as there was an oven-hot flash. My back slammed against the hard wooden leg of the pool table. The world spun as a bout of dizziness and nausea overtook me.

As soon as the smoke cleared—and also my head—I realized with dread that Turiel was gone. A part of me hoped he'd been incinerated in the blast, but somehow I knew it wouldn't be that easy. I wasn't sure if Caesar had told Angela I was alive yet. The last time I heard him plotting with Sarah about me, it had sounded like he might not have told her. Now I was sure she would find out. I shoved that worry aside for now. I'd deal with that later. My legs started to twitch; I could feel my toes again.

In all the chaos, I had lost sight of Paul. I could see he'd almost made it to the front door after freeing himself. I tried to get to my feet to go after him, but my body still wouldn't respond. All I could do was gasp and flop awkwardly onto my back like a fish on land.

Paul bounded for the door. There was a flash off to his left. *Sarah.* For one brief second, I thought he was going to make it outside. Instead, the brave fool turned back around, grabbed something out of his pocket, and extended it open with a flick of his wrist. His club. He slashed downward, striking Sarah across her clavicle … for all the good it did. She chopped a hand out, quick like a snake strike, knocking him off-balance. He hammered at her kneecap on his backswing, and there was a shrill crack followed by her shout of rage and pain.

Paul lumbered backward, arms flailing as I came to a knee, my hands igniting in a supernatural crackle of energy. I took aim at Sarah from my crouched position—

And Sarah grabbed Paul's neck, twisting it around viciously in the opposite direction. He didn't scream or utter a sound. His eyes went wide with shock and disbelief, and he dropped like a stone, unmoving.

Sarah's eyes met mine. For a moment, it was just us two in the smoke-filled room. She gave me one last, fleeting grin before hurtling out into the storm.

My vision tunneled to first fire-engine red and then pitch-black as rage roiled through me.

They are all dead.

Chapter 20

Larna

I'D TAKEN A HIT to the chest of what felt like a million amps of current. It hurt to take in air. A huge shard of glass was embedded in my shin, all the way down to the bone. I assumed it had gotten there when Caesar had blasted me out of the window.

My helmet had saved my life, preventing my skull from getting bashed in upon impact. I yanked it off in excruciating slowness, then went to work on my shin, grimacing. Once I'd jerked the glass out, I ground my teeth together, riding out the sudden wave of agony flooding through me. *The pain* will *subside.* I felt the zing of warm healing flow through me, quicker than I expected it to. *Gabriel's blood.*

I knew it was cold outside, because I could see the mist plume out in front of me with each torturous exhale, but I couldn't feel it. The rain came down in sheets so thick I could barely see ten feet in front of me. At my back was the thick outline of trees. I couldn't believe how far I'd been thrown from the cabin.

Even though I couldn't see the wildlife, I could feel their presence, perched in the trees for shelter, riding out the torrential weather all around me.

They were smart. Me—not so much.

I adjusted my one and only piece of leather armor at my wrist. Alastair had broken the other one during his fight with Sarah and Caesar previously. Fortunately, Gabriel had had another set stored away, which he'd temporarily loaned Alastair, and which I'd convinced him to take, instead of me—he was human and needed all the advantage he could get.

Across the way, past the field and beyond the circular gravel drive, I could clearly see the battle raging inside my dad's place. Strobes of blue-white light, which should have been lighting up the night sky outside, lit up the inside of the cabin instead. A sign of angels letting loose their ultimate fury.

The deafening concussion of each thunderclap shook me to my core. I'd only expected to see one angel tonight—not *three* of them. We were seriously outmatched on firepower.

Suddenly I heard someone let out a bloodcurdling howl that was filled with so much anguish, misery, and hatred that it instantly made my blood run cold.

Alastair. Oh no.

A renewed bout of adrenaline tore through me, taking with it some of the incapacitating pain that had kept me rooted to the spot. Whatever had just happened was bad. Very bad. My eyes churned bright with my *Sight*. I launched myself back to my feet, ignoring how much everything hurt—and ran.

Before I could get to the door though, a dark shape hurtled out of a parted curtain of rain, coming right at me.

There was a flash of silver in the darkness. I sidestepped out of the way, distantly feeling the hot sting of something scraping my shoulder. A fist shot out, and I moved under their wide swing, trapping their arm against my chest and driving an elbow up into their face at the same time. My attacker dropped what they were holding with a strangled yelp, and I caught the glint of metal sinking into the mud and muck at our feet. *Sarah.*

When I glanced up, I could see the hate burning her eyes a deep shade of blue, almost purple.

She'd tried to kill Corinth.

She'd tried to kill me.

Alastair too.

I could see my own reflection in her eyes. I raised my fists, a strange calm washing over me. Just her and me now. I imagined I looked like Alastair did when he displayed his mask of defiance. He didn't know it at the time, but he'd been training me for this exact moment. This was not the time to let my anger rule me—I could hear his voice in my head.

One of us wasn't walking away alive. I thought she had come to the same conclusion, because with a terrifying bellow, she closed the distance between us, her sharp, pointed teeth flashing. Her face lit up demonically in the gloom of the elements and night sky raging on above us.

Fights don't happen slowly like they do in the movies. There was no time for shouts or insults. This wasn't coordinated or planned or choreographed. It was ferocious and deadly and ugly. She was much faster than me, so when her knuckles slammed into my nose, it shattered upon impact. Blood gushed out like a fountain. My eyes blurred and burned. I could hear teeth snapping like a rabid dog's as she came at me again, relentless. Water washed the salt and blood down my face and into my mouth.

I blocked as many of her blows as I could, my arms jarring in their sockets with each impact. Pain blossomed up my face, neck, and arms where she struck me. I couldn't see much of anything, even with vampire *Sight*. I was soaking wet, and up close and personal, her mousy-brown hair stuck to her forehead and cheeks, making her skin look purple and puckered.

I fell back as she kept coming at me.

Throwing an arm out on instinct, her fist hit the bony part of my forearm, and I heard the crunch of knuckles breaking against my arm. And then there it was, hot agony washing over me—I pushed it to the back of my mind. It hurt, but I'd been through worse.

I kept my left arm up, blocking my face, letting her get closer with each strike, biding my time. Over confidence was her downfall. Hate was her downfall. Cruelty was her downfall.

The rain mixed with her spittle flying out of her mouth as she rushed at me again—already she was winded. She wanted to kill me too badly. I let her throw a few more strikes, blocking most of them until I saw my opening. I jabbed out, striking her across the jaw with one good, solid blow. She flapped her arms out to the side like an injured bird, stunned. Angry and exposed and hurt.

If I'd never trained with Alastair, I would have let my emotions cloud my judgment long ago. I also wouldn't have been in such good shape. Cardio was a blessing. She was exceedingly strong, but Sarah didn't train. I could tell by how tired she was getting after each bout she dealt me.

Alastair's training saved my life.

I heard the soft *shnick* of my blade releasing from its sheath, and on my exhale, as she charged, I drove the blade home, carving out the center of her chest, the knife going straight through her heart, out the other side in a spray of red and water and bone.

She stumbled back, a terror-stricken look crossing her face, bright green eyes blinking rapidly in disbelief.

I wiped a hand down my mouth, slowly letting my gaze travel to her chest.

Her eyes followed mine down.

Down … down … down …

Once she saw my leather armor still attached to the weapon sticking out of her chest, she let out a choked sob. I'd stabbed her with enough force that she'd ripped it right off my wrist as soon as she'd backed up.

Her heart's labored ticking was loud in my own ears. The copper scent of blood mixed with the smell of ozone. She only had moments left to live. But like a snake with its head cut off, she kept on thrashing right up until the very end.

With dizzying speed, she came at me again—

I jumped in the air, aiming for the armor still rooted in her chest. My kick landed perfectly, forcing the armor deeper into her rib cage. This time she crumpled, collapsing into a motionless heap on the saturated earth— those wide jade-green eyes staring up at me in incredulity and death.

Chapter 21

Corinth

PAUL IS DEAD BECAUSE of me. Paul is dead. Paul is dead because of me. Paul is dead …

Guilt and rage swirled inside me, obscuring my perception, turning madness into something corporeal. I felt like a champagne cork right before it bursts free—all compressed air and wrath. I was on the verge of explosion. My chest tightened as what felt like an external force tried to burst its way out of me in the form of arcing electricity.

Chaos ensued around me as I let loose a battle cry, and jumped to my feet, lightning shooting out of my fingertips, still curled around my blade. It snapped and sparked, sizzling blindingly bright. In my head, I played out all of the things I was going to do to Sarah—starting with frying her to a crispy, sautéed nub. I'd let her heal and then do it all over again.

The caged energy exploded out of my hands, destroying the rest of the thick material of my gloves. I had no idea how much power was coursing through me— all I knew was that it felt good. Really good. Without even needing to look in the other Grigori's direction, the one that was fighting Vinson and Al, I let loose the rippling tide of deadly lightning.

The angel barely managed to conjure a shield at the last second, but it didn't matter. I watched in equal parts fascination and awe as lightning crystallized into a sharp spike. The projectile plowed right past his defenses and through his chest, exploding of out his back, and on his silent exhalation of agony and surprise, he crumpled like he'd been made of only skin and bones—no muscle.

Across the room, I made eye contact with Caesar. I couldn't hide my pleasure at seeing him look so frightened. I might have imagined seeing a flash of regret in his eyes too.

I set my jaw in determination, stalking toward him, unafraid. He scrambled backward and cowered behind one of the wooden legs on the pool table. His fingers ignited like Roman candles, and he took aim at me from his hunkered position.

I threw my blade out in front of me, and in a shower of golden sparks, my shield flared to life, thwarting his feeble attack.

"*Coward!*" I shouted.

Caesar's eyes zipped around the room, assessing, looking for his next move or opening to kill me. "If I can't hurt you, Slayer, I'll hurt the ones you love." He grinned and took aim at someone off to my left.

The vibrations in the air reverberated around me like a tuning fork. My senses were heightened, so when I threw myself to the side, I moved with the speed recently gifted to me by vampirism to easily block his attack once again.

"*Stay behind me!*" I yelled to the rest of our group. I was the only person standing between them and Caesar's reign of terror. I'd seen what he could do. My chest constricted again as I thought about Larna out there all alone in the dark and stormy night.

I prayed she was still alive—but I doubted it. Not with that amount of power he'd put behind that bolt of lightning. I wondered if Gabriel was still out there. Something told me, not in this weather.

He opened fire right as I felt a hand on my back— Imani's.

My shield flared up again as his lightning struck it in a shower of sparks and sweltering heat. Vinson and Al were behind me too now—I could hear their breath sawing out of their mouths extremely loudly in my ears.

Caesar let out another volley of lightning—his attempt at trying to take down the entire cabin. He was no longer concerned about getting away. He wanted to take us all with him.

I reached for my *Sight*, embracing it this time—even the pain of hunger that came with it. All of it. Every part of my messed-up, melting-pot self. And I found it: A pulsing blue beacon in the inky abyss, waiting as faithfully terrifying as ever. A glimmer of insanity. I let myself get lost in it. Reveled in it. Bathed in its almighty glory—

Caesar jumped out from behind the pool table, kamikaze style, barreling into me like a freight train. There was no going back for either of us. His hands were already blazing bright. I grunted in surprise but managed to drive a knee into his stomach. He floundered back a step as my own hands burst into flames. I grabbed the front of his robe at the same time as he took hold of my vest. There was a blazing light and then blinding pain. I collapsed, taking him with me to the floor, our hands still tangled in the folds of each other's clothes. Dark brown irises, round as saucers, met mine.

Besides the pitter-patter of rain splashing on the wooden floorboards, the only sound in the cramped cabin was Caesar's sharp inhalation.

We both looked down at the same time.

No. Numbness spread through me at seeing the wound. It was almost comical, the gaping hole in my chest. Smoke curled up and out of the grievous injury. A part of me knew this was the end. I felt frantic hands on my back, pulling me away from Caesar. Maybe Imani. Maybe Vin.

I released my grip on Caesar and looked back to see him smiling up at me, all pointy teeth. "You made me do it, Corinth—look how many have died today."

Oddly enough, he sounded despondent.

I thought the person holding on to me was Vin, not Imani. I could smell aftershave. My vision blurred.

A steady buzzing of electricity and charged energy vibrated through the air. A ripple of power surged up and surrounded me in a strange golden light. I swore I felt something unfurl out of my back. *Like wings.*

The hands around me fell away, and someone yelped. I heard Al curse behind me. Imani let out an involuntary bark of surprise.

The hole in my chest began to fill in, the damaged skin miraculously stitching itself back together again. The numbness started to leave my limbs. I clutched at my chest in astonishment as it healed.

Slowly I got back to my feet.

Caesar gave a nervous laugh. "Corinth, you are … more *powerful* than …" He choked on the word before he could get it out. "Let's work this out. I know how civil you can be. I know you … I know—" he swallowed again "—you like to talk things out. I can teach you how to use all that untapped power coursing through you." He held his hand out toward me, pleading. "Come with me. I can tell you everything you want to know about the cure. You don't have to die … not like this. I can help you."

The wind outside howled its disapproval, answering for me, as I leveled my gaze on his outstretched hand.

I took one last look at Paul's lifeless form near the door. What I was about to do was for Paul. For all the lives lost back at the clan too. The broken glass on the ground near the window he'd thrown Larna through glittered like a flashing light.

I threw a quick glance behind me to see the stunned faces. Al looked stricken. I knew he wanted to go to Larna, but he was pinned down behind me. Waiting. Watching. Stunned. He wasn't going anywhere until I took out the last remaining threat inside this cabin.

The other angel was dead, blasted to smithereens. Turiel had escaped. Imani, Al, Vin were all alive, but … *Larna*, she was still out there—and she hadn't come back.

My head was buzzing. *Dead.* She was dead. He had killed her. Fury bubbled up inside me like a geyser, ready to blow.

"I'm long past civility," I told him with icy malice. "You want power? I'll show you power."

I threw everything I had at him, uncontained lightning pouring out of my hands with such force that the blast threw him backward. A high-pitched wail came out of him, not sounding even remotely human anymore. It rose to a fevered pitch for what felt like an eternity, before finally winding down to a mangled gurgle.

Chapter 22

Larna

ALL I COULD FOCUS on as I hurtled back into the cabin was the fact that Corinth had wings. Wings that were neither feathery nor cute—they were breathtaking but in a terrifying way—haunting and extraordinary. They looked like hot coals burning black and red in a fire. Dark and ominous shadows slinking behind him, only visible in the flashes of light. The fire radiating off him was like opening an oven door and being blasted full in the face by heat.

I had been able to heal faster than normal, thanks to Gabriel's blood—he had saved my life.

The air sizzled with so much static electricity and ozone that my hair stood on end. In school, I'd learned lightning currents moved over the surface of the body in a process called external flashover. Atmospheric charges could exceed three hundred thousand volts—so when Corinth had them exploding out of his entire body, I was sure his ticket had been punched.

Bile rose in the back of my throat at seeing what was left of Caesar's prone form at Corinth's feet. At least, I thought it was Caesar. He looked like the melted wax in a fragrance burner. The entire room was stifling, suffocating. My hair, which had been soaking wet when I'd come charging back into the room, was now dry. It smelled like an electrical fire. The heat around Corinth sucked the oxygen from the cramped living room. Whatever vortex folded around him was widening, and it looked eerily similar to a black hole.

"You're going to kill us all!" I tried to shout over the tumultuous roar of wind and rain and thunder from the open door behind me.

Imani, Vinson, and Alastair were all staring at Corinth in complete shock. It wasn't until Corinth turned his head toward me that I saw what they saw: hollowed-out sockets. His eyes had been replaced by lightning. A shiver worked its way down my spine. This moment reminded me of the first time Corinth had found his true power. The night my dad had died by Gabriel's hands. That hadn't been *true* power—*this* was.

Empty holes in his head flashed molten white as he turned his gaze on me, the weird light dancing in his sockets. I willed myself not to get sucked into those hollow eyes as I stepped forward, closer to him.

The shadows seemed to have sunk into the contours of Corinth's cheekbones, making him look almost like he was wearing makeup. I got a sick sinking feeling in the pit of my stomach—I couldn't bring him back from this.

I drifted closer on impulse, and someone put a hand on my shoulder, halting my progress. Alastair.

"Get everyone to the chopper. We'll be right behind you. *Go*," I told him.

"I can't leave him or you behind," he said softly,

throwing a backward glance toward the front door of the cabin.

I thought he meant Corinth. I was going to tell him that I would get him back, but when I turned to see what Alastair was staring at, my stomach dropped. There was a prone form lying stock-still near the doorway. Too intent on Corinth's self-explosion, I hadn't seen the body until now. I sucked in a horrified breath, trying to tamp down the sudden rush of loss coursing through me. *Paul.* I couldn't deal with it—not yet, or I'd break.

I went rigid all over and then finally found my voice. It broke, but I heard the force behind my words. "I just need you out of here now. *Please*, Alastair."

"What about Sarah?" he asked through clenched teeth.

"I took care of her," I hissed.

He gave Corinth one more brief glance before finally relenting. After that, all three of them disappeared out into the thunderstorm without another word, leaving me behind to deal with possessed Corinth. I shuddered and then stepped up to him.

I didn't know why I did it—even standing this close felt like being roasted alive. I could sense the overwhelming amount of mental anguish in him. I knew I was risking a lot by touching him, but I reached out anyway, placing a hand against his chest. The touch was galvanizing. A jolt arced between us, and even though it hurt to keep my hand there, I didn't dare move or back down from him. The hole around him widened, along with his wings.

The light dancing in empty sockets was unnerving,

which made it that much creepier, because I knew he was staring at me. Tiny sparks of electricity shot out of his fingertips, arcing over what was left of the material on his bloodied hands.

His wings flickered eerily—almost enveloping me in their blistering embrace as he stepped closer. If they touched me, I knew it wouldn't feel like fluffy feathers. The heat increased, and I started to feel woozy.

Corinth tilted his head to the side and then looked down at my hand on his chest. He shook his head. There was a tiny crack in his countenance as he tried to take back control. The supernatural energy surrounding him dissipated, and so did the wings at his back. His maple-colored eyes returned. I could see the glaze of pain in them.

He wrapped strong arms around me. "*I thought you were dead.*"

I returned his hug, suddenly overwhelmed by everything. "I'm okay. I'm not going anywhere. You're okay."

After a moment, his attention settled back on Paul, and then he left me to stumble over to him, sinking down to his knees, a pained expression on his face.

I followed suit, collapsing beside Paul, opposite Corinth.

Corinth's hands were glowing blue again. Before I could stop him, he held them above Paul's chest, and a surge of energy poured out of them, flowing down into his lifeless form. I wondered idly if this was how Corinth had been able to bring Alastair back.

I was choking on my own tears now. I didn't want to lose Paul.

"Can you bring him back?" I rasped.

"*I ... I can ... bring him ... back.*" He slammed blazing hands against Paul's chest, hard, performing CPR.

I let Corinth do it, hoping and wishing that maybe he *could* bring him back. He'd done it before.

Each time Corinth hit Paul, he said, "*I can bring him back.*"

It was his mantra. Mine too.

"*I can bring him back.*"

For one fleeting moment, I believed he could. But the longer he worked, with nothing happening, the more the rock in the pit of my stomach seemed to grow larger.

After a while, all I could focus on was the sound of hands pumping rhythmically against Paul's chest. Paul never moved or uttered a sound. There were no signs of life left in him. I don't know how long it lasted or when I slumped back, hyperaware of Corinth's hands slick with blood. His hair was stuck to the side of his face with sweat. How far would I let him go before I tried to stop him? He was going to kill himself.

After what seemed like an excruciatingly long time, I reached out to stop him, but Corinth gave me a look, and I pulled my hand back. I couldn't stop him. I didn't want to. *Paul.*

Alastair appeared beside me. I had no idea where he'd come from. He put a hand on my cheek, checking on me, his eyes searching.

"You came back," I breathed, unable to look at him.

"I never left," he said quietly.

My eyes finally drifted to Alastair's, but his gaze was fixed intently on Corinth. We both watched him work, enthralled. Corinth looked as drained as I felt, and even though the light still glowed out of his hands, I could see the lethargy starting to set in. His eyes were glassy, and his head started to sag with each zap of energy he sent down into Paul.

Alastair squeezed his eyes shut. His left eye was swollen closed, and half his face was covered in little spatters of blood. He cradled his right arm close to his chest, his wrist a gnarly shade of violet.

"I can't make Corinth stop … I … I don't want to," I admitted. "But I think he's hurting himself."

I tried to half-heartedly pull Corinth off Paul again. "*Don't try and stop me,*" he snarled, then yanked out of my grasp and, with renewed vigor, struck Paul's chest with a closed fist. Corinth looked ghostly pale in the darkened room.

I threw a hand to my face and crumpled to the floor, spent.

Alastair stepped up behind Corinth and swiftly wrapped his good arm around Corinth's neck, hauling him backward, away from Paul.

Corinth's hands curled around Alastair's forearm as he struggled against Alastair, but he had him in a tight choke hold—and Corinth was done, in more ways than one.

I heard Alastair speak softly in Corinth's ear, "He's gone. You can't bring him back." My heart broke seeing the power start to flood out of Corinth as Alastair whispered, "Sometimes gone is gone."

The sizzle of energy playing across Corinth's skin dissipated as Alastair squeezed tighter, cutting off just enough oxygen so Corinth would pass out. His eyelids fluttered closed, and Alastair gently guided him down to the floor, cradling his head so it wouldn't slam against the hardwood.

I crouched over Corinth to check his pulse. Unlike before, his skin was now ice-cold, and his slow, deep breaths told me he wasn't waking up anytime soon. The way his eyes moved rapidly under closed lids worried me.

"One of the Grigori got away … He'll go to Angela," I said quickly. "Corinth's in danger … especially unconscious."

Alastair lifted his shoulders and glanced back down to Paul. "We should get out of here. It's not safe." I detected a slight waver in his voice. "I couldn't save him."

Vinson stalked back inside the cabin. He said something in Russian and, after a brief pause, stilled himself, and then ever so carefully, he bent down over Paul to lift him off the ground. Without a backward glance, he carried him out into the rain. The soft tapping as it hit the roof sounded like tears falling.

Alastair clenched something tightly in his fist, his knuckles going white.

Imani was beside me, grabbing Corinth under one arm, while I took his other side. We stumbled out into the stormy night with him in tow, both of us exhausted. Imani's restrained silence spoke volumes to me. She really did care about Corinth.

As we carried him to the waiting chopper, Alastair stopped in front of Sarah's corpse, the object still clasped in his hand. Even with all those battle wounds covering his features, I could still make out the resentment on his face as he looked down upon her. Alastair gave me a sidelong glance and then dumped the object onto her corpse.

Curious to see what it was, I glanced down to see something shiny and silver in the dark. To my surprise, I realized it was his pocket watch, the one he'd taken from Wrentmore.

He gave me a pained, thin-lipped smile. "It's over."

Gabriel exploded out of the still-running chopper to help everyone on board. The rain had slackened off, and a thick carpet of wet leaves flew into the air as we took off.

After what seemed like a devastatingly long time, Gabriel made his way over to sit beside me. He squinted down at the slumbering form. Alastair moaned softly, his head lolling from side to side in my lap. He had refused to let me treat his wounds. He had also declined to take anything for the pain. Probably his way of punishing himself for not being able to save Paul's life.

"We needed Sarah alive," he said pointedly. "I could have used compulsion to get answers."

"She killed Paul."

"Let me get this straight—you lot didn't get any information on the whereabouts of the cure?" Gabriel turned to gesture at Corinth, who was still dead to the world, splayed out on the opposite side from us—next to Imani. "That gray pallor to his skin does wonders for his complexion. Keep this up, and he won't be around to reap the benefits of a cure at all," he grumbled. "Shall I tell my pilot to take us to my estate?"

I shook my head adamantly. "No. Nan's place. You know the address." My voice cracked. "We have to lay Paul to rest."

"You realize this is my helicopter, right? I can make my pilot take us anywhere without your consent."

I watched Vinson cover Paul's body with his trench coat. There was something jarring and familiar about Vinson's act of compassion. It reminded me of the night I'd lost my father. A wave of grief and remorse washed over me so strongly that I gasped from it all.

I put my head in my hands. "Please, *Stanton*, just take us to Nan's place. You can drop us off and leave."

Gabriel cleared his throat beside me as if he wasn't quite familiar with feelings of sorrow or hearing me plead—still, somehow I felt that he understood. He dropped his hand down, and his fingers brushed against mine.

Eventually, he wiped a hand across his mouth and said, "Miss Collins, your best friend, who is still *alive*, albeit debatably"—he gestured at Corinth again—"is dying. There is no time for this. I can better protect you all from one of my compounds. Please, see reason."

"You sanctimonious ass ... I didn't see you racing in to help until after the fight was over." I choked back a flood of tears, tasting salt at the back of my throat. "If you could have seen what Corinth did—" I ran a hand through my hair, glancing down at Alastair. He was snoring softly. My stomach did a flip as I thought about blood ... There was just so much of it—the scent was almost too overpowering for even my level of control.

Gabriel must have sensed it too, because he was

fishing out a metal flask from the inside of his jacket pocket. "Fine. We go to Nan's. But you're convincing her to let me stay there too. Where you go, I go."

He tried to hand me the flask, but I didn't take it from him. I didn't want to admit to him that his blood had saved my life.

"You should drink. This was for Corinth. It's my blood, but seeing as how you're so weak—"

"Why do you even care?"

He turned away from me, avoiding my dogged gaze. "I'm just protecting my investment. Look, you did your best to try and help your friend, but if you don't keep your strength up, how can you expect to help Corinth? Besides, by the looks of you, I'd say your next snack will be your boyfriend."

I tilted my head to get a better look at Gabriel. "You can sense it too? Something off about his blood … I thought it was just me."

Gabriel nodded. "There is something altered in him since he came back. I don't know what it is though."

He was right. I could feel the tips of my fangs growing. I felt wretched and ashamed, so I grabbed the flask out of his hand and drank.

Gabriel spoke so softly I almost missed it, "I'm sorry about your friend." And then he vacated the seat next to mine so quickly I thought I'd imagined him saying something.

Chapter 23

Larna

NAN'S PROPERTY WAS JUST how I remembered it: rolling hills, green meadows—Clark Kent's family home meets Martha Stewart's with bohemian flair. It had been repaired to exactly the way I remembered it before Gabriel and company had set fire to it. That was why it was all the more awkward bringing him back here with us.

Fortunately, Nan was in a forgiving mood, so she let Gabriel onto her property on the condition that he didn't bring any of his people with him.

I had fond memories of reconnecting with my dad here. And it was where I'd really started to fall in love with Alastair. It's funny how someone can breathe a little bit of their own life into you by simply sharing their past in confidence. That connection with him was all the more profound.

We buried Paul beside my father's grave. Paul didn't have much in the way of family—except for us—and I knew he'd want this to be his final resting place.

Alastair wrapped an arm around my waist and pulled me close. The setting winter sun seemed to express our sorrow through the evolution of color: purple, gold, and magenta—deep shades of a bruise; the clouds looked a lot like Alastair's face. Fortunately, his eye wasn't as swollen as it had been.

In this one solitary moment, there were no Grigori chasing us, no race for the cure … just Alastair and me watching a retreating sun, the shadows between the trees on the edge of her property starting to thicken.

I remembered the pond about half a mile down the trail, and I suddenly longed to visit it again. There was something so soothing about listening to the cacophony of frogs singing in the background. It was cooler out now, so I wasn't sure we would even hear them.

"You're warmer than I remember," I said finally.

He snaked a hand into his jacket pocket. "I'm freezing my buns off."

I laid my head on his shoulder. "Do you want to go back inside?"

"Are you kidding? And miss this sunset? Besides, Stanton is in there."

We were silent, enjoying each other's company for a while, before I said, "How do you feel?"

Alastair turned to regard me, his lips pursed in thought. "If you mean physically, I'm a little sore, but I was dead not too long ago … so I'll gladly take a couple of bruises."

I snorted. "Try a couple of bruised ribs, concussion, *and* a sprained wrist—"

He pulled me closer, effectively cutting off my listing of his injuries. "All of that fighting last night, and we couldn't save Paul … It just seems so …" He stopped, unable to find the right words, I thought.

Unfair. I could hear the hurt in his voice.

"Nothing is fair about any of this," I whispered.

We'd lost a great man.

"Me not being able to heal quickly means I might be a detriment to you. Maybe we should reconsider turning me …" He let his voice trail off.

I reached up to caress his cheek. It was pink from the cold. "No way in hell are we having the turn-me-back-into-a-vampire talk. Not gonna happen, unless that's what you truly want. But something tells me it isn't."

He shook his head against the top of mine. "Not craving blood is both strange and wonderful. I know it probably sounds petty, but I can finally enjoy the food I cook. That wasn't an option a few short days ago. To be able to get this chance now is"—he shrugged—"incredible. But it bothers me that maybe you don't feel the same way." He winced and rubbed a hand gingerly across his bruised jaw. "I don't mind the physical pain. Paul was family. And I don't have much in the way of family. That's the pain I can't take—losing someone else I love. You and Corinth and Vinson are it now. And even though Corinth is the sarcastic, whiny little brother I never had—"

I gave him a playful nudge as I said, "I want what you want. You've sacrificed everything—and I mean *everything*—to get to this point in your life. You saved my life. No way am I letting anyone take that away from you. How did you convince Nan to let Gabriel back on her property, anyway?"

Alastair sighed. "I didn't. Vinson did. I don't know what he told her, but it must have been pretty convincing.

Nan hates Stanton with a passion. I wouldn't be surprised if she's plotting to kill him right now. If we didn't need his"—he did air quotes—"*donation* to Corinth, I might kill him myself."

At the mention of Corinth, I took in a shaky breath. He hadn't woken up since we'd arrived. The state he was in was bad. We were no closer to getting the cure from Angela, and without Dave's help, we were lost. Corinth might not ever wake up again.

There was only one thing I could think to do, and I did *not* like it. Desperate times called for desperate measures though.

I said, "Speaking of Corinth, that was some crazy cosmic display he put on back at the cabin. I'm really worried about him."

He nodded his agreement. "It worries me how quickly he's deteriorating. It seems to be correlated with how much he uses his power. If he keeps going at this rate, he'll kill himself."

For the first time in a long time, I felt cold, and it wasn't from the frigid temps. I was worried about what the future had in store for us.

The sun crested the last hill and then ever so slowly sank below the horizon. I could have sworn it gave us one final wink as it did. I pressed myself against Alastair's side, listening to the sound of his strong, steady pulse.

He took a deep breath, and when he spoke, it was barely above a whisper. "I fell in love with you back at Stanton's manor—*before* you were turned. There was so much light in you that it was impossible not to notice. I think it counteracted all that darkness inside me." He paused, and I weaved my fingers through his and squeezed. His face lit up with a smile from ear to ear, which I'm sure had to hurt, but he didn't seem to mind. "I was trapped in a figurative well. It was just so damn dark. But every time you came around … it was as if you were shining a spotlight down into that well—into my soul. That light was everything. In those rare moments, I could feel the warmth again. I had been in the cold for so long. I thought to myself, maybe I'm not trapped down here all alone after all. You made me laugh. I'd forgotten what that was like." His gaze stayed locked on the place where the sun had sunk below the hill. "I'm sorry I never told you any of this until now. I should have …" His voice faltered. "When your father spoke about you, his eyes would always shine with pride. It was the only time I ever felt that he had, at one time, actually been a normal human being. He made for one intimidating vampire … It was why I was so curious about you when we finally did meet. Your father was a born leader—as are you. There's something about you, Larna Collins."

"He was never an intimidating dad," I said softly. "He was goofy and clumsy, and he came up with the lamest jokes ever. He was one amazing photographer. He had an eye for it. He hated cell phone cameras." I rubbed a hand under my nose. "You know what, Alastair Iszler?"

"What?"

"I never thought I'd fall for a blond."

Alastair laughed. It was a full-throated belly laugh. I loved it. It had seemed so long since I'd heard him laugh in this way.

"You know what I'm looking forward to?" he asked.

I shook my head against his shoulder.

"Growing old." Alastair's arm fell from around my waist. He turned suddenly to look me in the eyes, grabbing hold of both my shoulders. His blue eyes sparkled like jewels. "I was trying to make a point earlier, and I didn't have the courage to bring it back up. Even though I want to be selfish staying human … this isn't about me. It's about something bigger. You should turn me. There is going to be an epic battle coming. I can feel it. Once we have the cure in hand, I can choose to be human again."

His gaze searched mine as if he were looking for any signs of what he thought I might be thinking in response.

I took a moment to gather my thoughts before saying, "Even though your eyes are as hypnotic as ever, you don't have the ability of compulsion anymore, Alastair. Neither you nor anyone else is going to convince me that you should be turned back. I've never seen you happier, and you want me to take that away from you? In case we don't find this cure, at least you've gotten exactly what you wanted. A chance at a normal life. So, no, I will *not* turn you. No one else will either, for that matter."

He put his hands on his head, clearly frustrated, but I could see relief too. "I tried."

"And it was a very valiant effort," I added wryly. "You love me for saying no."

At that, he turned in a circle, his hands still on his head as he barked out an exasperated laugh. "More than *Star Wars*, more than *Miracle on 34th Street*; more than cooking, more than my leather jacket, and definitely more than anything else in this entire messed-up world."

Alastair enfolded me in his arms and leaned down to

kiss me. He smelled strongly of fresh soap, and his lips tasted sweet, as if he'd just eaten grapes. I melted against him as he drew me close. I felt light-headed from our combined body heat. It felt right, like we were two puzzle pieces snapping together. My cheeks flushed as his lips grazed my neck and throat. He trailed soft kisses over my skin, moving lower, toward the hollow point of my neck. I let out a soft moan as he pulled back for a second, his brows rising in his way of asking permission before continuing. I wanted to say, "Don't stop, dummy," but words had inconveniently left me.

Instead, I pulled him closer, my mouth tracing the shape of his. I knew he could feel the tug of my smile, because he matched it with one of his own—a fervent one. I'd never had anyone look at me the way he was looking at me. His hands snaked underneath my shirt, caressing bare skin at my lower back. I shivered under his electrifying touch. I could feel the need in it—pure and simple and carnal. He wound his other hand into my hair, not so gently tugging my head back to deepen his kiss, his breathing quickening. Okay, I'd never had anyone kiss me the way he did, either.

I didn't even realize we'd moved until his body was crushing mine against the house—on the far side of the wraparound porch—hopefully, away from prying eyes. Sneaking in moments like these were all we had right now.

We stayed locked together for a good long while, enjoying the warmth of each other's company, and by the time we separated, we were breathless, our hair a tangled mess and our skin on fire.

I put a hand to my lips and whispered, "I love you.

Chapter 24

Larna

I T WAS AS TENSE as a presidential cabinet meeting during a world-ending crisis when Alastair and I wandered back into the living room. The source of all that tension was poised on the edge of one of the kitchenette island barstools that overlooked the living area—the same place where I'd sat and watched Alastair cook bacon shirtless all those months ago.

It was extremely unsettling and weird seeing Gabriel Stanton in this safe space. One of his legs was folded over the other one as he so delicately sipped a cup of hot tea, his pinky finger sticking out.

That was the spot where I'd asked Alastair to tell me all about vampires. It had been extremely hard to come to terms with the fact that supernatural creatures existed in this world. Now I was one of them.

I noticed Nan sitting on the living room floor, perched atop a fancy tasseled rug in yoga meditation pose. I thought she was probably trying not to kill Gabriel. She looked just as stunning as when I'd seen her the last time—maybe a little bit less frightening. Her long silver hair was in an intricate braid running down the length of her back. I couldn't help noticing how her black skin contrasted with the gray slate of her eyes. She looked comfortably relaxed in a flannel shirt, tank top, and formfitting yoga pants.

Vinson was sitting on the stairs, silently drinking out of a bottle of vodka. He barely acknowledged us as we walked in. That had been Paul's favorite spot, situated closest to the door so he could slip outside to have a smoke whenever he wanted.

My heart started to ache all over again. I missed him. I even missed the scent of his stale cigarettes. I missed riding in the back seat of his trashed Beetle, which was parked in the driveway, and I missed the twitch of his long handlebar mustache as it hid his rare smiles.

Corinth was splayed out across one of the deep, spacious couches near the fireplace, a warm-looking fuzzy blanket thrown over his lower half, his arms wrapped protectively around himself—sleeping soundlessly.

The fire proved to have more life than he did as it spit, crackled, and roared.

My heart sped up at the sight of him. He had the same leaden tinge to his skin, only now it seemed to have gotten worse. He didn't appear to be well rested—his hair was matted to his forehead, and he was shivering despite the warmth of the room and close proximity to the fire.

Imani sat poised on the arm of the couch next to Corinth, as sleek and quiet as a cat, but she was a bundle of raw nerves, the tip of her long red fingernails beating out a rhythm against her thigh. She also had a slight twitch in her jaw that seemed to get worse the longer she watched Corinth sleep.

The heat was stifling now, and I tugged at my shirt collar in irritation. I would have complained about how hot it was, if it weren't for the fact that Alastair had moved to stand in front of the fireplace, his hands held out in front of him. By the way his back was set, I could tell he was just as troubled as I was by Corinth's condition.

Nan finally spoke in a clear and authoritative voice. "Larna, dear, I said if Gabriel Stanton ever stepped foot on my property again, I'd kill him. I have only reserved myself thus far because you all have asked me not to. And the only reason I have chosen to listen to your request is that I had the utmost respect for your father, and I told him I'd look out for you. I realize you have need of Gabriel's blood and his resources, but I have both of those things. I would sooner kill Gabriel and provide you with my own to aid Corinth. I can assure you it is just as valuable."

Alastair turned his back to the fire to glare at Gabriel. "She does have a valid point."

Gabriel, unperturbed, took a sip of his hot tea without comment, his lips twisting up at the corners in amusement. He had never looked so British in his entire life.

I said, "Trust me … Don't think I haven't considered killing him every single second since he's been with us. But we need him."

Everyone's head swiveled toward Nan as if this was a sports match and I'd just made a point for our team. It wasn't as if I'd challenged her to a duel or anything, but the way she growled in response made me realize how delicate a situation this truly was. He had burned down her house, after all.

This wasn't time to back down. Something told me Nan would respect me more if I stood up for what I believed in. Nan was the grandmother I wished I'd had, although *grandmother* didn't really fit her title description. Her confidence, warmth, and take-no-shit attitude made for the type of person you wanted to keep around for a lifetime. But in this moment, she was way more intimidating than Gabriel had ever been. I felt this decision might make or break us.

"This is your house—your rules. We have come here for *help* and to bury our friend. I will vouch for Stanton. If he does anything to break your trust ... you can hold me personally responsible." My eyes darted back over to Gabriel. His smug expression had disappeared, replaced by a flicker of something I couldn't quite identify.

I glanced back to Nan. "You can kill him *and* me both."

Alastair whirled around at hearing this, a look of pure abhorrence on his face. I made sure to avoid his pointed gaze.

One side of Nan's mouth quirked up. She seemed more impressed than imposing, but only just. I tried to suppress the slow tremor that worked its way down my spine. I knew that she was the type that would actually go through with my proposal if something did go wrong.

"It would seem you are better at negotiating than I remember. Just make sure he plays nice—'cause I handle up on all my pacts." Nan's gaze fell on Corinth. "As for your friend, I will try and keep him as comfortable as possible, but there is nothing else I can do for him at this point. This is beyond even my expertise. He needs his own kind—and by that, I mean angels."

I was worried about that, but I kept it to myself for now.

"Thank you, Nan. You have shown us kindness when you didn't have to," I said tiredly.

She inclined her head, a ghost of a smile playing on her lips. "Of course I had to. Especially after you lot came dragging in here looking like drowned rats. That was one magnificent storm last night."

An idea struck me so suddenly I jumped to my feet, excitement buzzing through my bloodstream. Corinth's own kind. Angels. Weather. Lightning. Storm.

"Do you have a laptop?" I asked suddenly.

Nan nodded. "Of course I do, child. I'm not afraid of technology."

Alastair perked up, turning his back to the fire. "What is it?"

"I have an idea," I said excitedly.

"What are you doing?"

I slammed the borrowed laptop closed, twisting around from the spot I'd claimed on the floor next to the couch Corinth was lying on. My mouth fell open as soon as I saw that he was awake, slow-blinking down at me, his eyes still glossy with pain and fatigue. It took me a few more dull-witted moments to realize he was actually conscious.

I threw myself into his arms and could hear his teeth chattering loudly in my ear. He still looked like death—

minus the warmed-over part.

"*You're awake!*" I pulled back. "And you feel like a block of ice."

He gave me a weak pat before extricating himself from my firm grasp on his shoulders. "Where are we? How long have I been out? Did you get Sarah?"

"We're at Nan's place. You've been out for almost a day. It's three a.m. Everyone is asleep, I think." I glanced away from those big chocolate-colored eyes of his. "Sarah is dead. We came here to lay Paul to rest. Gabriel is upstairs …"

I let the sentence trail off at that thought, thinking about how strange it was that Gabriel was actually here. *How have things been so turned upside down?*

"Were you the one to—"he cleared his throat"—get Sarah?"

"Yeah, yeah, I was."

He nodded, looking away, and I could have sworn I caught dampness at the corners of his eyes, but when he turned back to face me, he only said, "On a scale of one to ten … ten being the worst … how bad is my hair?"

I knew when he was avoiding dealing with his emotions, so I let it drop for now and reached a hand out to brush a disheveled lock from his forehead. "It's off the charts."

He groaned and then set to work patting his hair back down. "Guess I shouldn't complain. I mean, at least I get to die with a full head of hair."

I instinctively grabbed his hand in mine, my heart wrenching painfully. "You don't get to give up on me," I said. "We need to talk about what happened back there with Caesar—"

Before I could even finish the rest of the sentence, he barked out a quick "No," his body going tense all over. He must have sensed that I was going to argue, because he said, "Drop it, Larna, *please.*"

Oh no. That was his serious face. He only brought it out on the direst of occasions.

"Okay. Fine. But I'm resurrecting the topic later." After hesitating for a moment, I added, "Are you hungry?"

"Perpetually," he said, nodding. "But I could really go for some coffee right now. Comfort plus heat in a cup equals medicine."

I relocated to the kitchen to search the cabinets for the mugs and coffee while he raised his voice from the living room. I wanted to tell him it wasn't necessary, but I stayed quiet anyway, letting him speak.

"So … this is Nan's place … The last time I was here, I never got a chance to come inside, because of the repairs taking place. It's … nice. Simple." Corinth pulled the fleece all the way up to his chin. "I like the traveler vibe she's got going on. Makes me feel like I'm in Tibet or Kamar-Taj … like I had to climb a mountain or something to get here. Fetch me some more throw pillows, woman—"

I'd already thrown one at him, using vamp speed, of course. It hit his face, and he pretended to fall back wounded.

As I finished putting the coffee on, I traipsed back into the living room. "You can stop pretending you're okay." I forced my way back onto the couch beside him, lifting his feet to place them on top of my lap. He was still shivering.

Corinth was staring blindly into the fire now, watching the flames dance around the stacked logs. "Someone is playing a cruel joke on me, and I'm still waiting to get the punchline, because I'm a glutton for punishment." He rubbed a hand over his glazed eyes and then ran it down his face. "Can you do me a favor?"

"Anything," I said without hesitation.

He glanced around the room as if he didn't want to be overheard. When he was satisfied that we were alone, he whispered, "I want to call my family … to tell them …" He swallowed hard, shaking his head. "No … not me. I want *you* to tell them I don't care about what they're keeping from me. I know they thought what they did was for the best. I want you to look out for my family when I'm gone."

I hopped up, letting his legs fall back to the couch and he groaned.

I bit my lip. *Don't cry. Don't cry. Don't cry.*

When I was able to get my jaw to stop quivering, I said, "No way. That's your job. You have to call them and explain everything, Taylor. I know your mom and dad will hear you out."

I pretended to check on the coffee, dashing back into the kitchen to gain control of my emotions. If I kept eye contact with him, I really would lose it.

His voice once again rose loudly from the living room, even though he didn't have to raise it—I could hear him perfectly. "Larns, I know you're not religious, and I get that, I do, but I *am*. I believe I have these … *abilities* for a reason—and the blade …"

I risked a glance at him from across the kitchenette to

see he had rolled his eyes up to the ceiling.

"I think some people are meant to do greater things in life in a shorter amount of time than others because that's all they get. One quick, wild ride—the length of an amusement park roller coaster. That's my journey. So when I ask you to take care of my family, I don't ask it lightly."

Forgetting the coffee, I found myself drifting back into the living room, standing over him without even realizing it, my arms crossed protectively over my chest. "Of course I'll take care of your family. I promise, Corinth … but … believe me when I tell you that you're getting to the old-and-gray part of life if it's the last thing I do."

He closed his eyes and smiled a small, sad smile. "Tell Al he's not off the hook either."

The Beetle was filthy. There were cigarette stains covering the driver's seat, and the ceiling fabric hung down just low enough to hit the top of my head. I ran my hand along the inner-roof lining, thinking about the last time I'd been in Paul's car. Paul *was* this car. Even in death, he was helping me out. The key was still in the ignition. I started the engine and it rumbled to life—*Old Faithful.* The interior might be in poor condition, but it still ran well, and there was half a tank of gas left.

I checked the GPS on my phone again and then powered it down. It should be enough to get me to where I needed to go without having to hit a station to fill up. As I was putting the car into first gear and backing out, the passenger door flew open, and Gabriel hopped inside, a waft of his cologne coming right along with him.

I couldn't hide my surprise as I pressed down hard on the brake, stopping.

"*What do you think you're doing?*" I growled.

"What does it look like I'm doing?" He wrinkled his nose in disgust, glancing around.

"It looks like you're invading my privacy."

"Get used to it, Miss Collins. It's you and me now, up until the very end." He ran his finger along the dirty dashboard. "This car is filthy. What do you think about taking one of my luxurious rides instead? I can have my people here in less than ten minutes. If I were only to get Nan's gate code ..."

I spun around in the cramped seat to face him. "Seriously. *Get out.*"

Gabriel scratched at his scar in thought. "Okay—but I wonder what your boyfriend will think of you gallivanting off all by your lonesome." He opened the door and threw a leg out. "I'm sure he knows exactly what you're doing. I'll be sure to let him know I saw you."

"*Fine,*" I snarled through clenched teeth. "Get in."

He slammed the door shut, a satisfied smirk on his face. "Where are we off to, then?"

"To do something stupid," I said. "You sure you want to come?"

"Oh ... *absolutely.*" Gabriel gave me a sidelong look. "By the way you're dressed—combat boots, guns, and black fatigues—I assume we're going to stop the apocalypse from happening.

"We're going to find these angels and beat the cure out of them so I can save my best friend's life." I put the car in first, and it gave a jolt as I maneuvered down the long paved pathway. I was suddenly thankful my first car had been a stick shift.

Gabriel let me get out of the automated gate exit and then out onto the main thoroughfare before he spoke again. "This is what you get for having two boyfriends."

I tightened my hands on the steering wheel, ignoring his jab. "Look, this is just a recon mission—I'm coming back for Alastair and Vinson. You don't have to come with me; I can let you out right here."

"Sure. Recon mission," he said, not sounding convinced. "Not that I don't find your new attitude admirable—it's just that it isn't exactly raining angels around here. I assume you have a plan."

"Back at the cabin—when Caesar and Corinth were fighting—they harnessed the power of lightning. It got me thinking about weather patterns. Technology, detectors, these days can track phenomena like that, so I started looking for anything that might fit that description. Something popped up on the radar out of nowhere about sixty miles south of here. All I want to do is take a look. If there's anything to it, we'll call for backup." I lifted my wrist. "My watch is back in working order again, thanks to Nan."

Gabriel lifted his chin in understanding. "Let me guess … lightning strikes, no storm?"

I nodded and then threw the car into fifth as I gunned it up to the fastest it would go—seventy miles per hour. I'd been in England long enough to learn the roads, plus it was four in the morning and there weren't that many cars out, so I felt decently confident about driving on the left side of the road.

I had expected Gabriel's company. For someone who claimed to be a step ahead of everyone else, he sure was easy to read. Or maybe it was our weird connection that made that possible. Whatever the case, I needed to keep him close.

Corinth asking me to take care of his family had sent me spiraling down a dangerous path—

"I could have gotten us a driver—or a car that has seat belts," Gabriel muttered, not for the first time.

"I happen to like this ride." I patted the dash lovingly, thinking about Paul and his sacrifice. "She gets the job done."

Chapter 25

Larna

THE SMITHFIELD GREYHOUND TRACK was right off the highway on the southeast side of London. As we'd gotten closer to the dog track, I'd seen lightning crisscross the sky over the stadium, too bright and ominous to be natural—there were no other clouds in the darkened sky. The moon looked like a tiny sliver of silver against the black backdrop.

I parked about a block out of the way, positioning the Beetle in an empty parking lot next to some dumpsters, and checked the gun at my hip.

As I started to get out, Gabriel said, "I thought this was just a recon mission."

I shrugged. "In order to recon, I have to get a closer look."

He leaned over the driver's seat, craning his neck to look at me through the open driver's door. "Let me just get my people over here first—"

I grunted. "If you're scared, you can certainly stay right here where it's safe … and call for your army."

He got out, reluctantly, I noted, and then followed at a distance, muttering angrily to himself the entire time.

I kept a close eye out for security or cameras, but by the amount of graffiti on the concrete and walls, I was sure they didn't have any. Fortunately, leaping tall fences wasn't exactly a difficulty for vampires. All it took was a quick high jump over the ten-foot retaining wall, and we were inside.

There were no ticket takers or ushers, no one buying food at the concession stands. Besides the late hour, it looked like this place had been closed for quite some time. The smell of stale alcohol was thick in the air. The crunch of empty cartons under-foot and weeds jutting up through patches of concrete were key indicators that this place had not been in use for a while.

Gabriel's eyes darted to the shadowy corners of alcoves as we passed into the tunnel beneath the concrete stadium, his voice echoing loudly off the surrounding walls. "You were right about something being off about this place. I can feel it."

I didn't want to admit to him that I could too.

As we emerged out onto the track, I smelled the heady scent of burned ozone. A flash of lightning lit up the night sky overhead once again, and I ducked down on pure instinct. It had been so close.

There was a giant circle pattern, at least fifty yards wide, burned into the dirt track. I could still see smoke curling up from it. Something was carved inside the giant circle: intricate symbols and sigils too complex for me to commit to memory—I'd have to take a photograph to record it and study it in further detail.

I retrieved my cell phone from my back pocket, turned it on, and waited for it to power back up, spinning around. The scorch marks in the earth were still hot.

"Do those markings look like they were made with …?" I shared a quick glance with Gabriel as we both said "Lightning" at the same time.

"Any idea what this means?" I needed to go up into the stands to get the bird's-eye view for a better look. "It looks like we just missed them."

It had been an outside shot at best to find anyone still here, let alone angels who could easily transport themselves from one place to the next with nothing but a simple thought.

Gabriel was already making a beeline out toward the dead center of the track, his hand reaching into his pocket for his phone, I guessed, as he said, "It's time I called my people. I have experts who can decipher this."

I followed him, scanning the thick shadows near the entrances and exits, but stopped myself short as soon as he quit speaking.

"What?" I asked, my voice sounding shrill in the still night air. I suddenly had a very bad feeling about this, even though we appeared to have the place to ourselves.

Dave had made us see fangs when there were none. What else could these so-called angels do? Invisibility? The hairs on the back of my neck stood on end, as stiff as razor wire, and another volley of lightning threaded overhead— closer this time. More threatening and ominous.

My senses were firing off in all different directions. The hot prickle of warning hit the back of my neck, and it happened in an instant, that same soul-sucking snap of charged energy hitting me like a snakebite out of nowhere.

There was an advantage to having superhuman speed

though. I dropped my phone and was already throwing myself out of the way right at the same time as a clap of deafening thunder and blinding light ripped a hole wide open in the atmosphere exactly where I'd been standing only moments before.

Gabriel darted out of the way of one too, rolling into the soft dirt track, a trail of soft dust churning up behind him in the process. I shouldn't have been surprised at how swiftly he'd moved, but I was.

I was lying in the dirt, gawking up at the hole ripped wide in the ozone only a few feet from me. It looked like a swirling gray mass—vast and otherworldly. Then out of that vortex stepped a woman.

I saw that she wasn't wearing any shoes, and her pale pink toes looked small and delicate from my vantage point on the ground. Her royal-blue robe shimmered unnaturally as she moved. Black veins stood out vividly against the translucent pallor of her skin. They looked like tattoos. She had hair the silkiest shade of onyx I'd ever seen. It made her round, equally pale blue eyes stand out even more.

The robed woman lifted her hand, and a blue ball of flame burst into life in her palm. She gazed down upon me and smiled. It was an electrifying smile that had me sucking in a shocked breath. The energy in her hand danced and weaved through her fingers like a living entity.

So entranced by her appearance, I almost forgot that I was armed, or that I had on armor, or vambraces—or that I could even move.

Another figure dropped out of thin air to stand beside the woman in blue, closer to Gabriel. He looked just as regal in black robes, with curly blond hair and a square jaw. I could tell he used to have a symmetrical face, but his engorged nose had been broken one too many times. It made him look deformed and wretched. Even with the messed-up nose, I recognized him immediately. He was the one who had grabbed Corinth back at the cabin—the one who'd gotten away. I idly thought about how strong the person had to have been in order to do that sort of damage to an angel. *Corinth.* Corinth was strong enough to do that kind of harm to an angel.

I thought he said his name was Turiel.

My eyes skimmed back over to the woman. I couldn't not look at her. This was Angela. My blood ran cold. She had wreaked so much havoc. Created vampires. Killed so many Nephilim and humans alike.

There was a flurry of movement off to my left. Gabriel, keeping his distance. He didn't make a move to run away or go after them like I thought he might. I was more shocked at this realization than anything else that had happened tonight.

I started to get up, but the robed woman arched a dark eyebrow at me. "Stay where you are, child of mine."

She lifted her hand. The spinning ball of flame flickered brighter, angry, as if it were dying to be let loose upon the world. Upon me. "Two more vampires to bring into my fold. How fortunate you are to be here right now." Angela's eyes hovered over the deep gouges in the earth at her bare feet. "Turiel left a warning for the Watchers, but apparently, they are too cowardly to show up."

Turiel stepped up beside Angela. His voice sounded,

to my extreme amusement, nasal when he spoke. "She's with the Nephilim—the *boy*."

Her blue eyes narrowed as Gabriel took a step toward Angela, drawing her attention to him briefly.

He held his hands out to show her they were empty. "I am Gabriel Stanton, leader of clan Deimos." He gestured at me still on the ground. "This is Larna Collins. We mean you no harm. I'm not sure if you've heard of me or my clan before, but my influence is far-reaching. I have a vested interest in this girl and would prefer you not kill her. I assure you, we can work something out."

Angela's gaze darted down to me and then back up to Gabriel once again. "I know who you are, Gabriel Stanton. Leader of one of the largest vampire clans in the world." She paused, a hand going to her chin in thought. "*Larna.* I know that name … The son of Danel, the Nephilim, he called your name out when he was dying." Her smirk widened in amusement. "I was both surprised and revolted to hear that he is now vampire—worse than an abomination."

"Seems a bit contradictory to hate what you created," I growled.

Angela inclined her head. "You are one of my offspring. And so I truly hope you will work with me, to help create more like you—be a mentor, an influencer. I can give you anything you want in return. With your help, we can spread our agenda. All I need from you is to create more like you, vampires, as many as you can—"

I pushed myself up onto my elbows, heat flooding my face. "I will *never* work with you. Not in a million years."

Angela closed the distance between us, looking down

upon me in my position on the ground. She was so close now she could reach out and touch me with her foot. Her eyes lingered on my combat boots and then the pistol at my hip.

"Where is the boy?" she asked softly.

Gabriel spoke up quickly, inching closer to Angela. "She doesn't speak for both of us."

I shot him a look as I said, "Tragically, Corinth did not survive his wounds. We gave him a beautiful tribute. He wanted one of those Viking funerals where we sent his body out to sea. His favorite song, 'The Imperial Death March' from *Star Wars*, was played."

She laughed, and it came out as a soft trill that sounded a lot like the tinkling of a sleigh bell. "Come now, vampire. Do you really think you can lie to me? I know he is alive."

I said, "You tried to take his blade from him, and it ended badly for you."

I heard Gabriel's sharp intake of breath a few feet away, but I didn't look at him. In truth, I couldn't take my eyes off the hypnotically glowing death ball she was weaving through her fingers. Her features morphed from congenial to ugly in less than one second flat.

Making an angel angry enough to want to kill you: check.

The orb's pulsating seemed to increase with her temper. Angela shook her head, and her dark hair fanned out peculiarly around her head as if she were floating underwater. A halo of hair. I could see why Corinth had been so shaken when he'd talked about her.

She clucked her tongue in what I thought was regret

as she turned her attention to Gabriel a few feet away from me. "You are my servant, Mr. Stanton. I *will* be requiring your services very soon, but for now, you may go." She waved a dismissive hand at him. "You have the information my people sent to you on how to contact me?"

Gabriel put his hand in his pocket and pulled out a crumpled piece of paper, the same one I'd seen him looking at when I was in his room. He nodded.

"You lying piece of—"

I started to say but, Angela spoke up, cutting me off. "As for the girl, her death is of more use to me now."

Gabriel took a hesitant step toward me and halted. After a moment, his eyes swept over to mine, inscrutable. "Larna," he hissed, "don't be stupid. Join her."

I laughed. "That's where we differ, Gabriel. I don't bend on a whim to save my own skin. There is no way I'd ever go against Corinth. She'll have to kill me first."

He shook his head in agitation and then turned back to Angela. "I look forward to working with you."

My heart took a swan dive as Angela, again, made a flurry motion with her hand, shooing Gabriel away like she would a stubborn gnat flying in her face.

And just like that, he left me without so much as a backward glance. I watched his dwindling form vanish into the dark shadows of the tunnel, exiting back out of the passage we'd come through to get here.

Exactly what I'd expected from him. Coward.

Angela's eyes slid over me like an oil slick, calculating. "I've been around since the creation of this planet. You think a teenage *boy* can best me. Ever since Turiel informed me that Corinth had survived his wounds and that he'd been turned by one of your kind—given the virus *I* created—I knew he would not be long for this world. It's really quite fitting. His blood will eventually burn off the virus like a fever." She twirled her free hand in the air. "All you have done is delayed the inevitable. Even so, he must still suffer by my hands."

My mouth went bone-dry at hearing that.

Turiel stepped up beside Angela, drawing my eyes to the danger at hand. I watched in growing alarm as he formed the same type of glowing energy in his hands that Angela had created. The electrical surge bounced between his open palms, snapping and sizzling like bacon on a griddle, as if in anticipation of its next kill.

Angela raised her arm high. "Because Corinth killed my first lieutenant, Caesar, I think it fitting we send the Nephilim a message: your mangled corpse." I tried to hide the panic and fear on my face as she continued. "I have been waiting for the right moment to enter his mind. All I have to do is gain access to his thoughts in order to find out exactly where he is. I can deposit your body at his feet in less than the time it takes to kill you."

"Why haven't you done it already, then?" I goaded. "You've known about him being alive for quite some time now, but you have done nothing to find him. I wonder why that is. Maybe because you're scared of him and of what he'll do to you if you try."

Angela's mouth turned down at the corners, and her eyes blazed molten red. She looked like what I pictured the Devil might look like. "How dare you—"

I moved, reaching for my *Sight* and pistol in record

time—only to prove that it was a valiant waste of effort.

Angela had been right about being faster, because she'd lobbed the sphere right at me before I could even finish pulling out my weapon. It hit me square in my midsection, and the impact bowled me over. I went sprawling in the dirt, my gun flying out of my hand in the opposite direction, the breath knocked from my lungs. My nose was filled with the scent of burning flesh.

I was flat on my back, looking up at the last winking stars in the sky, feeling oddly disconnected from my own body. The world was blurry and off-kilter. I noticed dimly how beautiful and hazy the glow on the horizon looked as the sun started to rise.

It was at this point that irony hit me full force. If I wasn't about to die, I would have almost snickered at the thought that I wanted Gabriel Stanton, of all people, to get away. At least one of us would live to tell the tale. Maybe, just maybe, he'd go to Alastair and tell him what had happened to me. How I'd fought up until the very end …

A futile chortle bubbled out of my throat as I rolled over onto my side, my gaze traveling slowly down to see the fist-sized hole seared into my chest like a sigil. Burns hurt worse than any other type of pain. This was something altogether different. My ears buzzed. My head buzzed. Everything buzzed.

So much for recon mission.

From my fetal position on the ground, I could see my attackers' slow progress toward me. Turiel and Angela. Her bare feet left the smallest of imprints in the dark sand as she stalked closer, unhurried.

Turiel had already somehow appeared behind me from out of nowhere.

They threw their hands in the air at the same time, and the sky opened up on command. A clap of thunder rattled my bones and knocked my teeth together. I pulled my legs up to my chest and closed my eyes as the lightning poured down around me. The heat was too intense. The snap and crackle of energy felt like a rabid dog snapping at me.

As far as power goes, theirs was beyond frightening. I couldn't fight this. No one could. At this point, I wasn't even sure Corinth could. My fingers scrabbled at the watch on my wrist and then stilled over the tiny red button. I wanted to push it—more than anything—but I didn't.

There was no sense in calling for Alastair or Vinson or Nan. None of them could get here in time or help me—not by any regular means of travel—and Corinth wasn't nearly strong enough to transport himself here to fight these two off. I wasn't going to let him, anyway. Not for me.

I was on my own.

As soon as the lightning hit their fingertips, they combined their currents of energy to form an arcing cage around me, with Turiel at one end and Angela at the other.

Gradually they closed off the ring of fire around me, the temperature intensifying to an unbearable degree. Tiny electrical currents burst and crackled ominously, an electrified cage, blisteringly hot. I felt dizzy. The static made my hair stand on end. I tucked myself into the smallest ball possible.

Angela would hold true to her word about mutilating me. A pang of regret welled up inside me at the thought of Corinth finding my burned body at his feet. Already, I could feel my skin start to bubble. It was beyond any pain I'd ever felt before.

My eyes sought anything I could use—a weapon, something in my pockets. I wasn't going out like this—curled in the fetal position. I stumbled back to my feet, biting back a cry of agony as my right hand brushed the side of my sweltering prison. My skin instantly turned black and was scored with deep red gashes where I'd touched the light. It was healing but not nearly rapidly enough for my liking. There was something about angel energy that slowed the vamp healing process. I tried to suck in a deep breath, but the stifling smell of burned plastic and seared flesh gagged me.

Angela's eyes crackled, consumed with her madness—she was someone who clearly loved watching people being tortured; she was going to take her time.

I fumbled with the buckle on my armor with my one good hand. Maybe I could eject the blade and ram it down her throat when she got close enough, if I was even still alive by then.

Instead, a sudden faintness overcame me, and I sank to a knee, the deadly lightning now only inches from my entire body. If they stepped even one foot closer, I was dead.

Before they fried me crispy golden, I saw a dark shadow dart between the combined torrents of energy. A person. A primal, earsplitting howl ripped from their lungs as soon as they put themselves right in the path of fatal cross fire. That person was my savior. They broke the connection at the same time as they freed me from the death trap—using their own body to do so.

It was one of the bravest things I'd ever seen anyone do—and the stupidest—and when I realized who it was, my mouth dropped open in complete shock.

Gabriel Stanton.

Acid hit the back of my throat at hearing his strangled cries. There was no question he was dying. Angela and Turiel didn't seem to mind that they were killing him instead of me. They were fueled by their own bloodlust now.

Unable to keep my footing, and also horribly captivated by the lightning show, I fell hard onto my rump and scampered backward across the dirt track, my hand still burning. I just wanted to get away. Gabriel was regenerating and healing at a rate I thought was impossible—even for a vampire. The fact that he was still standing was impressive. I realized that this was how he'd survived Corinth stabbing him in the back, and probably generations of other attacks as well.

If I'd taken the brunt of what he was going through, there would be no question that I would be dead by now. The smell of boiling flesh was overpowering. His skin looked like melted plastic, and his head of dark, curly hair was now gone, along with all traces of the scar on his left cheek. His face *was* the scar.

He fell to his knees, hands balled into fists and extended out by his sides. His eyes snapped open to meet mine. The connection was terrifying and palpable, so profound it was as if he'd opened up a psychic link between us. Empathy was a powerful thing, and in those briefest of seconds, I felt everything he did. There had been a time when I would have left him to die. Hell, I was still on the fence. He deserved no less for what he'd done to my father, but he'd just saved my life—in the most agonizing way possible. I had expected him to cut and run. I couldn't let him die by their hands.

Besides, if anyone was going to kill him, it was going to be me.

I got to my knees, discarded my ruined and melted vambrace, and went for two thin shuriken blades in my vest pocket—blades gifted to me by Vinson. They were hot to the touch but not enough to stop me. I aimed one for Angela's exposed neck, right at her collarbone, and the other for Turiel, who was standing on the opposite side of Gabriel. I let them fly.

Fortunately, they were both too busy frying Gabriel to throw up shields. The blades sank into exposed skin at the same spot on both their necks, opposite each other. For only having one good working hand, I was impressed by my aim.

The combined torrents of power fizzled and flamed out as they staggered back, momentarily stunned.

The distraction had given me enough time get to my feet and race to Gabriel's side. He was convulsing and foaming at the mouth. I bit into the wrist on my uninjured hand, and shoved it toward his mouth without even thinking of the consequences. As soon as my blood hit his lips, his body seized up and his back bowed like he was a contortionist. His eyes went all black. No irises. A moment later he went limp in my arms and his fists fell open by his sides. And then, quicker than I thought possible, strong hands wrapped around my arm like a vise.

He drank from me with renewed vigor, an animalistic strength overtaking him in the process. I had never seen Gabriel lose control. Not like this. He drank. And drank. And drank some more … his pupils still blown out as round and dark as saucers, drawing me in.

"*Gabriel …*" I managed to half pant, half groan.

It doesn't take long for a vampire to drain the life out of their victim. It comes with the territory—the innate survival method for creatures of the night—or day. It meant less of a chance for a vamp to get caught feeding in an alleyway. *I would know nothing about that …*

My eyes flickered over to Angela and Turiel. They had somewhat recovered. They were also in no hurry to finish us off. I shook my head, noticing them already advancing on us once again, but there was nothing I could do to stop them with Gabriel still latched on to me.

He kept drinking with no signs of stopping, and my heart thundered in my chest, a splitting headache blurring my vision. My wrist had an unbearable ache that wouldn't let up.

"*Gabriel,*" I breathed. "*You're killing me.*"

I hadn't even considered pulling away from him, until it was too late. My vision went dark around the edges. I tried, but he was too strong now. I wouldn't even be able to keep my eyes open much longer.

And that's when my *Sight* flared to life in an instant. Another survival instinct. As soon as I met his glazed-over gaze, I knew I had him, if only for a moment. It was all I needed. This time it was surprisingly easy to slip into the inky corners of his mind. The hard part was staying there.

I felt weak from losing so much blood, but I managed

to whisper one word: "*Stop.*"

Gabriel sagged against me and then collapsed, his arms falling away from mine, exhausted, alive, and surprisingly pliant. He let out a soft moan, lifting his face to look at me. His eyes were like two dark pools. A dribble of blood leaked out from the side of his mouth.

"I knew the day would come," he wheezed, "when you no longer wanted to see me die a violent death."

Even with my blood to help him heal, he was still a badly burned mess. He tried to laugh, but his face was too scarred and damaged.

His eyes landed on my watch. "Corinth … will come … if you call him. My phone broke when I … jumped out of the way earlier—my people are too far away to get here, even if I could … contact them. Please tell me someone from your clan knows … about us being here."

"Alastair knows," I said quietly. "But it doesn't matter now. Corinth will kill himself trying to get here. I won't risk it. Besides, it's too late." My eyes glided back over to see Angela, who had stopped at my feet. She was twirling that deadly coiled energy between her fingers again, smiling lazily down at us.

"I don't want to die today, Larna." He reached up in a blur of motion and, before I could stop him, pressed the panic button on my watch.

I was fuming that he'd gone against my wishes—that is, until I saw his gaze lock on something across the way. The look of alarm on his face sent a shiver running through me, effectively cutting off my angry retort. I followed his line of sight. The Grigori were here. Like, *all* of them. They bounded out of those weird cloud-like portals, landing around the dog track to surround us.

Gingerly I pulled Gabriel's head into my lap, defeated.

He laughed softly to himself. "For once in my life, I did *not* see this coming. I did not see myself saving your life. I was well on my way out of here when something stopped me." He laughed again. "But it would appear that we are both going to die today anyway."

Chapter 26

Corinth

I OPENED MY EYES to find myself curled up on Nan's couch. I had been dozing fitfully. I remembered the nightmare I'd been having, a juicy one—chock-full of dark, evil, faceless things, things that would eventually morph into Paul's face. Then Benny's. Then Caesar's. Then Angela's. I had played out the moment Paul had died over and over again in my head.

There was no distinguishing real life from my nightmare now. Night terrors. The image of Paul's lifeless eyes—just like Benny's—when he'd stared at me in surprise and death as Sarah twisted his neck around, and I bolted upright, the hilt of my dagger clutched painfully in my hand.

I wasn't sure when I'd drawn it out, but now orange light flickered against bronze metal, the heavy fog of sleep still clinging to me—

Someone's hand clamped over my mouth and then another hand encircled the wrist that was gripping my blade.

Whoever had a hold of me tried to shove me back down.

With the help of a healthy dose of adrenaline and fear, plus a whole lot of vampire strength, I tossed my assailant off me as if they didn't weigh a thing. They hit the floor and rolled to a stop near the still-glowing fireplace with a wounded grunt.

I was on my feet and stepping toward them, my hands crackling with lightning by the time the figure started to sit up, rubbing at their head in apparent pain.

"I don't like you being a vampire anymore."

I blinked away the last remnants of my nightmare as soon as I recognized the voice. I should have also recognized that platinum hair poking up too, and those inconceivably blue eyes. "*Al! What the hell, man!* Are we under attack? Because if we're not, there are about a million different ways to wake me up, and none of them involve scaring the living crap out of—"

"Larna needs our help. *Now.*" Al held his wrist up to show me his watch. It was flashing bright in the dim lighting of the room. On it blinked one word, LARNA in bold letters, and then it changed, flashing her coordinates.

At that, my heart rate spiked, and I jumped back to my feet, my hand tightening on the hilt of my blade, still in my grasp.

"Let's get Gabe's chopper—" I started to say, but he stopped me with a look. I glanced around the empty living room. "What is it? Where is he?"

Al clutched at his injured hand, the one he'd hurt in the fight with Caesar, and moved quickly to sit on the couch. Reluctantly I joined him, suddenly feeling too pent up to sit still. I could see the remnants of his black eye in the golden firelight.

"I need you to trust me on this," he whispered. "She left a couple of hours ago."

"Why would Larna leave without us? And better yet, why would you let her?"

"She noticed a weird weather phenomenon on the southeast side of London a few hours ago. Unusual lightning patterns with no reports of storms in the area—" He raised an eyebrow. "Sound familiar? She went to check on it. She was supposed to be back by now."

I threw a hand to my head in exasperation. "Come on, Al, you know Larna is a crap magnet. Why would you let her go alone? Why would Vin let her go alone?" I searched his face, but it was a veritable steel vault. There had to be a good reason why he would let her wander off by herself—even if it was only a recon mission. I knew he was keeping something from me. I left it alone for now.

My main concern was for Larna's safety. And time was ticking.

"She's not alone," Al said. "She's with Stanton. Look, I know you're not exactly operating at a hundred percent here … especially after what happened at the cabin, but I need you to go after her."

I shot him an irritated look. "Come on, Al." I said "*Duh*" with an exaggerated eye roll. "Of course I'm going after her. More than one person exceeds the ride limit though. If you want me to bring her back, you know you can't come with me, right?"

He put a hand on my shoulder, his face set in resolve and determination. "I know. And I know what I'm asking of you … too much. I'm sorry, Corinth. Just bring her back. *Please.* Do you need anything? Any more weapons?"

"This is the only weapon I need." I said it simply, without ego, and held up my blade. "You're lucky I never took my Chucks off."

I knew it cost Al something to ask me to go, especially when he couldn't come along for the ride. I thought that hurt him more than anything else did. He clenched his jaw and held a hand out to help me up. I accepted it, ignoring the beginnings of a hunger cramp.

I can do this.

I thought about Larna and held my breath, counted to five, and then blew it out again. Nothing. I held my hand out for the watch. Al handed it to me. I concentrated on the face and the flashing coordinates.

After that didn't work, I thought about the one face I didn't want to: *Angela's.* I don't know how I knew it, but Larna was in real danger—and she was with Angela.

I squeezed the watch tighter.

Back when Angela had invaded my mind, right before I'd been stabbed, there had been a residual connection left between us. It was why I had been waiting to figure out a way to get back inside her head to get the cure. With Dave gone, it had become increasingly obvious that I would have to be the one to do it.

Fear's icy grip had stopped me though.

The room crackled with power and ozone as I concentrated on Angela's achingly beautiful face. *Take me to her.* If I was wrong, I was handing myself over, but I didn't care. I had to help Larna.

It happened quickly.

One second, I was breathing in the remnants of the embers in the fireplace, and the next, I was spinning helplessly through the endless chasm of light and chaos—

A second later I dropped out of the vortex, landing solidly on my feet in a clap of thunder—my blade held at the ready. The flood of power raged through my veins, leaving my throat feeling raw and my body achy. I was breathing in fast, ragged gasps, and I glanced down to see the faint traces of muscle and sinew in my forearm standing out, pulsating electric blue like lightning.

The smell of ash, smoke, and char had accompanied me through the portal. The scent was heavy in my nostrils, and the smell of scorched flesh banished any other thoughts from my mind. I looked around quickly, assessing.

As soon as I saw Larna, my stomach dropped. She was on the ground, surrounded by a cadre of Grigori, who were mere feet away.

The thing cradled in her lap drew my eye momentarily away from all the threats in front of and around us. Disgust manifested itself in the form of a flinch. The charred skin was so grotesque it barely resembled a person. It reminded me of dried beef.

Larna's eyes flashed up to meet mine. As soon as she saw me appear, I could see all the layers of complex emotion flickering across her face: anger, regret, fear—but not surprise. She looked sad, as if she had already resigned us all to dying.

I disappeared in a clap of thunder and dropped down in front of her, placing myself between her and the advancing Grigori.

"Corinth—you shouldn't have come," she said quickly. "Angela is here—it's a trap."

"Then why'd you press the button?" I said, stepping

in front of her, brandishing my dagger.

"I didn't." Her eyes flew down to the thing in her lap. "Gabriel did."

"You know me—I never miss a party," I said under my breath. "And, *shit*, that thing is Gabe?" I turned around, my eyes searching. "Where is she?"

Larna shook her head. "She disappeared, along with Turiel, when she felt you coming."

I looked around, chill bumps popping up along my forearms. We were in the center of some type of stadium. The loose dirt track went in a quarter mile circle and was as wide as a jogging track. There were strange burn marks etched into the ground at our feet. Somehow I knew the symbols were sacred, meant only for an angel's eyes. It wasn't written in English but an ancient language. A warning meant for the Watchers.

There was so much tension in the air, I could cut it with a knife.

The Grigori had spaced themselves evenly across the entire track. Each angel seemed taller than the next … over seven feet, to be exact—all with similar striking features. Giants built on a scale not meant for this world. They looked pretty too. Equally as pretty as *Lord of the Rings* elves, but without the pointy ears. They didn't have bows and arrows at their beck and call, because they didn't need them. The armor strapped across their chests was made of brown leather scored with patterns that looked a lot like old-school crosses. These angels had deadly lightning at their disposal … and they were all pointing it right at us.

I gulped.

"Corinth, get out of here," Larna ordered.

Her eyes darted from left to right, as if she were a caged animal. I suddenly caught the burn marks on her right hand, and I cringed.

"What the hell did you get us into?" I whispered to her out of the side of my mouth.

The dark energy swirled in my chest, winding its way through me, in much the same way it had back at the cabin. Caesar had been the by-product of what I'd unleashed, and I was about to do it all over again.

The thing on Larna's lap that resembled smoked meat spoke. "Oh, you know, the usual … mayhem and destruction …"

I jumped, grabbing at my chest. *"It's still alive."*

A voice rang out behind me. "Well, well, well … speaking of who is still alive, I thought I was going to have to hunt you down like prey … but here you are. I should have known you'd come for her."

I whirled around, my pulse racing.

Angela's emotionless voice was as chilling as I remembered. I hated noticing how she looked just as stunning and elegant as the last time I'd seen her. Even her long, velvety blue robe couldn't hide that exquisite figure of hers.

It felt like a boa constrictor was squeezing my insides to mush. I didn't know if this was by her doing or if I just couldn't take the sight of her staring at me like that.

Turiel was beside Angela. His appearance raised my blood to the point of boiling: curly blond hair, galling dimples, pale skin that made him look that much douchier than he already did. But to my extreme satisfaction, I realized his once symmetrical face was perfect no more. His nose was crooked and bent at an odd angle, bulbous really.

I remembered striking him in the face repeatedly at the cabin, and I smiled. That was my doing.

"I see you brought your pet monkey with you." It was out of my mouth before I could stop myself. I pointed at Turiel's face. "I like the nose job, by the way."

He stepped closer, his hands pulsating blue, fisted down at his sides.

Angela said, "I have misjudged your—" her eyes traveled up and down me. "—abilities."

"People always do," I said evenly. "And then it backfires on them."

She sniffed at the air and recoiled as if she'd been punched. Her perfect features transformed into something ugly and sinister as she studied me more closely. "So it is true. You *are* vampire."

I spread my arms wide. "I decided to become the best of both worlds—only because I knew it would annoy you, of course."

Larna whispered, "Corinth, what are you doing? We really don't have time for your banter." Her worried tone brought my attention back to the surrounding Grigori who had slowly started to creep in on us. They moved as one. "*Get out of here.*"

I couldn't believe how close they'd gotten already. Of course, they could easily just transport themselves closer in a fraction of that time, but I thought they were waiting on Angela to give the order. Speaking of, my gaze flitted back to her. I could see the pity welling in her eyes, directed at me.

"You have become worse than an abomination. It's a shame really."

I positioned myself between Larna and Gabe, stepping forward to protect them as she sauntered closer, brandishing my blade at the incoming Grigori on the other side. I couldn't protect us from all of them.

"What's that?" I said, stalling.

"How repulsive you've become."

"Thank you," I said, baring white teeth and fangs.

Her pale skin started to turn a bluish-gold hue—it was both arresting and captivating. She spread her arms out beside her, suddenly angry. A set of wings burst out of her back, bright as a burning star. Her eyes were ablaze with the same light. It was celestial and otherworldly and terrifying.

The way she moved wasn't of this earth. Her voice was harsh and piercing, like ice picks stabbing me in my eardrums.

Angela spoke only to me and in my mind. *Come closer.* She held her hand out, beckoning. Those wings were so lovely. Hypnotic. She was the most beautiful creature on the planet. I would be insane not to listen … Why wouldn't I get closer? What had I been thinking? I should have done this ages ago.

I hadn't been thinking.

My feet moved of their own accord, and I took a step toward her. She was so striking.

Somewhere at the back of my mind, I heard Larna scream my name.

But Angela's voice was louder than hers.

That's right. Closer.

My limbs felt warm, heavy, and malleable as putty. I shuffled forward another step. All she had ever wanted to do was take care of me. I so very badly wanted her to take care of me. I was within arm's reach of her now. Just a little further, and it would all be over … no more pain. Glorious nothingness.

Corinth, I can show you an infinite universe full of your wildest dreams and desires. We are all creatures of compulsion, are we not? You are merely a puppet—waiting to be controlled … You want me to control you.

So badly.

Her fingers stretched out toward me, summoning, and her blazing wings looked like a kaleidoscope of spellbinding colors—swirling round and round in fathomless depth and infinity. I wanted to dive in, go for a swim, sink to the bottom, and stay for an eternity.

I reached a hand out, brushing the tips of my fingers against hers—

Something hit my leg, hard, and light burst open in my skull, fracturing everything. With it came a searing pain, exactly what I needed to pull myself out from under Angela's compulsion.

My injured leg crumpled underneath me as I came all the way out of the trance, my eyes snapping open, blinking back the sting of confusion and agony. One more step would have done it. My stomach rolled with a new tide of fear at seeing how close I'd gotten to Angela. She was toying with me, of course. I knew she could just transport herself behind us at any opportunity she wanted.

Angela's pale blue eyes widened in irritation.

"*Corinth!*"

Larna was still shouting my name, clearly had been for quite some time, because her voice sounded hoarse.

Angela was laughing.

My eyes sought the source of the deep throbbing in my leg. A thin, star shaped blade stuck out from my calf. I struggled back to my feet, ignoring how much it hurt, and disappeared in a clap of thunder to reappear back at Larna's side before Angela could retaliate.

"You stabbed me!" I gasped in both irritation and gratitude, gazing down at the sharp object still protruding from my leg. "That's going to leave a mark."

"It was the only thing I could think of to break her hold over you—it worked with Alastair when you grazed him with your blade at the graveyard. I figured we didn't have anything else to lose, and I'm too weak to stand up."

I gripped Larna under her arm at her right shoulder. "You don't have to."

I closed my eyes, ready to beam us out of there. Now that I'd done it a few times, the ability to make myself travel anywhere I wanted seemed to come more easily. Natural. Plus being scared out of my wits was all the motivation I needed. All I had to do was think where I wanted to go. I felt the connection instantly.

"*No!*" Larna gripped my hand tightly in hers, preventing me from opening up another portal.

"Seriously?" I said, squinting down at her in confusion. "What now?"

"You can't leave him behind."

My eyes flickered over Gabe. Half of him was charred and crispy, and his breathing rattled wetly in his chest as he struggled to exhale. He looked like he was not long for this world—

I barely had time to glance up as Turiel rushed me, throwing one of those spinning orbs at me at the same time. The rest of the Grigori converged, disappearing and reappearing in blinding flashes of silvery light and deafening thunder. This was it. It shook the stadium, there were so many. War. This was war. It was already here.

I threw a hand out on instinct, and a shield bloomed up bright, brilliant, and divine—our saving grace—right as the ball of energy struck it with enough force to pulverize my bones. My Converse dug deep gouges in the earth as the force of it shoved me backward. I cried out in pain, trying to ignore the increasing discomfort in my calf where the blade was still deeply lodged in my muscle. It burned beyond belief.

Turiel had been waiting for this exact moment; I could feel the amount of hatred behind each shot he took at me.

Angela's eyes hovered over the shield I'd conjured up in the heat of the moment. Unimpressed, she waved a hand in the air, making a slow circling motion to the Grigori all lined up behind her like a firing squad: Take your time. Make it hurt. Enjoy their pain.

I shot a quick glance down to Gabe's mangled body as another volley of lightning hit my domed shield in a shower of sparks. I gritted my teeth and put a shoulder into it this time as Larna ducked down behind me. She threw a hand up to protect her face.

My shield shimmered weakly, flickering. I didn't think I could fend off another attack. I wasn't strong enough. It took less than a fraction of a second for my fight-or-flight response to kick in. I called up a portal in the span of a millisecond.

This has to work. Please let this work.

I didn't think of the consequences of trying to carry an extra person through the portal with me. There was no time. I knelt down beside them both, planting first one hand on Larna's shoulder, and then the other on Gabe's grossly disfigured arm, and I twisted back around. Turiel was barreling straight toward me with reckless abandon, his overly white teeth flashing as he gnashed them together in rage. I could see the saliva flying out of his mouth as he shouted something I couldn't discern.

On the opposite side, just a few feet away from me, Angela's entire body lit up in an eerie shade of gold, wings extended from her back in a display of power and light and fire—gloriously so.

I squeezed my eyes shut. The image of wings was burned onto my retinas as I plunged us all through the opening of the portal, to what I hoped was our escape.

Ice spread through my veins, scattering to my extremities. There was some type of resistance, like someone trying to drag me back from where I'd just come from. Someone like an angel. Someone stronger than me.

Angela's words reverberated inside my skull, her voice like a wrecking ball to my brain: *You cannot hide from me, child.*

Larna and Gabe were holding on to me as tightly as they could.

I will just appear right beside you when you arrive at your destination.

It felt like someone was digging into my head with a

garden spade, splitting it in half, hacking my brain to bits. I screamed. It was all I could do to hold on to my terrified passengers. I wondered idly what would happen to them if I did let go. They'd be lost forever. Time didn't work the same way in this place.

If you turn yourself and the dagger over to me, I will make sure your friends' deaths are as painless as possible. I must make an example out of you for the rest of the Grigori. Yours will not be painless.

I should have been terrified. I should have tried to shove her out of my head, but all I could think about was getting the cure. This was my chance. I tried to insert myself into her mind, thinking one word over and over again: *Cure. Cure. Cure.* I caught snippets of apparitions and people and otherworldly beings as they slid across my vision.

I saw faces—distorted masks. Horns. Sharp, pointy teeth. Fire. Spirals of light. Birth and rebirth. I couldn't make sense of any of it, which left me feeling like I was sifting through chaos and madness. *I* was the one going mad. There had to be something inside her head I could use. We hurtled through that chasm of sound and thunder and light as I held on to that one word: *cure.* A part of me knew I was dying anyway and that this would be my only chance, so I went for it—holding nothing back. It was torment. Everything hurt. I had never experienced anything so … different and unfamiliar. I felt displaced and fragmented, like I'd never find my way out of her head again.

Just when I thought I wouldn't be able to take it anymore, we slammed back to earth—hitting something solid.

I was painfully aware that I was on my side, hacking up blood with one bold image still emblazoned in my mind: trees, branchless and skeletal, their bark glowing eerily gray-white in the dark, leaves shivering … or wait, no, that was me shivering …

And then I was gone—*just gone*. Faded to black.

Chapter 27

Larna

FEAR SLICED THROUGH ME, just as sharply and piercingly as Corinth's cries of agony did. He was clutching his head in his white-knuckled grasp, and he wouldn't stop screaming.

When we burst back into existence in Nan's living room, several things happened at once: Vinson and Imani heard our arrival in a horrendous clap of thunder—everyone did once we'd arrived in the living room. Vinson helped Imani cart Gabriel off to one of the bedrooms to attend to his grievous wounds.

Alastair and I struggled to hold Corinth down while Nan pulled the blade out of his leg and said through gritted teeth, "I've got an emergency stash of blood for just this sort of occasion. I'll be right back. Hold him down until I get back."

She darted off before we could respond. I hoped her blood would bring Corinth out of his paroxysm. He was shaking violently under our grip.

"What happened?" Alastair asked. "What did that bastard do?"

By *bastard*, I knew he meant Gabriel.

"That bastard saved my life—I made a horrible mistake. We … we … were ambushed by the Grigori. They almost killed us." My voice wavered. "Gabriel put himself directly in the line of fire to save me."

"Why didn't you call me as soon as you got there?" he hissed, worry and aggravation dripping from his voice like acid. He glanced down to my injured hand on Corinth's stomach. "Larna, your hand," he gasped. "It's badly burned."

"I'm okay. I'm healing. There was no time. It wasn't an ambush meant for us … It was for the Watchers—"

Corinth let out a horrifying wail, drawing me back to his current predicament. My stomach felt like smelted lead. His hair was plastered to his forehead, and all the color had drained out of his face. He looked frail and weak now. I put my good hand to his chest. It came back sticky. What at first I'd taken to be sweat was actually blood.

I lifted his T-shirt up and took in a sharp breath at the sight. There were over a dozen cuts and stabs wounds on his torso.

My horrified gaze shot to Alastair's. "He's bleeding."

"Did this happen to him there?" I shook my head as he said, "Those are his old wounds coming back, aren't they?"

"No, no, no, no …" Corinth shook under my grasp, and I tightened my hold on him. When we finally managed to get him under control again, I murmured, "This is my fault. I asked him to take Gabriel with us … It was too much for him, and …" Tears formed at the corners of my eyes. I swiped at them angrily. "I shouldn't have asked him to do it. We don't have time to wait around until the cure finds us."

Alastair unconsciously released his grip on Corinth to put a hand on my arm. "It's not your fault. It's mine. You know as well as I do that you can't *make* Corinth do anything—"

Corinth went rigid and he shouted at the top of his lungs, "*GET OUT OF MY HEAD!*" And then he sagged back, his body going still as if in his final moments before death.

I reached out, my hand shaking, to check his pulse. "It's weak," I said, "but he's still alive."

Nan stepped around me to plunk a warm cup into Alastair's hands. "Get him to drink it." For the first time, I saw a crack in her all-businesslike manner, her steely eyes round and angry.

Alastair funneled the liquid into Corinth's mouth, for all the good it did, because by the time he was done, it didn't seem to matter—breath barely lifted his chest.

"Stanton is as hard to kill as a cockroach," Alastair said as he stumbled out onto the front porch to join me. He looked exhausted—but out of all of us, he seemed to have the most energy.

I'd been sapped of all mine since we'd gotten back, especially after having given most of my blood up to Gabriel, even after partaking in some of Nan's generous offering. She'd had plenty of her stash to go around, thankfully. But my sudden decline into depression wasn't helping.

I refused to meet Alastair's pointed gaze in my

direction as he sagged down onto the swing beside me. This was one of my favorite spots on Nan's wraparound porch. You could see all the way across the meadow to the crest of the hill. On the other side of that hill was where the barn sat. The normally swaying stalks of tall grass would have been more beautiful had they not been dusted with frost by the recent snowfall.

"Any change?" I asked him tentatively, afraid he might give me bad news.

He nodded. "Corinth is doing better. But there hasn't been a peep out of him since he stopped screaming. Imani is watching over him right now. I think the blood helped. His chest has healed up some." He paused, then said, "Your hand looks better too."

I glanced down to my bandaged hand, cringing. "I couldn't stand to see him like that—not again … not after … It brings back unbearable memories of that night." I shivered as a wave of nausea washed over me, stealing my breath away.

"What happened out there, anyway?" Alastair asked carefully.

"The Grigori were trying to call out the Watchers. We walked right on out into the middle of an ambush."

"Your plan didn't work. I'm calling it." He ran a hand through his blond hair, messing up the perfectly combed part. A lock of it fell into his eyes, and on pure instinct, I reached out to brush it out of his face.

He gave me a fleeting smile, pulled my uninjured hand into his, and drew it up to his lips, his breath tickling my knuckles.

"Corinth's condition isn't your fault. I pushed him

into going to get you when I knew he didn't have enough strength for it. If it's anyone's fault, it's mine. I guess the three musketeers always end up finding ways to get into trouble though."

I gave him a sidelong glance. "A movie reference? Say it ain't so."

Alastair held up a finger. "Actually, it's a book reference—Gatien de Courtilz de Sandras, *Mémoires de M. le comte de la Fère*, set in France in 1625." He stopped when he saw the look on my face and shrugged. "*And* you already knew that."

"No. I mean, wow … It's just … I've never heard you speak French before." I cleared my throat. "It's quite lovely."

He smiled again before saying, "'C'est cela l'amour, tout donner, tout sacrifier sans espoir de retour.'"

"What does it mean?" I asked.

"'That is love, to give away everything, to sacrifice everything without the slightest desire to get anything in return,'" he said quietly. "Corinth knew what he was doing. I just wish it had been me instead."

I drooped back into the cushioned swing, feeling exhausted and overwhelmed. "You can't always be the one to save the day."

"I can damn well try," he growled.

I smiled at that. It was just such an Alastair thing to say.

"Gabriel was close to my father, right? Before he turned him. I remember reading stories about my dad meeting Stanton in his journal." Alastair gave a slight nod as I continued. "Gabriel probably knows more about all of us than we know about ourselves … *He* is our only link to finding this cure. I *have* to put the plan back in play. We have to scour the city, boil oceans, go to the ends of the earth to find it. You're not going to like what I'm about to suggest either."

"Let me guess: it involves the billionaire?"

I nodded. "Unfortunately."

After a moment, one side of his mouth quirked up as if a light bulb had gone on over his head.

I sat up quickly. "What is it?"

He raised his eyebrows. "Oh, nothing … While you're dealing with Stanton, I'm going to scour the city, boil some oceans, and go to the ends of the earth."

Burns were painful. More so when eighty percent of your body was covered in them. Gabriel was propped up in a bed in Nan's spare bedroom, reading a book—and wearing nothing but a grin when I walked in.

Without looking at me, he flipped the page, unperturbed.

I whirled around, rubbing at my eyes in revulsion. *"For crying out loud, put some pants on!"* I screeched. "There is no *unseeing* that."

"Apologies, Miss Collins, but it's the quickest way for me to heal—fresh air on exposed skin, you see."

I rolled my eyes, disgusted. "Oh, I see *everything*, regrettably."

I heard the rustle of the bedsheets as he said, "I'm decent."

When I spun around, he was wearing sweatpants and

a T-shirt. Seeing him look so relaxed was almost as jarring as seeing him naked. I noticed he was right about one thing: he did look like he was healing at an exponential rate. His skin used to be charred and blackened; now it just looked more like a ripe avocado, except without the greenish-black tinge to his skin—it was red, raw, and swollen.

I could almost make out the faint scar line on his cheek, which was a marked difference. A little more like Deadpool, I thought.

"Does it hurt?" I asked.

Gabriel waved a hand. "I've had worse chemical peels."

"Too bad," I muttered.

He chose to ignore my dig at his expense and said, "You didn't bring flowers, so I'm assuming this isn't a social call."

There was a taupe chaise longue next to his bed, the kind that you could curl up on and stay for a century or two while reading a good book. This had been Paul's room when we had visited, and I realized I had never stepped a foot in here before. The pale blue and cream color scheme was a nice touch—simple, elegant, and not over the top. Curtains as rich as Alastair's baby blues were pulled tight against the burgeoning daylight.

Gabriel did not fit in this room. His tastes were way too ostentatious for any sort of domestic bliss. Nothing near this simple. He liked vampire chic.

I flung myself into the chaises' depths, curling my feet underneath me. The faint smell of cigarette smoke still clung to the cushions. I closed my eyes against the fresh wave of heartache. *Please don't cry in front of Gabriel. Anyone but him.*

When I opened them again, he was regarding me with an expression I almost mistook for compassion. But that didn't bother me as much as the silence did. It wasn't uncomfortable—no small talk necessary. I wasn't sure what that said about me. I did not want to feel comfortable in Gabriel Stanton's presence.

The man—I say that loosely—had a commanding presence about him, and I imagined he had never waited for anything in his entire life, but if my contemplation bothered him, he didn't show it.

He closed his eyes and started to hum softly to himself. It was a sweet melody, and it wasn't long before I realized he could carry a tune. It didn't sound familiar— maybe an old Irish folk song. I wondered if he could sing. By the sound of his range and tone, it sure seemed that way. Yet something else personal I had discovered about him that I didn't need to know.

I glanced up to find him studying me with an amused smirk on his face, his faint pink scar stretched down the left side of his cheek. We had been sitting in silence for a good long while.

"It's something my mother used to sing to me," he admitted softly. His eyes went wide for a second, as if he realized he hadn't meant to share something so personal with me.

Caught off guard, I finally asked, "Why did you risk your life to save mine?"

"Isn't it obvious?"

I shook my head.

"I have an agenda. I always have an agenda."

"You could have left me there," I said quietly. "Something tells me your agenda wasn't the only thing you were worried about. I think it's time you told me what's actually on your agenda."

"Is there another reason for this visit?" Gabriel sounded annoyed, as if I'd hit the nail on the head and he couldn't quite hide his distaste for caring about someone other than himself.

Something inside me knew he would never be forthright and open about his knowledge of the cure. He was going to keep everything a closely guarded secret until he absolutely couldn't, because that was the way he worked.

But seeing Corinth so close to death all over again had brought out a new kind of desperation in me.

I had to get the truth out of him once and for all— whatever it took.

I cleared my parched throat. "I think my father held the answer to the cure—or at least part of it. The only way I know how to track it down is by starting at the beginning. I need to know why you turned him. And seeing as how I'm pretty sure you won't give me a straight answer, I'll just have to take that answer from you."

My *Sight* stirred to life right at the same time as I sprang at him with steely resolve.

Chapter 28

Larna

I DIDN'T HAVE MUCH practice using my *Sight* on other vampires—especially one as old and strong as Gabriel Stanton. It was why I'd let him hum without interruption, and it was also why I'd remained silent until I knew I was ready.

It takes full mental, preternatural, and emotional focus to use compulsion. According to Gabriel, he was the only one who could compel another vampire—besides me, that is. Mind control takes up a lot of energy, and it takes a toll on whoever performs it. This was something altogether different. *Gabriel* was altogether different.

His weakened condition had made for the perfect opportunity to finally get some truthful answers out of him. The last time we'd been locked together in a battle of minds, we'd experienced each other's thoughts and emotions and memories, as if we'd etched a tiny part of ourselves into each other.

I'd hated every minute of it.

If there had been any other option, I would have taken it. The only thing worse than having an enemy was empathizing with that enemy. It wasn't as hard for me to understand him as I'd thought it would be. We all have reasons for doing what we do; his were just as valid to him as mine were to me.

For once, I'd caught him completely off guard—his eyes told me so. They were radiant and round, blown out, all black and no iris, just as spellbinding as mine were right now, I was sure. He wasn't going down without a fight though.

The pull was magnetic, peculiar—as if our minds were playing bumper cars, ramming awkwardly into each other as we both fought for control over the other.

Even wounded, he was incredibly resilient. It felt like I was swatting at Mount Olympus. I couldn't breathe, move, or bat an eye for fear of losing concentration. Sweat beaded on my forehead as we stayed locked like that for another full minute.

If he won, I would be in serious danger—I pushed harder, until I finally slipped through the tiniest crack in his armor. And then I was tumbling right through his defenses, straight into his memories. My skin tingled with the thrill of beating him, but the feeling didn't last long. An image flickered to life like old film on a projector starting up.

The first time I'd thwarted Gabriel's attempt at compulsion, I remembered seeing him holding a dying woman in his arms. I would never forget those stern inkblot eyes, the older woman's snow-white hair and bronzed skin weathered by the sun, kissed by age. I also remembered the tears pouring down Gabriel's face as he'd held her in his arms and wept over her body. At the time, I had no idea how I knew it was his mother, but I did. I thought it was because I could feel his love and heartache as if they were my own. We were connected somehow.

I saw a younger-looking, bearded Gabriel stretched out on the ground, holding his mother in his arms, her hand resting limply in his. She was dead—run through with a short sword still sticking out of her stomach.

My breath left me on a rush of air, and then the image faded as quickly as it had started.

Gabriel inhaled sharply. I mirrored his reaction. I had never felt so scared and exhausted, but also keyed up, in my entire life.

And then suddenly my vision swirled, and another strange memory surged to the forefront of my mind. I was standing on a clifftop in the middle of the night. White swells churned below me on one side of that cliff, and on the other, situated in a deep bowl-shaped valley, was a massive campsite. White tent tips spread out, vast and far-reaching, down below me. I lifted my face slightly to the soft spray of saltwater raining down on me. Lightning zigzagged the sky overhead. It smelled like seawater and fresh air and soil. But I also caught whiffs of body odor and fire and livestock.

A gust of wind whipped what sounded like a multitude of flags around in the distance.

This memory smelled and felt so real, but it was completely unfamiliar—

The sudden clang of weaponry brought me fully to attention. I jumped, scanning the area around me. The sound of faint voices carried lazily across the basin. This was an army.

I caught movement out of the corner of my eye and turned to see two broad-shouldered men, both with long hair and beards, marching toward me. They had bronze-colored skin, tanned dark by long hours outside, their faces cracked and weathered by time and harsh conditions. As soon as they were close enough, I saw that they were escorting someone, a man whose head was bent, with his shoulders hunched and his hands bound behind his back. His sandaled feet dragged across the soft dirt, leaving a trail in their wake as the two men hauled him along between them.

I had to remind myself that this was only a memory and I couldn't affect anything in it. Even so, I found myself falling in line behind them. I knew I was here for the man they held captive. They took no notice of me as I followed at a distance.

I took careful note of what the men wore, believing that it might give me a time period to go on. They had on dark leather armor, sandals, and had shields made out of wicker slung across their backs. I noticed the short swords at their hips too. Wicker shields. Sandals. Maybe this was early Roman Empire. Soldiers.

The men ahead of us had stopped to form a tight semicircle around their captive. I slowly made my way to the front of the group, a foreboding feeling forming in the pit of my stomach.

There was a large, lavish tent nearby, and the front flap partially covered the entrance. By the look of it, whoever resided inside was someone of great importance and wealth. Fine gold-and-silver tassels gleamed brightly in the soft light of several lanterns at each side. Several guards had positioned themselves at the four corners, spears in hand.

One of the men, upon seeing the soldier's approach, ducked inside the tent and then quickly dashed back out again, giving me time to position myself in front of the opening—and everyone else. I found myself more than a little curious about what was inside.

But the prisoner's head snapped up, drawing my attention back to him instead. As soon as I got a good look at his face, I stumbled backward, almost falling.

The captive shot one of the soldiers at his side a look of disgust. That action was just *so* him. Gabriel Stanton. His features were familiar, yet noticeably different. For a moment, all I could do was stand there studying him with my mouth hanging open. This was pre scarred Gabriel. Pre vampire Gabriel too.

One of the soldiers pushed him toward the front entrance of the tent. In the light, I could make out his face clearly. He looked to be only twenty years old. His dark, tousled hair flopped messily into his eyes. He had a short, trimmed beard and was wearing a knee-length brown tunic. Each of his wrists was wrapped by cloth. This was not the well-dressed, affluent Gabriel that I was used to.

The guards stepped up and held the front flap aside as an older man with a long, curly brown beard and cold, calculating eyes swept regally out from his extravagant shelter.

The man had dark skin, and across his collarbone, he wore a gold amulet: bird wings stretching the width of his chest. A tall gold crown was perched on the top of his head. He was adorned with a purple, floor-length silk tunic with a gold cloak slung over one shoulder, reminding me a little of how Sozo and his people dressed.

The regal-looking man swept a hand out toward Gabriel, flashing him a warm, serpentine smile—as if his mood might change at any second.

The two men at Gabriel's sides pushed him roughly to the ground. Gabriel, his hands still bound behind his back, pitched forward, landing face-first in the dirt at the crowned man's feet. The surrounding men laughed cruelly at him.

I cringed, knowing exactly what that kind of mockery felt like.

Gabriel raised his dark eyes up. His heated gaze landed on the dark-skinned man in front of him. The man motioned at the two soldiers behind Gabriel, and they pounced on him, viciously pulling him back to his feet, and when they spoke, it was in a language I did not understand.

I was able to catch one word that made my heart skip a beat: Ephialtes. A jolt of recognition tore through me at hearing that name. *Gabriel's birth name.* Was this Thermopylae? *Greece.* When had the Battle of Thermopylae taken place again? 500 BC, or something like that ... words like *Persians, Sparta,* and *last stand* came to mind.

I suddenly wished I'd had a chance to look up Ephialtes or paid more attention in history class. I wondered if he had played an important role in history. Lightning threaded the sky overhead, parting it in half, and I jumped in fright at the suddenness of it.

The conversation seemed to heat up. Gabriel was speaking animatedly, his entire body bent forward at the waist while his captors held him back. It looked to me like he was trying to reason with the man in the crown—pleading with him.

I knew a shake-down when I saw one. They wanted information. One of the soldiers at Gabriel's back shoved him hard again. Gabriel lurched sideways, falling to the ground at the royal's feet. Gabriel tried to roll onto his side as another guard kicked him in the gut, but it was futile, because the rest of the group joined in, beating, kicking, and jabbing him with the blunt end, and sometimes the sharp end, of their spears, until eventually he stopped moving altogether.

I turned away from the violent scene, sickened. I knew I couldn't do anything to stop them, but I couldn't help but try. I whirled around and advanced on the soldiers, placing myself between them and Gabriel.

I raised my fists and jutted my chin out just as several men raced right through me, their bodies flickering eerily in the process.

There had been a time when I would have loved watching Gabriel suffer. Now, though, I felt sorry for him. My gut twisted. I didn't want to be an observer anymore.

His pain was my pain.

Unfortunately, this memory wasn't something I could just walk away from. I glanced up at the storm-riddled sky, trying to scrub the image of Gabriel's bloodied and battered face out of my mind.

The crowned man stood off to the left, watching and waiting, his hands clasped behind his back as he slowly rocked back and forth on his toes and heels—enjoying the show, a cruel sort of smile twisting his lips. A curly-haired soldiers elbow slammed into Gabriel's ribs. He took another fist to the face and more shots to his body. Gabriel curled in on himself. All the while, I listened to his gurgled screams.

More men rushed up, sprawling him out on his face, where he lay spitting out dirt and blood.

The youngest soldier had a high, squeaky voice. When he spoke, it cracked. I heard the name Xerxes and froze. And then he said it again: *Xerxes*. Xerxes was another name I did recognize: the king of the Persian Empire. He was looking at the man in the gold crown reverently. The hairs on the back of my neck started to rise as my eyes swiveled back toward the man in the crown. *Xerxes?* The *Xerxes?*

Xerxes motioned for them to pick Gabriel back up, forcing him onto his knees, his hands still tied behind his back.

Even through all the blood covering his handsome features, I could see how much pain Gabriel was in. His spit more of it out onto the ground at the king's feet.

In a deliberate show of force, Xerxes took a short sword from the hands of one of the soldiers. I watched in dread as the king approached Stanton with it point down.

I knew what was coming a moment right before it happened.

He slashed downward with the sword, across the left side of Gabriel's—Ephialtes's—cheek, the blade shearing neatly through muscle and bone.

My thrumming pulse was drowned out by the sound of Gabriel's guttural bellow. His frantic howls turned into words that bubbled out of him like a busted fountain as he gave up the precious information he'd been too stubborn to give until now.

The last thing I saw before I was ripped from Gabriel's memory was the small triumphant smile on Xerxes's face.

I had to force myself to take slow, deep breaths as the pressure inside my chest built to an excruciating degree. My whole body was shaking, and I found myself blinking away fresh tears. It took me a whole minute to realize that I was back in the real world once again.

All I could concentrate on was Gabriel's scar, standing out pale and pink on his cheek. I had always wondered how he'd gotten it. Now I knew.

After what I'd just witnessed, I didn't want to revel in my win. I only felt shell-shocked, but I reminded myself that Corinth's life was still hanging in the balance. I had to be quick if I still wanted to get any answers out of him—the longer he was under, the harder it became for me to retain control over him. Because I did have control over him. Finally.

At the back of my mind, I kept thinking about how strong Gabriel had to have been to plant a future suggestion into Alastair's mind, when he'd gotten him to turn on us. I already felt the slow drain of energy seeping out of me.

"The paper you had in your pocket—the information on how to contact Angela—she must have gotten that to you while we were still in the clan. Are you working with her?"

Gabriel shook his head. "No."

Relief bloomed in my chest as I said, "Tell me why you turned my father. The whole truth."

Gabriel gritted his teeth as if he refused to answer. After a brief struggle, his eyes snapped back to mine, and he said, "Because I liked him."

"Explain," I snapped.

"All I wanted was information from a neighbor and a family friend of the Taylors. Your family hadn't even been a blip on my radar, but once I realized Corinth spent more time at your house than his own, that was when I started really digging into your life. Your father, Jack, was a well-known photographer who conveniently traveled often for work. I realized it would be the perfect opportunity to gather intelligence on the then-twelve-year-old Corinth. So I sent for Jack under the guise that he would take photos for my various business enterprises in England. When we met for the first time, we just so happened to hit it off. I found your father to be my equal—and utterly wasted as a photographer—from the very moment I met him. For the first time in a long time, I had found someone who wasn't dull. There was something refreshing and vibrant about his honesty. Your father loved to talk, but he wasn't afraid to share his truth. We had many late nights at The Swan, polishing off expensive bottles of bourbon, discussing politics, sports, business ... and, of course, *you*. He gushed over how much Corinth loved you—so much so that I came to realize that I didn't even need to use compulsion on your father. Jack was so starved for intellectual conversation." He gasped for a second, and I felt his resistance as he rasped, "Jack and I, we both saw something we wanted in each other."

My pulse was racing and I struggled to keep eye contact. "Let me get this straight. You turned my father because of your dysfunctional need for company? Friendship? Something more? You thought you were going to be one big happy family, so you took mine away from me?"

Gabriel gave a little shrug. "Deimos *is* my family. I was going to make Jack a part of it too."

"But why not just go after Corinth's family? Why mine?"

"Because I wasn't infatuated with Corinth's family."

He said it so matter-of-factly. Succinct and to the point. He was *finally* telling me the truth. I swallowed heavily. How was I supposed to take that? The rock in the pit of my stomach wasn't helping me stay in control. I didn't want to hear any more, but the truth was like water dripping from a tank: eventually, all of it would leak out.

It wasn't enough of an answer—not after everything he'd put us through. "Then why turn me?" I murmured.

"I turned you to get to Taylor—and Jack. I needed you to protect your best friend until he came into his own. My idea was to use that love you had for him. I never planned to turn you at first, but in the end, I thought you would be more comfortable staying with your father if you were like him. Vampire. When Jack wouldn't agree to join me willingly, it made me angry. I wanted him to make the choice without compulsion or force. You see, it was important he agree by his own free will. People are so much more loyal that way. Most beg me to turn them. I never do. But your father—he begged me *not* to. I guess you could say I made an exception—*twice*." Gabriel's eyes flashed. "The apple doesn't fall far from the tree."

I didn't have anything to say to that. I couldn't.

He continued, even though I didn't ask a question. "Control, Larna. It's always been about control. The only way I knew I was ever going to get Corinth's help was by turning someone he loved. You. I turned Jack and gave him a choice. I told him if he worked for me, I would wait to turn you at the age of eighteen. I also agreed to leave your mother alone. It took me a while to figure out Jack was working against me, and that he'd recruited Alastair to his cause. Again he fought me at every turn. But how would I get the dagger to Corinth? I had it in my possession—until I let Jack steal it from me. It was easy dangling little hints and clues in front of Alastair Iszler. Do you really think I would have chosen someone as caring and kindhearted as Alastair to watch over you at my manor?" He laughed mockingly. "I did my homework on him. Loner. Misfit. Outcast. Hates his own kind. It wasn't a coincidence you found your father's journal when you did. I delivered it right to your doorstep. I had my people hide it in your house when your mom started renovating. Jack didn't want you to find him. He tried fighting your fate, but you didn't. You walked right into it as if you had always known. When you came traipsing through the doors of my hotel, I knew it too."

Cold sweat trickled down my back. It all made sense, but it was still appalling nonetheless.

Gabriel said, "I wanted you to say yes to me—so I could hold it over your father's head, make him realize he'd lost his own daughter ... *to me*."

A shiver ran down my spine as realization dawned on

me. I'd lost control of my *Sight* without even knowing it, and he was still talking. He shouldn't have even remembered our conversation, but somehow he did. Maybe I'd never had the hold over him to begin with, or maybe we were connected in more ways than one.

He cocked his head to the side. "The only thing I couldn't control was how strong Corinth or *you* would become. You've had some of the answers in your possession this entire time. Jack entrusted you with his recordings. His thoughts … his voice … and you still have it in your possession."

Over the sudden erratic beating of my heart, I whispered, "*His journal.*"

Chapter 29

Alastair

ALASTAIR HAD TOLD LARNA he was going to scour the city, boil some oceans, and go to the ends of the earth to help get answers about Corinth's condition. It was the reason why he and Vinson had stealthily positioned themselves on the roof of a tea shop near Camden in London. They weren't there for the caffeine. He was watching the nightclub across the street.

This particular club was a vamp hotspot for clan Sangre. He'd heard rumors that they did all sorts of horrific, torturous things inside those well-protected walls. And it was just the sort of place you might go to in order to get answers about rogue angels trying to take over the world.

He pulled the scope of his rifle back up to his line of sight and watched as another vamp strolled up to the bouncer at the heavily guarded back door to the nightclub they had been watching for the better part of three hours.

This was one of the many places he would have taken down by now if he hadn't been so busy with avenging angels and Armageddon and everything else in between— like dying.

Alastair glanced back to make sure Vinson was still beside him. Sometimes he needed the reassurance. Vinson was a ghost, besides the fact that he had barely spoken a word since they had started their surveillance of the club.

That was why it was odd when Vinson pointed to Alastair's bulletproof vest and said, "Does that work?"

Alastair looked down. "Against bullets, yes ... anything else, no."

"Not vest." Vinson gave a shake of his head. "What you have in pocket."

Alastair handed the rifle back to Vinson and then drew out an object from one of the many pouches, knowing exactly what Vinson had been referring to. Vinson stared at the red liquid inside the capped syringe.

"Corinth's blood," he said. "I took it from the labs at Eleutheros, when I was following him." Alastair nodded down to where he knew the back entrance to the club was located. "I have a feeling we might need it tonight."

Vinson quirked a dark eyebrow in response.

"Oh, come on—don't give me that look. It's not that underhanded," he sighed. "My intention was to give it back to Corinth, but with everything that's happened recently ... well, I haven't had the chance, and then I forgot I even had it ... you know, because I died and everything. His blood can kill a vamp within minutes, and I expect he would give me his wholehearted permission to use it in this situation. I'll beg his forgiveness later."

"If kid is alive later ..." Vinson stopped himself short, letting the sentence trail off.

Alastair was sure Vinson saw the pained expression come over his face. Sorrow and regret. They both knew the cold hard truth when it came to death, but it didn't make it any easier to swallow. He'd seen that same look from many people over the years, and he knew he couldn't hide the way he felt from Vinson. He didn't want to.

As someone who prided himself on his stony indifference, he found his newfound *human* emotions quite annoying. Vinson was as good a confidant as a Catholic priest though.

"There is no reason to hold on to burden. He chose this life." It was the closest to sympathy Alastair had ever heard Vinson give.

"Yeah, after it chose him first," Alastair mumbled.

"Faster we move, faster we find cure for kid."

Alastair gave a curt nod, too overwhelmed for a minute to reply. Vinson caring about finding a cure for Corinth meant a lot to him. Deep down, Alastair knew Vinson was a family man.

"Something feels off about clan Sangre tonight," Vinson said, shifting the subject back to the task at hand.

"I feel it too," Alastair breathed. "You'd think these people would get more creative with their clan names … Clan Blood is not very imaginative for a bunch of vampires."

Sangre was a feeding den—they also drank alcohol, danced, partied, much like what you might find at any ordinary nightclub. It was rumored that they strung up and killed vamps for sport here. Anyone who infringed on their territory, or did something to piss them off, paid for their actions in front of a live audience.

Tonight, though, Alastair had watched Sangre members haul in, by his count, at least thirty human captives—all of them with hoods over their heads and hands tied behind their backs, forced inside like cattle to their slaughter. This was not like Sangre, or any other clan he knew of for that matter. Most clans were covert about their illegal activities. If you shone a spotlight on anything vamp-related involving humans, it left you open for retaliation from other vamps—and the like.

There wasn't an oversight committee on all things vamp-related. Vampires policed their own. This was just blatant disregard and carelessness, which meant they weren't afraid of other clans stopping them.

He exchanged a quick glance with Vinson. "Those people they're dragging in there are human."

Vinson nodded his agreement.

This place was definitely a mecca for the bad—and he was only too happy to put a stop to it.

Vinson and Alastair had borrowed some of Deimos's raid gear before heading out. Alastair had plenty of layers on because it was colder than a polar bear's toenails. Being human had its disadvantages, and susceptibility to the weather was one of them. He was wearing all-black boots, black camo pants, his leather jacket, and a vest over a long-sleeved thermal, and, of course, his armor buckled at each forearm. The vambrace helped keep pressure on his injured wrist too. He'd hurt it when one of those angels had grabbed him. They were tougher than they looked, apparently.

Alastair groaned in frustration. "That's fifteen more they've lugged in there in the last half hour."

Flecks of fresh snow dotted Vinson's dark uniform. Alastair couldn't help but stare at a flake that had landed on Vinson's nose. The ice was turning into puddles at their feet, but it was still too bitterly cold and blustery for his liking.

"I know what they do to people who piss them off," Vinson growled. "Dragging in humans for show means they care little for consequences."

Two jagged flashes of lightning knifed down, cutting the sky wide open and then vanishing quicker than Alastair could blink. If he hadn't been looking for it, he might have missed it completely.

The Grigori were here. At least they knew this was the right spot.

Alastair turned to Vinson, his blood beginning to boil as the all-too-familiar flush of heat started to color his cheeks. "You thinking what I'm thinking?"

Vinson growled his response.

Alastair refused to let innocents be killed or turned tonight. He did not like it when vampires took advantage of the innocent. "The Grigori have recruited Sangre to their cause. They're going to turn all those humans in there and make a spectacle of it. Vinson—I'm going in. I don't expect you to join me—"

Vinson growled again.

It was just the two of them, and they were seriously outnumbered. Alastair really hoped Vinson would come with him.

"You are human now, no? You will make for perfect distraction. Private club in back. No one gets in without invite. You need to get on main stage to free prisoners. Can you handle heat while I free prisoners in back?"

Alastair clapped Vinson on the shoulder, already

stripping out of his leather jacket. Next came his vest. He unfastened the leather cuffs on his forearms and then finally yanked off his long-sleeved thermal, leaving behind only a thin white cotton T-shirt that did nothing to cut the cold slicing through him like a knife.

Alastair had been sweating underneath all those layers, and he was sure the moisture was now turning into ice crystals on his skin. His breath plumed out in front of him in giant white puffs as he ran a hand through his neatly combed locks, disheveling it on top—emulating the style in which Corinth wore his hair.

He reached down to double-check the hidden blades in his boots. "How do I look? Do you think they'll recognize me?"

"Like human popsicle." Vinson pointed at Alastair's face. "Black eye is nice touch." In a blur of motion, Vinson reached out and, using one of his many knives that appeared in his grip as if by magic, sliced his own palm open. Blood blossomed up brightly against pale skin. Vinson planted a red palm print against the left side of Alastair's white shirtsleeve. "You are marked. They will take you to back, thinking you are volunteer."

Alastair flipped the capped syringe in the air before slipping it into his back pocket. He flashed Vinson a quick brazen grin and then threw his leather jacket on over his T-shirt. "How much time you need?"

"Fifteen minutes."

Alastair nodded. "Right." Vinson turned to gather his gear as he added, "Oh, and don't tell Larna I did this."

Vinson rolled his eyes as he slung his rifle over his shoulder, muttering something in Russian—his disapproval that Alastair was thinking about Larna and not the mission at hand.

Technically, he was thinking about both.

Alastair made his way toward the entrance of the club. The pulse and swell of the bass was already making his eardrums ache. The two guys stationed outside the door were vamps. Their job was to escort their "guests" inside once they'd received approval to get in.

He couldn't remember a time when his senses had ever been so dull, except for his taste buds—those had been the only thing heightened as soon as he'd become human again. The rest had gone to shit. His eyesight was one of them. He felt night-blind as he made his way over to the front of the line, especially with all the city lights flashing overhead, distracting him.

A red neon sign with the word *Sangre* pulsated brightly above him.

Everything pulsed like a heartbeat.

London had a heartbeat.

He'd always enjoyed nightlife. Now, though, he found he enjoyed daylight more. Maybe because it didn't bother him like it used to. There was a long line of vamps waiting to get inside to see the macabre show. Their bloodlust was palpable. His stomach twisted into knots at the prospect of watching humans turned into vampires for entertainment.

The turn was not a fun process—it was painful and brutal.

A group of young girls standing in front of him,

looking to be in their late teens, chittered animatedly to one another. They were probably much, much older than they appeared. They all wore vibrant, colorful faux-fur coats, short skirts, and patent leather high heels.

One of the girls, who had flaming-orange hair and a sharply contrasting purple coat, twirled around to give him a shy smile before turning back to her group.

He wondered if she could smell the vamp blood on him.

After the group of girls were let inside, Alastair made his way up to the bouncers guarding the door. For a moment, all they did was look him up and down with disinterest, their gazes lingering on his black eye. He noted that both of them had arms as thick as tree trunks, and legs corded with muscle. One of the vamps had a tattoo on the left side of his neck that looked like blood dripping. A little too tongue-in-cheek for his liking.

The second vamp stroked his shaggy beard in thought and, in what Alastair thought sounded like a thick Aussie accent, said, "This club's not for you, mate. Invitation only."

Alastair flashed them both a vexing smile before pulling his coat down to reveal the crimson handprint on his arm. *Marked.* "Here's my invitation."

The vamp with the sandy-blond hair shared a quick glance with his companion before sniffing at the air. Alastair saw the greedy hunger light up his eyes. Maybe they got credit for bringing in more humans, like commission. Either way, they weren't turning away a healthy "volunteer" who had been marked by another vamp. They could smell Vinson's blood and distinguish it from others'.

He shoved Alastair forward. "You better hurry up; it's about to start," he crowed. "Tom, escort this one inside and get him set up with the rest."

Tom led Alastair forward, through the door, a firm grip at his elbow.

Once inside, the first thing Alastair noticed was the insane amount of *red* everywhere. Varying shades of it—scarlet, crimson, burgundy, and maroon … the effect was dizzying. Even the hallway looked like a blood vessel.

He knew this particular venue had been a historic theater at one point in time. Velvet curtains, velvet ropes, velvet ottomans—all vaudeville, cabaret-style decor—the furniture was covered in velvet, with little gold tassels decorating the chair's arms. The ornamentation was meant to be suggestive, but he felt that it was the opposite. It was as if he had been transported back to Stanton's manor all over again. Alastair hated crushed velvet. He also hated over-the-top flashiness that went with the mythos of all things vampire.

For a second, all he could hear was the pounding rumble of music, feeling it reverberate in his bones as the melody amplified and increased. The sound washed over him, taking with it some of his nerves. It had been a long time since he'd been fully immersed in clandestine mode. Fear was an appropriate response to things outside people's control, but Alastair wasn't afraid—he was in control. He only felt a sense of calm right before the storm. It was always the same during a mission: he was the epitome of collected—afterward, maybe not so much.

Still, there was an inkling at the back of his mind he couldn't quite brush aside. He kept thinking about how far news of his resurgence and reemergence had traveled. He wasn't exactly a faceless figure in the crowd anymore.

The hallway stopped at an iron door guarded by five goons. Their eyes raked over Tom, who still had a hand at Alastair's elbow. Tom nodded at them and then they let them pass through the doors without comment.

Once they spilled out into the main theater, Alastair realized he hadn't been prepared for what awaited him. A playhouse of the macabre. The auditorium was filled to the brim with hundreds of ravenous vampires. He noticed no one was sitting in the fancy-looking scarlet fabric seats. Everyone was either standing, dancing, or swaying to the deep bass of music playing throughout the auditorium. Thick, matching curtains parted the stage in half. Balconies painted with gold accents lined the entire upper floor. He wasn't a movie goer by any means, but if this place had played movies, this would have been a nice spot to watch them from. The theater itself looked old—1920s, he guessed.

Tom led Alastair down the middle aisle, and as they made their way toward center stage, Alastair's eyes were immediately drawn to what was on it: twenty living souls, boys and girls alike, all spaced out evenly across the platform, their hands bound above them by rope. Most of the victims hung limply, resigned to their fate. A few others were actively trying to free themselves, their feet barely scraping the floor as they swung back and forth in their panic and fright. Of course, even the rope was crushed velvet. He cringed inwardly as Tom ushered him closer—front row and center.

They passed by a young girl with short, spiky blond

hair in the audience. She was holding a champagne glass delicately pinched between two slender fingers. It was filled with blood. Some of it dribbled down her chin as she drank.

Sharp fury worked its way up through him at seeing this place so jam-packed, standing room only—with no one making a move to help any of these poor souls.

The crowd of onlookers was clearly enjoying the show already and nothing had happened yet. This was wrong in so many ways. An image of Wrentmore, fangs bared, popped into his head, and Alastair stiffened involuntarily.

For what felt like an incredibly long time, all he could do was look around. Vamps had their hands raised in the air, licking their lips in anticipation. Some were clapping and whistling, and others were grinning, with bloodstained teeth showing. The metallic tang was thick in the air. He noticed a few girls on the very far left of the stage, crying for help. Their alarm was only serving to send the crowd into more of a frenzy—a soon-to-be bloodbath.

Alastair had to work hard at keeping his face a blank mask.

They were about to be turned in front of a very captive audience.

His stomach flipped at the sight of so much delight in seeing other people's pain. A side of vampirism he'd *always* detested. And Alastair didn't even realize he'd stopped until his escort shoved him roughly toward the stairs, heading straight up to the stage.

"What's your problem? This is what you signed up for, *human*," Tom said with a snort. "You should be clamoring to get up there right now. You almost missed your chance."

He could take out this guy if he wanted to. The way he carried himself with overconfidence would have made it easy to catch him off guard—throw an elbow to his face, take out a kneecap.

Instead, he let Tom guide him toward the rest of the livestock on exhibition without comment. As soon as they hit the stairs, Alastair tripped himself up so he could quickly palm one of the knives from his boots. He wasn't sure if they would search him or not.

Alastair's escort yanked him roughly back to his feet, grabbing his elbow as they made it up the stairs and onto the platform.

From up here the crowd sounded deafening, and so did the music.

Tom shoved him forward toward the right side of the stage, three people down from the end. He proceeded to spin Alastair around to face him, gesturing at his leather jacket. "I like that jacket … real leather. Looks expensive. I think I'll relieve you of it. Besides, you won't be needing it, anyway, will you? We gotta give them a good show, right?"

Alastair was suddenly glad he'd stowed the syringe in his back pocket and not his jacket. He shrugged out of it, handing it over, but before he relinquished his hold on it, he narrowed his eyes and said, "I'll be expecting it back in good order."

Tom snorted. "Whatever. Price of admission." And then he proceeded to string Alastair up with the rest of the group, like a side of beef in a butcher shop.

Alastair tried to move to his left, and agony shot up his shoulder from his injured wrist. Even though the rope was made of soft material, it still dug painfully into his hands, stretched up over his head. His fingers were already starting to go numb. His balance was also off, the way he was standing on the tips of his toes to get traction.

Now that he was front and center, Alastair could see and feel the ripple of fevered tension so strongly that he got disoriented from it all. He tried to squint past the blindingly bright lights aimed right in his eyes. Suddenly he was very glad that Vinson was his backup. *This is probably a very stupid idea. Scratch that—this is a very stupid idea. Not so calm and collected now, are you?* he thought.

Alastair's gaze traveled over the rest of the "volunteers" around him. A younger guy with dark skin and equally dark tattoos covering both his arms and legs was staring dully off into space.

He signaled to the guy, half yelling over the bass of the music. "*Hey!*"

The kid turned his head, and his eyes stretched wide in surprise as if he thought Alastair had appeared out of thin air. "Dude, were you there just a second ago?"

"Just got here."

The kid laid his head against the crook of his elbow, looking defeated. "Come to join the party?" he whispered bitterly. "They grabbed me after football practice. I tried to fight them off, but these guys are monsters ... literally ... I had no idea vampires *actually* existed." He shuddered.

Alastair glanced down to see that the kid was wearing cleats and a green-and-white striped jersey with athletic shorts. "Hang in there," he whispered. "I'll get us all out of this."

The kid stared stupidly back at Alastair for a second before letting his eyes drift to the rope holding him up. "Did you just seriously tell me to hang in there? Yeah … sure—like you're in any position to help, anyway."

The sound of cheering rose dramatically in the background as Alastair yelled, "*What's your name?*"

"*Nicola!*" he yelled back.

"Nicola, trust me when I say I'm getting us all—" A surge of clapping and shouting drowned out the rest of what Alastair was saying as someone took center stage.

He could see their outline as they moved back and forth, the lights winking out each time the figure walked in front of them. And then a loud-speaker squelched to life and the music died down. When the person began to speak, the crowd seemed to hang on to the announcer's every word.

"*Hellllllllllooooo, clan Sangre!*" This was met by another round of applause. "I'm DJ Maze, your host for tonight! And boy, do we have a special show for *yoooooouuuuuu!*" He swept an arm out wide behind him, gesturing at all the life-size blood bags strung up for their viewing pleasure.

Alastair clutched his knife between slick fingers, taking in slow, deep breaths. His ribs were pinched, and it made it hard to breathe with his arms stretched over his head. Tom did not like late arrivals, apparently.

"There is a lot to catch you up on tonight! We have the pleasure of introducing a few friends of the Grigori. *Angels are our future!*"

There came a lot of whistling and hooting in response.

"Now that we have partnered with the Grigori, the time has come for us all to take a stand. It's time to live out in the open. Among humans. They are *not* our equals. We are better. Unrivaled. Powerful. Greater. *Yet why are we the ones who are afraid to show them our true selves?*" He pumped both of his fists enthusiastically in the air as another round of applause broke out. "And look at this lot." The DJ turned back to face them, speaking to Alastair and the rest of the group on-stage. "Our newest members, ready to join clan Sangre. And even though you might not have chosen this way of life, this way of life chose *you.* You are among the elite now. We welcome you with open arms. *We* are the future."

Things had progressed a lot faster than Alastair had originally thought. They were building an army for the Grigori—working with one of the largest clans out there, besides Deimos, that is. He had known it was coming, but not this quickly. They were going to reveal themselves to the world, and sooner rather than later.

Just then a thunderous echo boomed out over the audience. Alastair would have clamped his hands over his ears if he could have. By the crackle and surge of energy rolling through the entire theater, he knew what was coming next. There was a loud, resonating bang, and a churning vortex of wind and light opened up in front of them. From out of its depths plunged two tall figures.

Alastair was breathing hard now, trying to ignore the pounding in his skull—the beginnings of a gnarly headache setting in. He couldn't even remember the last time he'd actually gotten a headache.

An emaciated angel with cheekbones sharper than a skeleton's appeared, along with someone else—and it took Alastair a moment to make his eyes work and see past the stage lighting, but as soon as he saw who was with the other angel, his heart began to thump irritatingly loud.

Turiel. The angel who had grabbed Corinth back at the cabin. Alastair ducked his head and hunched his shoulders in order to hide his face.

DJ Maze gestured to two vamps at the end of the stage, and they materialized behind one of the young girls at the opposite end from him. She couldn't have been older than fifteen. Her curly blond hair was tied back in a tight ponytail, and she had on a school uniform. She was crying softly to herself.

"We'll start at this end … our newest recruit." The DJ snapped his fingers, and the vamps grabbed her, and she screamed.

Alastair kept his head down, making himself stand incredibly still, thinking through his options. But he didn't get long to think, because one of the vamps, a broad-shouldered man with long chestnut hair, pushed her head to the side and bared his fangs.

Alastair snapped his head up and yelled over the applause of the crowd. *"Stop it! Leave her alone!"* There was a smattering of jeering and clapping before it died down. Everyone was looking around, confused at the interruption, even the long-haired vamp had stepped away from the young girl he was about to drain to look at him. *"Why don't you start with me instead?"* he goaded.

There came more insistent babbling and whispering

from the gathered crowd.

The DJ quieted everyone down, gesturing at them as he shouted into his mic, "Quiet, everyone! Quiet now!"

Maybe Alastair was only imagining it, but he felt Turiel's eyes rake over him. Turiel leaned over to Maze and whispered something into his ear. The DJ's eyebrows rose and then his gaze flickered over to him once again.

He could hear Maze whisper into his mic, "*As I live and breathe … well, well, well … who do we have here?*"

Vinson had wanted a distraction. Alastair figured he was about to get one.

DJ Maze whirled around, giving a little flourish of his hand, perfectly thrilled by this new turn of events. "It's come to my attention that someone up here is a traitor to our kind. *Someone* who has disparaged our good name." He pointed right at Alastair and said, "*Alastair Iszler.* Did I hear something about you volunteering to go first?" He turned back to the crowd. "Why don't we give him what he wants?"

There came laughter, and then shouts and boos, the masses now turning into a rising mob. Their rage was a palpable, living, breathing thing once they realized who Alastair was.

This wasn't the worst position he'd ever been in— he'd died and come back—but it was a close second.

DJ Maze appeared in a quick flash of movement to stand in front of him before he could even blink his surprise. He could see the DJ's face clearly now. He looked young, early twenties maybe, with mocha-colored skin and dark eyes and spiky russet hair. There was a fancy-looking fur-lined headset draped around his neck with a microphone attached to it. He looked every part the college disc jockey and MC.

Turiel was beside Maze too now, his eyes taking in Alastair. Greedy. He looked different from the last time Alastair had seen him. His nose was bent and broken and grotesquely out of proportion to the rest of his once-perfect face.

The DJ turned his back on Alastair, bowing theatrically to his audience, clearly loving the anticipation of the spectacle he'd built up.

The drama.

"For those of you who have been living under a rock these past few months, Deimos used to have a pretty big price on Iszler's head for being a traitor to our kind." He whirled around, gripped Alastair's hair, and yanked his head back to whisper in his ear, "You thought you could just waltz right on in here without being noticed? I don't know what you're playing at." He shook his head. "*Corto de luces.*" Alastair knew in Spanish this meant "not the brightest bulb in the box." In English, the DJ added, "Because your face is pretty noticeable, amigo ..." He addressed the rapt audience again. "Did you know he hates his own kind? That's why he abandoned you. *Us.* Iszler took matters into his own hands. He's *human.*"

It was a smart move, feeding them fear and violence. This was where mob mentality took over. The only thing Alastair could hear now was the sound of soft crying coming from several of the people tied up beside him on-stage. This only fueled his anger more. He'd had enough of this guy preaching lies.

The spectators were hanging on to his every word

until someone at the back of the theater shouted, "*Prove it! Prove he's human!*"

"He's deceiving you!" Alastair shouted into the silenced throng of onlookers. "The Grigori will make you serve them and then kill—"

Maze pulled Alastair up by his shirtfront, causing his toes to scrape across the stage, effectively cutting off the rest of his sentence. "*Shut up*," the DJ snarled at the same time as he covered his microphone so that no one else could hear him.

For the briefest of instants, his eyes fell on Alastair's hand, and then, without warning, Maze ripped the palmed blade out of Alastair's grasp. The DJ flicked the knife open and, in one fluid motion, slashed a long diagonal cut all the way across Alastair's chest.

A ribbon of red bloomed bright against the white fabric of his shirt. Maze pulled Alastair's shirt up. After a second, when the wound didn't close up, Maze bellowed, "See—he doesn't heal!" He sniffed at the air, moving in closer to Alastair, his eyes practically rolling to the back of his head. "*What are you?*" he whispered under his breath.

By now the crowd had erupted into a flurry of motion and shouts of panic. After what seemed like an exceedingly long time, Maze was finally able to calm the horde down long enough for him to speak again. "This is what the Watchers and the Slayer, Corinth Taylor, want to turn you into—*human*. He is living proof. *Look at him*," he hissed. "*What should we do about it?*"

The Grigori wanted to make Corinth out to be enemy number one. They were calling him a slayer.

Alastair heard the cries and shouts of the onlookers:

"*Turn him!*" "*Kill him!*" "*Bleed him dry!*" "*Break his neck!*" All suggestions equally as dark as the last.

Alastair thought he was doing a bang-up job of distracting, but he really wished Vinson would hurry up. There must have been more captives backstage for him to free than he'd anticipated. Or maybe something had happened … Wait, had it been fifteen minutes?

The DJ had worked himself *and* everyone else up into a bloodthirsty fervor. Alastair could see the purple vein pulsing at Maze's neck as he licked his lips at seeing the bright red on his shirt.

He wanted blood. *Alastair's blood.*

Sweat rolled into Alastair's eyes, slid between his shoulder blades, and ran down the crooks of his arms, which had been holding up the brunt of his weight. His shoulders ached as Maze pulled him even closer, stretching Alastair's arms out as far as the rope would allow him to go.

"Guess it's just a good old-fashioned draining for you tonight—gotta make an example out of you." His lips were parted, and the tips of his fangs flashed bright as he sank his teeth into Alastair's neck.

No more drama needed.

Chapter 30

Alastair

ALASTAIR MAY HAVE BEEN human, but when Corinth and Dave had brought him back to life, he'd felt altered somehow, and it wasn't until this very moment that he realized why.

Maze had stopped draining Alastair and was slow-blinking at him in confusion. He staggered back a step, a hand going to his throat as if he were making the universal sign for choking. Blood dribbled out of the corners of the vampire's mouth. His blood. After another second though, instead of the DJ finishing the job he'd started, he dropped like a stone, shaking violently and foaming at the mouth at Alastair's feet.

Somewhere at the back of Alastair's mind, he knew the audience had gone devastatingly quiet, but he had lost enough blood to cause pitch-blackness to creep in at the edges of his vision. He focused on the sound of his own pulse beating hard against his eardrums as he struggled to stay upright. His knees almost buckled out from under him, and his hands and wrist ached from the added pressure on the rope.

Alastair had over a hundred years' worth of training

and fighting under his belt, and those instincts didn't go away just because he was human. They had been honed and fine-tuned to the point where he possessed a sort of sixth sense when it came to fighting. He'd learned to read people's body language as easily as reading a book. He could sense what people were about to do even before they did it—a premonition that made him something more than just human.

A part of him still operated with that same preternatural perception. Adrenaline kicked in and sent his heart rate skyrocketing.

Turiel, temporarily caught off guard by the vamp's death, didn't see Alastair launch himself into the air until it was too late. Using the rope to pull himself up, Alastair wrapped his legs around Turiel's neck and squeezed—

At the same time as he heard the crack of a rifle. Vinson finally announcing his presence.

With his legs still twisted around Turiel's neck, Alastair flipped himself backward, tossing the Grigori end over end in the opposite direction at the same time as the rope snapped taut and broke. He sprang back to his feet without losing momentum, shedding what was left of the rope still wrapped around his wrists.

By this point, Nicola was staring at him with mouth gaping wide. "How the bloody hell did you do that? *Who are you?*"

The crowd burst apart like a flock of birds escaping from a gilded cage as chaos ensued.

Alastair flashed Nicola one of his half grins and shrugged. "I have twenty different black belts."

"You are one strange dude," Nicola said. "And I'm

not at all ashamed to admit that I love that about you."

Alastair fished the second knife out of his boot, cut Nicola free, and handed him the blade. "Can you take care of the others?"

"Sure thing, boss," he said and set to work without needing any more direction.

Most of the audience was running and screaming, heading for the already-overloaded exits. A few stayed to watch the show, while the rest were deciding whether to take a stand against Alastair. All of the remaining people tied up on-stage were shouting in fright and crying as they tried in vain to free themselves.

Off in the distance, there came another volley of rounds fired from Vinson's rifle.

The vamps who had decided to go after Alastair were falling around him like flies.

Alastair was going to help the young girl who looked to be about fifteen when a flash of blinding light whistled past his head, so blisteringly hot he could smell his hair burning. He staggered backward as Turiel bounded out of a strangely spinning, cloudlike vortex. The force of it bursting into existence was enough to knock him sideways, almost off the stage.

There was no time to do anything but meet Turiel's charge head-on. They hit each other and went down hard in a tangle of arms and legs at the edge of the stage.

Alastair took a blow to the gut at the same time as he rammed a knee into Turiel's sternum. An angel could stop his heart from beating in an instant, probably with a flick of a wrist. That was why he knew he had to take Turiel's hands out of commission—and quickly. He didn't have the healing ability anymore—if he got zapped now, he knew he'd be out for the count.

Wrapping both his legs around Turiel's outstretched arm, he used his hips for torque, twisting Turiel's elbow grotesquely in the opposite direction. The bone gave with a satisfying snap. There was a howl of pain, followed by Turiel's free hand igniting in an eerie shade of cobalt, flaring up so intensely that white blotches exploded across Alastair's vision.

Alastair tugged blindly at the syringe in his back pocket, uncapped it, and sank the needle deeply into what he thought might be Turiel's neck or back or arm—he couldn't tell which—injecting Corinth's blood into the angel.

Turiel stood back to his feet and growled, "Is that supposed to do something to me?"

"Yes," Alastair gasped. "*Distract you!*" he yelled at the same time as Vinson appeared from behind the stage curtains as if he'd been part of the final act all along, opening fire on Turiel.

Alastair threw his hands over his head, thinking about how Vinson loved making an entrance even more than Corinth did. Vinson emptied an entire magazine from his submachine gun into the angel's face, head, neck, and chest. It was enough to knock the Grigori back a step with each blow, all the way toward the end of the stage, until he finally teetered over it and disappeared from sight.

Alastair jumped to his feet and went after the angel, but as soon as he got to the edge of the stage, where Turiel had vanished, he realized that he was already gone. *Damn those angels with their teleporting abilities—*

Someone yanked Alastair backward off his feet from behind.

They had him fast about the chest, crushing his arms against his sides, and also his lungs. Whoever his attacker was, they were inhumanly strong. So strong, in fact, that they'd already hauled him halfway across the stage by the time he even had a chance to react.

Alastair kicked out blindly behind him, landing a blow to a shin.

Rough hands loosened their grip around his middle. He whirled around to face whoever had grabbed him. It was Tom, the vamp who'd strung him up and stolen his jacket. To make matters worse, Alastair realized that he was wearing it too.

He launched himself into the air and kicked out, striking Tom square in his jaw. The vampire squawked, doubled over, and grabbed at his head in pain. In the same fluid motion, Alastair whirled back around, kicking down hard at the side of Tom's knee. The vampire lurched sideways, almost falling down the stairs center stage.

Fortunately, all the captives had been freed by Nicola and had vanished from sight. No casualties except for the bad guys. And maybe him, he thought distantly.

Tom bared his teeth and started toward Alastair again, but before he could charge, Vinson took the vampire down with all the enthusiasm of a lion going after its prey, tearing Tom's throat out before Alastair could even think about lifting a finger to help.

He raised an impressed eyebrow as the rest of the theater emptied out, minus a few stragglers, in part, Alastair thought, because of Vinson's violent display.

A thunderous *BOOM* shook the entire auditorium, and the ozone thickened right at the same time as a cloaked figure surged forth out of thin air right behind him.

He recognized the skeletal sack of bones who had arrived with Turiel, and he wasn't as frail as he looked, because he clamped strong hands around Alastair's throat that felt just like iron bands. They crackled and sizzled with electricity and heat. Alastair gasped at the searing pain, barely managing to rip out of his grasp at the last second and roll to the side.

For all the good it did.

The Grigori had already let loose another wicked bolt aimed directly at him. Time seemed to slow down. Alastair couldn't move out of the way fast enough.

Vinson flew out of nowhere, jumping into the line of fire, taking the brunt of the impact and saving Alastair's life, but the blast sent Vinson soaring past the heavy curtains that blocked the rest of backstage from view.

Damn angles.

A group of about twenty Sangre members were circling the bottom of the stage like vultures, hindering Alastair's escape. Some had recovered after being shot, while others had arrived as Sangre's back-up shortly after Vinson had disappeared. He turned to go back that way, but he was met by Turiel and the bag of bones once again, blocking his exit. He could have fought off one angel, maybe … but not two.

They were moving toward him, their hands shining

bright like deadly glowsticks, lighting the dark aisles in front of them. That wild-eyed look they were giving him made it appear as if they had finally come into contact with the game they'd been hunting for centuries.

Alastair swallowed hard, taking everything in, contemplating his next move. From the rope swinging lazily above his head, to the two dead vamps at his feet. He could work with the rope, use it to propel himself into the approaching group. He cast his gaze around the rest of the theater. It was riddled with bodies. Vampires killed by Vinson. The DJ was by his feet too—deceased now after drinking Alastair's blood.

The Grigori prowled closer. They had him dead to rights. Their eyes were full of cold malice, but they weren't in any hurry to finish him off just yet.

Alastair gestured down at Tom's body, near his feet. "If this is going to be my last stand, do you mind if I get my jacket back?"

Slowly Alastair crouched down beside Tom's body, keeping a careful eye on the circling vultures so he could pull his jacket off the dead vamp. The entourage of waiting vamps and angels only stared at him as he shook his jacket out and then shrugged back into it, the smell of iron and leather strong in his nostrils.

There were no snide remarks or need for any more show.

Alastair turned to face them, lifting his fists and getting ready to fight to his last, dying breath. "Okay, I'm ready."

A golden sphere of light and sound exploded all around him. He thew his hands over his ears. Surely the earth was quaking apart beneath him. The ground shook and then shifted, and he dropped to his knees, trying to shield his eyes from the blazing light. It felt like being flattened by a steamroller. His eyes were watering, and when he did manage to look up, he saw five giant forms standing shoulder to shoulder, forming a tight, protective circle around him.

Only moments before, no one hand been standing there.

Alastair froze. He realized that a part of the light was the stage lighting glinting off polished armor. A tingling numbness ran through his entire body. His tongue felt thick in his mouth and his heart was hammering away a million beats per minute.

He found it impossible to stay upright.

A hand reached down, gripped him tight, and then they hurtled into a whirling vortex of light and chaos and a whole lot of nothingness. *Angels.*

Chapter 31

Alastair

ALASTAIR FLOPPED TO THE ground on a white sandy beach. Vinson was sprawled out next to him, both of them, amazingly, still alive. At least, he thought he was still alive. His arms were stretched out by his sides as he gazed distantly up at a cluster of palm trees overhead. The pounding of his head and heart were in sync. There came the gentle lap of waves breaking against the shoreline not ten feet away. The smell of brine was heavy in the air. This was exactly the opposite of where he thought he would end up tonight—or today rather.

Vinson put a hand up to shield his eyes from the blinding sun and popped up into a crouch, a hand going to his charred vest so he could pull out one of his many throwing knives. Vinson always expected trouble. To be fair, Alastair did too, but he was officially spent, having lost too much blood to the vampiric DJ.

He let his eyes adjust—it was so bright he could barely make out where he was. This amount of sunlight was a marked difference from London's nightlife. It was humid and warm, and he was already sweating through his leather jacket.

Alastair realized, half in dismay and half in relief, that the people—*angels*—who had pulled them out of the theater were now standing over them, watching in resolute silence.

It was off-putting that they could transport him anywhere in the world in the span of a few seconds.

They were nestled on a small stretch of land—an island with no inhabitants—and beyond that, as far as the eye could see, was only crystal clear water. There was nowhere for them to go even if they had wanted to run.

Obviously, the angels wanted privacy.

This was the second time Alastair had been thrust into that weird tunnel of light and elements, and he did not like it. He sat up, grimacing as a bout of dizziness overcame him, and threw a hand to his neck, feeling for the puncture wounds made by Maze. His white T-shirt was shredded and crusted with red. His wrist was aching worse than ever now, and he wasn't sure how much blood he had lost. Enough.

Out of the five, only one angel stepped forward to reach a hand out toward him. The angel had spiky dyed-blond hair. He looked to be of East Asian descent, or at least, it appeared that way to Alastair. He stared up at the extended hand but didn't take it, even though the guy had an honest enough face and a warm smile to boot.

These beautiful creatures were exceedingly tall, and they blotted out the sun as they moved closer, to tower over them both.

He didn't accept the angel's proffered hand. Instead, Alastair took a moment to take them in, squinting up in wariness at their overly polished bronze breastplates, which looked fifty pounds too heavy.

One angel in particular stood away from the rest of the group, drawing Alastair's eye to him immediately. He was shorter than the rest, but that didn't say much—they were all taller than he was. But this angel had pale blue-violet eyes, which stood out because of his raven-colored hair and equally pale skin. There was something decidedly familiar about him, but Alastair couldn't quite place what that was. He wondered why he didn't have dyed hair like the others, and why he was standing further away from the group—standoffish.

Behind Vinson's crouched form, were a dark-skinned man and woman. They stood at attention, their backs straight and arms crossed over their chests. Alert. Observant. Resolute.

To Alastair's surprise, the one who'd offered him his hand was still smiling genially down at him with his hand held out. He motioned at Alastair to take it again.

"I'm Ikari," he said cordially. "I saw what you did back there. That vampire who drank from you—he reacted like he would have if he'd drunk from one of us." Ikari tilted his head to the side, studying Alastair as if he were an extremely hard-to-figure-out jigsaw puzzle. "You're not an angel and you're not Nephilim. Yet you helped all those humans escape. Very noble of you. So you're not on the Grigori's side ... At face value you seem human—but you're not. Which begs the question, who are you? Better yet, *what* are you?"

Alastair noted that Ikari had an American accent.

"I'm—" he started to say but stopped himself short,

unsure of what else to tell them.

They had saved their lives, but that didn't mean he trusted the angels just yet. Still, he relucatantly took Ikari's hand—which turned out to be a big mistake, because once he was back on his feet, Ikari moved quickly, pressing a flat palm against Alastair's forehead.

His eyes fluttered closed before he could even think to mount a defense. For a split second, all Alastair could feel was a warm sensation flooding through him. And then there was a piercing presence in his mind, a tiny sliver of pressure at the base of his skull—and then it was gone, and he was breathing heavily, his chest heaving up and down as if he'd just sprinted a mile in two seconds flat.

The feeling was eerily similar to when Caesar had invaded his mind, but this hadn't been nearly as intrusive.

Vinson was on his feet in a flash of movement, his hand reaching for the sharp projectile Alastair knew was in his vest pocket, but then another angel, a woman with deep-caramel skin and mocha eyes, disappeared in a flash of light, only to reappear behind him, jumping out of a portal in a booming crash of thunder.

She put a finger to Vinson's forehead before he could react, and uttered one word: "*Sleep.*"

Alastair had rarely seen anyone move that quickly.

Vinson flopped down, landing on his stomach in the soft sand, deathly still, his eyes squeezed closed, as if he had been tranquilized.

Alastair rushed forward on instinct. "*What did you do to him?*"

Several strong hands pulled Alastair back before he could go at them. He struggled against their hold, dimly aware that he felt better than he had in ages. His wrist no longer hurt and the laceration on his chest had healed. He felt energized—as if he'd never lost blood in the first place—back to prize-fighting condition.

"It's okay," Ikari said quickly, trying to reassure him. "Your friend is only sleeping. We just needed to know if we could trust you … and that one there"—the angel pointed at Vinson lying in the sand—"looks like he's all about violence first and more violence later."

"What did you do to me?" Alastair asked, shooting a glare behind him at Ikari. His hands were still wrapped around Alastair's forearm like a vise.

"I healed you. Check your wounds," he insisted. "I read your memories too, but I promise it was only to make sure we could trust you. Can't be too careful these days," he added with a shrug, letting him go.

Alastair's fingers grazed the side of his neck where the puncture marks had been only a moment before. His skin felt baby smooth. There were no more blemishes. He pulled the sleeves of his jacket up and looked down, noticing the chafing on his wrists from rope burn was gone too. The skin under his eye was no longer swollen. No more black eye.

He nodded at Vinson, who was now snoring softly, a puff of sand wafting out from under his nose with each exhalation. It was the most peaceful he had ever seen Vinson. In fact, he had never seen Vinson sleep before. Ever. It was unsettling.

"Is he going to be okay?" he asked.

"It'll be the best sleep he's ever had." Ikari quirked an eyebrow. "We're called the Watchers. I see from your memories that you know of us already—and the last Nephilim." Ikari flicked a glance behind him to the others, who were looking at him expectantly. "I know where Corinth is." He turned back to Alastair. "But we'd rather you take us to him. We don't want to drop in unannounced and scare a house full of vamps—if that's okay with you, Alastair."

Damn these angels and their mind-reading ability. He'd never told them his name.

Chapter 32

Corinth

I WAS REALLY ENJOYING the absence of nausea, severe hunger pains, and fatigue. Everything would have been great—had I been awake.

This dream was as vivid and real as any I'd ever had. I ran my hand along the counter of my favorite hometown coffee shop: Four Star Coffee Bar. I used to get the best granitas in all of Fort Worth, Texas, right in this very spot—well, technically, *not* in this very spot.

The cool marble countertop kept me grounded in this alternate version of reality. Maybe I didn't want to wake up. Even though every single detail in this dream felt real— right down to the smell and soon-to-be-tasted coffee—I knew it wasn't. If this had been real, it would have been bustling with over caffeinated customers, the patrons buzzing around like bees, pausing only long enough to hover over their proverbial flowers—or cell phones. It wasn't hard to picture humans as anthropomorphic bugs in that respect. Speaking of cell phones, I missed mine terribly.

This was what happened when I let my brain run wild. I didn't mind the solitude. I knew I had been called here for a reason. I didn't get any bad vibes, so I was almost sure I wasn't meeting Angela.

I certainly didn't mind the heavenly smell of roasting coffee beans.

Propelling myself onto one of the barstools, I shoved my chin into my hands and waited. Just as I was about to explore the idea of trying the coffee, I caught movement out of the corner of my eye.

My heart skipped a beat as soon as the door to the kitchen swung open and Dave marched in, complete with that good-natured grin on his face. It said, "I know something you don't."

I bounded off the barstool, clambering around the other side of the counter to throw my arms awkwardly around him. I wasn't sure if we were at the hugging stage yet, but like a lot of things, I forced it there anyway.

In one breath, I said, "Where have you been? You saved Al's life. Was that you who pulled me out of the cabin?"

He barked out an uncomfortable laugh and then extricated himself from my embrace. I noticed he was wearing his usual beige linen suit adorned with matching hat. I watched as he skillfully maneuvered himself around the countertop. His hands, which had been empty before I hugged him, were now full with two Styrofoam cups.

Dave took a seat on one of the stools, and then set the drinks down. "I am sorry it took me so long to get back to you. I am glad to hear your friend Alastair is alive, and, I presume, human, as I suspected."

I nodded. "Yeah, and you brought him back from the frickin' *dead*. I am eternally grateful to you for that, and so is he."

Dave shook his head. "We can't bring people back from the dead. Angels can only heal. I didn't bring him back—*you* did."

At that revelation, the pit in my stomach dropped out as if I'd just hit a dip on a roller coaster. Gradually I sank down on the stool beside him, stunned. "*I* brought Al back? But how? I've never even healed anyone before, not even myself. I'm currently in a coma right now—unable even to wake myself up. Angela … she did something to me. How is this even possible?"

"It is possible because of that." He gestured toward the blade at my hip. "*And* I guided you through the process—that's why it took me longer to get back to this plane of existence." His eyes twinkled with what looked like pride as he gauged my reaction to what he'd just told me.

After a moment, I gestured at the full cup. "May I?"

He nodded. "Please."

I took a big sip of the drink he'd set down in front of me, not minding the silence stretching between us as I tried to put my thoughts in order. "Sugar and espresso." I wiped my mouth. "Absolutely as delicious as I remember. And here, in this place, I can actually taste again."

"I tried to access a fond memory from your past, a place where you would be more comfortable … chatting."

"This is definitely better than the field." I took another swig of my drink before saying, "Man, it's so good to see you." I stopped myself short. "Wait. I'm not dead, am I? Because the absence of pain is kind of freaking me out. And I don't crave blood …" This sudden realization hit me, and I gave a start, almost knocking over my drink in the process. I caught it between fumbling fingers, hating the fact that I had to keep reassuring myself that I wasn't dead.

"No," Dave said. "But you are dying." The way in which he pressed his lips together told me he was troubled by this turn of events. "Your body is riddled with the virus. I can buy you more time, but that's only part of the reason why I'm here. I've been trying to shield your mind from all angels. Now that Angela's been in your head, she'll send every single Grigori after you. You must learn to block her on your own."

A shiver ran down my spine. I took some time to think of all the worst-case scenarios if that were to happen. I couldn't put everyone in danger.

After a good long while, I whispered, "I saw something … in Angela's mind when she went after me. All I could snatch was one image: a grove of skeletal trees with white bark. It's not much to go on, I know, but does it ring a bell?"

"You went inside Angela's mind?" He ran his thumb across his forehead. "Corinth … what have you done?"

I already knew my situation was dire, but it didn't help hearing it out loud. I trembled, thinking about all that sweeping darkness trickling into me when I'd been inside her mind. I thought some of it had taken up residence inside me.

For the first time, I could see how truly worried he was about me.

"Technically, she was already in my head … It was like we were connected or something—I couldn't help it."

"Well, that explains your deteriorating condition."

He frowned. "You're way out of your league here, kid. You can't do that again. The more you use your powers, the worse you get."

Disappointment hit me hard.

His eyes zipped back and forth as if he were working his way through a problem. "What you have described could be any forest or heavily wooded area on this planet. Trees are bigger than we are. They are steeped in ancient religion, and they stand tall when we fall. There's the Tree of Life, the Tree of Knowledge, and the Giving Tree. There are fig trees. The Jesus Tree in Lebanon. Oak. Palm. Olive. It may even just be symbolic. A white tree though?" He shook his head again, clearly perplexed. "I don't know of any off the top of my head."

"That was you at Larna's cabin, wasn't it?" I said. "You pulled me back before I could go nuclear on Caesar and Sarah. I almost killed Paul."

He nodded. "That was me. We travel through lightning. And you have it mastered quite nicely, by the way."

"I appreciate you stopping me from doing something I would have regretted. I just wish I could have saved Paul. Why couldn't you help me back there? Sarah killed him and … even with all this power I possess, I still couldn't save him. I couldn't bring him back. That's what I need to learn to control. How do I do it again?"

Dave took his hat off and raked his fingers through his hair. "You can't do that again, or it will kill you. I was too weak after helping you bring Alastair back to save Paul. I'm so sorry. I only had enough energy to pull you through the portal. I know this is hard on you. The only reason you were able to bring Alastair back was because he still had Nephilim blood in his system, and I guided you to do it—giving you some of my power in the process." He paused for a second and then said, "Look, there's something I should have told you a long time ago ... I just didn't quite know how to start this conversation, or even think I was going to have it in the first place."

I opened my arms, glancing around at the empty coffee shop. "You have my undivided attention. I don't ever want to leave this place again."

He tapped his fingers nervously on the countertop.

I didn't even think angels could get nervous. My stomach did a flip in anticipation of what he might tell me. What more could there be? He was throwing a lot at me already.

"I have been around for centuries, and during that time, there have been many angels who have met humans and fallen in love. Many sons and daughters have been born—*Nephilim*—like you." He cast his gaze away from mine, wrapping his fingers around the drink in front of him. I sensed it was more out of the need to keep his hands busy than anything else. "All Nephilim have been systematically wiped out by the Grigori, thousands of lives lost. So many of our kind killed just because they were born." He spoke softly now. "Let me start with my real name—it's Danel, not Dave."

I sat up straighter at this. "That's what Angela called you."

He nodded. "Nephilim have *always* had a target on their back, and I have worked tirelessly to make sure you were safe until at least your eighteenth birthday. *We all have.*" With a shrug, he added, "You're my son, Corinth."

A tiny part of me had played out this very scenario. That part of me still hadn't seen this coming. Those few words slammed into me so hard that I hopped up off the barstool before I realized I was moving.

I wanted to tell him that he was full of it—of course he wasn't my biological father—but someone had to be, right? I mean, I was part angel, which meant I had to come from someone other than the people who had raised me from birth.

Dave mirrored my reaction by getting to his feet too. He stepped toward me, but I put a hand out to stop him.

"I *am* your father," he said again, more forcefully this time, but it came out raspy, as if his throat was raw. His tone had a hint of empathy in it that was a nice touch too.

I knew he was trying to urge me to believe him, but I didn't. I couldn't. I wouldn't.

I pressed a fist to my stomach and, after a moment, said quietly, harshly, "That was funny. You forgot to shove a fan in your face to sell the whole Vader thing. You saw *Star Wars*—so what? That doesn't make you my father." I was babbling now, but I couldn't stop myself. "Did Larna put you up to this? Because I don't find the humor in it … and I find the humor in *everything*. You're making jokes over here, and I'm dying. Maybe we are related."

Dave wasn't smiling. In fact, he was giving me the patient look a parent might give their child when they're on the verge of throwing a tantrum or about to have a meltdown. It was enough to make me clamp my mouth shut tight.

I almost bit my tongue in the process, and my breath was hissing out of my lips in shallow, desperate pants as I tried to piece things together. "My parents have … been together—" I swallowed "—for … thirty years. They were high school sweethearts … My dad is retired Air Force. He raised me. You had nothing to do with it—none of what you're saying makes any sense."

It felt good to lash out.

I needed time to mentally prepare myself for news like this, and clearly, I hadn't, because I staggered back, knocking over the heavy barstool in the process.

He threw his hat onto the countertop and ran a hand through his hair again, reminding me of my signature move. How had I not seen it before? I couldn't unsee it. My height suddenly made more sense. The strong curve of his jaw was similar to mine, and my wild mane had definitely come from him, although he had thinning hair. If I'd only looked a little closer, paid a little more attention to his mannerisms …

A dimple popped up on his left cheek as he gave me a half grin. I idly noted that I had one in the exact same spot.

After what I thought was the longest dramatic pause in the entire universe, he said, "Your mother and father have been a part of each other's lives for a very long time. You are correct, they were high school sweethearts, but technically, they haven't been together for the *entire* thirty years." He made sure to meet my gaze when he spoke again, and it felt weird, him speaking about my parents with any sort of familiarity. "They broke up briefly when Jonathan first joined the military. During that time ... your mother and I met. Susan was still in college. I was a professor—*not* her professor—"

I put a hand up. "Whoa, whoa, whoa. One of the most powerful beings on the planet, at war with other angels, just ups and decides to become a professor? And not to mention the creep factor of you forming a relationship with a student. What aren't you telling me?"

"It's not like that, Corinth." He sighed. "Susan was leaving campus one day. We were on opposite sides of the street at an intersection, waiting to cross the street. When the light turned green and she started to walk, a car came out of nowhere. The driver had passed out at the wheel, and he swerved right into her. I ... I witnessed the whole thing. It was on that day that I made the decision to save her life ... to heal her ... Look, it's a long story, but everything else after that happened because we were in love. I *loved* her."

Dave shot a glance down to his hat, his fingers curled tightly around the brim. "Passing on knowledge has always been of the utmost importance to me ... but ..." His gaze flickered back to mine. "This is harder than I thought it was going to be. When your mother had you, I knew you'd eventually be hunted down for what you are. So I ended our relationship, and she went back to your father when he returned home. Your adoptive father is a good man—he took her back because he loved her—and he cared for you without question, never batting an eye that you weren't his biological child. Your mom knew the dangers—you being the last Nephilim ... We went through a lot to hide you."

We?

My adoptive father.

Adoptive.

No, no, no, no, no.

Deep down I knew he was telling me the truth—I'd known it for quite some time—but coming to those terms was something quite different.

I let out a scornful laugh. "You mean to tell me my dad and mom knew everything about me? And they never told me? No way, I'm not buying it. *No.* I *don't* believe you. How did you even convince them of the truth?"

"It didn't take much convincing."

The air around him shimmered and churned as wings unfurled out of his back. I watched in awe as they flickered like a hologram. The sight was just as arresting as it had been before. They spread wide, the entire length of the room, smoldering red and coal black. The light reflected on his face shadowed the contours of sharp cheekbones—his eyes were shining bright with golden irises. The wings at his back shimmered once, twice, three times, and then disappeared, reminding me a little of how it looked when my blade appeared magically in my hands whenever I needed it.

I couldn't imagine what my dad's face must have looked like when he'd witnessed such an incredible supernatural display. Probably like the face I was making now. I guessed it wasn't hard to imagine my family wanting to help an angel. They were God-fearing people, and their son was one of them.

The hairs on the back of my neck started to stand on end at this realization.

Their son is *one of them.*

What must they think of me?

My parents must think I'm a freak.

The sound of my breath rasping in my throat echoed hollowly in my ears.

Dave might get odd looks out in public for his height, but he didn't stick out like a sore thumb—people wouldn't peg him for an alien life-form. He could get away with teaching. I could maybe see why my mom might possibly have liked him. He exuded a quiet confidence, and that smile plastered on his face looked like he had a secret that nobody else knew about. Plus those wings and golden eyes …

"I am truly sorry to tell you in this way. I never wanted you to know. It was always too dangerous to possess any sort of knowledge about this. You have been hunted your whole life. You never even knew it. I did my job well—that is, up until now. You are the last one, and if the Grigori get their hands on you, they *will* make an example out of you. Not only because of how much all of us have lost on both sides of this war but because you're a symbol. A symbol of hope for the Watchers, and a symbol of devastation for the Grigori. They don't consider you a living, breathing person with feelings, kid. Especially since you're part vampire too. You're a *thing* to them. An obstacle that needs to be dealt with."

I could almost feel his shudder from where I stood rooted to the spot—I had a matching set of tremors in my own hands to prove it.

I started pacing, suddenly feeling more and more agitated by the second. So much time lost. Dave watched me walk the entire length of the checkered path in front of the counter, my mouth gaping open and then snapping shut again as I thought.

I finally stopped near the door to the shop with my back turned to him. I hung my head, feeling too overwhelmed to move or breathe or think.

He said, "There's something else you should know. I came here to warn you about Gabriel Stanton. Angela has recruited him to her side. If history repeats itself, the way it always does, he'll take her up on her offer to be ruler of one clan over all the others—*his* clan."

I strode back over to the counter and picked up the overturned stool from the ground, gesturing to the empty seat again.

We both took a seat next to each other. I kept my eyes trained on an irregular spot on the countertop: a deep gouge in the marble. It had been chipped at over time, worn down and smoothed, as if the people who'd sat in this very spot day in, day out couldn't resist rubbing their fingers across it—such a minor detail that hadn't been overlooked in this dream world.

Eventually I glanced over at him. He was staring at me as if I might drift apart and vanish at any second, *Avengers: Infinity War* style.

He nodded. "War is most certainly coming."

My gaze settled back on the countertop. Maybe if I stared at it long enough, all of my problems would go away. What did I say to that? I had nothing.

"You can't trust Gabriel," Dave insisted.

"I can't believe I'm defending the douchebag ... but he's kind of helped us a lot lately. Plus I don't feel all that bad using up his money."

"The cure isn't a controlled narcotic. It's not a prescription drug to be doled out, Corinth. Do you really think that once Gabriel finds this out, he'll side with you?" He paused to let this sink in. "He doesn't want a cure for himself; he wants to control it. He'll be your downfall. He is keeping you close because he is waiting to act."

This time I did swivel around in my seat to look at him. "Are you asking me to do what I think you're asking me to do?"

Dave ran a hand through his hair again. "I am not asking you to kill him, no. But I need you to know the truth so that when the time does come, you will not hesitate to act. Vampirism is a blight on the human race—a plague that must be stopped. Only *you* can bring about the end of it."

I laughed at that. Ironic. "I *am* the thing you want me to bring an end to. I *am* the blight. Vampire."

He cleared his throat, uncomfortable. "I realize this is a hard decision, and you don't want to go against your friend Larna, but what's more important here? You are my son. My *only* son. If you don't start making tough decisions now, you won't survive this war. What will you do if there is no other option but to take his life?"

A stab of anger tore its way through my gut, burning fiery hot like a poker left too long in the embers. Especially when he mentioned Larna. What did he know about her? "You're not my father. You didn't raise me. You know, you sound a lot like Angela right now. You have been at each other's throats for so long that you've lost perspective—"

Dave's hand shot out, and he gripped my shoulder, his fingers digging painfully into my skin as he squeezed it tight. I didn't think he meant to hurt me, but the damage had already been done. I let my icy gaze travel down to his fingers.

He faltered for a second, his eyes following mine, and then he blinked in surprise and drew his hand back as if he'd just realized what he'd done.

"Why now?" I asked quietly. "Why tell me any of this now?"

"Because you need to know the truth."

I was angry and getting angrier by the second. *Wrong thing to say, Dad.* Heat started to rise in my face. "If you actually cared, you would never have had me in the first place." It was out of my mouth before I could stop it. Of course I didn't mean it, but I wanted to make him feel just as hurt and out of sorts as I did right now. "You had me when you knew the Grigori were still hunting"—I stabbed a finger against the countertop on each word—"every—single—Nephilim—out there—and killing them. Dave, or Danel or whoever you are, the part I keep struggling with is why you put me in the line of fire in the first place. Unless you wanted to make a weapon out of me." I licked my dry lips as realization started to dawn on me. "You only became a professor so you could meet someone. You *wanted* to have a child with a human. I was just a plan to you."

Dave's whole body slackened as if someone had pulled a lever at his back and turned him off. His head drooped down so low his chin touched the top of his chest. An angel laden with the weight of guilt.

I am right. Wow. And the hits keep coming.

I don't know why I care.

I didn't know him.

I said, "You said it back when we first met. You wanted to see the Grigori get served justice by the very thing they hated the most: *Nephilim*. You never wanted a kid—you only wanted a *weapon*. Well, let me tell you what I told Larna's father: *I—am—no—weapon.*"

Up until now, he had just been someone trying to help me out of a jam—funny, because he had put me in this jam in the first place. Even with all the information I'd lined up so rationally in my head, why did it feel so damn *irrational?* I wondered if this was how Larna had felt, learning that her father was vampire. She must have been devastated. I felt so much closer to her all of a sudden.

I swiped a hand under my eyes, feeling moisture there. "So … you never wanted me in the way a father wants a son?"

Why did I keep digging at this wound when I already knew what his answer was going to be?

Dave ever so slowly raised his chin, looking at me from under hooded eyes. Liquid swirled in place of his eyes, making them look as luminescent as a thousand treasure chests filled with polished gold. "I have always wanted you," he said firmly. "The Watchers made a pact with each other. The first born child of our group would be our last hope. There were seven of us up until recently. You have no idea what any of us has gone through to get this far. Benny—he died trying to save you. The Grigori killed his twin sons when they were just two years old. He never fully recovered from it. Samyaza, my number two, could not bring himself to have children. Tamiel, my war chief—her neither. Ikari's wife was an expectant mother—they butchered her in front of him. Diniel's child made it to thirteen before they found and killed her." He tapped a finger on the marble, his eyes drifting down to the Blood Dagger resting in its sheath, strapped to my leg. "I wish I could tell you everything …"

I felt sick. I always knew he'd been keeping something from me. But this? The dagger felt heavy, strapped there now, weighing me down. The way Angela looked at it, and the way angels looked at it—with reverence in their eyes—told me so. So many had paid for it with their lives.

Dave stood, placing his hands on his hips. He stared vacantly across the bar. I knew he was contemplating some other distant memory, thought, or recollection from his past. He looked like he was a million miles away. "There's something else. Something you need to know about that blade you carry."

My head snapped up at that. "There's *more*?"

"Have you heard of the Spear of Destiny?" he asked.

Spear of Destiny. I most definitely had heard of it before. I tried to push down the deep, yawning pitch-black abyss rising up to greet me. Oh no. I knew where he was going with this. The world spun nauseatingly around me. The blade. Thunderblade.

"*Yes,*" I croaked. *Breathe in. Breathe out.* My chest was rising and falling rapidly now. *Breathe, Corinth.*

"The Blood Dagger," Dave began, "was made from the tip of the spear used by the Roman soldier who pierced

Jesus's side when he was crucified."

What a cosmic joke. I wanted to laugh, but I couldn't find my voice. God was probably laughing right now, finding all of this very amusing. Growing up in a Christian church, of course I'd heard of the Spear of Destiny. It still had Jesus's blood on it. Correction: Jesus's blood was in my hands.

Black bled its way inward at the edges of my vision, whittling it down to nothing. *Don't black out.* I staggered dizzily to my feet. *Breathe.*

The dagger was sitting on top of the countertop. I didn't know how it had gotten there. I didn't remember relieving myself of it. I realized I didn't want it anymore. I needed to be as far away from it as possible.

The price.

The burden.

It was too heavy.

It was all too much.

I unconsciously rubbed my now-sweaty palms across my jeans.

Dave's hand was on my shoulder, but this time it was supportive, and I felt his care from this one simple action. "Breathe, son."

I licked my lips again—*son?*

"*Why me?*"

"Look, I wish I had time to convince you of how worthy you are to carry this blade." It was in his open palm in a wink of light. He turned my hands over and plunked the dagger into them. "But you have to convince yourself. To be worthy does not mean you have to be perfect. The faithful see the invisible, believe the incredible, and then receive the impossible. This is the moment for which you have been created."

"Will you stop giving me the fake fortune cookie advice. Be real with me. Tell me this sucks. Tell me you got saddled with a cowardly son. Why don't you step up to the plate and help?" I asked, trying to stifle the raw edge of hysteria in my voice. "If you haven't noticed, I'm currently in a *coma* after taking a thrashing from Angela. I am dying. I am only eighteen. You ask too much of me, *Danel.*" I emphasized his name, making sure he knew I wasn't going to call him Father. The burden on my shoulders was too great.

I threw the blade across the room as hard as I could. It hummed loudly as it whirred through the air, but before it could break out of the window in the fake coffee shop, it vanished in a blur of motion and light, only to reappear strapped at my thigh once again.

I closed my eyes and fell to my knees, my hands covering my face. "WHAT DO YOU WANT FROM ME?"

"To finish this," he said quietly.

For a brief instant, I could see how much anguish and torment was running through him—but then it was gone, and he was flashing me his brilliant smile again.

"I am going to do everything I can to wake you up and give you enough strength to get you through this next trial. As soon as you entered Angela's mind, you sped your condition along significantly. With the virus running through your veins, I am not even sure how much I can help. Once I do this, I won't be able to come back. You will be on your own."

"What do you mean, you won't be able to come … b-b-back?" My voice faltered.

He picked his hat back up and put it on his head. "You will do great things, Corinth Taylor."

"I don't deserve that look you're giving me … that look of admiration. I don't want your help. Not if it means you can't come back. For Pete's sake, I just found out you're my biological father. There has to be more time to sort this all out. I'm still furious at you, and I don't want this to be our last interaction. This is all next-level bizarre, but we can work things out … have a family picnic every year or something … Look, you've thrown a lot at me … *please*, can we talk about this? Isn't there some other way? At the risk of sounding like a whiny brat … this isn't fair." I rubbed a hand through my hair again, distressing it to a fine point. "I need to talk to my mom and dad … my *family*. I refuse your help. I don't want it—"

"Here's some more fortune cookie advice for you, kid: Because you are a survivor of the unfairness of life, you're much stronger than you give yourself credit for. And you are capable of achieving far more than you believe." When Dave spoke next, I could hear the regret in his voice. "There are things we don't want to happen but have to accept, things we don't want to know but have to learn, and people we can't live without but have to let go of. You can finish this, son."

And with that, Dave placed a hand on my shoulder and then winked out of existence.

Chapter 33

Corinth

MY EYES FLUTTERED OPEN. There were many things vying for my attention. Like an overpowering smell of burning incense. But everything else went out the window as soon as I realized a warm, slender body was sleeping next to mine.

And that person had their arms wrapped around me … and a leg—and they *weren't* attacking me. *Bonus*. At first, I thought it was Larna—and I was perfectly okay with this, even though it had been awhile since I'd had any sort of romantic feelings for her. I just wanted familiarity and comfort after what I'd just learned. Thoughts of Dave's confession invaded my mind. My father had just sacrificed himself in order to save my life.

I turned my head, expecting to see Larna, but when I realized it wasn't her, my heart skipped a beat. It was Imani. There was something decidedly intimate about the way she lay snuggled against my side—even fully clothed, I mean. I had to admit, it was nice waking up in the arms of a beautiful woman.

Her hot breath hit my eyelashes. I sighed deeply, and it was enough to wake her up. Her dark eyes popped open to meet mine, and she drew in a sharp breath as I threw the covers back.

"You're awake," she breathed.

I was wearing a T-shirt and sweat pants—not exactly debonair or anything. Imani, on the other hand, always looked good no matter what she was wearing. She must have been here for a while, because her red romper, which revealed quite a bit of thigh, was wrinkled.

We blinked awkwardly at one another before she finally detached herself from me and sat up, arching her back in just such a way that sent a shiver of pleasure running down my spine.

Do I like Imani?

My libido said yes.

Her black, wavy hair was sticking out on one side of her head. I was pleasantly surprised it wasn't perfectly styled as per usual.

She rolled her eyes at me gawking at her. "Calm down, Sparky. You were shivering so badly that the only way to stop it was by good old-fashioned skin-on-skin contact—I guess it worked. You're welcome."

I knew my cheeks were bright red, but I didn't care. She'd used my line back on me. Yikes. For once, I felt semi normal, until my conversation with Dave came flooding back again. Anger like fire built up in the pit of my stomach. He was dead because of me. He didn't give me a choice. How many did this make? Benny, Paul, the twelve souls back at clan Eleutheros.

Imani's gaze darted away from mine for a second. "We didn't think you were going to wake up ... You were screaming so loudly."

For once, I was speechless. It felt nice to have one thing go right and to have someone else care about whether I lived or died. And I was awake, but it didn't take long for that sinking feeling to come back as I glanced around the room, taking everything in.

It was as if I had been transported back to my favorite Indian restaurant—they always had copious amounts of little burning sticks standing straight up in a bowl of sand. I'd apparently traded the overly comfy sofa in Nan's living room for one of her spare bedrooms. The bed I was lying on wasn't nearly as comfortable as her couch though. I didn't know how long I'd been out, but it had to have been long enough for me to warrant dehydration. My back ached on both sides in the exact spot where my kidneys were located. I felt sticky and gross, and I knew I needed to take a razor to my face. I sat up, pulled my T-shirt away from my chest, and realized my entire torso felt stiff. I pulled my shirt up to see a large bandage taped to my chest and ripped it off. There were no wounds—but the bandage was covered in blood.

Dave was gone for good. I didn't know how to feel about anything anymore. He was my biological father, but I didn't know him. However, if it hadn't been for him, I would be dead right now.

Imani's eyes widened as she took in the sight of my newly healed chest. She reached a hand out. "You were bleeding to death. There were so many cuts … What Sarah did to you … *I'm sorry*. I had no idea what you went through that day of the attack on the clan. I should have been there with you, but they would not allow me back inside his office. You didn't trust me. And that was entirely my fault. Sozo had wanted to speak to me about the vampire that attacked you—the one I killed—he'd confined me to my quarters for my own safety. Not even Gabriel could get through all that security. He tried."

A cold shiver worked its way down my spine as my eyes drifted to my chest and then back to the blade on the nightstand next to the bed.

"Imani, I—" I started to say, but the door burst open, and Al poked his head inside the room, interrupting us.

I could see the flicker of worry and then relief in his eyes as he took me in. And then he took in Imani and me in bed together, and his eyes widened in surprise and something else—amusement.

"Am I interrupting something?" he asked slowly, quirking an eyebrow in the process.

I reflexively reached for my blade and, in a quicksilver flash of light, had it in my hand in an instant. I cupped my face in my hands, feeling the cold steel of the hilt biting into my palm as I did so. I tried to hold back the flood of emotions rushing through me. Not fair. I felt overwhelmed.

Imani jumped beside me, her eyes going wide.

"Sorry," I told her. "Force of habit." It took me a moment to find words again. "No … Come in, Al … You look like you have something important on your mind."

Before Imani got up, she rubbed my back in a surprisingly simple, sweet gesture. *Is that genuine concern for my well-being?* I looked up to meet her penetrating gaze.

"I'll give you two some space," she said quickly, and without a backward glance, moved toward the open door before I could comment on it. I tried to keep my mouth from gaping any wider as I watched her leave and close the door behind her.

Al strode the rest of the way into the room, giving me a quick nod, and then he inclined his head toward the door that Imani had disappeared through, giving me an all-knowing smirk. "You two sure looked … *comfortable.*"

"Not a word," I grumbled.

He raised his hands in the air, but his grin faded as he sat down on the end of the bed to regard me. Al rubbed at a spot on his forehead, clearly troubled. "You don't know how good it is to see your scrawny butt awake again. We weren't sure you were even going to pull through."

"I know that's your way of being endearing, but we gotta work on that." I sniffed and wrinkled my nose. "So, you guys are gassing me with incense to hide the fact that I really need a shower?"

"That was Imani's doing. She thought meditation might help snap you out of it." I thought he wanted to ask me more about Imani, but instead, he said, "You saved both Larna's and Gabriel's life. It was one of the bravest, stupidest things I've seen anyone do, by the way. But when you came slamming back here with them in tow, you started screaming, and then you fell into a coma, and those cuts came back."

I shook my head and was about to answer, but I stopped myself short as soon as I started to study him. There were no bruises or cuts or scrapes on him from our earlier escapade at the cabin. "Do you have a tan?" I sat up straighter, sniffing the air. The sleeves of his favorite jacket had dried vampire blood on them. "Dammit, I'm down for a few hours, and things go to hell … Why do you look fresh as a daisy? I know you got hurt back at the cabin … I remember the black eye. Please tell me that you're not a vampire again."

Al reached up, unconsciously rubbing at his neck, and then laughed softly to himself. "So it's weird that I look refreshed? Scratch that … In our world, that *is* weird. You've been out for a few days, by the way. And thanks to you, I didn't get drained dry by a bloodthirsty vamp."

I sat up straighter. "What do you mean, thanks to me, you didn't get drained dry by a bloodthirsty vamp? What happened?"

"Vinson and I took on a clan—Sangre. They are working with the Grigori, turning innocent humans for their own purposes to create an army. One of them attacked me—bit me and then died right there on the spot. Apparently, when you brought me back from the dead, you passed on some of those angel genetics to me."

I glanced down at the blade still resting in my hands. "Your blood is … toxic? So … that means you can't be turned."

"It would seem that way," he said. "Corinth, look, the Grigori are spreading fear about you—calling you a vampire slayer."

I threw a hand up in frustration. "That's preposterous, since I'm part vamp now—"

"You and I both know that," he said, interrupting. "But not everyone else does. The Watchers showed up at the last second to help us take them down. They healed me—hence why I look 'fresh as a daisy,' and then they asked me to bring them here to see you. They contacted

Dave and told me that he would be able to help you more than they could … I'm sorry for bringing them here without asking your permission first, but we had no other choice."

I thought about what Dave had said about sacrificing himself to save me, and also about killing Gabe. Dave really was—*had been*—my biological father. Why did this hurt so much? The fact that he'd saved my life and then vanished right back out of it once again was more than infuriating … but these Watchers could hold the answers to all of my questions.

"It's okay, Al. I need to see them as soon as possible." I threw a leg over the side of the bed, suddenly alert. "I got into Angela's head and was able to extract one image from her—I think it has to do with the cure, but she got inside my head, and I couldn't shake her. Dave showed up while I was under and helped me—" I cleared my throat. The truth of what Dave had really done for me sat heavily in my chest, but that didn't mean I wasn't still mad.

Al's voice rose an octave as he said, "That's huge news, Corinth. What was the image? We have to tell Larna. Let me get her. She'll want to know that you're awake. There's a lot you need to catch up on." Al glanced around the room. "Where is Dave, anyway?"

I rubbed at my eyes, suddenly drained. "He … he won't be coming back this time … It was too much for him." I glanced down at my chest.

Al's eyebrows bunched together in comprehension, and he reached out to put a hand on my arm. "Does that mean he's …?" I nodded slowly as he whispered, "I'm really sorry, Corinth. I wish I could have done something to help—he saved my life too … He was one of the good ones."

"Don't," I said evenly.

Al frowned and looked away.

He was only trying to help, I knew that, but I couldn't stand for him to say something sentimental right now. I didn't know why I couldn't tell him Dave was my biological father—maybe because I hadn't even had time to process it myself. I couldn't even tell him about the blade's origins.

"I need to talk to the Watchers away from prying eyes and ears. Can you have them meet me in the barn? Alone. Don't tell anyone else."

Al got silently to his feet, but before he could disappear, I grabbed his arm with the hand not holding my blade, stopping him. "Can I ask you something?"

He turned back, his bright blue eyes searching mine. "Anything."

"My body—the cuts on my chest." I gestured to the bandage I'd ripped off. "Is it …?" I faltered, searching for the right words as the rock in the pit of my stomach seemed to grow larger. "It's coming back, everything Sarah did to me …"

"Not if we can help it," he said resolutely. "You have to keep the faith."

I laughed at the irony, aware that the blade felt a little heavier now. "I was wondering why I feel so … ordinary. I mean, I shouldn't be susceptible to dehydration. My organs should be rapidly healing themselves. But … they aren't."

Al rubbed at the scruff on his chin. "Things are

turning around. The Watchers are here. They can help. The cure is close. I can feel it. Get dressed. Grab a shower. I'll let them know you want to meet in the barn—in say, thirty minutes?"

I nodded.

After Al had left and I'd gotten up, I realized someone had bandaged the back of my calf, where Larna had stabbed me to stop me from giving myself over to Angela. That wound had healed too, of course, so I pulled the bandage off.

I drained about a gallon of water from the tap in the bathroom sink and then had a quick shower and a shave. I couldn't heal on my own anymore, even with Gabe's or Nan's blood to tide me over. What Dave had done to help me was only temporary, and I knew the more I used my abilities, the sicker I would get.

In the closet, someone had neatly hung up my assortment of black camo pants and long-sleeved thermals. I got dressed, but unable to find my Converse, I turned back to the bed. I sank down to my knees, peering underneath it, and breathed a sigh of relief when I found first one and then the other shoe.

In hindsight, I should have been more worried about where my dagger was rather than my shoes, because when I stood back up, I nearly had a heart attack.

Gabe was standing near the nightstand with my blade clutched between his meat hooks, and he was using the sharp tip to clean underneath one of his fingernails, a smug expression on his melted face. The burns had turned to a deep-reddish shade, the color of peeling skin after a bad sunburn.

He was wearing all black—black slacks and a black formfitting polo shirt. He looked about as relaxed as I'd ever seen him, like he was just about to go golfing.

I rolled my eyes. Knowing what I knew now about the dagger, I felt compelled to jam my foot up his ass—but instead, I calmly stretched an arm out and beckoned for it. My eyes churned and burned bright—along with something else. In a blaze of light and glory, the weapon winked out of his hands and reappeared in mine.

Gabe's jaw dropped as he glanced down at his now-empty hands in disbelief.

I wiped the blade on my pants and then glanced back up at him. He still had a shocked look on his face, but he'd managed to close his mouth at least.

A deep cold seeped into my bones, raising the hairs on the back of my neck. This was a kind of cold that wouldn't let up no matter how many layers of clothing I put on. I rubbed at my arms as the slow sap of energy hit me, and then threw myself back down onto the bed before my legs gave out on me.

I said, "You look a lot less charred than when I saw you last."

"I didn't know that was one of your party tricks," he said slowly.

"I'm full of surprises. What are you doing here, Gabe?"

He cleared his throat. "Not many people can be credited with saving my life."

I cocked an eyebrow, but when he didn't continue, I said, "Careful, Gabe. People are going to think you might actually like me." I shoved a hand into my pocket to hide my trembling, unable to get Dave's words of warning about Gabe out of my head.

His smirk was back on his face now that he'd had time to recover. "If you tell anyone I like you, I'll kill you."

"And that's the problem we keep having," I muttered.

"Your people are downstairs waiting for you. They arrived in style—in a clap of thunder and lightning—carrying your now-human Mr. Iszler like a sack of potatoes ... and Vinson."

"My people?" I squinted back at him. "Does it bother you being surrounded by so much virtue? Feeling a little out of your element?" I snapped. "What are your intentions? Why are you here? I need to know—*now*. If I have to constantly watch my back around you, then what use are you to me?"

He opened his arms wide. "I merely came to admit you saved my life—"

"What if I told you the cure isn't a drug that can be doled out?" I blurted.

Gabe stiffened, his ink-black eyes narrowing. "I'm listening."

"I need to know that once I put things into motion, you won't jump ship, because if you do, things won't go well for you." I let this hang suggestively in the air, tapping the hilt of my blade with one finger.

Gabe's gaze settled on the weapon I'd strapped back at my thigh. "If this isn't hypothetical, then I guess I'd like to know how you came by this information ... for *starters*."

"Dave told me." I tried to gauge his reaction—I felt it was important to tell him the truth so he would believe me—but he was a great poker player, and the only thing I noticed was one side of his mouth curling up at the corner of his burned lips.

He paused for a moment as if considering his response and then said, "I suppose you wouldn't believe me if I told you that changes nothing."

I shrugged. "You're going to need to convince me."

"You wouldn't believe me even if every single word out of my mouth *was* the truth." He barked out a quick, short laugh, but his eyes flashed dangerously. "Have you told Larna or Alastair about this?"

I cast a glance down, still pondering if I could kill him in cold blood or not. "I could just force the answers out of you. Or you could try and compel me—" I stopped, wondering if my anti-*Sight* would backfire on me now that I was vampire. Maybe they'd cancel each other out.

It felt wrong—but also right—threatening him. I gave him a dark sort of grin as Dave's voice echoed in my head: *You can't trust Gabriel.* Danel had given his life for this cause—for me. He believed Gabe would turn on us— that he already had. Angela had recruited him. I believed Dave. Gabe wasn't innocent. He'd killed who knew how many people in his lifetime.

Maybe there was a way to test him and *not* send him packing to hell. Or maybe it just had to be done. I knew what I had to do though. I had to hand him over to the Watchers.

Chapter 34

Corinth

NAN'S BARN SAT A half mile from her house, over the crest of a hill. The doors were open wide, creaking ominously in the wind, and a mushroom-sized cloud had formed over the farm, all but fit to burst, looking heavy as lead.

A blizzard was brewing, and it had caused temperatures to drop below freezing. The frigid temps didn't do anything to help the fact that I felt like I was suffering from hypothermia, which came from the forces vying for domination inside me: Nephilim versus vampire. An epic battle.

I had slipped out of the door on the back porch. I wasn't sure what to expect, meeting the Watchers for the first time. It was intimidating, and I'd wanted to gather my thoughts before I did.

The scent of mildew and rust hit me as I paced the entire length of the empty barn. The straw strewn on the ground was wilted and dead. This place hadn't housed livestock in a very long time. I wondered why it hadn't been kept up like the rest of Nan's property. My eyes wandered to the metal chair bolted into the ground. The straps on the armrests gave me the willies. I thought about what Nan did out here. *Rated R for violence—that's for sure.*

The dagger hummed in anticipation as I tugged it free of its sheath. The familiar weight was comforting. Instead of it being cold to the touch, the hilt was surprisingly warm. The blade whistled as it sliced through the air, speaking a language I understood fluently. I felt more proficient with it than I ever had before. The calluses on my hand were proof of that. I had practiced with this thing every day for months yet never known how important or powerful it truly was. Thunderblade provided me with a boost of strength and grace I would never have possessed on my own. Only some of these abilities had been born of habit and repetition—the rest my bloodline had gifted to me.

A pang of guilt welled up inside me as I thought about Dave once again. Dammit.

What would Luke Skywalker do in his darkest hour? *Kill Darth Vader.*

I had an excuse to run away and never look back.

But if I did … I'd still be hunted down—I'd still die. I wondered if I should go home and spend my last few days with my family. I wondered if Jimmy, Pete, and Zoey missed me as much as I missed them. I'd thought about calling my dad several times over the last half hour, but the conversation I wanted to have with him wasn't going to be over the phone. I guessed I'd just have to survive so I could talk to my parents face-to-face.

I yanked off the heavy winter jacket I'd borrowed from Nan and tossed it onto the chair. The cold prickled my forearms. It helped me focus on something other than impending doom.

"You've chosen a good place to avoid everyone."

I twirled around to see Larna standing in the open doorway of the barn, backlit gloriously by the setting sun. Her jet-black hair was sticking up in complete disarray, going every which way, golden highlights creating a glorious halo around her head. In a way, the messiness made her look that much lovelier. I still couldn't believe how much she'd changed over the past year. The muscles on her arms were a key indicator of that. She was wearing black pants and a green thermal with the sleeves rolled up to her elbows, revealing the glint of gold buckles and leather armor underneath. The cold didn't seem to bother her like it did me.

She ambled inside, glancing around uncomfortably as she whispered, "This place still creeps me out."

I bounced on the balls of my feet, trying to warm up. "I came out here to get rid of some pent-up energy before I meet the new houseguests. I mean, they're staying here too, right?"

She lifted a shoulder in a one-sided shrug. "Unclear. Nan has a guesthouse about a kilometer from here. Supposedly, they've been there for the last day. But it's not like we can keep track of them. They can jump to whatever location they want to with a snap of their fingers. They're a secretive bunch and they keep to themselves. They're … strange … to say the least. Especially the dark-haired one who calls himself Leo."

I watched her make her slow way over to me, and when she was within arm's reach, she yanked me into a quick, hard hug. I put my chin on the top of her head, wrapping my arms around her shoulders, enjoying the warmth she provided.

It always felt right, embracing her.

We stayed locked together in silent companionship for a moment longer before she said, "Thank you, Taylor, for coming after me."

"I'll always come after you," I murmured. "And I don't mean that in a creepy way."

She pulled back, big hazel eyes gazing up into mine, searching. "You know I would do the same for you in a heartbeat."

I gave her shoulders another squeeze. "That's what makes us such a great team."

She took in a shuddering breath. "About the new houseguests … even though they saved Alastair's and Vinson's life, and I'm eternally grateful for that, I don't know if we should trust them. There has to be a reason why Dave never introduced us before. He had plenty of opportunity to do so, but he never did. We could have used their help many times over, especially their healing ability. Why did Dave shepherd us to a vampire clan when we could have been with them this entire time? Protected. I'm worried we might have done something we can't undo. Something doesn't add up about all this. Did Dave tell you anything?"

I turned away from her. There was so much I wanted to tell her. I wanted to tell her about Danel being my father. I wanted to tell her what he'd said about not trusting Gabriel Stanton. That there was a war coming. I wanted to tell her about my blade. I wanted to tell her that losing Paul made me feel as if someone had ripped my heart and lungs right out of my chest and then replaced them with deflated balloons. There was just so much … I still hadn't dealt with Paul's death. He wasn't gone to me. Not yet. I should have been able to bring him back.

Instead, I said, "What's up with you and Gabe? I know something is going on between you two."

Larna's face was inscrutable and expressionless, something she'd learned from Al, no doubt. When she spoke though, her tone told me to proceed with caution. "He's not the monster you think he is." She paused briefly before adding, "I … I think … he's on our side."

"Not the monster I *think* he is?" I choked out. "Larna, the guy killed your father—"

"You don't think I know that?" she said, her voice rising almost hysterically.

I raised an eyebrow. "Do you? Because you're not acting like it. Everyone around here seems to have forgotten that he's tried to kill us on more than one occasion, placed a bounty on our heads, ruined our lives … He made Al break my arm. He turned you against your will. For all we know, he's working with the Grigori … and you two are all chummy now. You gonna have popcorn-and-movie night next?"

Larna put a hand on her head, looking hurt. "I can't do this with you, Corinth. Not now." She stalked back to the open doors and marched through them, leaving me alone to fume on my own. I didn't follow her. She didn't have the information I did. Maybe I should have told her everything, but something stayed my hand. The way she was with Gabe … what if he'd managed to sway her? I didn't think he could compel her—but still, I just couldn't take the chance of anything getting back to him.

What is wrong with me?

I brought Al's martial arts lessons to the forefront of my memory. He had taught me that practicing precise, controlled movements repeatedly turned into habit. Habit increased reaction time. *The habit of persistence is the habit of victory*, he'd told me on several occasions. When you take the guesswork out of it, your mind takes shortcuts— makes you anticipate things more quickly. I would need every single advantage I could get when dealing with vampires and Grigori.

All I had to do was think it, and my blade was in my hand. It felt different now that I knew the truth about it.

Al had taught me some variations of kali—a form of martial arts that uses weapons techniques. Like if I got caught in a knife fight, he had explained that I should always expect to be cut. That was just the nature of the beast.

Balance and center of gravity—both of these things were of paramount importance when doing katas. I planted one foot in front of the other, letting muscle memory take over, letting it wash away the remnants of my heated conversation with Larna.

Traveling the entire length of the barn, I slashed at the air with the blade, twisting, moving, hacking, and chopping, meeting imaginary foes head-on. It suddenly felt good to work the stiffness out of my muscles, to only think about what I was doing in that particular moment.

Nothing else mattered.

I lunged forward. Each thrust and slash was executed with power and control and precision. Slash, slash, move. Slash, slash, move. Close-quarter combat was the way to go. It was also why a lot of vampires wore armor on their forearms. I'd seen Jack do that very thing against Gabe. This was my arena.

So focused on the task at hand, I lost track of time. Lunging. Hacking. Chopping. Jabbing and parrying. *What if I can't control this other half?* The half that required drinking blood to keep me alive. Since I'd been turned, I'd found every possible way to discount the ever-increasing pull of bloodlust. Of course, I had the use of Mother Nature at my disposal. I hadn't been vampire back then either.

I was starving. Without even realizing it, two sharp incisors grew out of my gum-line. I pulled a hand up to feel the pointed fangs, suddenly disgusted with myself. My heart thundered in my ears—*thump-thump-thump, thump-thump, thump-thump-thump*—and a strangled sob tore out of my throat as I fell to a knee, dropping the blade. Hunger. Food. Blood.

The room thickened with ozone and moisture, and with it came the slow-burning sensation of something unraveling in my chest. The ground rumbled its pleasure beneath me. I was drenched with sweat. Somewhere at the back of my mind, I knew I should be reigning all this power in. It was too dangerous and I was too weak … but I was just so angry and confused and grief-stricken.

After a minute, something began to shudder against the floor. When I cast my gaze down to see what it was, I saw that it was my dagger, shaking as if a poltergeist had hold of it. It was angry too, I supposed.

A particularly vicious wave of emotion hit me. My blood sang in my veins. I curled my fingers around the dagger's handle, reconnecting with the strangeness of it—both good and bad—and in the space between a deep breath and an exhale, I found what I was looking for.

Just then I caught movement at the barn doors. When I looked up, I saw the glint of a whole lot of armor and steel and somber faces staring at me.

Al swept into the room behind the Watchers, his eyes going wide at seeing my skin crackling all over with blue currents of energy. My *Sight* clung to me. Deep-rooted. Comfortable. Violent. With the greatest reluctance, I let it go. As the power seeped out of me and finally dissipated, so did the rumbling beneath our feet.

There were five of them in total, and they proceeded all the way into the barn, cautiously. Tall, regal, backs erect—armor in superb, overly polished condition. They all had dyed-blond hair—all of them except one, who I noticed had oppositely styled hair, as dark as a raven's feathers. This must have been Leo, the one Larna didn't trust. He was standing at the back of the pack, looking obviously out of place among the rest of the group. Almost sullen, I deliberated.

The angel with the dark skin, with one of the broadest chests I'd ever seen, took a step toward me. He had a severe frown on his face, and he was equally as tall as Dave. I noticed the color of his skin was in deep contrast to the platinum of his hair. It shimmered like fish scales in the sun as he marched closer, his eyes skimming to the blade at my hip and then back down to my Converse.

Al crossed his arms over his chest and followed him, looking strangely enough, like my bodyguard.

There was a long pause as the one who stepped forward, said, "I am Samyaza." He reached a hand out. "It is an honor to meet the son of Danel."

Al's eyes lingered on me for a second, and I could see the question in them as I closed the distance between Samyaza so I could shake his hand. "It is an honor to meet you, sir."

Samyaza turned to a second angel closest to him. "This is Ikari."

Ikari stepped forward, and when he did, his gold breastplate blinded me as it caught a ray of sunlight through the open barn doors. I couldn't get past his spiky, unnaturally golden, shining hair either. It looked like he could impale someone if they got too close. He also had a wicked-looking curved sword strapped to his back. There was a certain grace to his movements. Ikari was all light.

He seemed to notice me staring at his hair, because he shrugged and said, "Just because I'm an angel doesn't mean I can't have a little style."

Samyaza turned to another fierce-looking angel, skin equally as dark as his, who was standing just on the other side of him. She wore a stern expression and had hard gray eyes and a long golden-silver braid running down the length of her back. "This is our warchief, Tamiel."

She gave me a curt nod but didn't move to shake my hand.

He pointed at another angel, a girl with hair the color

of brass, with beautifully smooth caramel-colored skin. "This is Diniel."

She leaned her head to the side but didn't say anything in greeting.

"And that's Leo over there," Samyaza finished.

Leo was casually leaning against the wall near the barn doors, looking bored. He twirled a thin gold knife between nimble fingers. His body language told me he was relaxed and at ease, but there was a sort of tension running beneath the surface like a live wire, a controlled restraint to his movements. I could somehow sense the danger and unpredictability resting in those bright eyes as his gaze flickered to meet mine. They were an incredible shade of light blue that looked almost violet.

He flipped his knife into the air and caught the handle with a deftness that I thought was quite impressive. After a moment, he strode the rest of the way into the barn, stopping only well within my personal space. Without a word or comment, his eyes raked over me, taking me in—judging, I decided.

I extended my hand, but he didn't make a move to shake it; he only stared at it. I stood to my full height, pulling my hand back awkwardly, trying to pretend that his tall stature didn't bother me. Out of the group, he was the shortest—I'd peg him for at most six foot six. Still, he was taller than my six-foot-four frame.

"Al, would you give us a minute?" I whispered, not taking my eyes off Leo. There was something about him that I couldn't quite put my finger on.

Al gave me a curt nod. "I'll be right outside if you need anything."

I watched him slink out as silent as a shadow, a shaft of winter sunlight cutting through the partially open doors, sparking light off the blade in Leo's hand.

He pointed it at me. "So ... *this* is the vampire." His eyes flashed wickedly, and I noticed the rings of violet separating blue irises from dark pupils. I also caught the hint of a British accent when he spoke again. "Vampire hunter *and* vampire all in one. That must get confusing, huh?"

I shrugged. "It's like a two-in-one shampoo and conditioner—more bang for your buck."

He flipped his knife into the air again and caught it. "I have to say, I'm not impressed."

"I get that a lot," I said dryly. "Look, you don't have to be impressed, you just have to listen." I turned back to face Samyaza, who was still studying me with arms crossed regally over his broad chest. "I am assuming you all know that the blade is made from the Spear of Destiny."

Samyaza stepped closer to me, brushing past Leo in the process. "Yes—the Blood Dagger. We needed something that could contain all of our combined powers."

I pressed my lips together and lifted my head to the ceiling. "Why would you all agree to do this? I don't understand ... According to Dave—*Danel*—placing your powers into the blade weakened you."

Leo snorted. "Speak for yourself ... and for the record, I was outvoted. I never wanted to put all our hope in one little Nephilim—not even a full-blooded angel—"

Samyaza put his hand up, stopping Leo. "We have all lost much ... friends, spouses, daughters, sons, mothers, and fathers during this war. We are ready to put an end to it. We wanted to meet you long before now, but Danel hid you away from everyone—even us. He was very clear about that up until the end ... but now that he is gone ..."

I couldn't hide the bitterness creeping into my voice. "So Danel ... he really is gone?"

Suddenly Leo threw his knife across the room. It stuck point down into the chair that was bolted to the ground, and in a clap of thunder and lightning, he disappeared.

As far as storming out goes, I thought he had pretty much cornered the market.

Samyaza looked unperturbed, as if he were used to Leo's antics. "Some of us are taking it harder than others—but yes. Danel *is* gone."

I ran a hand through my hair. "I haven't exactly had time to process everything y'all are throwing at me here. I only recently learned I'm his son."

Samyaza's eyes glowed like melted metal. "It was hard on him. I am glad he finally told you." He inched closer to me, getting into my personal space. "I never thought it possible for a vampire–Nephilim to exist—but here you are. Your eyes glowed like one of them—with vampire *Sight.*"

I shrugged, my eyes darting to the rest of the angels dispersed throughout the barn.

He said, "Can you travel through lightning as well?"

I realized the cold was starting to get to me, so I blew air into my hands and paced back to the chair to throw on the borrowed woolen coat, and that was when I noticed

Leo's knife was gone. I wondered vaguely how he'd done that. Apparently, angels had similar gifts, which, now that I thought about it, made perfect sense. He controlled his own weapon the same way I did the blade.

Offhandedly I said, "Uh, yeah—it sounds way cooler than it feels though."

Samyaza tilted his head slightly, studying me more closely. "Your condition worsens."

If there was ever a time to be intimidated into silence, this was it. I didn't want to look weak in front of them—they had definitely expected more out of me. Everyone did.

Samyaza shook his head. "Your friends—Alastair and the vampire Vinson—fought bravely at the nightclub."

"Yeah, they do that a lot," I agreed.

"We were there to save the humans' lives—the clan was going to turn them for their own purposes," he continued. "The Grigori are building an army. They have amassed thousands of followers. Vampire clans from all over the world have joined them … They are turning as many humans as possible—to start the epidemic."

The anxiety in my chest felt like a heavy stone. These angels had put all of their faith in me. I let my gaze drift back over them one by one. They were all staring at me expectantly, as if I held all of the answers for how to stop Angela. *Why did Dave have to put all of this on me?*

"There are only five of you left?" I asked finally.

Samyaza straightened to his full height, which was saying something, because I had to crane my neck to look up at him when he spoke. He inched closer, his breastplate almost touching my chest. I didn't back down from him, even though he was a giant and I really wanted to.

"We are stronger than you think," he said softly.

I detected the warning behind his words.

"I meant no offense. I barely escaped with my life the last time I confronted Angela and the Grigori. There were so many of them … All I'm trying to say is that if they have an army, shouldn't we have one too?"

Tamiel spoke up. Her voice was rich and thick with an accent I couldn't quite place. "The Nephilim has a point, Samyaza." She faced me, her lips quirking up at the corner. "That is why we must recruit more to our side."

I threw a quick glance at her. "How? Who?"

"We will rally those who are willing to help. Sozo's clan, for one."

I blew out an exasperated breath. "He is stubborn. I've tried to get him on our side. Besides, numbers won't mean a thing if I don't even know how to find the cure. I gleaned information from Angela: a forest or grove of trees. The bark was white …"

Ikari chimed in quickly. "You got this from Angela?"

I nodded.

Samyaza's dark eyebrows drew together and he said incredulously, "*From inside her mind?*"

"Why does everyone sound so surprised when I tell them that?"

Tamiel drifted closer to Samyaza, a hand going to her chin in thought. She was looking at me differently now. Maybe with a little more hope. "Because Angela is a master at mind control and manipulation and reading memories. Why do you think so many have sided with her? None of us can get into her head. The only one who had enough control to try was Danel."

Ikari crossed his arms over his chest, clearly offended. "I'm standing right here."

Tamiel rolled her eyes. "You're okay at it … I suppose."

Ikari snorted. "Perhaps you can try it again, Corinth. With my help this time."

"You can teach me?" I could feel my excitement start to grow at that.

"If you're willing to learn."

"Yes," I said a little too eagerly. "I could use all the help you can give me. I've been floundering around, trying to figure all this stuff out on my own, and it's been more than frustrating. Dave tried, but …"

"What about Gabriel Stanton?" Samyaza interjected. "Did Danel tell you about Gabriel? That he is a liar and a traitor? He is working with Angela. And he is here—staying with you right now. If you think he is going to side with you, you're wrong. You must kill Gabriel Stanton."

I clamped my mouth closed. He had hit upon the very thing that I was going to bring to them—

A soft creak came from above us, halting my thought process.

My eyes darted up to the rafters as there was a flash of cobalt—vampire *Sight*—and then there was a streak of darkness as a form moved lithely across the beams above us.

I caught the sight of a scarred cheek and burn marks. *Gabe.* The word *spy* came to mind immediately. He had to be working with the Grigori. He'd heard every word, eavesdropping on our conversation, and he was probably going to report back to Angela as soon as possible.

Dave had been right about him all along.

My blade was in my hand before I knew it. The rage stirred to life inside me, my pulse burning with the promise of spilled blood. I dove into the heart of the darkness, right into the glacial clutches of the very thing that was killing me. My teeth clacked together so hard I thought I was going to break my jaw. I'd never felt cold like this before.

I am *going to break.*

I threw the dagger into the air, calling for the sky to open up and rain glorious destruction down upon Gabriel Stanton.

Chapter 35

Corinth

MACABRE IMAGES FLOATED ACROSS my vision: Sarah stabbing me repeatedly with a scalpel. Me bleeding out on that table in the warehouse. The redheaded vamp kidnapping my little sister, Zoey. Me killing that rogue vampire, Sherry, on Larna's front lawn. Stabbing Gabe in the back at the cemetery. Melting Caesar's face off. Paul's neck snapping like a chicken bone. All of this because Gabe had meddled with my life. My breathing slowed and became shallower. It sounded distorted in my head. All the emotions I'd been holding at bay for so long burst forth in the form of a deafening crack of thunder and lightning.

It felt good to dole out some vengeance.

There was something strangely addicting about using my *Sight*. Not like when I harnessed the power of lightning—that felt less alien. I'd been avoiding using both at the same time since I'd come back from the brink of death.

Outside, drops of rain pattered against the barn's roof. The forecast had not called for rain—*but I had*. Time halted. I could see everything as if in slow motion. The barn doors started to swing wide in slow increments. Lightning struck and then stuck to the sky like tape. I could see it streaking toward the earth, the dizzying array of colors swirling inside it were mesmerizing: azure, green, purple, and orange.

The Watchers had started to raise their hands, all of them aiming for Gabe. I was faster though. Wind whipped up, throwing snow and leaves into the air outside. The debris drifted round and round in a lazy cyclone. There was something to be said for controlling lightning, but *time* was altogether different.

And then it was speeding up again, rapidly, as several things happened at once.

Larna flung herself through the barn doors right as Mother Nature's sharpest knife made contact with the roof, cutting through it as if slicing through warm bread. The strike was powerful enough to knock Gabriel out of the rafters like a spider.

I could hear his ragged pants, see the register of shock on his face as he fell at the same time Larna looked skyward, toward the roof, her mouth dropping open.

The source of the storm's power burned as bright as a star inside my chest. I needed to unleash it. Static lifted my hair as the elements funneled their way inside the barn, spiraling and twisting around me—centering me in its eye. I wasn't afraid of it hurting me. I controlled it.

Leo was beside me. I had no idea where he'd even come from. He flung that sharp golden knife in Gabe's direction, but Gabe landed gracefully behind Larna, surprisingly sure-footed for having just been forced out of the beams by lightning.

His knife hurtled straight for Gabe's face, a spinning blur of metal—

Gabe yanked Larna in front of him, using her like a shield, while Al barreled through the barn doors behind them a moment too late.

Leo made a flicking motion with his hand, and right before the knife struck Larna between her eyes, it stopped midflight, hovering an inch away from her face.

Then the blade vanished in a wink of light, only to reappear in Leo's outstretched hand, and I would've been more impressed with how fast Leo moved had Gabriel not hauled Larna back against him, the tip of his knife kissing the bare skin at the side of her neck.

Al skidded to a halt behind them, a panicked look crossing his features.

Somewhere at the back of my mind, I knew I should stop myself. The ground quaked. Wilted straw lifted off the ground, floating around everyone, looking a lot like snow falling in reverse. An old horseshoe tacked to the wall near the ceiling shook violently, trying to tear itself loose so it could streak off into the cosmos.

A pulsating charge of energy crackled through my body as a gust of wind and leaves soared up around me. Before I could make the storm *really* dance to my tune though, I heard shouting.

The sudden and insistent nature of the shouting increased.

Al was staring at me with mouth stretched wide, his face pale and waxy in the darkened entrance of the barn. Thunder rumbled outside, as dark and ominous as my mood.

Larna closed her eyes and pressed her lips into a thin line as a ribbon of blood threaded down the side of her neck.

Gabe was not one to bluff—but neither was I.

He should not have done that.

I squeezed my eyes shut as an image of me standing on top of a pile of ash and cadavers and bone flashed across my vision. Corpses littered Nan's front lawn. Blood and gore painted the scorched earth, remnants of a deadly war zone with no survivors. My bloodlust wasn't just a yearning … it was an ache inside me that wouldn't be satiated unless I killed.

I can't go back …

Something hit me hard on the back of my skull.

I sank to a knee, my hand still extended toward the sky, and then ever so slowly the power seeped out of me, and I found myself staring dazedly up at Leo, my head reeling.

He was holding a short sword in his hands, pommel facing down.

"You can thank me later, *hybrid*," he drawled.

Chapter 36

Larna

OT BREATH HIT THE back of my neck, and I flinched. "I'll kill you if I have to—you know I will, but you're coming with me."

Gabriel.

"Gabriel—" I started to say, but I quailed when he pressed the cold knife harder against my skin. He was so close I could feel each rapid rise and fall of his chest against my back. There was something warm and sticky sliding down the side of my neck. My body tensed up like a bowstring.

He half whispered, half panted, "This is self-preservation. They want to kill me. I heard them plotting."

"This is not the way to conv—"

"Shut up," he snarled.

My eyes briefly sought the angel standing behind Corinth, his fingers curled around the pommel of a short sword. He was the one with the dark hair and pale blue-violet eyes. Leo. He stood over Corinth, surprisingly calm and collected, his eyes sparking with a mixture of curiosity, irritation, and surprise as he looked down upon him.

The angels were shouting at Gabriel and at each other. Everyone was shouting, actually. Alastair was shouting behind me. Straw and dirt and wood chippings floated back to the earth, swirling in slow, lethargic circles to land on Corinth's prone form and settle into his dark hair.

The rest of the angels' hands were lit up with a torrent of energy aimed directly at us.

This was how I was going to die.

Gabriel snaked an arm around my waist, making sure I shielded him from the angels' line of sight, keeping me uncomfortably close. Very carefully he started to back us out of the barn, with me in tow, the knife's razor-thin edge pushed against my throat.

In my peripheral vision, I could see Alastair. He had his gun aimed at Gabriel's head. He lowered it as soon as we got closer. We made eye contact with each other. Alastair's eyes narrowed down to two tiny slits as we passed. He looked wretched—the helplessness on his face almost made my knees buckle out from under me. This was his worst nightmare. And at this point Gabriel was almost dragging me, anyway. I held Alastair's gaze for an unbearably long time and then shook my head, telling him to stand down. I had a fleeting thought that this might be the last time I'd ever see him again.

Alastair snarled, "*Gabriel. So help me …*"

I knew Alastair didn't have the power of *Sight*, but it sure looked that way to me as his eyes flashed blue. His chest was heaving, and there was a stark topography of veins sticking out on his hand as he clenched his weapon tightly against his leg. I could see how much it hurt him not to come after us.

Gabriel's lips curled back into a ferocious grin, the tips of his fangs showing. "Don't even think about following us, Lover Boy. You know I don't bluff."

Stanton guided me back up the hill, back toward the farm, a hand to the small of my back, the blade never leaving my neck as we left Alastair and the angels behind. They didn't try to portal themselves behind us, surprisingly. I thought they might be taking Gabriel at his word that he was going to kill me. It meant something to me that they weren't trying to kill him. They could have traded my life for his. Maybe they did care about who lived or died.

Back at the top, near the house, I could see Nan, Vinson, and Imani waiting for us, blocking our escape to where a sleek black helicopter had landed just south of her massive lawn.

The wind from the rotors lashed at my hair, whipping it into my eyes, blinding me. I didn't even know how he'd gotten his clan here so quickly, unless they'd been here the entire time, or nearby.

"Nan, as always, it's been a pleasure!" Gabriel shouted over the roar. "Thank you for your hospitality, but we'll be taking our leave now. Sorry this is so disconcertingly similar to the last time I was here, but I can assure you, I won't burn your house down unless I have to." His gaze drifted to Imani. "Are you coming with me?"

The corners of Imani's mouth curled up. She spoke loudly over the noise of the rotating blades. "Not this time, Gabriel."

He nodded as if he had expected her to say that.

"*Pity.*"

Nan looked fierce—her eyes were twin sapphires of dancing light. She inched toward us, her hands spread out in front of her and fangs bared, ready to pounce. She didn't need a weapon, she *was* the weapon.

Vinson, on the other hand, was armed to the teeth, and he had his shotgun trained on Gabriel—but he didn't take the shot. The troubled expression on his face sent a spike of adrenaline coursing through me. *Vinson never worries.*

Gabriel fisted a hand into my hair. I gasped as the cold metal scraped my windpipe. "I wouldn't, Vinson. You see that long line of cars outside the gate? All I have to do is give them one signal, and they'll swarm the farm. I don't want to kill her—but I will."

Gabriel reached out, tugged my watch off my wrist, and then unbuckled the armor at my forearms. He chucked everything on the ground and said, "Give me your knife—the one with the bone handle. I know you still carry it on you."

Slowly I stuck a hand into my pocket and drew out the small knife Alastair had given me. Gabriel plucked it from my fingers and threw it on the ground next to my other weapons.

"Gabriel—you're making a huge mistake," Nan hissed. "We'll rain down vengeance upon you and your entire clan if you hurt that child."

"I was forced into this. The angels want me dead." He cocked his head to the side, a strange urgency in his voice now. "*This is about my survival. I'll be keeping her for insurance. Tell Mr. Taylor that if he or his friends decide to come after me, Larna* will *die.*"

Gabriel shoved me into the chopper and jumped in nimbly after, and then we were lifting off, leaving behind a trail of dirt and dust and snow fanning out below us as his pilot skillfully maneuvered the helicopter into the air. By how well this exit had been executed, I was guessing Gabriel had had this planned for quite some time.

Gabriel Stanton had wedged himself uncomfortably next to me, the tip of the blade still pressed to the hollow point of my throat. My stomach did an agonizing flip, and he glanced down to the trickle of blood, immediately pulling the knife away, apologetic, he seemed.

We were alone in the spacious cabin of a different aircraft from the last one—definitely fancier. And a lot more comfortable, with leather bucket seats. I watched as he slowly placed the knife on his thigh.

"My intention was never to harm you."

I rubbed absentmindedly at my neck. The cut had already stitched itself back together again as if I'd never been cut in the first place. "You could have fooled me." My gaze flickered to the knife in his hand. I imagined taking it from him and ramming it into the side of his neck, just like I'd done before …

And I'd started to move when he said quickly, "I wouldn't." He motioned toward the back corner of the cabin. I turned my head sharply to the side to see a dark shape swathed in a robe the color of parchment lurch to their feet.

The form had blended in so perfectly with the

background that I hadn't seen or heard them move until now. Angel. A hood hid most of their face from view. Even so, I could tell the person was a hulking monstrosity. They could easily have been rising out of a grave instead of a seat. He or she was huge—at least eight feet—and on the creepy scale, I'd give them a five hundred.

Lurch had meaty, hairy hands that crackled portentously with white-hot electricity—deadlier looking even compared to the type of energy Corinth generated. I watched in horror as the figure pulled the hood of their cloak back, revealing a disfigured face underneath.

Okay, so maybe it was a *he* and not a *she*. If you could call it a face. He had tanned, leathery skin that hung down around his neck as if it had been melted off. His eyes were red streaked and bulged out of his head, making the right side of his face look that much worse than it already did. A scar ran horizontally across the length of his forehead. Where his ear should have been, there was only a deep gouge of skin and a hole.

Angel? Or something else entirely?

I wondered what could have done that kind of damage to his face. Nothing good.

"Don't test me, Miss Collins. If you try and compel me, or fight back, my winged friend here has orders to go after your boyfriend. All it would take is a simple drop-in by this angel to grab Iszler." He lifted his eyebrows. "A drop from this height … well, I bet it would do some real damage to a human. Who do you think would get to Alastair first? Your Watcher friends or"—he thumbed a hand toward the giant—"this guy?"

My heart rate quickened, drumming loudly in my

ears. "So, you sided with the *Grigori* … Where was he when you got yourself crispy fried back at the track?" I shook my head in disgust at my gullibility. "Why would I believe anything out of your rotten mou—?"

"I didn't side with the Grigori. He's not with the Watchers either," Gabriel said. "Once I saw Corinth's and the Grigori's *abilities*, I knew it was time to fight fire with fire—or lightning with lightning in his case."

"So he's a hired hand?"

Gabriel shrugged. "He's a free agent."

"Why not just keep to our deal?" I muttered. "We were on the same side. Corinth saved your life even … You saved mine."

"Corinth changed the deal. He was plotting to kill me with those angels." Gabriel's eyes sparked from black to blue and then black again, as dark and polished as the surface of an oil slick. He clenched his fists together, the knife flashing in his grip as he got up, pacing.

I wondered why we were alone, besides Lurch in the back corner, silently sulking. My guess was that he didn't want me to try and compel any of his clan members to turn against him, which meant he thought I was strong— and he'd planned on taking me with him. I had to think this through, be calm about my actions. Of course, it was exceedingly hard to concentrate with the way his hands shook holding the knife.

After a second, he moved to the opposite end of the cabin, to one of the overhead storage lockers. I thought about going after him—even with his angel of doom watching my every move. I almost didn't care. *Almost.*

I took in a deep, calming breath. There wasn't much

I could do while we were a few thousand feet in the air, besides get myself killed, or Alastair killed. I could wait this out—be patient, figure out a plan. Gabriel had warned Corinth not to come after us. I didn't have my watch. No weapons. No cell phone. I was on my own. I idly wondered if Corinth would even listen. I hoped he would. The way the storm had obeyed his every whim had been beyond frightening. I was scared for him. I was scared for all of us. I didn't need saving—*he* did.

So lost in my own head, I didn't realize Gabriel was back in front of me again. He still had his knife, and he tapped it impatiently against his leg as if he were coming to a final decision. He drew something out from behind his back: a pair of heavy-duty handcuffs, the kind they had put on me back in the fight at his armory.

At the sight of them, I almost bolted to my feet, but I made myself stay absolutely still, grinding my teeth in agitation.

"Put these on," he ordered.

My gaze locked on the hired thug, who had moved even closer. I could smell the sudden change in ozone as his hands sizzled with uncontained power—apparently he was ready for me to fight.

He was right.

My eyes blazed up bright with my *Sight*. I felt my fangs elongate. "*No.*"

I may not have a weapon, but I didn't need one. Not when I could compel Gabriel. I was a lot stronger now, and he knew it. I was going to try, anyway.

"Think about Alastair," Gabriel insisted.

"Why do this?" I hissed between clenched teeth.

"We're not friends, remember? And you've seen what I do to my enemies." He reached down and unceremoniously snapped the cuffs onto my wrists, and I let him. I couldn't take the chance he would go after Alastair next. He was lucky I let him.

The metal felt brutally cold against my skin. Final.

"Corinth forced my hand. He told me something …" He faltered.

I perked up at hearing that. "What hand is that exactly? What did he tell you?"

His pinched and strained expression made the pit in my stomach drop out so suddenly it was as if we'd hit a bump in the air. "You're going to turn me over to Angela. After *everything* … Corinth was right." I laughed softly to myself, feeling winded and stupid. "Is that all it takes to sway you? You really are spineless."

"He was going to kill me. I had to act—"

"I would have gone to bat for you. I would have convinced Corinth not to do it. You saved my life—and for *nothing*." I lifted my manacled hands. "If you turn me over to her, she *will* kill me."

"I know," he said, regret lacing his voice.

Chapter 37

Corinth

I WAS SUDDENLY GLAD Nan's living room was so spacious. Imani was examining a fingernail with interest when I fumed past her for the fifth time. Even from across the room, I caught the hint of raspberry and mint coming off her. This was the vamp part of me—increased olfactory sensitivity. VEP. Her eyes kept flashing to mine. I could tell she wanted to say something to me, but she kept her mouth clamped closed, her lips two thin red lines.

Larna didn't have a phone. Gabriel had dumped her watch and weapons before they'd taken off. *Dammit.*

The second they'd become airborne, I'd tried to home in on her location using my newly acquired supernatural skill set—to try to snatch her out of Gabriel's clutches—but I couldn't locate her no matter how hard I tried. It was as if she'd just vanished off the face of the planet.

And I couldn't stop thinking about why that was: *Because she's dead.*

Ikari was sitting cross-legged on a tatami mat with his eyes closed. Finally, after what seemed like an eternity, they popped open. He hissed something in another language—Japanese, I guessed. "I can't locate her—something keeps blocking me."

I couldn't stop shivering. Icy fingers of dread kept stabbing me in the stomach over and over again. If there was an angel blocking our attempts at trying to find Larna, then that meant we were too late. She was with the Grigori. I shivered. *With Angela.* Gabe had handed her over to them. She was as good as dead.

My fault.

My fault.

My fault.

Larna had been taken because of me. If I hadn't overreacted back there, everything might have worked out. Instead, I let Gabe snatch her right out from under me. I kept catching furtive glances from everyone. They were all thinking the same thing: I was the loose cannon.

Vinson was in the kitchen, staring into his vodka glass, wearing one of his surly scowls. Samyaza, who I was going to start calling Sam, was huddled near Tamiel and Diniel, or Tami and Din—I hadn't quite decided on their shortened names yet.

He was speaking quietly with them, trying to come up with a plan of his own, I guessed. I knew they were trying to get me to see the bigger picture, that there was more at stake than just getting Larna back, but I didn't care.

She was what mattered most.

Leo was the only one who looked unruffled by the situation, lounging on the couch near the fireplace, his legs stretched out in front of him—all he needed was a beer in one hand and a remote in the other, which would have been an entertaining sight to behold, because he was still wearing full polished armor and gear.

Maybe what Larna had said about not trusting them had been right. His flippant attitude was making me more livid by the second. Plus he'd knocked me upside the head. I clutched at the back of my skull, thankful that the bump wasn't too bad. I got why Leo had done it, but it still hurt.

Nan was in the kitchen, making tea—keeping herself busy as she quietly stewed to herself. I knew how angry she was at me. We had all let Gabriel come here, allowing him to sleep in one of her spare rooms. We should have shackled him from the get-go. Of course, Larna had vouched for him. A tiny voice in the back of my head said, *And look where that's gotten her.*

Al was the only one not in the room. As if on cue though, he stormed back inside, marching past Imani, his jaw set. He looked positively murderous. Furious creases were cut into his forehead. His cheeks and nose were red. He'd been outside for a while—snowflakes had whitened his already-blond hair, making it look silver in the soft light of the dimly lit room. He had Larna's bone-handled knife clutched in one of his fists. The dark shadows under his bloodshot eyes stood out even more against the pallor of his skin. I watched him roll up the sleeves of his black-and-white-checkered flannel before he marched up to me.

"Al, I don't kn—" I started to say, but before I could finish getting the rest of the sentence out, he wound his fist back and clocked me across the left side of my jaw. I staggered back, too stunned to react.

Al yelped in pain, clutching his hand to his stomach.

Gingerly I reached up to caress my cheek. The skin was already starting to swell. After a second, I found myself moving stiffly into the kitchen. Even though I knew it wasn't the same situation, it reminded me of the night he'd broken my arm while under Gabe's influence, except this time he didn't look like a blank canvas. I swallowed hard, tasting blood, as a deep silence settled over the room.

Nan had stopped busying herself to stare openmouthed at us.

One of my back teeth felt loose. I spit blood into the sink, and the tooth went with it, circling the drain. Everything had gone down the drain.

I made my way back into the living room, stopping to stand directly in front of Al.

I deserved it, I told myself. I deserved more.

He was holding his wrist, but there was still fire in his eyes—he wanted to hit me again; I could see it. His chest was moving rapidly with each ragged breath he pulled in.

I spread my arms out wide. "Go ahead, Al. Take another shot. Have as many as you like." I glanced around the room, rubbing my jaw. "Anyone else want to have a go?"

Sam was squinting at me, and so were the rest of the angels, all of them except Ikari, who still sat silently with his eyes closed as if nothing had happened.

Din put a finger to her chin as if she was highly amused by the sudden outbreak.

"Get an eyeful, everyone. This is who you put in charge of the Spear of Destiny." I pointed at Tami. "Are you

impressed? I'll tell you who wouldn't be impressed … *Dave.*" A hysterical laugh escaped me. "*Dave* would definitely *not* be impressed. You know why? Because he's my father. But guess what. He's gone. And he's not coming back."

Al was giving me a funny look as he whispered, "*Spear of Destiny?*"

I stepped up to Al, getting in his face this time. "Did you know Dave was my father?" I shoved him and he lurched back, only to regain his balance, quite agilely, in fact, and it only served to annoy me more. I didn't care that he'd lost some of the fire in his eyes, or that he was looking at me with pity. "Are you done? Come on, brother," I spit. "*Hit me.* I've seen you fight. I know you have a lot more in you." I flicked a gaze around the room, and then it landed on Imani.

She was standing on the threshold of the front porch, her dark eyes inscrutable. Her black hair was tied back with a red silk ribbon. I had no idea what she was thinking. "Come on, Imani. Why are you even here? Shouldn't you be with Gabe right now? You could be plotting to destroy the world with him … Did he leave you behind to spy on me?"

I wanted them all to hit me—to take away some of the despair and pain slowly eating me alive.

Al raked a hand through his silvery hair, snow melting between his fingers, running down the side of his face. His forehead knitted in just such a way that reminded me of a jigsaw puzzle. He shot a gaze toward Vinson, who was sitting on the stairs, drinking out of an economy-sized bottle of vodka now. He didn't have anything to offer up, I noticed. He only frowned. I hated how he wasn't outside patrolling, like he normally would be. He had given up too. Larna was gone.

"COME ON!" I shouted, daring each of them to come at me.

No one did.

I couldn't take their disappointed looks in my direction for one more second. I shot past Vinson and then Imani, flying out the door. I heard the distant clap of it slamming closed behind me as I exploded out into the blizzard, ignoring the stinging sleet pelting me in my face.

The grass was heavy and wet, and the air was thick with moisture. It clung to my lungs. They burned and my muscles ached as I ran as fast and far as I could. Out past the barn a half kilometer away, past the frozen pond, out into the waist-high weeds, and beyond.

For a second, the only thing I could focus on was the sound of my own labored breathing as the air left my body. My muscles screamed and my legs burned. I sounded like a rabid dog, panting and huffing, my arms and legs pumping as fast as I could move. Which was at light speed. I didn't stop until I made it to Nan's property line—the fence was at least twelve feet high. I didn't try and climb it or jump it. Instead, I doubled back. I wasn't sure how far I went, but by the time I stopped, I couldn't catch my breath, no matter how much I fought for it.

My socks and Converse were drenched through. My face was wet and my hair was matted to my forehead. I hadn't put on a coat. After all that exertion, the biting cold had just started to seep back in when I realized where I had stopped. Paul and Jack's graveside.

I didn't mind the fact that my fingers were numb or that my chest was unbearably tight, or that I hurt everywhere. I sank to my knees in front of their side-by-side graves, curling my fingers into my hair. I bent over, touching my forehead down to the icy muck and wept. I mean I really let it out.

At least I had good company.

Finally, after a few stretched-out, torturous minutes, I spoke through a wavering voice. "I did … something … stupid, guys. Larna … she's gone … because of … me," I gasped. "I don't know how to get her back. I don't know how to find the cure. I just found out who my biological father is—*was*—and now he's gone … again, because of *me*. I am dying. I sure do miss your sage, unapologetic advice, Jack, and, Paul, I miss your cool levelheadedness and that mustache." I ran a hand down the side of my bruised jaw. "Jack, you'd probably tell me to quit messing around and go find your daughter." My voice hitched. "I'm trying to, sir … but I don't even know where to begin—"

"You think you're the only one who's lost someone, kid?"

At hearing the voice at my back, I quickly sat up and swiped a hand down my face, wiping off the moisture, suddenly embarrassed about making such a spectacle of myself. *Great. Out of all the people who could have found me, it was this guy.* I cast an irritated glance behind me.

The one person here I didn't like had followed me. Leo was spinning that gold knife of his in between his slender fingers. The way he skillfully navigated the blade across bare knuckles seemed vaguely familiar to me. If he had witnessed my emotional outburst, he didn't show signs of it, which I was thankful for.

Sleet hit his gold armor. I watched it melt into slush, fascinated despite trying not to be. I could almost see the heat rising off his body in waves. Angels ran hot, apparently. More droplets of water ran in rivulets down his breastplate, gleaming bright in the moonlight. I was guessing the cold weather didn't bother him either. I begrudgingly admitted to myself that he did look a tad bit intimidating.

I blew out a deep breath. "If you're here to gloat or knock me out again, you can just turn right back around and march your holier-than-thou self right on out of here."

"Holier-than-thou." He grunted. "That was funny."

I looked up to see if he was being sarcastic, but I couldn't tell—he had resting ambiguous face. "One of my many attributes … You can also add 'getting all of my friends and family killed or abducted' to that list too …" My voice trailed off as I turned to stare at the two mounds of dirt in front of me.

I stood back to my feet, sopping wet and shaking.

"You're not the only one who has lost family."

My head snapped around at that. "You mean the rest of the Watchers?"

He lifted his shoulders, a faint smile clinging to his lips. "Yes … but I'm also talking about my birth family."

"Birth family?" My mouth fell open.

"I am not one of the angels who fell to earth," he clarified.

"I don't understand. I didn't think angels were born."

"When the angels came here, over time, they began to take on human traits and qualities—losing power but gaining something else—the ability to have children. I am the offspring of two of the original angels who came here in the beginning."

I ran a hand over my mouth. "So your parents are—"

"*Gone,*" he finished for me.

"I'm sorry," I said, and meant it.

I found myself studying him more closely. I realized he did look younger than the rest of the Watchers—if I had seen him out on the street, having never known him before, I would have guessed he was a little older than me. Maybe twenty at the most. His eyes were a strange color of blue mixed with violet. Unnaturally so. He looked like he was wearing contacts, but I knew he wasn't.

"Look … none of what happened back there in the barn was your fault," he explained. "Stanton was the one who took your friend by force. You were merely trying to stop a threat—on an obnoxiously massive scale, like using a bazooka on an ant."

I ran a hand through my hair. "Is that why you hit me?"

Leo flipped his gold knife into the air and caught it deftly by the handle. "That was for fun." After a brief pause, he added, "Your friend Larna, she seems very capable—like she knows how to take care of herself. I would have hated to see her get caught in the crosshairs of friendly fire. If I were you, I'd give her the benefit of the doubt. From where I was standing, she didn't look scared of him—she looked scared of you … Everyone did."

A spasm of anxiety gripped me tight as I staggered

back a step, clutching a hand to my chest. He didn't hit me again, but it sure felt that way. I wondered if I looked as pale as I felt. He was right.

"Why do you even care about my well-being, anyway?" I lifted my arms, glancing around. "You don't seem excited to be here. What do you want, Leo? Did you draw the short straw to come and talk to me?"

"I don't."

I lifted an eyebrow when he didn't follow that vague statement up.

"Care about you," he clarified. "I just have a vested interest in getting you to the endgame—that's all."

I huffed, and a puff of white mist escaped my lips in the process. "Finally some honesty."

"Gabriel Stanton has had centuries to learn how to get into people's heads. Not to mention the fact that he turned your friend. They have a peculiar connection. Don't tell me you haven't noticed."

"How do you know that? How do you know he turned her? Did Dave tell you?"

"I make it my business to keep track," he said simply. "Danel has kept you in the dark about a lot of things— and for good reason." Leo's voice was dripping with aggravation, and something else I couldn't quite put my finger on—a certain bitterness that hadn't been there before. "Danel never mentioned me to you before, did he?"

I shook my head. Actually, now that I thought about it, he had brought up everyone else *except* him.

Leo stepped up beside me, his eyes glazing over as if he were staring at something I couldn't see. After a moment, he shook his head as if to clear it and laughed softly to himself. "Danel and I never really saw eye to eye on anything."

We stayed quiet for another minute or two, and for some strange reason, even though I didn't know him well, I was suddenly glad for his company.

He bowed his head and stepped back, letting me finish paying my respects to Paul and Jack.

When I turned back to face him, he said, "For someone who was just handed the most powerful weapon on the planet, I think you handle it … okay. Most of us would have done a *lot* more damage with it by now. It would be like someone giving Thor's hammer to a chimpanzee."

I couldn't help it; I snorted as I gave him a sidelong glance. "Did you just compare me to a monkey? You know, I mistook you for a real a-hole when you first showed up. But *Thor*? Seriously, I never saw that coming … not in a million years."

"Oh, I'm still an a-hole," he said darkly, and with that, an unbridled clap of thunder and a blaze of light flared up so bright I had to shield my eyes from its intensity. When I was able to blink past the pain of it and clear my eyesight, I realized he was gone.

"Duly noted," I whispered. "*Thor* fan."

Chapter 38

Corinth

AL HAD HIS BACK turned to me, stoking the fire with a poker when I walked back inside, shivering from hypothermia, my pants stiff and coated in mud and frost.

All of the angels had disappeared to who knew where—Nan's guesthouse, I assumed. It was the one place I hadn't run past.

Between rattling teeth, I gasped, "I'm so, so sorry, Al. Larna is …" My voice broke.

Sparks from the fire shot into the air. They looked like fiery hornets. I imagined Al just as mad as those hornets.

The soft hiss of oxygen breathing life back into the flames reminded me of camping with my dad. I inhaled the smoke and ash and soot as a flashback hit me: My dad holding his favorite mug, standing over a smoldering campfire with that look on his face that told me he was thinking about pouring lighter fluid all over it again. I was an eleven-year-old who looked to follow his example. The moment my father had caught me staring at his favorite mug, a simple green tin, he gave me an all-knowing smile and handed it over so I could have a taste.

That was the first time I'd ever had coffee.

Some teens relish getting the chance to have their first sip of beer with their dad, but coffee had always been our thing—it was what we'd bonded over.

Why does it feel like I am about to pour lighter fluid all over everything?

Al's head swiveled in my direction. I could see the sharp contours of angular cheekbones in his profile—both light and dark. He moved into the kitchen and came back holding a tin that looked eerily similar to the one my dad had handed me back when I was eleven.

He thrust it into my frostbitten fingers. I took it between trembling hands as he shoved me toward the fireplace to get warm. His way of apologizing for hitting me, I supposed.

Normally, he would have had some advice to share, but this time I didn't think he could find the words. I knew that if something happened to Larna, we'd both shatter into a tiny million pieces. I guess we didn't need to say anything to each other.

Imani came up behind me. I could feel her body heat rolling over me like a tidal wave.

"In the past, I wouldn't have stayed. I would have left with Gabriel." She shook her head and then laughed softly to herself. "I used to care only about myself. But there's something about you ..." Her voice trailed off for a moment, and then she said, "I stayed because I believe you are a leader capable of making tough choices for the greater good. But I can't have you doubting me again."

I squinted up to meet her fierce gaze. Those dark

irises pulled me in, glittering like sun dapples on the water. She looked both confident and beautiful. The kind of look she was giving me could melt Ken's plastic shorts off his plastic body.

I swallowed and glanced back down, unable to handle the intensity of her glare.

Al groaned and turned back from his spot in front of the fire to face us. "So, what does this leader want us to do next?"

I suddenly felt the hot sting of tears at the corners of my eyes. I planted my palms against them. Having Al back in my corner meant everything to me. I felt a weight lift off my chest.

"Gabriel's reaction is my fault. I told him there was a cure for all vamps and that it isn't a vaccination to be controlled. I had to know if he was truly in it for the cure. I guess we know the answer, because he failed miserably. Now he's running scared."

Al's eyes hardened, and when he spoke, I couldn't ignore the sharp fury in his voice. "I just can't help feeling that you made an awful mistake going to him first. You should have come to us—we could have devised a plan together." He stormed across the living room and grabbed his coat from the hook by the door.

I had let myself sink onto the couch out of pure exhaustion, but I bolted to my feet again. "Whoa, where do you think you're going?"

Al shrugged one arm into the sleeve of his leather jacket. "I'm going after her."

"Do you think that's a good idea?" Imani interjected softly.

It was nice she was with me on this. I needed backup.

"You tell me, *Imani*." Al turned to her in anger. "You were Stanton's minion."

Imani gave an indifferent shrug. The gold bangles on her wrist clinked together. "So were you."

Al grunted and then crossed his arms defiantly over his chest. He had yet to put his jacket all the way on, and the empty sleeve flopped dramatically down by his side as if he had a third hand. "I'll kill the bastard myself if he hurts her."

I pinched the bridge of my nose, thinking. "If we focus all of our energies on finding the cure, this will be over. *All of it.* Larna will be human again, and so will Gabe. I don't think he's going to kill her. He'll want to use her as a bargaining chip—to get me to do what he wants. That's what he's said all along." I turned to Imani. "You know Gabe better than any of us. Am I right in my assumptions?"

Imani's black eyes met mine briefly before darting away from my piercing gaze. She seemed almost reluctant to speak. Eventually, she murmured, "He'll turn her over to Angela. It will be his way of asking for clemency—he'll join the stronger side because you made your intentions known that you were going to kill him. I am sorry, Corinth. Larna is as good as dead. That's how he operates."

My pulse slammed through my veins. *No.* "Do you have a way to contact Gabriel?"

"Yes. But you aren't turning yourself over to him to save her," she whispered. "I won't let you—not to save one person. You realize not even Larna is worth that price."

I pressed my lips together. "Dammit. Give me his number, Imani," I growled. "Maybe we can track him."

She laughed at my ignorance. "You can't track Gabriel Stanton unless he wants you to track him."

Al shrugged his other arm into the sleeve of his jacket, a pinched expression on his face. "If you can tell me you've got a plan, I'm in. Otherwise, I'm going after her. I'll storm Gabriel's place all by myself if I have to. She may be one person to you, but she's *everything* to me."

"Gabriel has any number of places around the world he could hold her at," Imani chimed in. "You'd only be wasting your time going back to his manor."

"I have a plan," I said calmly. "Take your jacket off, Al."

The door flew open ominously, and Vinson fumed in, stomping fresh powder snow and slush onto Nan's living-room floor. He'd always had a way with entrances, but I had never seen him look this livid before—and that was saying something. Apparently, we were all mad that we couldn't do more to find Larna.

His eyes landed on Al, who was still standing on the threshold of the room as everyone else turned to look at Vinson. He growled at the unwanted attention and stalked toward the kitchen.

Knowing what Vinson was going after, I said, "Bring me some too, comrade."

I didn't really drink, and alcohol didn't effect vampires the same way as humans. I just couldn't seem to get warm—that, and I needed to numb the rampant thoughts of what Angela would do to Larna if Gabe did turn her over to the Grigori.

I set the tin full of still-steaming hot java back on the tabletop.

Vinson eyed me from across the room and nodded.

I pulled a furry blanket around my shoulders right as another stab of pain tore through my gut, a form of icy acupuncture I wouldn't pay for.

Al raised a questioning eyebrow as he came slowly back into the living room. "So what's this plan of yours?"

Before I could answer, my hair whipped into my eyes as Vinson appeared out of thin air, holding the vodka out to me. After pushing my mop of hair out of my face, I took the bottle from him and drank down a generous gulp. I wiped my mouth as the pleasant warmth hit my belly. The slow creep of heat made me close my eyes for a brief moment in respite. But as soon as it had started, the sensation wore off, and I was reduced to feeling like a giant popsicle all over again.

I rubbed at my arms. "I'm going back inside Angela's mind. I can find out where she is."

Al shook his head adamantly, ticking off each of his fingers as he spoke. "First, you don't have the strength to do that. Second, I saw the state you were in when you got back from saving Stanton and Larna. Lastly, Angela put you in a coma for two days … What makes you think the second time will be any different?"

"That was back before I had a few angels on my side. They can teach me how to block her. I can tap into their energy and use it. Dave told me I needed to learn to control this. I'm trying to lead—if you'll let me, Al."

Al shook his head. After a moment, instead of saying what I thought he was going to say, he glowered down at me and said, "Fine. I'm in."

Chapter 39

Larna

I SAT CROSS-LEGGED IN the expensive leather seat in the cabin of Gabriel's six-seater helicopter, my hands still cuffed in front of me, poring over the contents of my dad's journal. It wasn't easy to turn the pages either. I had stowed the notebook in my pocket right before the incident in the barn. It had been over an hour since we'd left the safety of Nan's property. Occasionally I would glance up and catch Gabriel staring at me, but he would look away as soon as I caught him. I noticed that he had completely healed from all the burn wounds. Even his hair had grown back exponentially fast. The only scar marring his face was the one Xerxes had given him before he'd been turned.

He had been on his phone most of the time we were in the air, speaking in hushed tones that I couldn't quite make out, even with my supersensitive hearing. The blades chopping at the air made it hard to concentrate on anything else, mainly because they sounded like hands on a clock winding down. I knew what he was doing—contacting Angela's people to set up a meet for my exchange. I wondered if angels even needed cell phones.

I thought about Corinth, and a pang of guilt welled up inside me. He was under an incredible amount of stress. It stressed me out too, knowing he only had a short number of days left to live. I had to get that cure no matter what.

If that meant going through Angela to get to it, so be it. This was why I didn't try and take Gabriel out.

I forced myself to concentrate, trying to keep my mind off the fact that Alastair must be worried sick about me. My stomach churned at all of the possible scenarios probably playing out in his head. Worrying wasn't going to get me anywhere.

My plan, which Alastair had begrudgingly decided to go with, was trying to get Gabriel to join our side. I hoped Alastair still trusted me, that I could make this work.

Gabriel had abandoned all pretenses and was drinking.

He sat across from me, his legs stretched out in front of him, looking relaxed, but there was something seething just below the surface of all that composure—a chink in his armor just waiting for me to rip it wide open. For some reason, I didn't think he was okay with his decision to turn me over.

When I glanced up again, I found him dissecting me with those dark eyes of his again. I may have been in restraints, but that didn't mean I wasn't in control. Pretending not to notice him noticing me, I stretched my arms over my head and yawned. I wondered who had the better poker face.

"Jack used to keep a picture of you tucked into a pocket in that ugly duster of his. He didn't know I knew about it," Gabriel said. "He didn't like cell phone cameras. Find anything of interest in that journal?"

I didn't bother to look at him as I awkwardly turned another page. Nonchalantly I said, "I searched for *Ephialtes* and *Persia* on the internet—and guess what I came up with." I saw him stiffen out of the corner of my eye as I went on. "Most of the articles I could find on the subject say you betrayed the Greeks by revealing a path behind the Spartan lines."

He swirled the contents of his drink in his glass, his voice frighteningly soft and frighteningly alarming when he spoke. "What do you know about that?"

"I know that that's not what really happened," I explained. "Because I saw it all. *Everything.* I mean, yes, you gave them up, but only after being tortured by Xerxes, or the *Immortals* or whoever they were." I lifted my cuffed hands to point to his left cheek. "That's how you got that nasty cut on your face, right? With a short sword ... done by Xerxes himself."

His eyes stretched wide. They looked like dark pools.

"You think that if you keep betraying people and never let anyone get close, you'll live forever. It's what's always worked for you. Why mess with a functional formula? It must be such a lonely life."

The only reaction I got out of him was the tightening of his lips around the corners of his mouth.

I felt my eyes churn with my *Sight.* "I know what your secret is."

He took a sip of his drink, uncrossing his legs. "What's that?"

"You haven't always been the deserter or traitor or

cutthroat you make yourself out to be. I saw your mother dying in your arms. It was horrible. Stuck through with the same short sword Xerxes used. They killed her, didn't they? The Persians … *Xerxes.*"

He jumped to his feet, lowering his drink, and in a blur of motion, his face was inches from mine. I pressed myself further into the seat unconsciously. "You know nothing about my mother. Be careful with the next words out of your mouth."

My heart skipped a beat. I tensed up as his breath rustled my hair. He was so close I could see the veins jumping out at his neck. If he was going to kill me, I would make him work for it at least.

I tried to keep my voice steady, but my mouth was so dry. I just needed to press him a little further. "You used to be an honest man. A noble man. I witnessed it. What happened to that man?"

Quick as a snake strike, he stood back up and threw his glass across the cabin. It shattered to dust. *"He's dead!"*

My heart was thumping wildly now. "Is that what your mother would want to hear?"

He sank down beside me, suddenly deflated.

"Did you see *my* memories, Gabriel?" I pressed. "I know you did. I could see how they affected you. What did they look like? What did they feel like?"

He put a hand on his chest, over his heart, and whispered, "I … I … d-d-don't know …" He was blinking rapidly now, seemingly searching for something beyond what I could fathom. "It hurts."

To my utmost shock, I realized he did have feelings bottled up somewhere deep inside him. I'd accessed them—and all I had to do was get him to acknowledge them. To open up. How long had it been since he'd thought about his own mother? What had he seen through my eyes?

He stared at the backs of his hands as if they didn't belong to him. "You shared a kiss with Alastair." He cleared his throat, suddenly looking lost, his eyes zipping back and forth, pensive. He'd been alone for so long; I could see it reflected in his eyes.

It was so completely out of character, I found myself instinctively reaching out to him before I realized it. I pulled my shackled hands back. *What am I thinking?* This vampire had wreaked so much havoc in my life, killed my father, hurt Corinth, and was planning to turn me over to the enemy … yet …

His fingers gripped the sides of the seat like a vise. I could see every vein on his knuckles standing out against copper-colored skin.

"I saw you on your front lawn—with Corinth, having a picnic at night. He was explaining in excruciating detail everything he knew about the constellation Canis Major." He dropped his gaze away from mine. "You were sharing a bowl of popcorn and looking up into the sky as he pointed out the Dog Star—his favorite star. Canis Major represents the bigger dog following Orion … I couldn't care less about what Mr. Taylor's favorite star or constellation is—or that fact is now emblazoned on my brain. I absolutely detested seeing that look of contentment on his face. And your heart … your heart … was just so *full*." He looked like he was going to be sick, I noticed. "You liked him a lot, before Alastair. I *knew* you

two were close … but … I … I didn't know how it *felt*."
He shook his head. "I don't know how you stand it, all
those emotions flooding through you *all* of the time. It's
exhausting." He opened his mouth to add something else,
but his eyes fixated on something near my feet.

I turned to see what had grabbed his attention.

My dad's journal was face-down on the ground. I
must have dropped it when he rushed me. The pages were
bent and spewed apart. Gabriel moved around me to pick
up a piece of paper that had fluttered out between the rest
of the pages.

Not paper but one of my dad's old photographs.

He turned it over. "Where did this come from?"

I glanced at the Polaroid clenched between his
fingers, realizing it was the one my dad had taken of the
skeletal tree with scraggly branches reaching for the
heavens. The one I thought was ethereal looking. This
particular photo had grabbed my attention too. I wasn't
surprised by his curiosity. It really was a work of art. One
of my dad's best actually.

He read the words written on the back: "'*Trembling
Giant.*'" His eyes darted back up to mine. "You've had this
picture the entire time?"

"Uh … yeah … Why?"

Fully engrossed in his own thoughts, Gabriel lowered
himself back down beside me, tapping it against his leg.

I looked at it again and then pulled the photo from
his hand, the cuffs bulky and heavy around my wrists as I
studied it with renewed interest. "Trembling Giant …"

Shaking his head, Gabriel said, "Your father had the
answer tucked between the pages of his incessant drivel

this entire time." He fished his phone out of his pocket and pulled up a search page on the web. He plugged in the words *Trembling Giant* and pushed enter.

It had never occurred to me to research this further. I had always thought my dad had liked the picture and that was that.

He said, "I overheard Corinth talking about how he was able to glean an image of trees from Angela. This has to be more than just mere coincidence."

Immediately an article popped up.

We both skimmed through the editorial: the *Trembling Giant* was one of the oldest known single organisms on Earth, a grove of about forty-seven thousand trees all interconnected by one root system.

I sucked in a deep breath as soon as I read that the grove of quaking aspens could be well over eighty thousand years old. This had to be it. *Trees* …

"My dad knew." In awe of my father's brilliance beyond the grave, on my exhale I said, "He *knew*."

Gabriel's eyes flashed. "It's in *Utah*? The cure is in the States …? But of *course* it is." He peered down at my bound hands folded together in my lap. "Corinth, he told me that the cure, it isn't like an injection or a pill. It's a cure-all for every single ascended being out there. If it's enacted, all of us will be turned human once again. Do you really want that?"

I found myself searching his eyes. "No. But I won't let Corinth die either. Not if there's something that I can do about it. Being a vampire isn't as important as losing someone I love. Tell me the truth, Gabriel. Your intention has always been to control the cure like a drug, to dispense it to those willing enough to pay your price. Now that you know it doesn't work that way, you're bailing … just like you've always done."

Gabriel reached into his jacket pocket, and I tensed up, ready to make my move if he tried to attack me, but his hand stilled as he said, "You're right. This has always been about the cure. Whosoever controls it controls the world." Gabriel jerked his hand back out of the lining of his jacket, his fingers curled around something in his fist. "I will *not* become human again."

He was going to trade me to Angela after all—or kill me right here and now, and be done with it. I knew too much. He wouldn't let me go with this kind of devastating information for all vampires.

A small crease appeared in between his brows before he showed me the object in his hand: a handcuff key.

"I *can* let you go. Tell Corinth that the next time I see him, I won't be so generous. Because he saved my life—tell him we're even." Gabriel laughed softly to himself—I could hear the irony in it—and then he glanced to his hired goon Lurch, who was still sitting silently at the back of the cabin. "Take her back."

then she pulled her hand back.

"You know, the last time I did something like this, I was used as a human pincushion. Accessing Angela's memories is something I'm not looking forward to."

Imani lifted an eyebrow. "Don't be a baby."

"I mean, is it really such a bad thing to be a baby? Have you considered the possibility that we might not need therapists if we all cried a little more? Got it all out of our systems?"

"You talk too much." Imani rolled her eyes but she was grinning. "This world is filled with way too much whining as it is."

"Maybe … but I still got a chuckle out of you. I heard it."

She gave me a sidelong glance. "I admit, you're slightly funny, but I don't want it to go straight to your head."

"Oh, it's too late. Your compliment has gone straight there. Do not pass go or collect two hundred dollars." I spread my arms out wide. "I'm talking big head syndrome here. I won't be able to fit through a door—"

Imani slapped me playfully on the arm and we both grew quiet for a moment before she added, "You don't think it's weird? Me being—" she cleared her throat "—older than you?"

I sat up and turned to face her on the couch, hiking a leg up underneath me. "Well, this just took an interesting segue. Are you trying to tell me you like me? Because you look like you're my age, and the only thing that's weird is if you like me, because you're way hotter than I am."

Chapter 40

Corinth

THERE WERE TWO THINGS that helped me Zen out: *Mortal Kombat* and *Star Wars*. There was something soothing and cathartic about carrying out brutal fatalities on your enemies—in a game, I mean. But because these days I felt more like Raiden in real life—albeit a less cool version; I didn't have the hat—I decided *Mortal Kombat* might not be my favorite video game anymore. Besides, I didn't have a console with me, so I would have to make do with Nan's cozy couch and fireplace.

I rolled up the sleeves of my shirt and then immediately regretted it. The cold seemed to leech the life out of me, as quickly as diving into subzero temperatures. She had already provided me with a generous donation of her blood, but I didn't feel any better.

I eyed the fire appreciatively as Imani sidled up next to me on the couch, her thigh brushing against mine.

"I'm sorry about what I said," I started.

"It's okay. I haven't always been the best in moral decisions as of late. I'm sorry about your tooth." She reached out as if she were going to caress my cheek, but

She inched back, and her eyes landed on the dagger sheathed at my thigh. "You should be so lucky."

"You can say that again." It was out of my mouth before I could stop it.

She put a hand to her lips and cleared her throat, but I could have sworn I saw the hint of a smile on her face. "So, *Sparky*, how do you expect to steal Angela's memories from her?"

I couldn't help but crack a grin at the nickname. It felt special, as if it was an inside joke meant for the two of us. Except my lifted mood didn't last long—the thought of going toe to toe with Angela wasn't so appealing.

My grin faded, and the intimate moment between us fled. "It's not like I have an instruction manual for this sort of thing. I have no idea what I'm doing."

"But you do have a bunch of trained warrior angels on your side now," she said thoughtfully. "I believe in you—you *can* do this."

Ikari wasn't like the rest of the Watchers. For one, he'd traded his armor for workout gear. It wasn't just his smaller stature that set him apart. His waist was as wide as my pinky, and his shoulders were broad and corded with muscle. I was certain he could easily take me in a fight. I glanced down at my shrinking waistline and curled a lip in agitation.

He inhaled deeply and cracked an eye open. "Like that. Did you see what I did there?"

I lifted my eyebrows and glanced at the rest of the Watchers, all standing somberly around me, watching.

No, I didn't see what you did there. They were all trying to pipe up and give me advice on how to block Angela and get inside her head. It was exhausting.

"Sorry—Leo is distracting me." I glanced at him from across the room again. He was sharpening a very pointy short sword. The repetitive *shnick* noise it was making on the whetstone was grating on my nerves. He was the only one *not* trying to give me advice, I noticed.

Everyone else was staring at me expectantly.

Ikari spread his hands out in front of him. "Hey, man, this was your idea. I'm just here to help you get inside Angela's melon to find anything about this cursed cure … and to get your friend Larna back … You know, just the fate of the world hanging in the balance here—while you keep staring strangely at Leo."

I ran a hand through my hair, ruffling it up on top. "*I'm sorry.* Everything is distracting, since I have vampire senses that won't let up."

With spiky bleached-blond hair, eyes closed in concentration, Ikari was the picture-perfect enlightened beach bum. He looked like he was in perfect harmony with the world. This angel knew what the meaning of life was, and he wasn't going to share it with the rest of us poor saps.

He reminded me of Dave.

"Why do y'all dye your hair blond?" I asked.

He pointed at his head. "You mean this doesn't look natural?" He sounded mock offended. "It's a family thing."

"As in bloodlines or cult?" I asked sarcastically.

Ikari rolled his eyes as if I were slow to catch on. "We

are warriors—a bond that connects us. We dress alike and look alike for intimidation tactics. Besides, do you think our outward appearances are what we actually look like? Have you seen flashes of our wings or halos? Our exteriors are only a small glimpse of what we are."

I remembered catching snatches of war-torn, smoldering wings from Angela and Dave. I shivered.

"You aren't like the rest of the Watchers. You have this youthful hipness about you the others don't have, like nothing affects you."

He shrugged. "I live in California, bruh."

I couldn't quite hide my surprise at his use of American slang. "I thought you guys all lived off the grid in a cave or something."

Ikari rolled his eyes again and pointed to his face. "You're crazy if you think I'm going to hide this winning smile of mine in a cave."

Flustered, I said, "I mean, all the rest of the Watchers seem so intense all the time."

"I'm an angel and a human groupie. I like to tease … and if you can't joke, what's even the point of living?"

"I like you," I told him. "So, why are there only five of y'all left?"

"The Fallen, or Grigori, chose to follow Satan when they fell to earth. They blamed humanity for God's attention, so they went after it." He put a fist to his heart enthusiastically. "So some of us, the Watchers, volunteered to leave heaven on a one-way mission, to go after the Grigori—the Fallen—and protect all of humanity. But on the flip side, understanding humans is not a simple task. Love is a key component to living—and it's kind of a rite of passage here. So some of us fell victim to the very thing we had sworn to protect." He shrugged. "We had kids, lived life, and then the Grigori punished us for it. They eradicated our offspring because they thought Nephilim were abominations. We went to war—and that war lasted centuries, eons. It has been gory, and the casualties many." Ikari dropped his gaze, going silent. When he spoke again, I could hear the emotion building in his voice. "The Grigori believe humans are beneath them—the Nephilim are a by-product of that hatred. I believe you took out one of the Grigori's top soldiers—Caesar. I owe you for that one."

I thought about how many times I'd been stabbed by Sarah at Caesar's command. "Yeah, well … it cost me a lot." My eyes traveled over to where Leo was still sharpening his blade. "So, what's with him?" He doesn't have the same hair color, and he seems to have a chip on his shoulder the size of Texas—"

"With good reason," Ikari said quickly. "None of us has the right to each other's story. If you want to know his story, you'll have to ask him. I'd like to tell you mine, Corinth, if you'll let me. You have to understand, the Grigori don't fight fair. We have lost many because of their willingness to do whatever it takes to hurt anyone who gets in the way, especially humans. Gabriel Stanton has amassed one of the largest clans out there. Angela has recruited him to her side. We aren't the bad guys here. *War* is the bad guy. *War* is messy."

I grunted. "You don't have to explain yourself to me. Gabe has tried to kill me on more than one occasion. I still can't help thinking how deceitful I feel about all of this …

everything. I don't like making these decisions. I know Larna doesn't want a cure." It suddenly felt good to admit my true feelings and insecurities to someone other than Al or Larna, to someone who could understand what I was going through. "It's been weighing on me ... the fact that we don't necessarily see eye to eye on this. She knows where I stand though. If I have to shove that cure down her throat, I will. I think she feels like she'll do what she has to do in order to save my life." My throat constricted. "If I do this ... we can't ever go back to the way things were."

When I glanced back up, Ikari was nodding, but his eyes were burning with anger. "We've known about Deimos for a long time. Stanton *will* join the stronger side ... You do realize that's the Grigori, right?"

"Larna is with him, she'll do what she can to change his mind," I said slowly, wishing I sounded more confident about that fact. A small part of me thought, *Or will she?* "If I only knew she was okay ..." I put a hand on my dagger and felt its hum of anticipation running through me. My skin tingled as the charge started to build up under my skin. "I have to know she's okay." I glanced up, fire licking my insides, giving me some relief from the cold for the first time in forever. "If Gabe has turned her over to the Grigori, I *will* turn him into a pile of smoke and ash."

Sweat glistened on my forehead as I blew out a shaky breath. Ikari had been trying to teach me how to wriggle my way into his own head, but it was proving to be much harder than I'd originally thought. I mean, how hard could it be to get into an angel's subconscious? *Impossible.*

I ran a hand across my brow. "This sucks."

I was dripping sweat and out of breath, but Ikari was the opposite—looking fresh and alert. He opened his eyes and stretched his neck from side to side.

"I don't understand why you don't just go get the information from Angela yourself. You're clearly *way* better at this than I am."

"Because it would be like Godzilla stomping around Tokyo … She'd see me coming from a mile away … whereas you're more like a pint-sized church mouse, virtually undetectable. Besides, we transferred most of our power and energy into the dagger, making it an impossible task for any of us to complete—not enough strength."

I threw my hands up. "Wow … and the hits keep coming—pint-sized church mouse? How about Chihuahua at the very least? Won't she be able to detect the vampire in me? Have you seen my paltry will at work? I don't need all of this riding on my shoulders, Ikari. I feel horrible that y'all bestowed this power on me. Seriously, I am soooo underserving."

"We don't think so." Ikari's eyebrows knitted together. "And neither should you. The answer to your question about the vampire part of you—no. I think I can ward you from prying eyes. The dagger will help. Look, if you can get into *my* head, then I'll know you're ready to try to get into hers. Dave couldn't even do that, by the way." Ikari laughed at the look on my face. "Relax, dude, you'll be fine—have a little faith."

It was my turn to chuckle at the irony of an angel

using the words *dude* and *faith* in the same sentence. I squeezed my eyes shut. I was drained from my earlier display of power in the barn, but it didn't matter how tired I was. If I wanted to find Larna, I had to do this.

Ever so slowly, I reached for the source of my will, letting that strange energy fill my chest with a crackling charge of electricity. It came to me as easily as oxygen filling in my lungs. Ikari had said that I'd been going about accessing it all wrong.

I had thought the dagger worked as a conduit, but the blade wasn't the conduit. *I* was. The weapon was only a means of focusing my control. It contained unconcentrated power from seven incredibly strong angels. Instead of using my power externally, like throwing lightning around, I needed to use it *internally*, to shoot those wisps of subconscious into Angela's mind—to draw power from her.

She'd been trying to do the same thing to me. Fortunately, I'd had some pretty good back-up shielding me from her as of late. Ikari had said it took years to master what he was trying to teach me in just a few short hours. I learned that each angel had different abilities that they were better at than other angels. For example, Ikari was good at mental stuff, like psychic links, mind control, and manipulation. Tami could move incredibly fast and teleport more easily. Sam was the brawn—the fighter. Leo was good at conjuring weapons out of thin air and making them dance to his tune. Din could put anything or anyone to sleep—and I didn't mean that as an insult.

So with all that taken into consideration, I thought my training was going pretty well. Maybe I was a mishmash of all those things, because that was what they'd imbued the blade with, thereby blessing me with their talents. I just had to learn to control them.

I closed my eyes, imagining the thin tendrils of my will morphing into tiny snakes, fanning out toward Ikari's mind. This strategy seemed to work. I knew where the term *third eye* came from now. His halo was there to protect him from spiritual attackers. I could see it clearly now, and it was terrifying. A cracked and charred crown of hooks and spikes encircled his head, digging into his skull—it looked painful and not at all angelic. It was radiant and fiery and biblical—also scorched, singed, and battle-scarred.

Is this what I look like too? Maybe he'd lost a part of himself when he'd come here, and could never get it back—or maybe this was because of the blade. Whatever the case, guilt swelled in my chest, filling me with the dread of disappointing him.

I found my way around the singed protrusions, searching for a weak point inside. Trying to find a way past his defenses was cumbersome and tedious. This was nothing like using vampire *Sight*. After poking and prodding for what seemed like hours, I realized I needed a little science to help. It sounded weird, but that was what I was good at. If I could turn the energy into vapor or smoke or a gas-like state, in theory, I should be able to pass right through his fortifications. Gas is one of the four fundamental states of matter. Scientific experimentation 101—gas him. It didn't sound mature, but if the strategy worked, I didn't care how immature it was. All of this was in my head, imaginary, of course.

After coming to that conclusion, I visualized my mental-self rolling right through his defenses like a fog—

A blinding bright light hit me square in my eye … well, third eye … and my vision cleared so suddenly and unexpectedly that when I did come out of it, I was blinking past bright patches of light.

So surprised was I by this sudden change in scenery, that I almost lost the connection I'd established with Ikari. My surroundings flickered briefly before I got it back under control.

Then I found myself whole again, standing in a tiny room. Not Nan's place.

A draft of air hit me, and soft light flickered from a candle on a wall sconce. For a brief second, the light sputtered as if it were about to go out, but the breeze from the open window died down, and the light came flooding back, bringing everything into sharp focus once again.

I took in my surroundings. I'd seen *The Last Samurai* enough times to recognize the architectural design of domiciles in East Asia. Maybe early twentieth-century Japan. There was no buzz of electricity or rumble of cars or horns blaring in the distance outside the open window.

Two tatami mats lay side by side near my feet. A scroll as tall as me hung on the wall above one of the only pieces of furniture in the room—a wooden cabinet. A set of tortuously complex symbols were scrawled across it in another language I couldn't read—kanji, maybe.

It was dark outside, and I recognized a familiar musty odor in the air. A pungent scent of manure drifted in through one of the open windows. If this was Ikari's memory, it seemed real enough to me. There came a faint murmur of someone speaking quietly in another part of the dwelling.

A dividing screen woven out of bamboo separated the living room from the rest of the house. I noticed two pairs of shoes arranged neatly near the front door. It appeared that whoever was speaking was in the kitchen. There came the bubbling, steaming hiss of meat roasting over on an open flame. Fresh fish and spice ... Each smell more complex and aromatic than the last hit me. There was something different about the aroma of food here—or it could have been that I was slowly starving to death and I was always hungry. I'd been lulled into the peacefulness of no road noise or buzzing electronics. The warm breeze coming in through the window sent a wash of calm over me.

Shadows dipped and elongated in the adjoining room. Inching my way quietly—I didn't know why, as they couldn't hear me—over to the bamboo partition, I was able to make out hushed voices coming through the thin wall.

Unfortunately, it didn't matter what they said, because they were both speaking in another language and I didn't understand them anyway.

The candle beside me sputtered again as another gentle breeze wafted into the room. The shadows through the partition were as crisp and sharp as if they were standing in front of me. I recognized Ikari immediately from his shadow. He had to be six foot seven—even sitting down, he was still a head taller than the other person was. Ikari wore his hair in a high bun on the top of his head. I had to suppress a chuckle at the fact that he was setting trends before they were even trends. Something told me the Japanese were a wee bit more traditional than today's California though.

I could hear the feminine lilt of a woman's voice. It was soft and delicate. When she got up to check the food, I gave an involuntary gasp. Her shadow stomach was fit to burst with the expectancy of new life. She waddled over to Ikari, stretching up on tiptoes to give his cheek a peck. He bent down and brushed her forehead lightly with his lips. They laughed. A part of me knew I could just walk right on in there without them even saying a word, but I suddenly felt awkward for intruding on this particular intimate memory.

Ikari let out a throaty laugh right at the same time as the front door behind me burst open in a shower of wood—

A group of masked intruders exploded into the cramped living room.

I whirled around, my heart launching up into my throat. My pulse thudded away in my veins, and I raised my hands up ready for a fight on instinct. The remaining bits of lumber splintered apart as a crack zigzagged its way down the wall from the force of their incursion.

One of the things that stuck with me was how eerily silent they all were—no shouts or cries of warning or yelling. I hadn't even heard them approach. Thirteen figures filed their way inside, their hands glowing and sizzling with angel energy.

I wanted to scream, to warn Ikari, but I knew that it would do no good.

The intruders stood shoulder to shoulder, all of them

wearing Kabuki masks—a Japanese horror flick come to life—and I knew they did it for added effect. A torment meant only for Ikari. I put myself between the couple in the opposite room, my blade in my hand in a heartbeat, already reaching for my power—

It crackled to life, lightning arcing between my fingertips, lancing across my forearms, the energy writhing and uncoiling like a live wire under my skin. My entire body shook with rage. I let loose a bolt of energy at the first masked angel. It soared right through the Grigori, not so much as moving a hair on their head as it disappeared through the wall on a puff of air.

The masked figure I'd tried to take down stalked forward. He or she wore dark brown leather armor strapped to their chest. I looked closer, noticing the notches of dark leather scored into it. The intricate design crisscrossed the entirety of the breastplate, reminding me of the Crusader's cross I'd seen in history books—a large cross with four smaller crosses in each of the four quadrants around it.

The soft light by the candles made them look even more ominous.

Ikari burst through the bamboo wall, soaring right through me, to land on the ground, crouched in a fighting stance. He raised his head and gave them each a stare that made cold chills run down my spine.

The person in front of me was not the relaxed angel I knew him to be; he was an intimidating warrior. Ikari had on a dark russet tunic with matching pants, but he didn't have shoes or armor—unlike the group closing in to surround him on all sides.

It was clear he'd been caught off guard, all of this having unfolded in mere seconds.

His fists exploded with fire and lightning at the same time as I turned around to see a young woman standing behind him, one hand over her mouth, and the other on her belly, her cheeks rosy and skin glowing. The white-as-snow kimono she wore had tiny little cherry blossoms handwoven into the fabric, and a jade comb was pinned through the bun at the top of her straight black silk hair. She was quite the vision.

I turned back to Ikari.

The ever-increasing tension had steadily been building between the silent warriors and him. Nothing good was going to happen in this memory. I remembered Ikari telling me how he wanted to share his story with me. I hadn't realized like this. *Not like this.*

The only sound now was the unattended stew bubbling over the brim of the pot, hissing as it hit the fire. The uncontained power inside me fumed. If I *had* been corporeal, everyone's hair would be standing on end. I brandished my blade all the same.

The man who had stepped forward ripped his Kabuki mask off with dramatic flair, and a jolt of recognition tore through me. It was hard to hide that scowl and those perfectly symmetrical features, curly blond hair, and piercing blue eyes. *Turiel.*

I glanced at each of the Grigori, wondering if one of them behind the mask was Caesar. I balled my hands into fists, my whole body teeming with electricity. I wondered if this was how Dave had never recognized Caesar at the clan for what he truly was—he'd never shown his face before. Benny had found out who Caesar was—he'd tried to warn me.

I stepped forward, putting myself between them. "*Turiel*, so help me—"

He spoke in English but not to me. "You know the rules, Ikari, but you chose to break them." Turiel held his hand out, gesturing at the pregnant woman in the kimono. "Give us the expectant mortal, and no harm shall come to you. Angela will accept you back into the fold once more. We just want the unborn child."

Ikari gritted his teeth and hissed in English, "Any of you *brothers* or *sisters* touches my wife, and it will be the last thing you ever do." He turned his head slightly, speaking to the woman. "Aiko. Go. Now."

The rest of the Grigori, behind Turiel, inched forward, ready, silent, and waiting. Aiko did not run. She seemed rooted to the spot, staring at the glowing hands of her husband as if she'd never seen him before. Clearly, she'd never seen this side of Ikari.

Turiel dropped his gaze, lowering his voice threateningly. "It is not too late to come with us, old friend. Don't make us do this."

Turiel thought he was on the right side of things, that what he was doing was virtuous; I could see it in his face. Acid hit the back of my throat.

"*Please*, brother. We only do this for you." Turiel's eyes locked on Ikari's wife, who stood frozen in shock behind him, a hand pressed delicately to her parted lips.

Ikari waved her back, his hands still glowing with deadly light. "*Go*, Aiko. Run."

"Allow us to help you end this with a bit of *dignity*,

Ikari. We will not let her suffer … We give you our word."

I turned my attention back to Aiko. Maybe I could do something. Help. I could bring people back to life … Stranger things had happened.

Ikari was so focused on the immediate threat in front of him, he didn't see the figure materialize in a ball of light right behind his wife. There was no clap of thunder or zing of ozone or wind to announce an angel's presence, like there should have been.

When I saw who emerged in the quick flash of light, to land right behind Aiko, my heart shot into my throat, and without thinking, I dove through the hole Ikari had created, lunging toward the woman standing behind Aiko.

Angela.

And I went sprawling through her like vapor, an intense cold washing over me as I landed face-first in the fire-pit. It did not harm me, and I did not catch fire like I thought I might, or even make a mess.

She was just as breathtaking as I remembered her, in the most terrifying way possible, like how a panther stalking its prey in the wild is terrifying.

My eyes ticked upward to halt on that beautifully cold face of hers. Her onyx-colored hair was tied in a long ponytail at her back. It went all the way past her waistline. She looked like a sadistic Grim Reaper. Those eyes though, they were what gave me pause. They were zeroed in right on me … *Impossible.* She couldn't see me. This was only a memory.

My mouth fell open, and she held a finger up to her lips; her blood-red smile saying it all. *I see you and I am coming for you.*

"*Angela.*" I jumped back up, going for her throat, but something stopped me, pinioning me in place. It was that same invisible force weighing me down, constricting me like before, when I'd been held captive in my dreamlike state. She was here.

And then Angela gave me an all-knowing wink, pulled a thin blade out of the wide sleeve of her robe, and in one smooth motion sliced through Ikari's wife's throat.

Chapter 41

Corinth

A SCREAM TORE FROM my own throat as I came all the way out of Ikari's recollection, collapsing in on myself at the same time. The feeling of being completely helpless slowly faded as I reoriented myself back to reality. I knew I was in Nan's living room, sweating through my thermals, but I still couldn't stop shaking like a leaf, my nose planted firmly in the tatami mat I now lay curled on.

The image of Aiko's face right before Angela killed her wouldn't leave me. Something hot and sticky seeped through my shirt, but I ignored it to pull the flannel jacket tighter around myself. It had belonged to Paul.

There were people surrounding me—Al, Vinson, and Leo … Al reached out and put a hand on my shoulder as I sat up, his eyes filled with concern. I tried to make the stars of rage exploding across my vision go away. The zing of static was still thick in the air, and my hands were lit up. Sparks jumped precariously off my skin, and Al jumped back in alarm.

"Angela," I gasped. "Sh-sh-she knew I was there … She winked at me." I couldn't catch my breath no matter how hard I tried.

Ikari's eyes popped open to meet my horrified gaze. He gave me a pacifying look as if to say he understood my reaction, he'd lived it over and over again.

"I'm sorry you witnessed that particu—"

"*Angela*," I gasped again, more insistent this time. "*She saw me in your memory. She saw me!*"

Ikari was shaking his head. "She didn't see you, Corinth. What you saw was traumatic ..." His eyes lifted to the ceiling. "We have all lost so much. This isn't just a mission. It's about our family. I had to show you that memory, as hard as it was to see."

He must not have seen what I saw ... If he had, he wouldn't be so calm right now.

I thought about Dave and his admission, and then about my own family back home: Zoey and Pete, and Jimmy and Mom and Dad. What would I have done in his place if that had been my family? I shuddered. The look on Angela's face as she'd acknowledged my presence was going to haunt me for the rest of my numbered days. Actually, scratch that—I was never going to sleep again.

Suddenly the air shimmered, and churned and thunder shook the ground as an angel portal opened up beside me. My first thought was that it was Angela making good on her promise to come after me. I flew to my feet with a burst of renewed energy right as a figure hurtled out of the light and noise, and landed in a ball on the ground.

My eyes blazed bright. I wound my fingers around the hilt of the blade in my hand, about to lay waste to the small form crouched on the ground, when Al flew past me, blocking my line of sight. I barked out a frustrated cry as Al pulled the prone form toward him, wrapping his arms protectively around whoever it was …

"*Larna*—" he breathed.

Their relief to see each other was as palpable as anything I'd ever felt before. She buried her face in his chest.

"Are you okay?" He cupped her face and pulled her closer. "Are you hurt?"

When she finally looked up, I could see the tips of her cheeks had turned bright pink. She didn't look hurt—which made my heart start beating again.

I curled an arm around my stomach. Too many emotions had slammed into me as of late, and I didn't know what to do with them. *She's okay.*

I didn't know where Sam or Nan had come from, but they were in front of Larna now too.

Finally Nan had to pull Al off her so that they could get some answers out of her.

Larna's eyes met mine briefly, and then her gaze swept away from me. I was ashamed I'd almost killed her back in the barn. I knew she blamed me for what had happened to her. She wouldn't forgive me for that.

Then, surprisingly, she was in front of me, her neck craned so she could look up into my face.

I chose to gawk at the floor instead of her. "Larna, I—"

She didn't let me finish before she threw herself into my arms. Her embrace was warm and welcoming. I squeezed her tight, suddenly too overwhelmed for speech. We held on to each other for a few minutes until I felt like my legs might collapse out from under me.

She must have sensed how much I needed to sit down, because she was pulling me over to the couch near the fireplace, with everyone else was on her heels.

"How did you get away?" I asked quickly. "Was that an angel portal you just popped out of?"

She pulled her dad's journal from her pocket. "Gabriel … he … he let me go—I think I know where the cure might be." She plucked something from the thin pages and held it up. A photograph of a white tree with branches that snaked their way into the sky. "Is this what you saw in Angela's mind?"

My skin began to crawl as if a thousand ants were running across my flesh and I swallowed heavily. "*That's it.*"

Chapter 42

Larna

W E HAD ALL TAKEN up residence in Nan's living room, and it was packed. For the most part, everyone stayed quiet while I shared what I knew about the location of the trees my father had so cleverly left for me to find.

I sat smashed between Corinth and Alastair on the couch. Both of them seemed overly protective of me, as if they thought I might disappear at any second. I didn't mind it so much, considering just an hour ago I thought I was going to be handed over to Angela. I still had one hand intertwined with Alastair's as I showed Corinth the photograph of the tree again and then pulled up the aspens in Utah on the internet. They did look eerily similar to the one tree in the photograph.

After I handed off the laptop, Nan shoved a hot cup into my hands. I gratefully drank the warm life-sustaining substance while they let me regale them with what had happened to me while in the company of Gabriel.

The Watchers seemed like an intimidating bunch with their gleaming armor, tall statures, and somber faces. They stood rigidly at attention, listening without comment. I didn't really know them that well, and I wasn't sure if I trusted them yet, even though I knew Corinth and Alastair did.

Corinth was nodding as he said, "That's the place, all right." His gaze flickered to mine. I could sense a strange undercurrent of tension running through him. "So … Gabriel just let you go out of the kindness of his heart? Because we all know he doesn't have one."

Alastair's fingers squeezed mine harder.

I said, "You were right about him not wanting a cure-all. He thought he could regulate it like a drug—control it. He would be one of the most powerful people on the planet. Back in the barn, once he overheard you talking about him, he got spooked and ran."

Corinth averted his gaze from mine. "About that—I am *so* sorry, Larns. I saw him and I freaked out. I thought about everything he'd done to us, and I … I … just wanted to kill him …"

The only one who seemed completely at ease and unperturbed by anything I'd just shared was Leo, the angel with the opposite of platinum-colored hair, and his eyes were a shade of pale blue that reminded me of a periwinkle. A hint of lavender, maybe. There was something unsettling about him, the way he twirled that gold knife between his fingers.

What did I find so off-putting, yet familiar about him?

He caught me staring and flashed an aggravating scowl in my direction. I quickly turned my attention back to the matter at hand.

Corinth ran a hand through his wild brown locks. "I

still don't understand how I'm supposed to glean information from a bunch of trees. How does this help me get the cure? I mean, do we start bringing shovels and climbing gear? Is the cure hidden in a hobbit-like dwelling? *Is* it a tree? Maybe it's the *sap* from a tree … the bark …" He glanced at each of the Watchers, who were all standing in front of the kitchen bar across the room, watching Corinth with their arms crossed over their chests. "You guys are supposed to be providing me with answers here."

Samyaza stepped forward, dark eyes glittering. "Angela is the only one who knows how to enact the cure. We must go to Utah. We separate in order to amass an army—this clan Eleutheros, and any others who are willing to fight. Gabriel will tell her what we are planning. She will be there with her own army."

Alastair spoke up suddenly. "For all we know, Angela planted that image in Corinth's head on purpose—to force his hand. Maybe that was her plan all along. To trick him into going there."

Every eye in the room ticked over to Corinth. He slowly stood to his feet, a hand curled around his stomach. He didn't look well, I thought.

"I feel like this is the moment where I give everyone a moving speech or something, or tell y'all what we should do next—"

Leo flipped his blade into the air. It vanished in a wink of light, and then he was propelling himself off the kitchen bar he had been leaning against to march imperiously up to Corinth.

I could hear the slight British lilt in his voice as he said, "The only way to figure out how to get the cure and set it in motion is to pluck it out of her head—which you're clearly not going to do, because"—he pointed at Corinth's hand on his stomach and cocked an eyebrow—"look at you. *Or* we come up with another plan ... one which I have been working on for a very long time."

Corinth conceded the floor, sitting back down and looking more noticeably relieved. "I didn't want to make a brilliant speech, anyway," he muttered.

"Leo's plan involves trust and risk," Samyaza interjected. "We have been kept in the dark about it for good reason—only Leo knows the details. Danel was aware of this plan too, but since he is no longer with us ..."

I knew Corinth was remembering Dave's words about not trusting anyone. At the back of my mind, I kept thinking about why Dave had never introduced us to the rest of the Watchers before now. There had to have been a reason, and that reason was what set my nerves on edge. Clearly, Dave didn't even trust his own people when it came to Corinth. Something wasn't adding up.

I sat up quickly, pulling my hand out of Alastair's. "Dave's plans have blown up in our faces—*literally*. Angela blew Dave to smithereens in front of me, and then had one of her minions stab Corinth, repeatedly." I pointed at each of the Watchers in turn. "I don't trust you." I put a hand up before Corinth could say anything, standing to my full height, which wasn't saying much, and then gave Leo one of my piercing glares. It was like looking up at a giant. "*You* especially."

Leo rolled his eyes and gave Corinth a brief glance. "We could have killed you lot a million times over by now if we'd wanted to," he said arrogantly. "Besides, who else are you going to trust? Stanton? Or maybe you'd like to speak to clan Sangre. If you think you can fight the Grigori alone, be my guest to carry on without us." He paused for a second to scratch his head. "Look, I realize not all of Danel's strategies have worked in the past … but this will work, because it's my plan."

I crossed my arms over my chest. "Maybe you tell me this brilliant plan of yours, and then I'll decide if we can trust you or not."

Leo gave me a grim smile in response. "Samyaza, Corinth, Vinson, and I will prepare for battle here while you and Alastair go with Diniel and Tamiel to Eleutheros and gather volunteers."

I threw a hand to my head, frustrated. "Okay—even if we do leave to gather an army, that still doesn't explain what you plan on doing about Angela."

"That's the part I can't divulge. Hence why the rest of the Watchers don't even know about it."

Corinth glanced from me then to Al and back to Vinson. "What do you think, TL?"

Vinson lifted his shoulders slightly. "I like plan."

"*What plan?*" I shouted. "Seriously, guys … we can't trust them."

Corinth turned to Al and me. "I'm dying and we're out of options. But if you don't want to do this, just say the word. We're a team. I want all of us on board, together. I can say that for some reason I *do* trust the Watchers, and … I'm putting my trust in Leo."

I mashed my lips together and narrowed my eyes at Leo. "If anything happens to Corinth, I'm coming after you first."

My head was in Alastair's lap. I lay looking into the fire, mesmerized by the flames licking at the smoldering, charred wood. It broke apart in a burst of orange flame, giving a crackle and hiss. I was angry at being kept in the dark. But according to Leo, that was the way it had to be … which sounded like a good reason not to trust him. I stewed about this some more.

I knew we didn't have time to sit around—Alastair and I were about to head off to speak with Sozo, to gather as many people to our side as we possibly could, but we wanted one more moment to ourselves before things got really dicey. I didn't like separating.

Fortunately, we had the room to ourselves, as everyone was gathering their things and getting ready to head out to our final destination: *Utah*.

Alastair pulled my hand into his, lightly brushing his lips across my knuckles. After a second, he fished something out of his pocket and then dumped the object into my palm.

I glanced down to see the bone-handled knife he'd given me so long ago—before I was vampire.

"Let's not make loosing this a habit, okay?"

I couldn't help but smile as I cupped my hand around the pocketknife, holding it close.

"Do you think we can trust the Watchers?" Alastair asked.

I didn't answer at first. Instead, I mulled it over for a second before saying, "I don't know what else we can do."

He nodded, unusually silent for once. Maybe he could sense the impending doom as much as I could.

I gazed up into those baby-blue eyes of his. He was staring at me as if I were the most precious thing on earth. I inhaled sharply. *Why was he so devastatingly handsome?* I reached a hand up and drew him slowly down toward me, arching my back to kiss him lightly on the lips. I felt him sigh against me, his chest rising and falling in time with my own. After a moment, he reluctantly edged back. He seemed troubled.

"What is it?"

"He didn't hurt you, did he?"

I shook my head, knowing he meant Gabriel. "No, but I don't want to talk about Gabriel. No matter what happens, we're getting that cure for Corinth." I pulled his arms tighter around me—suddenly needing to feel the safety of his arms around me. Security for one small, measured moment. We were together and that was all that mattered. "Promise me you'll take me to Paris after this."

He grinned down at me, the fire reflected bright in those big round eyes of his. "*Oui, madame. Ce serait un plaisir.*"

"With the risk of this sounding extremely sappy ... I love you," I whispered, adding, "More than anything."

Alastair's brilliant smile could ignite a match. He ran his thumb across my cheek, and then he swept aside the hair on my forehead so he could lean down and lay a kiss on it. "You are *so* beautiful. I think it every single day, but I should have been telling you every single day too." My throat was tight with emotion as he added, "It scares me, how much I love you." He sat back up and wiped a hand across his mouth. "I have to admit, when I thought I'd lost you … I blew up. I hit Corinth—"

I quickly sat up, searching his eyes. "You hit Corinth?"

He nodded and then frowned as if ashamed of his behavior. "I couldn't stand you being gone and not knowing what had happened … I thought Corinth was going to kill you back in the barn—I saw all that darkness and rage roiling through him. I know it's not his fault and that he's dealing with forces inside him that none of us can even come close to comprehending … But when Gabriel put that knife to your throat, I had this horrifying flashback of him turning you. Jack found you after he'd done it, but by then it was too late. I hadn't been there to stop Gabriel, because he didn't *want* me to. He had been controlling me for months. I was the one who gave him the code to Nan's gate. *I* snuck away so he could infiltrate her place. You were turned because of *me*. It kills me that I couldn't prevent him from turning you, even if I had been there to stop him. I probably would have watched him do it—*I might have*. I don't remember." I could hear the anguish in his voice now. He let out a deep breath, as if this had been weighing on him for quite some time. "I let him take you … and back there in the barn … I just … I couldn't …" He broke off. "I took it out on Corinth, and that was wrong of me."

I fit myself into the curve of his side, laying my head under his chin. I could feel the pulse thumping in his neck, his warm skin against mine. *Human.*

"Have you told Corinth any of this?" I asked slowly.

"Sort of … not really. I need to. Did he tell you his

father is Dave? And that Dave isn't coming back? And that the blade he carries is the Spear of Destiny?"

I jerked back up into a sitting position at hearing that. "*What?* You're just now telling me this? *Holy* relics …"

"A lot has happened since you left," Alastair whispered softly. "Dave must have told him when they met the last time, while Corinth was still in his coma. He sacrificed himself in order to give Corinth the last of his strength. It's a bad deal all the way around."

"*Oh, man.*" I threw my legs off the couch and pressed a hand to my head. "He must be an emotional wreck. Dave is gone for good. No wonder he was so upset back in the barn—it makes so much sense now. Why didn't he tell me?"

Alastair shrugged. "I think he's still processing everything."

We went quiet for a moment, and then I turned to face him. "Is that why you want me to be human again?" I asked. "Because of what Wrentmore did to you, and because of vampires like Gabriel Stanton? Because not all vamps are bad."

Alastair blew out a deep breath. "Wow, you're eerily intuitive sometimes … You know I hate the idea of Gabriel controlling anything. It's simple really: I want to take that away from him. And I know not all vamps are bad …"

"Alastair, promise me you'll stop blaming yourself for everything. Me being turned wasn't your fault—Gabriel was compelling you without your knowledge. I do know one thing though, Stanton knew where Corinth was his entire life, and he kept it secret from the Grigori. I think he was protecting him—I mean, obviously for all the wrong reasons … but he could have sided with Angela long before now. There's good in him, and I saw it—if only for a moment. Maybe what he said about us being on the same side was right—he just doesn't know how to get back to that person he used to be."

"You don't get to defend his actions, Larna." His voice came out whisper soft, but it didn't feel that way to me. He might as well have been shouting. "Stanton doesn't do anything unless it benefits him in some way. He wanted to devise a way to get the cure from Corinth, thinking it was just about his bloodline—but it's more than that—"

I was going to tell him about Xerxes and Thermopylae, my views on why I didn't want to be human again, but Corinth shambled back into the living room right at that exact moment, interrupting my train of thought.

I stood suddenly. "Corinth, why didn't you tell me about Dave? He's your biological father? And your weapon … It's the Spear of *freaking* Destiny."

There were dark half-moon shadows under his eyes. Feverish splotches marked the tips of his cheeks, but he appeared stronger than he had before.

"Al told you …" His eyes darted to Alastair, who was still sitting on the couch, his head bowed, and then Corinth glanced back to me. "Danel. That's his real name. He … was … my biological father."

"Why didn't you tell me?" I pressed. "That's too much for anyone to handle all by themselves."

He raised an eyebrow. "Well, aside from Gabe

abducting you before I had the chance … we're all kind of dealing with a lot right now. I'm still coming to terms with everything. I'm not sure I can even tell my parents how I feel at this point."

I crossed the room in two strides and stood up on my tiptoes to rest a hand on his shoulder, peering into his honey-colored eyes. "Whatever you need, I'm here for you."

His lips hitched up on one side in that classic grin of his. "I know."

My gaze landed on the red Converse on his feet. I looked back up at him questioningly.

He lifted his shoulders coolly as if to say, "So what?" "If I'm gonna die, at least I'll go out in style."

"You're not dying. None of us are. And since you're wearing your Converse, I'm going to wear my dad's duster." I shot a glance back at Alastair. "You wearing the leather jacket?"

"That jacket goes with me everywhere," Alastair answered.

I turned back to Corinth. "You sure about us leaving you behind with these angels? I don't like us separating. It feels wrong."

Corinth pulled a face. "If there's anyone you can leave me behind with, it's going to be a handful of elite warrior angels. Besides, I like Ikari and Sam. I need to get to know Tami and Din. We'll have to have a barbecue in order for me to really get to know them all. I need to suss out what type of movies they like—"

I smacked him playfully on the shoulder. "What about Leo?"

He shrugged. "Oh, he's a Thor fan—"

I smacked him again and he grabbed his arm, acting mock offended. "I don't know why, but there's something about him that makes me want to trust him. You've got to let me go, Larns. I'll be all right, I promise. And you forget, I can transport myself with a snap of my fingers. If there's danger, I'll hightail it out of here and meet you at the clan."

That actually made me feel better.

Nan marched into the living room from her extravagant bedroom, situated off to the left of the stairs, toward the rear of the house. She was adjusting brown leather vambraces at each wrist, and wearing a tactical vest over a dark green T-shirt and matching pants. Sharp gray eyes offset her braided silver hair and black skin. Strapped to her back were two very wicked-looking samurai swords. I wouldn't want to go up against her, that was for sure. All of our jaws dropped collectively at seeing her so … armed to the teeth.

Corinth opened and closed his mouth like a fish sucking air, but before he could say anything, I beat him to the punch.

"You're coming with us?"

Her severe expression was beyond frightening. "Too many of us have lost our lives over these fools—the Grigori. Jack and Paul were my family, and now they're buried on my property. It's time we found them some justice."

"Are those vambraces?" I asked, pointing at the leather armor at her wrists.

She tilted her head to the side, her gaze icy. "Who do

you think taught your father how to use them?"

Corinth swallowed heavily and, too overcome by his burgeoning emotions, could only nod at her gratefully.

Imani sauntered in from outside, the porch door swinging open as she entered along with a cold breeze. I noticed she was wearing all red leather tactical gear. Corinth did a double take. If he had been drinking something, I was sure he would have spit it out. She had on a belt with several of those round grenade devices hanging from it, and sheaths wrapped around her thighs with multiple throwing knives tucked into tiny slots.

"You ready, *Sparky?*" she asked Corinth.

I noticed the rush of blood flooding his cheeks as he cleared his throat. "Good grief," he mumbled. "She's going to be the death of me—but what a glorious death that would be indeed."

Alastair grunted as Vinson walked in from outside, behind Imani, stomping a fresh smattering of packed snow onto Nan's floor. She gave him a stern look as he stormed in. He was wearing a white coat, white pants, and matching combat boots, and his rifle was slung over one shoulder.

Alastair was beside Corinth now. He gripped Corinth's forearm. "I'm sorry I hit you, brother."

"I deserved it," he said with a toothy grin. "It's up to you now, *brother.* You and Larna go to Eleutheros with Tami and Din. Bring back as many volunteers as you can, and meet us in Utah in two days' time. We're going to need that army."

Alastair pursed his lips and then nodded. "There's something I have to say. I didn't have a big family growing up. I knew it would be easier to go dark—to ghost everyone. Being a loner was my thing, and I used to be damn good at it." His gaze drifted over all of us. "I had been involved in so much scheming and subterfuge in the past that I didn't know who to trust. That's no way to live. I didn't know how to claw my way back to humanity until I met Larna—and you, Corinth, Nan, and Vinson, Paul and Jack—You all became my family. I can't think of anyone more worthy to carry that blade than you, Corinth. Take care of yourself until we get back with reinforcements. That means don't do anything stupid with those powers of yours."

"Dude," Corinth said. "With speech skills like those, you are *totally* going to win Sozo over." He glanced between us again, beaming. "Seriously, guys … don't worry about me while you're gone." Corinth yanked Alastair into a tight hug and then stepped back, clapping him on the shoulders. "You just admitted we're family. No take-backs. And I promise to keep my mouth shut about having a geriatric brother."

He laughed. "You're pretty good at winning people over yourself. Watch your six. It might get bloodier before it gets better."

"Not if I can help it," Corinth said confidently.

Chapter 43

Larna

WE DROPPED DOWN INTO the center of my dad's cabin on a cyclone of wind and a crash of thunder. Having two angels by your side definitely came in handy. Tamiel and Diniel had whisked Alastair and me to my dad's cabin—a pit stop on our way to Eleutheros.

I glanced around, staring openmouthed at our surroundings. Tamiel strode over to the front door and stepped outside to keep watch, I assumed. I wondered if she and Vinson would be a good match for each other. They were like two peas in a pod with their edginess and no talking and love for weaponry.

I tried to exchange a mystified look with Alastair, but he was gazing around the room in wonder too.

There was a fresh coat of eggshell paint on the walls. The lightning-shaped hole in the ceiling had been repaired, and so had the broken window that I'd been blown out of—not to mention all of the electrical outlets and lamps had been replaced. There was a tablet computer sitting on top of a brand-new wooden coffee table. Displayed on the screen were six panels of live security footage from the perimeter of the property—all upgraded. Even the pool table had been cleaned and set up to actually, well, play pool. The covered back porch had new wicker furniture.

The blood and gore from our earlier battle had all been scrubbed up as if it had never been there. The only scent assailing us now was citrus cleaning solvent and fresh flowers.

Yellow daisies were on the kitchen counter, arranged neatly in a fancy vase, and more were in the living room. I believed Nan's favorite color was yellow. The color of her house was fresh squash. Even my father's grave had lovely little yellow flowers dotting it.

There was a note with my name on it sitting on top of the pool table, in the corner of the room. I drifted over to it with Alastair by my side.

I picked it up and read aloud, "'Larna, I took the liberty of fixing up the place for you so that you can come home to a fresh start when all of this is over. A bit presumptuous, I know. I hope you like the new paint and furniture. Best wishes, Nan. PS Paul's Beetle is parked out front. I think he would have wanted you to have it.'"

I put a hand to my mouth, overwhelmed, as Diniel came up beside me, silent as an apparition. Her light-brown eyes scanned the room for possible threats.

Diniel did not meet my concerned gaze, but her voice dropped considerably. "We should go. I don't know how secure this place will stay—the Grigori have been here before, which means they may still be watching it. I'd hate for this new paint job to be ruined so quickly."

I nodded, and then set the note back down. "I'm glad

Nan has enough faith in us."

"She wouldn't have bothered fixing the place up if she didn't," Alastair agreed.

"Remind me to thank her profusely." I turned to Diniel and then glanced to Alastair. "Can y'all give me a minute?"

Without waiting for them to answer, I was already stepping over the threshold of my dad's bedroom. After a moment's hesitation, I slipped inside and then closed the door behind me, taking in a deep breath before looking around. I wondered if there would ever be a day when I didn't need to prepare myself to enter this room. Or a day when I didn't think of it as my dad's room. I still missed him terribly.

I thought about my mom too, and how she had been through so much since the start of this ordeal. It wasn't fair, keeping her in the dark—but it was a necessity, especially after her freak-out after witnessing vampires trash her front lawn. Vinson had compelled her to travel abroad, mostly on different cruise lines, at least until I could get word back to her that it was okay for her to return to her everyday life. It had only been a tiny nudge, but it hadn't taken much to tip her to go. She had worked as a nurse for over fifteen years of her life, with few vacations spent for herself. I didn't feel guilty for pushing her into taking a break.

The funds I'd transferred to her bank account from what my dad had left me—thanks to Paul and his incredible record keeping on behalf of my dad—were enough to last her for a few more months at least. Vampire compulsion came in handy; she had never questioned where the money kept coming from.

My father's black-and-red checkered blanket sat at the foot of the meticulously made bed. I ran my hand along it, thinking about him. I thought about Paul too. He had been as much a part of this place as my father had been. My heart ached.

I wished I'd gotten a chance to speak with him one last time. A pang of regret welled up in me, the longing so profound my eyes started to brim with fresh tears. They spilled down my face, hot against my cheeks.

I hastily wiped them away, wishing so badly that both of them could be here right now to see how far we'd come. Also, I selfishly admitted to myself that it would have been nice to have their help. I hauled the photo from the nightstand into my hands—I was seven years old on a park swing, not a clue in the world about what life was about to throw at me.

I didn't recognize the little girl in the photo anymore.

So much had changed since then.

The last time I was here, Paul had stocked this room with some of my clothes. I yanked my T-shirt over my head and pulled on a black tank top I'd gotten out of one of the dresser drawers on the far side of the room. A lightweight, sleek-looking tactical vest was in one of the many plastic tubs my father had left behind. I threw it on over the tank and then put on a black turtleneck over the vest.

Next, I checked both vambraces at my wrists, ejecting the blades one at a time. They were just as sharp and deadly as when my father had worn them. Nan had provided me with a new set.

I searched the rest of the room, not even knowing what I was looking for until I reached the last tub. In it, I found a gleaming Japanese short sword and accompanying adjustable leather sheath—meant to be strapped to the back.

The blade was shorter than two feet in length. I checked its weight and balance in a one-handed grip. It was perfect, seemingly made just for me. I didn't remember finding this the last time I had been here, but a lot had happened, and I hadn't had much time to search through my father's belongings—besides the fact that I'd been out of my mind with grief.

I hurriedly affixed the scabbard to my back, making the necessary adjustments to fit my smaller frame.

Once satisfied, I moved to the closet. Inside, I found what I was looking for: my dad's brown duster.

Nan must have had it dry-cleaned, because it was hanging in a clear plastic bag and it smelled of starch and detergent. I took it out and shrugged into it, thinking about how cool my dad had looked when he'd worn it the night he fought Gabriel. For some strange reason, it fit me perfectly. And then it hit me: Nan must have had it altered for me to wear. I wanted to hug the woman. It felt right. For the first time in a long time, I felt the heavy burden of despair lift from my heart.

For you, Dad.

Finally, I stepped into the attached bathroom, flipping on the light switch. The image in the mirror showed me how much I'd changed these last few months. Even with vampirism aging me extremely slowly, I still felt older—to me, I looked older.

My eyes were red rimmed, and I could see the sharp, shadowed contours of my cheekbones standing out in the harsh light. The tips of my cheeks were pink from the cabin's draftiness. I ran a hand through my short hair, spiking it up on top. Chunky blond highlights and jet-black locks made my wide hazel eyes stand out bright against alabaster skin. Gone was the awkward girl. I mean, I was still awkward in many other ways—nerdy, quick to blush; a pop culture queen, those things would never change—but I was definitely more confident than I ever had been in my entire life.

When I walked back out into the living room, I heard Alastair's sharp intake of breath before I saw his gaze halt on me.

My heart lurched in my chest. He was looking at me with a strange sort of pride mixed with desire, his gaze so heated it froze me in place for one flattering moment.

I didn't think I'd ever get used to the way he looked at me. He had no idea what effect he had on me … Okay, maybe he did, because as soon as he saw my cheeks light up, his devilish grin widened, all flashing white teeth and charm.

He looked beyond hot in his onyx motorcycle jacket, combat boots, and neatly combed blond hair. The only things that set him apart from the fifties look were the two pistols, strapped to each of his thighs. *Firefly* chic meets *A Streetcar Named Desire*. It only served to make him look that much more striking than he already did.

The door flew open, and Tamiel marched back inside with a gust of wind.

I tucked a strand of hair behind my ear and joined

them, pulling Alastair's hand into mine. I gave Tamiel and Diniel a quick nod to let them know I was ready.

"Let's go meet Sozo," Alastair said.

We dropped down into the center of clan Eleutheros's meeting hall, wind and thunder whipping through the chamber. It echoed chillingly loud around the domed ceiling.

The gallery was standing room only, just like it had been when we'd first arrived, only this time, we had two very intimidating angels by our side. And we were armed. Thankfully, Sozo had expected our arrival and appropriately warned everyone.

Our entrance was quite the spectacle nonetheless. I watched as people murmured to one another, their jaws collectively hitting the floor at the same time. I knew how fearful they were of angels. I had been here for the aftermath of devastation and destruction wreaked by one Grigori—*Caesar*.

Sozo stood at the head of the huge iron table, his hands clasped in front of him as we approached. He wore a silver robe with gold filigree on the ends of each sleeve. His dark, wavy hair was smoothed back, barely touching his shoulders. I glanced around, noticing how many more guards they had added to their ranks, their hands hovering inches over those electrical baton devices at their sides.

Sozo put his hands up, asking for calm. The crowd of onlookers had started their buzz of excited utterings. I could sense their unease; it hit me like a tidal wave. There were some familiar faces in the crowd too.

I hoped that they would listen to what we had to say. Corinth was counting on us.

Alastair gave my hand one last pump before moving up to stand beside Tamiel.

Tamiel's gaze was penetrating as she turned to Sozo and started to speak. "If we can garner a fraction of help from your people, it would make all the difference in this fight—"

"*Fight?*" Sozo's voice sounded like a gong over the hushed crowd, riveting everyone and stopping Tamiel from continuing her speech. His gaze slid over mine and then landed back on Tamiel. "We were blindsided … given warning by the Grigori to turn over the last remaining *Nephilim* or be invaded. But it didn't matter what we decided—we were attacked regardless of our decision, slaughtered by one of your kind as a distraction to get to Corinth Taylor. The Grigori only left because they thought they had gotten what they came for. The Nephilim's life … *They* fought bravely—not you. Why should we help you *Watchers?*" He almost spit out the last word, and I couldn't help but notice the contempt in his tone.

Tamiel's dark eyes landed on Sozo. I could suddenly see why she was Samyaza's war chief by the stare she was giving him. Most people would have shrunk back from her probing gaze, but Sozo didn't. He stood regally tall, his back erect and rigid as he waited on her response.

I knew she was sizing him up.

After what seemed like an uncomfortable amount of time had passed, she said, "I am sorry for the loss of your people. Benny was one of ours. He lived among you. He lost his life here too. He was your chief engineer for many faithful years. We know much about sacrifice and suffering. There are so few of us left. If we perish in this battle in two days, we take with us any hope of your clan remaining a free and happy people—whether it be as human *or* vampire. The Grigori seek to turn all of your kind against the human race. You will be exposed, hunted, and ultimately forced to turn everyone so that the Grigori can swoop in at the last minute and look like saviors. They will vilify you, make you out to look like monsters. They will then systematically wipe out *all* of you so that they may be worshipped." I heard the hint of pleading in her voice as she continued. "Don't you get it? Your race will not survive. There will be war regardless. You will be annihilated and used just like you were when you were ambushed." A flurry of motion and frantic shouts broke out around the cavernous hall. "If you think you are safe, think again … We can materialize out of lightning and make it do our bidding—"

Alastair stepped forward at this, speaking out of the side of his mouth. "You're not winning them over—you're scaring them." He glanced to Sozo, who nodded for him to go ahead and take the floor, giving his permission.

Alastair raised his voice over the frantic cries so that they could hear him, his voice sounding firm and steady and commanding. "*I died two weeks ago.*" He paused, letting this shocking bit of information sink in. "*And I was brought back human.*" They wanted to hear what he had to say. It was important. I could see everyone leaning forward on the edge of their seats to listen. He was the celebrity, so to speak.

I felt my pulse quicken as the vivid memory of his death assailed me. Even I wanted to know where he was going with this.

"I can only speak to my experience of being human again. When I stand in a patch of sunlight, the world turns into the brightest, whitest, purest thing. It is warmth. You have the chance to choose your own fate. Being human again is … my second chance. My choice. To start a family. Grow old without having to worry about where my next iron-enriched meal is going to come from. Maybe it could be your second chance too. You might have it good here, but out there, the world is hurting. Outside, this place is filled with violence and chaos." Alastair pointed at several of the people in seats in the front row across the way. "I believe most of you want exactly what you've been preaching. Peace. Vampirism was created as a means of control, and you are the key to stopping it. What if humanity can bring you that peace?"

There were boos coming from several people in the auditorium who were sitting in the seats higher up. A vampire with long dyed-white hair, who looked to be in his early thirties, jumped to his feet and yelled, "We don't want to be human. You're telling us that our only options are to join you and fight, or to be enslaved by the Grigori—so that they can force us to turn humans for their own purposes? Well, that doesn't sound like the worst idea to me … fresh blood all day long."

More applause broke out, but the majority of vampires and humans in the room had shot to their feet, appalled by his words. The drone of everyone talking at once drowned out the rest of what he had to say. These people were finally starting to realize how important this decision was going to be.

I glanced around, gauging the audience. How many would side with us? How many would leave to join the Grigori? Would we have to fight them here and now? I wondered how many of these conversations were happening all over the world right now. Word must travel fast through the clans.

Sozo's voice boomed out over the assembly once again. "Please, everyone, hear Alastair Iszler out first, and I will address any concerns afterward."

Alastair lowered his hands to his sides, his fists clenched tight. He shouted over the din of people still talking. "*We are seeking the cure.* I've seen the way your clan works. I have seen your advanced technology, medicine, and innovations. Why are you a peaceful society? The Grigori will turn you into something you're not. Why do any of this"—he gestured around him—"if it means nothing? Are you telling me that you would rather let hundreds of thousands, possibly millions, of people die just to stay *vampire*?"

"*That's exactly what we're saying!*" someone shouted.

"*They can join us!*" someone else cried out.

"We are not asking everyone to fight, but we are asking for as many of you to help in whatever way you possibly can."

"We'll help fight."

A group of five vampires stepped out onto the main floor, heading toward us. They were wearing baseball caps and jerseys, definitely not the normal clan Eleutheros attire. The one who'd spoken stepped past the rest of his group to stop in front of me. He sized me up at the same time as I did him. He had on a Yankees hat. Dark, curly hair poked out from underneath it, and he had one of the thickest necks I'd ever seen in my entire life. The rest of his group was just as ripped as he was.

He held his hand out to me first. "John."

I took his hand in mine and shook it. "Larna."

I thought I caught a hint of a New York accent as he said, "Your friend Corinth, he's a good guy. I've seen what he can do … and for what it's worth, me and the guys here, we stand by him—and you too."

I nodded at each of them in turn. "Thank you, John. Your help is most appreciated. I know if Corinth was here with us right now, he would tell you the same."

They filed into line behind us.

When I looked to Sozo again, I saw the ghost of a smile playing across his lips as he imperiously took the stage once again, stepping up to the head of the table. "We have much to discuss. Larna and Alastair—you are our honored guests, along with the Watchers. Please make use of your old rooms while we come to a decision. Of course, our council has final say over such important matters. We will convene in twelve hours' time—I am afraid that is the earliest we can come to a decision on such an important matter."

Alastair and I shared a look as Tamiel said, "That's not a lot of breathing room to gather up volunteers and get to Utah."

"No … no, it is not," I whispered.

Chapter 44

Corinth

LEO EYED ME UP and down. "You look good."

I caught the edge of tension in his voice, as sharp as the gold blade he twirled in between his fingers. I met his eyes briefly in the mirror. They were startlingly bright—if you stared at them too long, you might get lost in blue-violet fire.

"I look like a kid trying to play dress-up in their father's … uh, armor." I ran a hand along the smooth, highly buffed breastplate. "I draw the line at dying my hair blond though. *Blech.*"

Leo huffed. It almost sounded like a chuckle, but not quite. "Not one to judge, mate."

The armor gleamed gold in the reflection of soft light in Nan's full-length mirror. I had to admit, I did look a tad bit intimidating in it. Nan had graciously let us borrow her bedroom so that I could try on the gear. I don't know why I bothered. It wasn't me.

I looked around. A perfectly made wooden four-poster bed with a fluffy maroon comforter sat in the middle of her spacious bedroom.

In one corner sat a dark brown leather settee and a

window that overlooked the meadow at the side of her patio. Folded neatly at the end was a fur-lined black blanket. It would be a nice spot for reading, I thought. On the opposite wall, across from the bed, was a giant ancient-looking redbrick fireplace framed with bold brass accents. This space didn't have the bohemian vibe that the living room did. It was simpler.

I also didn't see any portraits or family photos adorning the walls. I wondered idly how old Nan really was. Her blood sure was potent enough to help me not feel like I was starving to death, at least for a good thirty minutes.

The house seemed strangely quiet now that Larna and Al were gone. Sam and Ikari were off preparing for battle who knew where, while Vinson and Imani were outside, keeping watch. I thought he grudgingly let her join him. Those two weren't exactly best buds. Maybe Imani was trying to win Vinson over, but you really couldn't win Vinson over—unless he deemed you worthy enough to fight alongside him. Things were happening so quickly. I was nervous now that we had a direction to go in—Utah. I'd never been there before.

Presently it was just Leo and me in Nan's oversized bedroom. He was showing me how to adjust the straps on the sides of the armor to fit it to my frame.

I rotated my arms in small circles, trying to get used to the restricted range of motion. I didn't understand how anyone got used to wearing this stuff. It felt rigid and confining.

I tried to both ignore and hide the fact that my stomach was growling again. It always growled. The hunger pains would not let up. I didn't tell anyone, but every single one of my old stab wounds had been slowly coming back—not enough to incapacitate me yet, as long as I kept the wounds tightly bandaged. I just needed a little more time.

I groped at the curved piece of metal covering my shoulder. "What's this called?"

"A pauldron," Leo said, his knife disappearing in a wink of light. "It's there to protect your upper arm and shoulder area."

"And they make this hard to get on and off, because …?"

He frowned, seemingly irritated by my attitude. "It's not meant for comfort. It's meant to keep you alive. Armor used to be fitted for the individual wearer. Think of it like a tailor measuring someone for a suit. This particular breastplate was made before the collapse of the Roman Empire—so it's a little outdated and, technically, made for a broader chest."

I cocked an eyebrow. "Duly noted," I added wryly. "So, who did you pry this off, anyway?"

Leo was staring off into space, as if a million miles away. Distantly, he whispered, "We can stand against any spiritual forces of evil's onslaught, wearing the armor of God." He shook his head as if to clear it and then nodded at my chest. "This used to be your father's armor."

As soon as he said it, my stomach dropped. Man, I could be an a-hole sometimes.

He continued as if I hadn't just said the worst thing ever. "Danel wanted me to give it to you. It was forged with angel fire long ago. Angels didn't use to need armor.

But the longer they lived on earth, the more they became, in a way, human—weaker than before they came here. It's what eventually led them to craft a material strong enough to withstand bolts of lightning." Offhandedly he added, "That's the real reason why Angela hates Nephilim so much. She believes they are to blame for her loss of power."

"Why would she think that?" I asked.

He slow-blinked at me as if I weren't catching on fast enough to anything he was trying to tell me. "Because you are the product of a union that should never have happened in the first place. You are a weak link in the chain. Over time, that chain eventually breaks."

"It almost sounds as if you believe what Angela is spewing …" I let the sentence trail off, glancing at Leo's reflection in the mirror again. I couldn't get a read on the guy. He was a steel vault.

After a second of awkward silence stretching between us, I said, "So why didn't Danel ever wear this? He always had on that dorky linen suit and hat."

Leo pointed at my feet. "Probably for the same reason you wear those red shoes. Like father, like son."

"Were you close with Danel?" I asked hesitantly. "I mean, back in the barn, when I mentioned him not coming back, you seemed … so angry."

"What do you want to know?" he asked, flicking a glance at me before making some minor adjustments on the steel plate at my back. It seemed to me like he was trying to avoid meeting my sudden scrutiny.

"I don't know. I just found out he was my father and now he's gone. What kind of, uh, angel was he?"

When I glanced back up, I caught a flicker of something in his eyes—a hint of dark jealousy, maybe, that hadn't been there a moment before—and then it was gone, and I was left wondering if I'd only imagined it.

Leo's voice came out sounding hoarse. "You should know, he sacrificed himself for you because he believed you could end all of this. Was he right?"

I went quiet for a second, pretending to study myself in the mirror, wishing I knew what else to say—wishing I could say yes. Suddenly my chest felt constricted. I couldn't breathe. "Can you help me out of this?"

Leo inched closer and reached out to polish a smudge at my shoulder. It seemed an odd sort of gesture to me. And then he was yanking off the piece at my back and jerking at the straps at my sides, helping me out of the armor in quick, brusque movements. As each piece came off, I started to breathe a little easier.

Lastly, he tossed the chest plate onto Nan's bed. I could tell he wanted to say something else. He was clearly frustrated, but I had no idea why. He turned his back on me, his hands on his hips. His own armor glittered like fish scales. He looked way more put together than I ever would in mail.

"Was it something I said?"

"Why trust me at my word?" he demanded, whirling around to face me. "I didn't tell you anything." He sounded conflicted and guilty and resigned all at the same time.

I lifted my shoulders in an exaggerated shrug as a tiny alarm bell went off in my head. Something *was* definitely wrong. I couldn't quite put my finger on what gave me this feeling. Maybe it was his precise and controlled movements. Everything he'd been doing since he'd walked into the room seemed … off.

"What do *you* want?" I asked slowly.

His eyebrows drew together and he looked puzzled for a second, as if he'd never been asked that question before.

"When all this is over," I clarified.

Leo's glare was as off-putting as his relaxed manner was. Mainly because I knew he wasn't relaxed. A strained sort of tension buzzed around the room, settling between us.

He tilted his head to the side. "I don't think I can imagine a day when this *will* all be over. It'll always be something else … It's why I have to take matters into my own hands. Desperate times, desperate measures and all." He was looking down now, his eyes zipping side to side as if he were deep in thought.

I cracked an uneasy half grin.

"The way you're talking makes it seem as if you don't want me to trust you. What does your plan really entail? I need to know before I do anything else, Leo." My heart sounded distorted as it echoed disturbingly loud in my eardrums. "What aren't you telling me?"

When he finally spoke, his voice sounded as icy as tundra. "I've learned that in war, unpredictability is how you win." He chuckled softly, and it sounded like the tinkling of a bell in the dead of winter—emotionless and distant and yet decidedly familiar. *Why did that laugh sound so familiar?* "I need you to come with me."

"Uh, I am coming with you—what are you talking about?"

"You're smarter than I expected, Cor. Can I call you Cor? Didn't you ever wonder why Danel never introduced us?"

My neck prickled. I made myself stand completely still with my fists clenched at my sides, even though every single one of my nerves was screaming at me to take him down. He was now standing in my personal space. I didn't even realize how he'd gotten that close. I didn't back down.

"I know we don't know each other that well, but you sound … off."

"This isn't going to make any sense to you," Leo said. "It makes what I'm about to do that much easier. I *am* sorry you'll find out the truth, all of it, in the way you're about to find out." He shook his head, and a lock of charcoal-colored hair fell into his eyes. "You see, Cor, my plan has always been to turn you over to Angela."

There came a sudden hum of warning from Thunderblade, strapped at my thigh. The compressing tautness of power crackled in my chest, beginning as it always did right before I called down lightning.

Leo felt it too. He shifted on the balls of his feet, ready to spring. I wondered idly which one of us would win out in a fight. *Me.*

My dagger was in my hand in an instant. I spun it once, keeping it close to my body at the same time as Leo grabbed at me, flinging himself right into the path of my blade.

The blade slid off his polished armor, doing no harm whatsoever, right as his hand found my shoulder, and he quickly uttered the word "*Sleep.*"

My limbs were too heavy to hold me up any longer. Thunderblade slipped out of my grasp. Darkness furled from the edges of my vision like the petals on a closing flower, and then a most welcome and overpowering sense of peace hit me. *Peace.*

Before I hit the ground, I heard him whisper, "Don't worry. I'll take good care of you."

Chapter 45

Larna

AT LEAST THIRTY VAMPS stopped me after the meeting, shaking our hands, giving me their devotion, pledging to help in whatever way they could. I hadn't felt this elated in a long time. Hope bloomed in my chest. Maybe this was a sign that they would side with us.

On the other hand, the halls became crowded with people trying to leave too. Vampires and humans alike packed up their meager belongings and were evacuating. I had no idea where they were going. Maybe they didn't either, or maybe they were going to join the Grigori.

As we were rounding the last corner to our quarters, I saw a girl with wide round eyeglasses and black hair tied up in a messy bun approach us. She pushed her glasses up the bridge of her nose and stopped in front us, her head bowed shyly.

After a second, she seemed to find the courage to speak up. Her voice was soft, and I could barely hear it over the drone of people surging past us. "I think I've found a way to help you."

I perked up at this. Her eyes skimmed to meet mine

as I said, "We would love any help you can provide."

"My name is Pearl, and I work in the labs. I am one of the few who ha—" she glanced around "—had access to Corinth's blood work. It … has certain properties, as I am sure you're already aware. Properties that can be used against vampires." I shared a quick look with Alastair as she continued. "I hope you don't mind that I took certain liberties to engineer a weapon using samples of his blood."

I swallowed hard, my mouth suddenly going dry. "What type of weapon?"

"Poisonous darts."

Alastair gave her one of his brilliant grins before saying, "Pearl, how many did you make?"

She pushed her glasses up on the bridge of her nose again. "About a hundred darts and also the guns to deploy them."

"And you're giving them to us just out of the kindness of your heart?" I asked slowly.

She pushed her shoulders back. "On one condition, yes."

I nodded. "What's that?"

"I have been alive for a hundred and sixty years—the love of my life, my partner, was with me for forty of them. She was one of those unfortunate enough to cross Caesar's path when he attacked. If you promise me you'll bring down every single one of these Grigori, then you can have everything I've made."

Diniel and Tamiel were the only ones I hadn't really had a chance to get to know—well, actually, all of them, especially Leo, were still a mystery to me. But there hadn't been time to socialize until now. Our rooms looked the same: white fluffy down comforters and green-and-silver accented floating bed frames.

Diniel was scowling at me from across the room, her arms planted one on top of the other as she tapped an irritated foot against the white-tiled floor. She looked to be about thirty-something, but I knew looks could be deceiving, especially for a bunch of angels who had been around since the dawn of time. Her hand moved to the hilt of the gleaming short sword strapped to her hip. She did look imposing.

Waiting was always the hardest part. It didn't help matters that I knew how little time Corinth had left to live.

I glanced around. "Where is Tamiel?"

"Checking in with Samyaza," she told me.

Alastair was taking a shower in his old room, and because I didn't know Diniel, and we were about to fight alongside one another, I figured I'd try to get to know her better. "So … how are you?"

"How am I?" Diniel laughed, her dark eyes seemed to glow golden in the low lighting in the room. "We are the only five left out of a slew of angels who have been doing nothing but fighting the Grigori for centuries—most of it done in the shadows. Now we must rely on a Nephilim teen to end our war. How do you think I'm doing?"

I rubbed at my brow in embarrassment. "I know, I know, I'm horrible at small talk, and I most definitely don't have people skills … Let me start again. I just need to know if we can trust you. I need to know if we can trust Leo. What is his plan?"

"In answer to your question about Leo, I trust him with my life—and his plan is one that was enacted by Danel long ago, when he found out about Corinth." She looked down, and her long, dark eyelashes fluttered, scattering light as they hit her bronzed cheeks. "I suppose I can tell you more now that the Nephilim isn't here. He is braver than I thought for agreeing to Leo's plan—"

"Have you heard from the council yet?" Alastair asked as he ambled back into the room, which had once been Corinth's, through the other connecting door.

He had shed his tactical gear and was wearing a gray T-shirt. The thin material did nothing to hide his washboard abs. He had thrown on a pair of tactical pants with matching combat boots, and he faltered as soon as he saw my panicked expression.

"What is it? Did we get news already?"

I shook my head.

"I was just telling Larna that the Nephilim is braver than I thought," Diniel said. "Mainly because they are meeting with Angela ... by themselves."

Alastair sank down onto the bed beside me, a hand going to his jaw in concern, at the same time as I blasted to my feet.

"*What?*" I bellowed. "We didn't agree to that. It's way too dangerous ... She wants him dead, for crying out loud ... Why wouldn't Leo or Corinth share this with us?"

She glanced between us. "If word got out about what Leo has planned, Angela would never fall for it. She's been inside Corinth's mind. If he knows something, Angela knows it too. We had to be very careful about giving away too much information—especially to the Nephilim.

Danel and Leo were quite clear on this. It's why Leo hasn't always been with us when we discuss tactics, why he leaves—why Danel never taught him his true potential. His plan is to let Angela root through his mind to show he is faithful to her. If he knew what we were doing, she would know it too."

Alastair ran a hand through his damp hair and turned to me quickly. "Your watch. Track his GPS. Get ahold of him … *now*."

My watch worked just fine, but when I pulled up Corinth's profile, his GPS came up blank. Cell phones didn't work in this place, surprisingly with all of their technology. I thought it was probably a way to make sure their location stayed hidden.

"Take me to Corinth." My eyes flickered to Diniel's. "I have to talk to him before he does something stupid. This was a mistake—"

Just then the outer door to the room swooshed open on a rush of air, and Tamiel marched in. She'd been coded to the room just like the rest of us. I wondered why angels even bothered using doors when they could transport themselves anywhere at any given moment. Maybe they used up too much energy doing that.

Diniel gestured at Tamiel. "They request news of the Nephilim. You have word?"

Tamiel's eyes narrowed as she moved to stand rigidly in the center of the room, her chin held high. "They're gone."

My heart was thrashing wildly against my rib cage now. "What do you mean they're *gone?*" I turned to see that Alastair was bone white. "They left to see Angela without us? Do you know how that worked out last time?"

"It is too late to change anything now. The course is set. We will meet them on the battlefield—at the aspens," she said evenly. "If we even have a small margin to gain supporters, we must use it. Gabriel's clan is thousands strong—if he sides with Angela, this battle is over before it even begins. We must stay focused on the mission."

I turned in a frantic circle, a hand on top of my head. "We have to go back, trace him—*find* Corinth. I need to talk to him. I have to—"

Alastair was on his feet and standing in front of me, his hands on my shoulders, looking me in the eyes. "Corinth will be okay. He knows what he's doing. Remember what he said."

I nodded, not at all feeling confident about that fact. *Not without us*, I wanted to tell him.

Alastair guided me to his room, and as soon as the sensors detected movement, they slid silently open. He led me through, a hand at the small of my back. We left the angels behind as he sat me down on his bed, the door closing softly behind us. He smelled of fresh soap and laundry and his old-man deodorant.

"I don't like it. They sure are too guarded about all of this. It has *defector* written all over it, Alastair," I whispered. "What if Leo or the rest of the Watchers sided with Angela?" It was something I'd been thinking about a lot lately. We had all been so desperate to end things.

"They wouldn't have gone through all this pain and suffering to just give up now and side with her," he said assuredly.

Lowering my voice, I said, "Wouldn't they?"

Chapter 46

Corinth

THE PLEASANT WARMTH OF deep slumber didn't last long. I was still in a state of semi consciousness when my eyelids fluttered open briefly. My senses felt dull and sluggish. There was a heavy weight on top of me, like a blanket. I was lying on a hard, flat surface, with a rock digging painfully into my shoulder blade. I couldn't keep my eyes open long enough to get a good bearing on where I was though. Wherever it was, it was not climate-controlled. Even with the weight of something resting on top of me, I was still trembling violently, frozen as the stone underneath my back was.

I inched my hand out to my side, searching for my sheath, and the blade I hoped was nestled safely inside it. I could feel the holster strapped to my thigh, but my hand came up empty. Leo had taken the blade from me.

I concentrated for a few seconds, trying to connect with my power, but for the first time ever, I couldn't feel the blade or open up a portal to transport myself out of here. There was only a faint buzzing, popping noise in my head. After a few more futile minutes, a sinking feeling hit me right in the pit of my stomach. I was powerless—at least for now.

The place reeked of mold and mildew. I wondered what type of danger Leo had dragged me into. Maybe he'd buried me alive in an Egyptian tomb. I kept envisioning myself surrounded by a bunch of snakes. I shuddered at the thought. It was deathly quiet, so probably no snakes, but still … *Why do I always end up like this? I blame Larna.*

It was exceedingly frustrating that I couldn't pry my eyes open either. Something was definitely wrong with me.

I tried to play out the conversation I'd had with Leo again to try and make sense of it. *I am sorry you'll find out the truth in the way you're about to find out. You see, Cor, my plan has always been to turn you over to Angela.*

The scuff of boots pulled me back to the present, and then someone was pulling the heavy weight off me. Cold air prickled my skin. I started to shiver all over again. By how my body was reacting, I assumed the temperature had to be in the low teens, maybe colder. I couldn't feel my fingers or toes.

I thought for sure my adrenaline would spike as soon as I knew I wasn't alone, but the leaden thump of my pulse seemed to stay the same. I must have drifted off again, because when I came to, I could suddenly hear two people conversing only a few feet away from me.

"Why now? Why bring me the child of Danel? Even when you know what he is to you?"

Angela.

It was true then—*Leo is a traitor*—he'd turned me over to her. *No.* Their voices echoed eerily around me, bouncing off an enclosed space—a small cavern or chamber, I guessed.

"He means nothing to me," Leo snapped. His voice sounded thicker and more menacing.

"Leo, I am more than surprised you've made contact with me after all these years," Angela said. "I must search your mind to make sure you have not been lying to me."

I heard Leo give a grunt. "Do what you must."

It went startlingly quiet for a few minutes until I heard the sound of harsh breathing. I wished I could see them, but I presumed Angela was rummaging through Leo's thoughts and memories, checking to make sure he wasn't lying to her.

After what seemed like an eternity, in a whisper-soft voice, she said, "I have always hoped you'd come back to me. But this … what you have done … bringing *him* here …" I could practically hear the shudder of excitement coursing through her. "You've proven you are more than worthy of ruling by my side. I saw it in your head—your fierce desire to lead." I could feel her eyes rake over me as she growled, "Is he dead?"

Leo let out a low, scornful laugh. "Not yet—he's hypothermic. He's been out for at least eight hours, exposed to the freezing temps to keep him sluggish and confused. Angels run hot as the sun, as you well know. The hybrid can be quite difficult to control otherwise … We both know how powerful he is when he's fully conscious." So focused on how blasé he sounded about me freezing to death, I missed what he said next, but then I caught the word *mother*, and my heart shot up into my esophagus. "*Mother*, I've always been on your side. I wish only to be with you … Father always did bore me to death with his ideals on humans and their equality—blah, blah, blah."

I couldn't hear anything after that. The world slowed to a dizzying halt, and my stomach roiled with nausea. *Mother?* Mother … *Angela is Leo's* mother? All my hope of Leo putting on a ruse vanished. *Oh no … I am so royally screwed.* He had said he was born from two angels, but he'd told me they were both dead. No—he'd said *gone.* So who was his father, then?

Suddenly things started to click into place. Now that I thought about it, he did have exceptionally dark hair and pale blue eyes—just like Angela. The other Watchers must have known, but why not tell me? They walked me right into a trap on purpose. Well technically, I'd walked myself right into the trap and slammed the door closed and locked it behind me.

I reached for my power, tapping into every ounce of strength inside me, but as soon as I connected with it, my head exploded with pain and my breath evaporated in my lungs—surely someone was stabbing me behind my eyeballs with ice picks. I curled onto my side, moaning. It felt like I'd been submerged in freezing cold water. It was a deep ache that wouldn't let up.

"*He wakes,*" Angela murmured. A moment later gentle fingers brushed a lock of hair from my forehead, like a mother might do to a sleeping son. The sudden contact was jarring. Angela's skin and breath were warm against my raised flesh. I sensed kindness in this action. It only served to distract me long enough so that she could slip into my mind. She sifted through my recollections and stopped on the last encounter I'd had with Leo in

Nan's bedroom. The shock of seeing Leo's betrayal all over again was like a slap to my face. The cold didn't just go bone deep; it crept into my soul. Then she was leaving my mind, and I was shivering all over again, violently, my teeth chattering.

"Where's the Blood Dagger?" Angela asked hastily.

I could hear the cold amusement in Leo's voice when he spoke. "In a safe place for the time being. It belongs to me now. I will use it as a token of my authority."

I tried to spit out, "Like hell you will," but it wouldn't come out no matter how hard I tried to speak.

A hasty laugh rang out, and Angela said, "You truly are my son, Leo. All ego. You have been gone for so long. Why stay by Danel's side all this time?"

"Because dear old Dad hid the Nephilim's location even from me, from all of us, until the very last moment. Danel never trusted me. He guessed there was a plant in the Watchers. I have been patiently waiting for the day when my brother would finally reveal himself."

I suddenly remembered how angry Leo had gotten when I'd told him Dave wasn't coming back. The jealousy in his eyes when he'd given me his armor … it all made sense now. I had misjudged the situation—read everything wrong. I jerked upright, almost flopping off the raised platform, trying to shake off the ice water in my veins. *Brother?* I felt sick, and the ringing in my ears started up again. I wasn't sure if it was because of what they had done to me or because the truth of that statement was finally sinking in. *No.*

I rolled over onto my side, one foot dangling over the edge. Almost there … *"You're my … brother?"* I finally gasped. "Dave w-w-was … y-y-your father?"

Angela lowered her voice ominously, snapping her fingers once she realized I was trying to rouse myself. "He is your half brother," she corrected me, and I presumed she was gesturing wildly at her minions, because she snarled, "You two, get him under control."

Rough hands gripped my shoulders, forcing me back down onto the unforgiving stone. I wrenched my eyes open to find myself gaping up at two very stern-looking Grigori at the same time they were gazing down at me, the fear evident in their glowing eyes.

They mumbled words like "Sleep," "Be still," and "Calm down" over and over again, but I struggled against their suggestions, taking in one single deep breath and reaching for every bit of power I had left inside me—

In an instant, it flared back to life. My chest tightened up excruciatingly, and the energy uncoiled. I let it loose on my captors. They flew backward, hitting the stone wall behind them in a bone-shattering heap, unmoving. My fangs were on violent display too, protruding out of my gum-line. I growled in anger, every part of me ready to fight, and rose up, vaguely aware of my surroundings, bleary-eyed and ill.

I was inside a dank mausoleum—resting on top of a stone coffin jutting out of the ground. Weeds and vines overhead hung low, groping for me—zombies digging out of their own graves …

Then suddenly several more angels appeared out of nowhere to seize hold of me, their arms winding around my throat, forcing me back down on top of the hard surface—my own grave. A macabre thought flitted through my mind that this would be my final resting place.

I was too cold and too tired.

There were scrabbling fingers and dark faces and glittering eyes and it only proved to rile me up as more Grigori surrounded me on all sides, panting and growling from the exertion of trying to hold me down. With all their debilitating and icy power trickling into me, I finally found myself succumbing to their commands. Together they were more formidable.

"*Whoa, whoa, whoa!*" Leo shouted, sounding winded. "What are you doing? I had him under control. You provoked him."

A queasy fatigue washed over me. I slumped back down, their voices melodic and soft and distant in the background, like the lingering feelings of a bad dream all but disappearing. I closed my eyes, feeling my *Sight* dissipate. They were just too heavy to keep open any longer. I didn't want to.

Angela's voice came out sounding sweet and husky. "He is stronger than he appears, darling, which means he must die *now*. I saw through your eyes, Leo, how he attacked you with his blade. And I also saw how you looked upon him with hate and jealousy. But there is no need for that any longer. He is an insect meant to be squashed, that is all. We can be done with all of it right here and right now."

"I set it up so that we could have an audience," Leo said quickly, almost desperate. To me though, his voice drifted along softly, like waves lapping gently at the shore. "Doesn't that sound better? After all your hard work getting to this point. He is the last. *The* very last Nephilim. All that planning and sacrifice … just to kill him on top of this dingy memorial stone in Skardu, Pakistan. Come now, Mother, he killed your favorite soldier—Caesar. He's thwarted you on multiple occasions. A teenage boy," he scoffed. "You must sacrifice him at the Tree of Souls. A perfect ending to this Nephilim's life."

I could practically hear Angela's head snap around and her eyes stretch wide at this revelation from Leo. Clearly, she had not been expecting him to know any of this or speak to her in such a manner. It told me everything I needed to know too. I had been on the right track with the vision I'd stolen from her.

"How do you know about that?" He had her completely on the hook now, her voice rising significantly. "No one knows about that."

"You have your ways of finding things out, and so do I. But what I have always been curious about is *how* to enact the cure. What do the aspens in Utah have to do with this? Now that we have the Nephilim under control, surely you can tell me." He had just the right amount of sweet curiosity and brazenness and awe to sound convincing, smooth even. "I must know."

Angela paused briefly as if considering what he'd said. "You know … you are right. But only if you are the one to do it—to make a grisly show of his death in front of all the gathered angels and vampires … He is your half brother after all."

"Very well, *Mother*," he said, and even though he spoke quietly, his tone was dripping with malice. "In one day's time, we will arrange for everyone to be there to witness his death, show all of those who oppose us how truly powerful you are, kill him slowly—he deserves nothing less. I'll send word to our enemies—the Watchers."

Chapter 47

Larna

"WHY ASPENS?" I ASKED slowly, reading over the details of Pando once again. The quaking aspens in southern Utah were one of the largest living organisms in the world, spanning over a hundred acres, situated in hilly, rugged landscape.

Alastair raised an inquisitive eyebrow. "Good question. I know Pando means "'I spread out'" in Latin. Maybe that has something to do with the virus somehow."

He was back in full fighting gear as we waited out the last hour for word from the council as to whether their clan would be joining our fight. I was trying to keep myself from freaking out. No one had heard from Corinth or Leo in at least twelve hours.

"Do you think Corinth is okay?" I asked again, worriedly picking at a fingernail.

Alastair boxed up the last of the dart ammo we'd received from Pearl, both of us now sporting the special guns she had so generously provided us with. "Corinth can take care of himself."

I rolled my eyes. "Have you *met* him?" I changed the

topic. "And fighting through a thicket of trees doesn't sound optimal or easy—"

"War is never easy," Alastair said, interrupting. "It's bloody and horrible and deceptive."

He had that faraway look on his face again, just like the time right before he'd saved Corinth's life and ended his own.

"Watching my father get killed right in front of my eyes … and then you." I shook my head and stopped, unable to finish the rest of the sentence. "I know how horrible it is."

Alastair had stepped up to the foot of the bed and was watching me. I had plunked myself down right in the middle of it. His blue eyes were exceedingly bright. He gave me a beautiful smile that transformed his face.

We were alone in his room, the winter wonderland looking like a lodge in the Alps. The faux sunlight streaming in through the curtains was just as brilliant as his smile. It felt normal. Right. Being here with him. The soft, natural-looking light highlighted the smooth lines around his eyes. It was enough to make my heart swell. There was a softness to him that hadn't been there before he'd become human. The hard edge of his self-criticism had smoothed over, maybe. He'd finally allowed himself to heal. I could see his steady pulse beat out a rhythm at the hollow of his throat. I so badly wanted to feel it beating against my skin. It was a constant reminder that he was here with me. *Alive.*

He placed his hands on my thighs. I could feel their feverish warmth through the material of my pants. There was a tug of pleasure in the pit of my stomach, and it came with a sudden longing to feel his hands elsewhere on my body.

We were about to go off to war—there was a high probability of us dying—and suddenly all I wanted to do was lose myself in him completely. I wanted to forget about how much stress I was in for just one moment. I was afraid we'd never get this chance again. Even though I was nervous, and my heart was trying to beat its way out of my chest, in this second, all I wanted was him. Every part of him.

"Come here." Alastair said it so provocatively my breath caught in my throat. He hauled me toward the edge of the bed and enfolded me in a tight embrace.

I placed my head against his chest, listening to his steady heartbeat. After a while, he tugged my legs apart and wrapped them around his thighs so he could pull me even closer against him. My mouth went bone-dry at the way he was looking down at me with a hunger in his eyes.

"Is this okay?" he asked thickly.

"Very okay." Butterflies erupted in my stomach. "But ... there's something you should know. I ... um, have never ... you know ... We haven't really talked about it ... getting intimate ..." I cleared my throat, hoping he would know where I was going with my awkward rambling. This was something I wasn't used to, being completely vulnerable with someone else. There had always been something going on—never a moment for us to just relish each other's company. I wanted to know what it would be like to wake up in his arms every morning. That was something we rarely had time to explore. I was a bundle of nerves.

"We don't have to do anything you're not comfortable with. It's nice just to have a moment to ourselves. And even though I really would like to explore every inch of your skin … while I take my time with you"—his fingers caressed my cheek—"we can take things as slow," he drawled, "or as *leisurely* as you want."

Heat spread through my belly like wildfire. "Oh, I'm very comfortable with that," I said, flashing him a grin, but then it faltered and I glanced down. "This might be our last chance to spend time with each other—and I don't want to waste another minute of it talking." The heat rose in my cheeks so rapidly that I suddenly felt flushed and light-headed.

There was something to be said for how he affected me the way he did.

He tipped my chin up so I was looking into those wide blue eyes of his once again. I sucked in a sharp breath. That would be my luck—I would pass out right before we even had a chance to get to second base.

He had never even seen me with my shirt off—no one had for that matter. In the past, I'd always been self-conscious about my weight. My body. My self-image. Now, though, I knew he would accept me no matter what shape or size my body was. That was the sexiest thing about him.

I had accepted myself, and all the curves that went with me, and so had he.

I closed my eyes as his hands moved down my chin to rest at the base of my throat. He bent down to lay a kiss on the side of my neck. I draped my arms around his shoulders. My hands trailed across the hard line of muscles on his arms as he inched onto the bed, moving with me. I could feel the ridges of each ab flexing as he slowly lowered himself on top of me.

We fell backward onto the bed, and then I was pulling him closer, my hands exploring every inch of him. His arm was the only thing bracing us up as his other hand encircled my waist. My shirt had ridden up, and his fingers felt hot against the bare skin at my back.

I gasped as he started yanking at his vest, as if he couldn't get out of it fast enough. I could hear the anxious need in his shallow breathing. "You … can tell … me to stop," he panted.

"Shut up," I said, only too obliged to help him out of his vest. My fingers fumbled at the Velcro, and because I had vampire super strength, I managed to rip one of the straps completely off. The vest slid away. Alastair laughed as he tossed the mangled remains onto the floor.

A shiver of pleasure fluttered down my spine. His amusement at my expense was infectious and easily the best thing I'd heard in a very long time. I joined him, giggling giddily as he bent down over me, his lips brushing mine teasingly—

And a knock sounded on the door, interrupting us. We were already breathless by this point, and as we broke apart, I heard his groan of frustration.

I ran a hand across my lips, the ache of desire still lingering. The screen on our side lit up to show us a silver-haired woman standing on the other side, hands clasped in front of her.

She spoke through the door, knowing we could both see and hear her. "Mr. Iszler and Ms. Collins, we have reached our decision."

My gaze moved over the hundreds of gathered people in the meeting hall. They all looked the same. Scared and confused—everyone in a state of chaos. Pearl was standing out in the crowd, speaking with several other vamps who looked just as worried. Sozo was the only poised one in the room—well, him and Diniel and Tamiel.

I tried to take a page out of their book and remain impassive, standing stock-still, my hands behind my back, carefully taking in all the anxious squints in our direction. We stood at the other end of the iron table as everyone finally took their seats, and a hush fell over the gathered crowd.

My eyes met Sozo's. He looked just as majestic as every single time I'd seen him: dark, wavy hair swept back over his shoulders, regal-looking silver robes, and penetrating, dark eyes. I could see why he was their leader. He had a commanding presence about himself.

Even though Caesar had been here for duplicitous reasons, I still remembered the reverence he'd held for Sozo when he'd spoken about him.

Sozo addressed the packed assembly room once again, his voice booming out over the crowd. "Thank you, everyone, for attending this emergency meeting. We all know that in light of recent events, nothing has been orthodox in our decision-making. After having met with the council, we have come to a decision that was not made lightly. It has become increasingly difficult for us to stay in hiding with our heads buried in the sand. We have all agreed that it is time we take a step into the light." He paused, letting his words sink in for the still-stoic masses. "We will not force anyone to leave—this place is still our home—but we must take a stand … with the Watchers and the Nephilim, Corinth Taylor."

Relief bloomed in my chest, so great that my legs almost buckled out from under me. They were going to help us. I shared a quick glance with Alastair. His eyes were shining with the same relief. Finally some good news for a change.

Sozo went on to say, "Much is about to change, and we want a say in the matter before it does. We believe that if we do not act now, the Grigori will win this war, and it will be the tipping point for all humanity, and us too," he added. "Now, I must inform you all that we have received word Deimos sides with the Grigori."

Whispering broke out in the gathered crowd. My heart plummeted at hearing this. I wished Gabriel had chosen differently … I had been so sure I'd gotten through to him. A vivid image of Xerxes slashing Gabriel's face came to mind. I shuddered at the memory that was now mine.

Something stirred in my chest, a pang of regret and sorrow.

Fear took on a virulent form as it ran around the room, all wide, panicked eyes staring back at me. Could we really ask these people to risk so much?

"We have heard from many other prominent clans that have joined with the Grigori: Sangre, Jīn, and Obsidian, to name a few. I have reached out, and with the help of the Watchers, sympathetic clans, such as Ark and

Prosper, have joined our cause. Anyone who is able to make it to Utah in a day's travel time—we are all converging at the Trembling Giant. I know this is most unprecedented, but we ask that whoever is able to join with the Watchers steps forward."

Alastair's lips were parted. I could see he'd been less than optimistic about their decision, and now he just looked stunned. Even Tamiel seemed taken aback. Her usual scowl had softened. She swallowed heavily and lowered her head in, I thought, part gratitude and part prayer.

No one stepped forward except for John and his crew, and they had already volunteered to go with us. I took a moment to look around at all the scared faces. These people weren't warriors—hell, I was barely one.

We were asking a lot. A ripple of trepidation ran through the gathered hall, washing over all of us.

Leaders become great not because of their power but because of their ability to empower others—and I saw it in Sozo as he stepped around the table, sweeping his hands out in front of him in a grand gesture. "I am in charge of your care *and* your way of life here. It is my job to ensure that you are safe and protected, and I believe in order to do that, it is time for me to set an example—to help secure our future." Sozo turned to Tamiel and gave her a slight nod. "Therefore, I will volunteer to fight alongside the Watchers."

A slow murmur worked its way over the crowd, and then, as if this had been the one thing everyone had been waiting for, people started to rise from their seats and join us.

Chapter 48

Vinson

THEY HAD ARRIVED AT Fishlake National Forest in Utah—at Pando—in a valley about a couple of kilometers from where he and his group had decided to station themselves while waiting for Alastair, Larna, and the rest of the Watchers—and anyone else for that matter—to show up.

As Vinson gazed out over the expanse of aspens, rocky terrain, and icy conditions, he realized he had been in worse situations. But not many. This was going to be his last stand. *In America.* He growled.

There were at least a thousand vampires dispersed among the trees.

Snow covered the craggy hillside around them. He was suddenly glad he'd thought to wear all white—that included covering his rifle in white cloth so that nothing about him would stand out in the winter wonderland. There would be blood spilled, but not on him. Vinson was now starting to think that none of it really mattered, though. They were grossly outnumbered. He watched the vast array of black shapes, dots really, on the horizon, which he knew to be clan Deimos and Sangre as they arrived in droves.

Imani sidled up next to Vinson, pressing those red lips of hers together into a hard, thin line. She was still wearing her red leather gear, and she stood out like a sore thumb beside him. His lip curled up in disgust, although, a tiny part of him liked her brazenness.

"Ikari says Corinth is in a dense copse of trees in that direction, inside the perimeter fences." She pointed just to the south of where they were situated. "And he says there are at least fifteen Grigori, including Leo, surrounding him, all of them simultaneously using their power to keep him under *control.*" She snarled that last word, Vinson noted. Imani blew out a deep breath before adding, "They must be terrified of him if they're going to all that trouble … I knew we shouldn't have trusted those bloody angels."

Vinson didn't need to look at her to know she had feelings for the kid. He knew why the angels were so scared of the kid too. If Corinth let loose half the power he possessed, he'd probably wipe out this entire valley, and all the trees right along with it.

He wished the kid would. *Brave but foolish.* The vampire–Nephilim had gone on a suicide mission and trusted the wrong angel. *Leo.*

Vinson wanted to make sure he had the honor of killing Leo first. He had foolishly trusted him because he'd helped save Alastair's life back at Sangre. Lesson learned. Vinson reached a hand up to his forehead, idly remembering how easy it was for the angels to put him to sleep.

He hated them.

Nan strode up beside them, wearing dark brown

leather armor strapped across her chest and a severe expression on her aged face. A long silver braid ran down the length of her back all the way to her waistline.

Vinson did admit to himself that she looked a modicum of intimidating with those wicked-looking swords strapped at her back.

"Stanton just arrived in his chopper," she growled. "Just on the outskirts of those aspens behind us. Most of the vamps are Sangre or Deimos, but there are some stragglers not associated with clans. Our numbers don't even come close to theirs. We've got perimeters set up so no unsuspecting tourists go traipsing into the woods and get caught in the cross fire—not that there would be many hikers out in this dreadful weather, anyway. We've also compelled the forest rangers in the area to spread the word that Pando is closed due to dangerous hiking conditions. The rest of our vamps on the perimeter will compel and catch anyone that wanders too close and send them on their way … but like I said, I doubt we'll have any surprise visitors, not with the storm approaching. Looks like it's going to be a nasty one."

Vinson nodded his agreement right as a portal opened up in an ear-shattering clap of thunder. Wind whipped Nan's braid out behind her as Samyaza dove out of the vortex he'd created to land in a graceful crouch beside them both.

Samyaza's dark skin was in deep contrast with his golden hair, but he looked no less intimidating because of it. The breastplate he wore looked like it weighed at least fifty pounds, and so did the sword strapped to his hip.

With all that gleaming armor, at least they were a

formidable-looking bunch.

Nan didn't bat an eye as Samyaza's gaze halted on her. She said, "Are you sure your guy is still on our side? Because Leo sure did look comfortable down there with those Grigori. Corinth is in deep shit if Leo isn't with the Watchers."

When Samyaza spoke, it came out low and guttural in the back of his throat. He sounded like he was growling. "Leo is honorable," he assured her. "The terrain is too poor for an all-out charge, and we don't have the numbers for it—not even with the hundred or so from Eleutheros. Angela is holding her people back. She will want to kill the Nephilim in front of us—it will be a spectacle for her, to show us all how truly powerful she is."

"*Corinth*," Vinson snarled.

Samyaza cocked his head to the side questioningly.

Vinson snarled, "Kid's name is *Corinth*."

Just then a thunderous *BOOM* shook the earth at their feet as another tunnel of light and wind opened up nearby. Out of its center bounded Alastair and Larna, accompanied by the two female angels.

Larna's face was strained, and she looked white as a ghost as they advanced toward their group. He had seen that look many times before, from infantrymen right before they went into battle. Her hazel eyes flickered for a moment, first over Imani and then Nan, before finally landing on Vinson.

She nodded at him in respect.

It was funny how much he'd grown to like her. He would never admit it out loud, of course. He had kept her apprised of the situation, but she still looked shocked being here, looking out over all of the enemy forces interspersed among the trees and dense foliage and beyond. This was what the brink of battle looked like— *never good.*

Alastair seemed combat ready too, with two pistols strapped at his hips, except for the motorcycle jacket covering his tactical vest—Vinson didn't understand his affection for that piece of clothing.

Larna's eyes glided to Samyaza's. Without warning, she strode forward and took a swing at him at the same time as his shield flared to life. She bounced back, landing on her rump, momentarily stunned, her hair standing on end.

Samyaza seemed unfazed by her reaction, as if he'd expected this from her. Judging by her expression, Vinson could see how angry she was at him. Her face went from bright red to a shade of purple like a plum.

"*You son of a bitch!*" she shouted, and she was already back on her feet again, going after him, but Alastair was there to catch her up, pulling her against his side. She jabbed a finger at Samyaza. "*Angela has Corinth.* How could you let this happen?" Her voice faltered, and she had to take a minute before adding, "*You let this happen on purpose … You wanted this to happen.*"

Samyaza's face remained impassive for an excruciatingly long moment before a flash of doubt and something else lit up his dark eyes—anger. "Leo will *not* steer us wrong. He has fought by our side against the Grigori for centuries, bravely sacrificing everything. Leo's father is Danel, father of—" His eyes settled back on Vinson before he added, "Corinth Taylor. I could not reveal everything to you, because Leo had to convince Angela of his intent to join her—his commitment to her side. If his memories showed anything other than his anger or jealousy, she would have seen it. Leo is Angela's son, and Danel, Corinth's father. All it takes is one slip-up from Corinth, or Leo, for them both to be exposed. He had to convince Corinth of his duplicitous nature most of all. It's why Danel never introduced Leo to Corinth before now ... or any of us for that matter."

Larna's hand flew to her mouth. "Angela is Leo's *mother*?" She sank down to her knees. "I just need time to wrap my head around this. That means—"

Samyaza nodded. "Leo is Corinth's half brother."

Barely above a whisper, Alastair said, "How is that even possible?"

Vinson noticed even Alastair looked pale now. All of this was news to him, but he failed to see how it was important.

Samyaza raised an eyebrow. "When we came here, we became susceptible to human traits and weaknesses, but also their blessings. Leo is a product of such a blessing. Out of the offspring born to angels, most of them sided with the Grigori, *except* Leo."

Nan, who had been quiet up until now, stepped up to Larna, a hand going to her hip. "Corinth left you a note. It was on my bed." She reached into her weapons belt and pulled out a folded-up piece of paper and then handed it to Larna.

Chapter 49

Corinth

I CAME TO SMELLING the crisp, clean mountain air. I cracked an eye open to see that I was standing right smack in the middle of a copse of trees. Cold air hit me full in the face, and I sucked in a shocked breath, coming fully awake. A gust of wind blew a lock of hair into my eyes. I tried to reach up to brush it out of my face and realized with a growing sense of dread that I couldn't move anything except for my head.

I glanced down. The red of my shoes stood out harshly against the pure white of the snow under my feet. I was standing rigidly at attention, my hands behind my back, a force I knew quite well holding me in place, against my will. Not exactly the most pleasant way to wake up, I had to admit.

There was a familiar crackle and sizzle in the air. I tilted my head to the side to see that there was a long line of Grigori behind me. They were using their powers to keep me restrained. I might have been able to break free had there only been six of them.

By my count there were fifteen.

Even though it was incredibly hard, I didn't fight

their hold over me—not yet. I needed to reserve my strength for now.

I'd broken out of Angela's grasp before, and she'd been extremely powerful—but I'd never had to fight off this many angels before, besides the fact that I didn't have Thunderblade. Its absence was making me angrier by the second. I had never gone this long without it. But I didn't reach out for it—not yet.

In the middle of the row of angels, I could see a throne made out of an old, gnarled white tree trunk. Ivy and obsidian-colored roses snaked up and around the base, and white bark curved around to form the back of the seat. Tiny red berries lined the top of the throne, sparkling like little red rubies. Of course there was a throne. There was always a throne. My eyes ticked over to the woman perched regally on the edge of the seat. Angela didn't look like an angel. She looked like the Devil incarnate—or an executioner, I thought. The hood of her robe hid most of her face from view, but her overly white teeth and startlingly blue eyes stood out—eyes just like Leo's.

Leo is my half brother. That lying snake.

A part of me still didn't believe it. I craned my neck around, searching for him, but all I could see were the thousands of vampires dotting the craggy hillside and beyond in front of me. They looked like pepper flakes in a mound of salt. Angela had walled us off from the rest of her forces. I could see the faint outline of shimmering light, the telltale sign of an angel barrier. Turiel, Leo, Angela, and I were the only ones inside the shield she'd formed around us.

She wasn't taking any chances this time—not with an army out there. I took in a deep, calming breath and then another, taking in my surroundings again. The trees had that same white-and-gray bark as the throne, their branches stripped of leaves during the winter months, spindly, bare limbs reaching toward the heavens. *Trembling Giant.* It was both eerie and surreal being here. Mainly because I knew this was where it was going to end.

It was a breathtaking sight. The fresh powder snow. The forest. The vast wilderness greeting me on all sides. It chilled me to no end, thinking about all this beauty being wiped out in one sweep of ugliness and violence. I knew what was about to take place.

I'd seen it in my nightmares often enough.

I had been standing atop a mountain of skulls and bones and gore. I had slaughtered everyone and everything around me. I'd taken pleasure in the crunch of brittle bones beneath my feet. It was as satisfying as walking on seashells at the beach. The feeling of wanting more blood and devastation on my hands—to feast on it—had always lingered long after I'd woken up from it.

Please don't let that be a premonition.

A flicker of movement in front of me brought me fully back to the present—a familiar face dropped in front of mine, so close I could feel their hot, rancid breath on my face. Blond hair. Perfect dimples. Once-upon-a-time-good looks. That ugly mass of pale, puckered skin surrounding that horribly broken nose … *Turiel.*

He smirked, and when he spoke, it sounded like he was pinching his nose. "I'm going to make sure you pay for what you did to me."

I barked out a laugh. "It sounds like you've just inhaled a hot-air balloon's worth of helium." I added dryly, "*Totally worth it.*"

Turiel planted a flat palm against my forehead.

My eyes slammed shut. When I opened them again, I found that I was no longer on solid ground. I was fully submerged in a cold, endless ocean—deep underneath the water's black surface. I couldn't breathe. I could barely see. My lungs were already on fire. It was terrifying.

I kicked out, trying to swim toward that tiny patch of teasing light above me. As hard as I was kicking now, I should have made *some* progress. Somewhere in the back of my mind, I knew Turiel was making me see this, but my ears screamed with the piercing pain of being so deep underwater.

I held my breath for as long as I could, but it only took one more minute for me to start swallowing burning salt water into my lungs—

Right before I could finish drowning, I burst out of my delirium, gasping and choking, but not on water … on air.

Turiel's smile greeted me, and it said, "I bested you."

"I'm going to make you regret living," he breathed. "*Drowning.* Everyone has that fear, right?"

I don't know how long Turiel forced me to believe I was drowning. It could have only been minutes at a time, or an eternity. I had moments of lucidity where I didn't feel like I was dying. I'd break out of the hallucination, convulsing and gasping for air, my chest heaving up and down like I'd just sprinted fifty miles in two seconds. I wasn't actually underwater, but it sure felt that way.

When I came out of this round of torture, I realized the mist had thickened, threatening to turn into sleet at any moment.

My gaze drifted to his gloating face. His upturned broken nose suddenly looked piggish in this light. I imagined him with a corkscrew tail and laughed. And kept laughing. I dry heaved and then tried to double over, but my body refused to give an inch.

Turiel didn't find my amusement amusing, apparently. He had been looking down on me with a slight smile tugging the corners of his lips, but when he saw me chuckling, he drew his brows in with effort and flew at me, wrapping strong hands around my neck in an iron grip, efficiently cutting off my oxygen.

"You could … do … with a breath mint," I gasped.

For a moment, everything dulled to a fine point as bright patches of light exploded across my vision, the hum of electricity faded—

Someone collided with Turiel, hard. He went down on his knees, slipping in the ice and sludge, panting and red-faced.

As I caught my breath and my vision cleared, I realized in a dazed stupor that the person who'd attacked Turiel was *Leo*—just the guy who'd planned on killing me in a few short hours, maybe less.

"What do you think y-y-you're doing, Leo?" Turiel spluttered angrily.

Leo's pale blue eyes flashed dangerously. "You were going to kill him." He wiped a hand across his polished armor. "That's my job."

Turiel got to his feet, scrubbing at the caked-on mud

on his cloak, his eyes narrowing in suspicion. "I never liked you, Leo—I think you're lying about being on our side." His eyes skimmed over to Angela, who was watching the two have their showdown. "You know you were the only one of us who joined the Watchers." He spit on the ground at Leo's feet. "We all know you love humans."

"I'm just finishing the job you couldn't," Leo said icily.

"That's enough." Angela held up a hand, stopping them both. "Leo has proven himself. He will be the one to end the Nephilim's life, *but*," she said, "Turiel is still free to entertain us while we wait for the Watchers to join us. The hybrid deserves no less."

I mumbled, "We can start a line for all those who want to torture me … It'll be in a more orderly fashion that way."

I was the only idiot wearing a thin black T-shirt—not by choice—but I was beyond the point of shivering. I didn't feel the cold anymore, even though I knew it was below freezing out.

I glanced up at the sky, watching the gray, rain-bloated clouds moving in. A lone buzzard flew overhead in slow, lazy circles. I hoped it wasn't an omen of things to come. It had happened the same way in my nightmare too—the rain coming down in sheets, dripping off my face, pouring down my throat, choking me—

And then I was choking all over again, gasping for precious oxygen.

Turiel might as well have forced my head underwater. The sensation wasn't any less real. I bit my tongue, and it instantly reminded me of when I'd broken out of Angela's grasp. I fought back, pushing against his mental invasion, using the same technique I'd used against Ikari and Angela. I felt his mind recoil instantly, and then his presence disappeared. I came out of it, only this time he was the one gasping for air and not me. Turiel grabbed his head and sank to a knee, too surprised to speak.

"Let it be known that *Turiel* will be the first one I strike down," I snarled.

His headful of curly blond hair shook as he laughed, but he didn't try to torture me again, or get up for that matter.

Leo eased my blade free of the sheath at his hip. A part of me was insanely irritated that he had it in his possession. The other part of me was glad I finally knew whose fingers to pry it out of. There was something decidedly deadly about those precise mannerisms, as if he were a predator assessing his prey before an attack.

He flipped it once and caught it deftly by the handle, pointing the blade at Turiel. "Mother, make your pet stop," he snapped. "I'm trying to think, and I can't with the *hybrid* gasping for breath every few minutes … In fact, I believe it's my turn." In a sharp flicker of movement, Leo was beside me. I couldn't help but notice how smooth and pale and deadly his hands looked curled around the hilt of my dagger. His armor gleamed unnaturally bright in the storm-darkened gloom, no trace of sunlight in sight.

I couldn't quite keep the furious undertone out of my voice when I spoke. "I take it family dinners at your place are out of the question."

"I thought about revealing the big secret to you many

times over, but in the end, it doesn't matter." I heard the bitter crispness in his voice, and something else—concern, maybe.

"You almost sound like you care what happens to me. I would ask you why Dave didn't mention you before now, but it seems obvious … He wanted to hide the truth from me about you … *and* her. How disappointed in you he must have been." My gaze slid back over to Angela, who was now watching us closely, perched on the edge of her ivy-covered throne, a fingernail resting on her chin in thought.

I glanced down to my own weapon he had pointed at my jugular. "You do realize I can take that from you."

"I know that." His pale blue eyes sparked as he said, "But Angela doesn't."

I started to say something snarky but then stopped myself short as soon as his words sank in. "Wait, what?"

"Remember what I told you back at Nan's—how I would take care of you."

I couldn't read his blank face. *What is he playing at?* I didn't think he sounded vehement. Actually, it was the opposite. I could hear a hint of fondness in his voice, like how an older brother might really sound if he was looking out for his younger brother.

"You're doing a bang-up job so far," I said carefully.

He leaned in closer, his British accent back in full force. "I *will* keep my word," he insisted. "Angela has no idea just what you and this blade are truly capable of. Are you ready to show her?"

With a dark grin, I said, "I'm dying to."

"She trusts me now. I have been trying to convince

her to tell me how to enact the cure, but in order to do that, I think I'm going to have to goad her into it. You'll know when to act. This is my apology in advance."

I heard the promise in his voice, and something else, but he was already gone before I could answer. I pushed down the sudden flood of hope flaring in my chest. *Conceal, don't feel. Please let that mean what I think it means.* I wasn't alone. I wasn't putting myself through this torture for nothing.

In the distance, I could see the blurry shape of a dark figure approaching. When the form got closer, I was able to make out a stylish onyx full-length tweed coat, and then the faint pink scar on the left side of that olive-toned cheek. Stanton. *Of course he is here.* Dave had been right about him all along. He wore fashionable black leather gloves.

I watched him enter our little inner sanctum, the shield dropping just long enough so he could pass through it to join the rest of our merry band.

He stopped in front of Angela and bowed slightly.

I rolled my eyes. *Oh, brother.*

With a flourish, she said, "Nice of you to join us, Mr. Stanton."

"I am happy to be here, as you commanded, *Angela*."

The way he said it made me think he wasn't happy at all. But if Angela caught the hint of sarcasm from Gabe, she didn't show it. Instead, she formally dismissed him with a wave of her hand.

He moved away from her and stepped up beside me, his gloved hands clasped together in front of him, looking straight ahead without a word or comment, pompous as usual.

"I really wish you would stop wearing that cologne." I turned my head slightly so I could look at him out of the corner of my eye. "*Seriously?* You look like someone just ripped right into one of your birthday presents at your own party. Normally, you'd have one of those superior, stick-up-your-butt looks on your face right now—you know, 'cause I'm all trussed up, ready for sacrifice." I hesitated. "I guess I just never thought I'd see the day when you were the subordinate … the lower class … the underling—"

"I chose the winning side," he snapped, refusing to meet my glare. "That's all you need to know, Mr. Taylor."

Behind us, Leo was already back by Angela's throne, a hand slung over the top of it as he leaned in to speak to her in a hushed tone. With my vamp hearing, I could still make out what he was saying.

"Where exactly is this cure? Surely you can tell me." He gestured toward the towering shield separating us from the rest of the vampire army. The sharp tip of my blade glinted bright as a patch of sunlight escaped through a brief parting of clouds. "Don't keep me waiting."

She held up a finger. "All in due time, child—the Watchers must be here to see you kill their precious hybrid first. And then I will tell you anything you want to know."

Chapter 50

Larna

Collins,

Just to be on the safe side, don't tell the Watchers what's written in this note. Angels can experience someone's thoughts and memories as easily as reading a text message. Vampire abilities mimic angel abilities. Think compulsion and anti-Sight. My guess is that Angela might be able to listen in, or search memories of other angels and vamps. Like how she got into my head and vice versa. It's why Leo didn't tell anyone his plan. For some reason, I trust him. I don't know why. I barely know him, but I do. I guess if I'm wrong about him, he'll kill me. Also, you should know that I don't have a fail-safe in play if he is an evil douchebag. It was my plan to go at this alone, so don't be mad at me.

Tell Al thank you for everything he's done for me. Vinson too. Al's like the brother I never wanted. Tell him to stop crying—he'll get over it.

PS Please take care of my family. Tell my dad and mom I understand why they did what they did.

Love you, Larns.

Taylor

I crumpled the letter up tightly in my fist as fat

teardrops rolled down my face. My head felt like a maelstrom of complex emotions, all of them swirling and melding with one another: fear, regret, love, hurt. The tears wouldn't stop.

"That *idiot*," I finally muttered.

Alastair ran a hand through his hair, tousling his perfect part at seeing my reaction to reading Corinth's letter. When I looked up at him, I noticed how his eyes narrowed expectantly, as if he were getting ready to hear bad news. I handed him the wadded-up paper, and he uncrumpled it and read, his eyes zipping back and forth over the page.

Once he was done, he looked up at me, a muscle jumping out at the side of his jaw as he said, "He's not doing this alone."

It took me a full minute to compose myself. I swiped a hand under my nose. "That idiot is sacrificing himself so he can get the cure," I said angrily. "*Not on my watch.*"

Vinson moved up to stand beside me. He put a hand on my shoulder. I knew it was his way of saying, "Not on *our* watch." And coming from Vinson, that meant more to me than anything else could right at this moment. I needed his faith that we would see this through. I needed his stoic stubbornness. I needed his detached outlook. I nodded at him, unable to put into words how much his help really meant to me. Whatever happened, we were at least in this together.

"Eleutheros is here. Most of them, anyway, including Sozo. They're just on the other side of that ridge." I pointed behind us, through the thicket of trees just up ahead.

Tamiel adjusted the short sword at her hip. "Diniel and Ikari will stay back and organize our fighters. Upon my signal, they'll move in from this position—"

A clap of thunder erupted around us, interrupting Tamiel.

Lightning crackled over Ikari's skin as he sprang agilely out of the portal to land beside me. His platinum, spiked hair glittered from the sleet that started to come down in a drizzle. He took two long purposeful strides and stopped in front of Samyaza. He'd been the one to get close enough to relay information about Corinth.

Ikari grimaced before saying, "One of the Grigori scouts relayed a message to me. Angela wants us to come to her. She wishes to show the rest of us mercy if we"— his mouth hardened around the edges—"were to witness the last Nephilim's death. I await your orders."

Samyaza said, "Ikari, you will lead the charge from the opposite side, through that section of trees from the south, where the other clans are positioned—a little over two hundred of them. Make sure to protect as many of our new vampire allies as you can when you get the signal. Diniel will lead those on the side closer to the lake—to the north. Tamiel you're with me." Samyaza pointed at the rest of us. "Nan, Vinson, Alastair, Larna, and Imani— you're with me. We're going to see Angela."

The wind picked up ominously, knocking the tree branches together as we moved out. They looked like they were telling us to turn back, waving their bony hands in the air in warning. We picked our way across the rugged terrain, toward the fenced-off area. Inside the fence, I knew we would find Angela and, hopefully, Corinth, *still alive.*

I had this sinking feeling that we would be too late. I wanted the Watchers to teleport us inside straight away, but it was important we see with our own eyes how many vampires and Grigori were actually out there waiting for us. How many we had to go through and fight. To kill.

No one spoke. We were all thinking the same thing—that this was going to be brutal and ugly, our last stand.

I checked the dart gun at my hip as we began to pass more and more vampires. And the closer we got, the more Grigori we started to see, their hands sparking with that cobalt-blue energy.

I kept thinking how this had come full circle. It felt eerily similar to the night we'd fought Deimos. Back then the vamps had stood silently watching us like ghouls in a graveyard as we'd approached. Now our opposition had spread themselves out sporadically among the quaking aspens, arms crossed over their chests with wolfishly hungry looks in their eyes.

Most of them wore the familiar black of Gabriel's clan. *He's chosen the wrong side.* My chest constricted at meeting Gabriel once again on the battlefield. There were so many. Hundreds. Maybe thousands of his people out here.

Alastair must have been thinking the same thing, because when he came up beside me, I felt his fingers brush mine. I wondered if he needed the physical contact just as much as I did. It still amazed me how electric his touch felt.

I found myself studying him out of the corner of my eye. Even with him being human now, he still maintained a refined grace to his movements. Maybe it was all of his martial arts training—he was so in tune with his body and with nature that it made him something more than just human.

I sucked in a deep breath before saying, "When I saw you die …" I halted for a second as we came across a gnarled tree trunk looming out of the mist ahead of us, blocking our path. Alastair bounded gracefully over it and put his hand out to help me across it.

I didn't need his assistance—I was vampire and lithe—but it was nice to know he still thought about being chivalrous. I dropped my gaze from his and took his hand as he helped me over.

He turned back to me expectantly. "You were saying?"

"It's something I can't go through again."

After we lagged behind the rest of our group, Alastair said, "I'm not going anywhere. *I promise.*"

I stopped and turned to look him in the eyes. "You can't make that promise."

"I damn sure can," Alastair said vehemently. "Besides, it's Corinth we need to worry about. His plan relies on Leo."

I could only nod my agreement—my throat felt tight and constricted. We were so close now I could smell the overwhelming tang of ozone in the air, feel the crackling surge of charged energy. We passed more and more vampires, and Grigori too. The forest was thick with the opposition. No one came at us though. They all held their ground. Orders from Angela, no doubt. One of them, a gangly-toothed vamp, shouted obscenities as we passed by him though.

Alastair took a moment before he said, "If it comes down to it, let me be the one to kill Stanton."

I found myself stopping again, and so did he. His gaze landed on the outer perimeter of the ten-foot-high security fence looming up ahead. The rest of our group had already started to clear it with ease.

Alastair had this grim look of determination on his handsome features now. "I know you and Gabriel share this … bizarre bond with each other." He glanced down, almost as if he hated admitting it aloud. "But you can't hesitate. Not with Stanton. Let me be the one to take him out."

I was going to argue with him, tell him he was being ridiculous, but something made me clamp my mouth shut and only nod. He was right.

Satisfied with my answer, he whirled on his heels and started forward once again to head to the fence.

I moved up beside Vinson, and he cocked an eyebrow at me, dug his feet into the soft snow, and jumped, clearing the top by a few feet to land effortlessly on the other side. I followed suit, right behind him.

"Show off," Alastair murmured from the other side. He started to climb his way up and over, but Tamiel gripped his elbow tight and transported him right through it, the portal spitting him out beside me. His arms pin-wheeled out to his sides as he slid in the soft slush. "A little warning goes a long way," he grumbled.

I could have sworn there was a slight tug at the corner

of Tamiel's lips as she continued on ahead of the group.

Nan and Imani were already in front too, their steps leaving deep imprints in the powder as they moved on. Samyaza was the last to follow, taking up the rear. His head swiveled from side to side, scanning the area for any signs of danger. Tamiel, at the front of the line, was just as watchful. I wondered if we looked as fierce as I thought we did.

The trek after that point didn't take long. As we emerged out of the woods, I stopped dead in my tracks. Everyone else did too. The word *legion* came to mind as soon as I saw them.

Appearing as if straight out of my nightmares were lines of strategically placed Grigori, all awaiting our arrival. Every single one of their hands arced portentously with that unrestrained blue lightning. Thick, dark cloaks hid their faces from view. Eerie and ominous.

A vivid flashback instantly transported me back to Nan's farm—when clan Deimos had swarmed over her front lawn like ants, all armed to the teeth. This was what we were in for—grossly outnumbered by angels on all sides.

Just behind the Grigori, as far as the eye could see, was a dismaying tableau of vampires dotting the landscape. Some were from different clans; some I could tell weren't even associated with a clan. Some wore all red, while others had on Deimos's black, and then there were the stragglers who wore only dingy jeans and T-shirts— with no armor, no coats, no guns, nor any weapons in hand.

But they all had one thing in common—their eyes

shone bright with their *Sight*, fangs on cruel display for us to see. Most of them were just kids, their faces devoid of emotion, eyes sunken in slack expressions, taut skin stretched over bones sharp from hunger. I could see the hate they had for us. I could feel the cold fury radiating off them.

Nan moved up beside me. "This is unprecedented. I've never seen this many vampires in one place before."

I swallowed hard, taking it one step at time, finally stopping beside Samyaza. He seemed as if he were just planning on taking a stroll through enemy territory and not minding it one bit. He was battle hardened. A part of me wondered just how many conflicts he'd been in over the span of his lifetime: hundreds, maybe thousands.

This part of Pando was not forest—a relatively flat valley opened up in front of us. But beyond that, using my gift of vampire *Sight*, I could just make out a faint shimmering quality to the air—a magic barrier of some kind, and then, further past that, another thicket of trees. That was where we would find Corinth.

I strode forward, toward the throng of waiting Grigori and vamps, fire coursing through my veins.

Time to get my best friend back.

Chapter 51

Alastair

T HE HIKE TO THIS point had taken enough time for Alastair to ponder every possible way this could go wrong. He had seen a ton of bad in his lifetime, and because of this, he knew when things were going to go south even before they went south. That same feeling of intuition tugged at him as soon as he saw the faintly bluish wall glowing up ahead of them. His nerves screamed at him to go running in the opposite direction. He ignored them, like he always did, letting the calm before a battle wash over him.

The dome of light served to separate their small group from the rest of the Grigori, Angela, and … *Leo*. This was how Angela planned to keep them contained so they could watch the show without interfering. All he kept thinking about was how in the hell they were going to get through it.

They'd passed hundreds of vampires to get to this point, but when he saw Corinth and the fifteen Grigori spread out in a line, their hands pointed at his back, Alastair had to force himself to not go charging at them all.

Larna was beside him. He heard her sharp intake of breath as she lifted a hand to point at the wall of light and then at Corinth. "There he is."

Alastair studied Corinth. He was standing stiffly at attention, and from what Alastair could tell, the way he was "posed" looked extremely painful. His hands were wrenched up behind him at an unnatural angle, and his head was down. Damp, wild locks curled up along his forehead, obscuring his face from view.

Alastair could see no rope or handcuffs or other restraints holding him in place, which meant the Grigori were using their powers against him, their tactics obviously meant to hurt and humiliate him. His heart gave a tormented lurch.

Barbaric.

A renewed bout of anger swelled inside him. This was why Alastair had been a loner his entire life—so he wouldn't have to deal with annoying emotions. At least Corinth was still alive. He took in a calming breath and then another. Taylor could be in much worse shape, he thought.

On the other side of the barrier, Alastair could make out a woman sitting on a throne.

"Is that a throne made out of a tree?" he asked.

Larna nodded. "Yeah. A little cliché for my taste."

Alastair noted Angela's eyes were the color of an impending storm, glowing dimly from under a large hood covering half her face.

A thicket of vines, red berries, and black-as-night roses adorned the throne. It looked both lovely and wild, and the image evoked a feeling he had had when he'd read

Lord of the Flies. The book was about kids marooned on an island. They regressed to the point of killing each another by the end of the novel. They were primitive in their thinking—and so were the Grigori. Killing their own kind—Nephilim—because they were not born like them. Nephilim was humanity. Empathy. Something the Grigori were entirely lacking.

He had never seen Angela before, but he could suddenly see why Corinth and all the Watchers had been wary going up against her. She looked as deadly as anything he'd ever seen—a coiled viper ready to strike.

"We're only twenty-five yards away from him," Larna said through clenched teeth, "but it feels like we're on opposite sides of the earth."

He set his jaw. Alastair wanted to shield Larna from all of this, to whisk her away, but that feeling was only fleeting. He knew she could handle whatever anyone threw at her. It was the hurt in her voice that made him feel this way.

Vinson stood stiff, his rifle held at the ready as he came up on the other side of Alastair. There was a certain heat to his detached calmness now. On most days, Alastair wasn't even sure Vinson had a pulse. Today Vinson had a pulse. He knew Vinson wished he was roosting in a tree somewhere, picking Grigori off and starting the violence already. Actually, Alastair was surprised he'd stayed this quiet up until now.

Behind Angela stood Leo, discontent flashing in those kaleidoscopic eyes of his. Now that they were together, with a jolt, Alastair realized Leo *did* look a lot like his mother. Both of them had sharp, angular cheekbones, exceedingly dark hair, and those pale, pale eyes ringed by violet fire.

In one hand, Leo clutched Corinth's blade. He had it draped languidly across the back of Angela's throne—seemingly not a care in the world.

Lastly, Alastair's gaze halted on Gabriel Stanton. Fire spread through his belly at the sight of Stanton. He couldn't seem to clear his head of the guy. Alastair glared at him, his temper rising by the second. Why did this have to be so personal? He knew the answer to that question immediately. Stanton was Wrentmore. It didn't help that he looked unfazed by everything going on around him, standing beside Corinth, his gloved hands clasped in front of him like the traitorous zealot he was. He hated Gabriel more than he hated anyone else.

Stanton's eyes locked on Larna as soon as their group stopped in front of the glowing barricade, and one side of his mouth quirked up in amusement.

Fat raindrops hit the wall in front of them with a sizzle and crackle, the skies threatening to open up at any moment. The electrical buzz of energy served to block out some of the blustery wind and noise of the impending storm as Alastair stepped forward on impulse, an inch away from touching the wavering light, his hands balled into fists by his sides. He knew that if he touched the wall, he'd probably be blown out of his boots, but seeing Corinth, his shoulders hunched and the pallor of his skin ghostly white, made him want to take that chance.

He was supposed to watch out for him. Corinth was his annoying little brother ... Older brothers were meant to protect their siblings. He had once again failed miserably to keep those he loved safe. Maybe he'd go after Leo first. Leo was supposed to be Corinth's half brother.

Turiel's head of blond hair bobbed back and forth as he paced in front of Corinth, itching to be the one to kill him, no doubt. He obviously hated Corinth for what he'd done to his face. There were so many choices for who to go after first—he owed Turiel too. Now to get over this wall …

Samyaza strode forward to stand on the other side of Alastair, near Vinson. Alastair was sure Samyaza could sense the tension building, because he said, "No one take any action. We can't use our lightning to break through this barrier. There are too many of them, and it will rebound back on us. We need to find out how to stop the virus. Patience isn't simply the ability to wait; it's how we behave while we wait that matters most."

Imani stepped up behind Samyaza. "I'll show you how I behave." In her fingers, she gripped one of those round bomb devices. Her hand was trembling.

Alastair glanced at Imani.

Her eyes flashed with *Sight*, and he could see the tips of white fangs over red lips. Her attention on Corinth was laser-like. Alastair recognized that look well enough: reserved anger. But it was mixed with something else—a certain affection he only recognized because he'd seen it on her face before, back at Nan's when he'd interrupted Corinth and her together in bed.

Samyaza squinted down at the device in Imani's hand. There was a flicker of something in his eyes, but then he was shaking his head. "You'll only hurt yourself and all of us in the process. Corinth is not on his own though."

"For your sake, I hope you're right about him," Alastair snarled.

The rest of their solemn group had all moved up to stand shoulder to shoulder in front of the wall, resolute and silent.

Larna, Nan, Vinson, Tamiel, and Samyaza—they all seemed equally as bleak. They were about to be forced to witness Corinth's death, and they acted like there was nothing they could do about it. Alastair felt sick at the thought. He scanned the tops of the trees, far above them.

"Can you jump it?" he asked. "Don't angels have wings? Why can't you just fly over?"

"We can't fly—not anymore," Tamiel answered.

He felt a hand on his shoulder, and he turned to see Larna pointing behind them. He followed the direction she was indicating to see twelve more Grigori erecting a second shimmering barricade at their backs, walling them off from the rest of the outside world.

No turning back now.

Alastair knew that once they watched Corinth's execution … theirs would soon follow. The rest of the Watchers were on the outskirts—ready to fight to their deaths. He wondered if they would even make it through the perimeter fence in time to be of any help.

Stanton spoke first, his voice carrying loudly over a sudden gust of wind. It sounded oddly distorted behind the barrier of spectral light raining down around them. "Larna, your father's coat looks good on you."

Larna stood up straighter and adjusted the collar on her duster, giving Gabriel a cold, hard glare right back. They were all beyond words—but her face said it all. She was going to go after him first.

Alastair clamped his jaw so tightly he heard something crack as Gabriel continued. "I see you've brought Nan out of retirement."

Stanton's eyes lingered on Nan's armor and then ticked to the wicked-looking swords strapped to her back.

At this, Angela finally stepped down from her throne, her bare feet gliding smoothly across the frozen earth, as if the cold didn't bother her in the slightest. Her light footsteps barely left imprints in the snow. She looked elegant in her royal-blue robe. When she stopped beside Gabriel, she traced one long fingernail along the top of his broad shoulder.

After a brief pause, Angela pushed her hood back to reveal her entire face. Her smile was cruel and her teeth pointy. She gazed at her rapt audience. According to Samyaza, she had been waiting eons for this day to arrive—and it showed.

"I had no idea the *first* vampire was going to be here," she purred, and her voice sounded melodic and rich all at the same time. "Welcome back, dear child." She spread her arms out wide. "Tell me, do you like what you have shaped? All of these vampires … your progeny … it seems right that you're here to witness the beginning of the end."

The shock of those words slammed into Alastair. He gave Gabriel a quick glance. Stanton, for once in his life, didn't look superior or exultant. He seemed completely caught off guard by this news, his eyebrows disappearing up into his dark hairline—no trace of any burns, he noticed.

Alastair turned back to Nan. Angela was staring at

her. Just how old was she? There was a hard glint in Nan's gray eyes that hadn't been there before, and that leather armor strapped to her chest served to make her look that much more severe. She had quite the reputation for being one of the oldest vampires alive. There had been many rumors about her age. This was the reason why she'd stepped away from violence. *She is the first vampire. Can it be possible?*

Nan rocked back on her heels as if she'd been slapped. Apparently, *she* didn't know she was the first vampire ever created either. Her eyes were round and wide, and when she opened her mouth to speak, nothing came out.

"You don't remember?" Angela said, disappointment lacing her voice.

Nan held Angela's gaze, and after a moment, she stepped up to the shimmering wall and squeezed her eyes shut. "*I didn't know.* I was fifteen. I'd awoken in the middle of a field, not knowing how I'd gotten there, burning up with fever. I thought maybe I'd wandered off in a delirium. I lived—" she licked her lips "—in Constantine, a village called Cirta—in Algeria, four thousand years ago. My parents tried to help. They took me to the local healer, and ..." Her voice wavered. "I didn't know what was wrong with me. I was starving but not for food ... The healer was the first I turned." Her voice was barely audible now. "I had no idea ... that I started all of *this* ..."

Everyone was staring at Nan with mouths wide open now.

Angela gave a sharp laugh. "I had many failed attempts, but you have to go through a lot of bad apples to find the perfect one ... You are a masterpiece. Vampires need humans to create more vampires. Vampires crave each other's blood over human blood. Thus, the cycle keeps going ... on and on and on again ... Genius, don't you think?"

"Yeah, well, this *masterpiece* is about to kick your ass," she growled.

Alastair felt tired all of a sudden. His gaze slid back to Larna. He loved the smell of her hair, the floral-scented shampoo she used. He loved the way she made him laugh. He loved how she didn't care about what anyone else thought about her. He loved her strength. How she never gave up. He longed to feel her back pressed warm and soft against his stomach. He wanted more moments like those, *everyday*—and he aimed to get them.

He didn't come back from the dead just so he couldn't enjoy life. Suddenly that tiredness went away, replaced by a fire in the pit of his belly.

Angela turned to Leo, and she snapped her fingers at him as if he were a dog that needed to come—Alastair was pretty sure if she had a rolled-up newspaper in hand, she would have swatted Leo with it. His eyes flashed with something that looked a lot like hatred, but it vanished so quickly Alastair thought he'd imagined it. Then he stepped behind Turiel, gripping Corinth's dagger tightly in one hand.

Corinth's chin was resting on his chest now. The steady rain dripped off the tips of his hair and ran down his cheeks in rivulets. He was just so deathly still. Freezing to death in that thin T-shirt. For one agonizing moment, Alastair thought Corinth had stopped breathing—but then he saw his chest rise and fall again, if weakly. Turiel was standing over him with a wicked grin on his face. He had done something to Corinth.

In a sharp flicker of movement, Leo was beside Angela, obeying her like the good dog he was. Leo's eyes flickered over their group before he turned his attention back to his mother.

"Let me introduce my son—*Leo*. I credit him with all of this. He is the one who brought me the last Nephilim." Angela threw a quick glance at Corinth, who was still and unmoving beside her. "Samyaza, dear friend, it really is good to see you again. You and Tamiel and the others can still join me. It is not too late."

Samyaza's frown deepened. Alastair could hear the cold drizzle pelting his armor as he stepped closer to the wall, his face set in determination. "Angela—you can change all of this … Stop what you are doing. Give yourself up, and I will be lenient with you."

She laughed at this. "Too bad Danel is gone. I would have loved for him to witness the death of his son. I am sure he would have loved to see his one *true* son disfigure the hybrid … I so wish he was here to enjoy this moment."

"You will not touch a hair on his head," Larna hissed from beside Alastair. There was a raw, savage edge to her voice now. "He's supposed to be your half brother, asshole. And *you* … don't even get me started …"

Alastair could see why Larna was so upset. Leo was checking the sharpness of Corinth's blade, running his thumb along the keen edge in anticipation.

Before he could stop her, Larna struck out blindly at the wall—

Alastair shouted "*Nooooo!*" right as the wall exploded in a shower of fiery light, blowing her backward off her feet. She tumbled across the frozen, hard-packed earth, heading straight for the second barrier behind them.

Vinson disappeared in a flash of movement at the same time as Alastair started to run. His legs felt like they were stuck in a vat of syrup; his reaction time was infuriating.

Before Larna could bounce off the wall, Vinson caught her up in his arms, and they skidded to a halt in a tangle of limbs an inch from striking it.

Alastair slid down beside them a second later, his hand going under Larna's neck. The moisture and tears glued her thick eyelashes together. Her short hair was standing on end, and little wisps of smoke curled up from her chest.

Rain was coming down heavier now, causing the scraggly white bark of the aspens to blend in completely with the background. Everything was gray—desolate.

Larna clutched a hand to her stomach, looking green around the edges as she sat up. "I can't watch this. *Please …* someone," she gasped, "do something …" Her gaze settled on Vinson, who was still holding her gently in his arms.

In fact, Alastair had never seen Vinson do such a thing in all the years he'd known him. He was sure *gentle* wasn't even in Vinson's vocabulary.

Larna's eyebrows drew together. "Why won't Corinth look at me? I can't reassure him if he doesn't look at me … I can't reach him …" Her voice cracked.

"Пожалуйста, не плачь, маленькая гусеница," Vinson said in Russian.

Alastair understood enough Russian to know Vinson

had said, "Don't cry, little caterpillar."

Angela's laughter rang loud and thick sounding through the barrier, interrupting them.

She was standing just on the other side of the wall now, taunting, her thick black hair untouched by the falling rain. "I wouldn't try that again. You're lucky I want you to witness what is about to happen."

Surprisingly, Imani put her hand out to help Larna up, and after a brief hesitation, Larna accepted it.

Larna set her shoulders in determination as she stepped back up to the barrier to glare at Angela. The thin wall was the only thing separating them. "Why don't you take this wall down and see which one of us wins in a fight?"

Angela waited patiently for their group to line back up before she said, "Your pain is the Watchers' fault. When you witness the Nephilim's death, know that it is a necessary cost. A small death for the betterment of us all. I can see your blame directed at me—"

Larna flicked a hand out toward Leo, who was still standing closely to Corinth, his blade clutched in his hand. *"Leo. Don't do this—"*

"They created abominations—half breeds unworthy of carrying the title of *angel.* While I"—Angela turned to the rest of the Grigori fanned out behind her, Corinth, Leo, and the throne—"have created perfection right here. It is time Leo earns the right to rule beside me. The only way he can do that is by proving his worthiness, by killing the Nephilim—slowly, of course, to set an example for all those who have chosen to oppose me."

Leo waved the blade in the air in front of Corinth's face and said, "This should be fun."

Chapter 52

Larna

LEO WAS GOING TO torture Corinth in front of us. I felt weak after I'd hit the shield, but I couldn't help myself … I wanted to beat my fist against the wall until it was bloody. Beat it until the whole thing came shattering down around us. I preferred the physical pain to the pain of having to see Corinth tortured to death.

I glanced around, trying to devise a way out of this, but when nothing came to me, I finally let my gaze drift back to Corinth for the five hundredth time. His soggy hair was curled around the side of his face and forehead. He looked half-frozen, his T-shirt soaked through. Who knew how long he'd been exposed to the frigid temps. I closed my eyes and squeezed my hands into tight fists. I couldn't make myself *not* watch.

Someone put a hand on my shoulder. I expected it to be Alastair, but when the person spoke, I realized it was Samyaza. "Have faith in Leo."

I opened my eyes again and could see that Leo was leaning in closely to Corinth, speaking to him in a hushed tone that none of us could make out—I didn't think even Angela could hear what he was saying, because she had edged back closer to the throne, away from us.

Everyone was waterlogged except for Angela and Gabriel, I noticed. Angela was somehow supernaturally protected from the rain, and Gabriel was holding a large black umbrella over his head, staring straight ahead, avoiding everyone's heated gazes in his direction. I wondered what he was thinking.

With a dramatic spin, Leo turned around to face us, speaking loudly enough so we could hear him through the hissing coming off the wall as rain hit it full force now.

"How about a little entertainment while I work … Mother, why don't you tell us all about the cure—how you created it—seeing as how the Watchers will be at their end soon enough. They are gathered here to witness this auspicious occasion; you might as well entertain me."

Angela cocked her head to the side, gazing at him with all the interest of a bird staring at a worm digging in the earth at its feet.

"Very well," she said. "For each cut you make to the hybrid, I shall grant you one fact about how I created the virus. As you can imagine, I have a lot to share … so you should get started. I want to remember this moment for a lifetime."

I shook my head in disbelief. "We have to do something." My gaze shifted from Tamiel and then to Samyaza and lastly Vinson. "*Do something.*"

This wasn't happening. It couldn't be happening.

Vinson fired his rifle at the shimmering wall. Bullets bounced off the translucent barrier, ricocheting uselessly off it in a spray of flickering energy. The rounds ripped into the dirt and slush at our feet, lobbing debris into the air, making it look like snow floating in a glass globe.

Vinson's eyes narrowed to two tiny slits, and he immediately stopped wasting his ammunition. None of us could stop this, and he knew it.

Then it happened quickly, the blade a streak of metal. I didn't even see it make contact, but I knew Corinth had been cut on the right side of his cheek as soon as the blood welled up and spilled down his face in ribbon like streams. For a moment, there was nothing, and then I heard Corinth's delayed cry of pain. It gave me hope. It meant he was still alive. I knew he was trying to hold it in, but he still refused to glance up at us or look in our direction. His lack of eye contact unnerved me more than anything else did. He was avoiding us. Maybe he didn't want us to see how much pain he was in.

His whole body was shaking. I watched in helplessness as the water washed dark globs down his collarbone, the red glaring against his pallid skin.

Turiel was pacing back and forth in front of Leo now. I could hear him muttering, "I could do a better job than that ..."

Angela inclined her head at Leo and tutted. "Yes, Leo, I know you can do better. *Oh, very well ...* The virus had to be tied to something living and something ancient in order for it to spread—something that I knew would be around for a very, very long time. The Tree of Souls. This place contains ancient life." Her gaze bounced from one tree to the next. Then she looked up, raising her hands to the sky. "These very aspens are among the largest living organisms on earth. They themselves hold the weight of all humanity in their roots. Souls. Eighty thousand years of life, to be precise. The interconnected root system beneath our feet spans over a hundred acres. Miraculous, is it not?" She whispered, "*Leo*, I do believe it is your turn."

Leo slashed out with Corinth's dagger again, and it was as if the cut appeared out of nowhere. A sizable gash across Corinth's other cheek. It appeared deeper than the last laceration. I threw a hand to my mouth as a sharp pain lanced through my chest, almost as if I'd been slashed through with the blade too. It was too much.

Corinth didn't utter a peep this time, only kept his eyes cast down at the ground.

Alastair reached out to grip my wrist, his hold on me firm.

I sought Gabriel out—maybe the one person I could convince to act. His hands were wound tightly around the handle of his umbrella, but he had a strained expression on his face that told me he wasn't exactly comfortable with what was happening to Corinth either.

As if he could feel my gaze upon him, his eyes locked on me, and then he quickly glanced away.

"*Gabriel!*" I shouted. "*Do something!* Are you really just going to stand idly by while they do the same thing that was done to you by Xerxes?"

Gabriel took a faltering step backward, caught off guard as soon as I said *Xerxes*. For once in his life, he seemed at a loss. His eyes flashed with indecision and something else. Fire. Rage. Wrath. I knew deep down Gabriel wanted to help, but he had been so far removed from making decisions based on morality and decency that he didn't even know how to begin to act. But there was something in his eyes that told me I'd gotten through to him.

"*Dammit, Gabriel, grow a spine!*" Alastair shouted.

Turiel threw an irritated glance at us. "Shut your mouths before I shut them all for you," he snapped.

Gabriel stepped toward Turiel, and dropped the umbrella at the same time as he unsheathed a sword from the handle. His teeth were bared, frighteningly so. In less than a second, his dark hair was plastered to his forehead by the driving rain.

He raised the sword over his shoulder and took a threatening step toward Turiel as Angela said, "I wouldn't think about doing anything stupid, *vampire*."

Angela's hands were glowing, and she had them pointed right at Gabriel. He gave me a quick glance and then dropped the blade to the ground at his feet, acquiescing, but I could still see the fire in his eyes.

Vinson growled behind me. I knew everyone was equally upset, but I didn't think I could watch anymore of this. I buried my face in Alastair's chest. He wrapped his arms around me. I could hear his rapidly beating pulse in tune with my own.

Angela looked displeased now. "Leo, really, you are dreadful at this. I guess I will have to show you how it's done."

I turned back to see Leo twirl Corinth's blade in his hand, his face impassive as he held the hilt out toward Angela, his lips slightly parted. His breath puffed out in front of him even in the driving rain. "Show me how it's done, then."

Chapter 53

Corinth

L ARNA'S SHOUTS OF CONCERN grew silent. They had sounded strangely distorted and muffled through the shimmering wall that separated us.

Still, I kept my head down—no matter how badly I wanted to look up at them, to see my friends who had so bravely come to watch me die. I knew what it had cost them. The cold rain washed the blood down my cheeks and into my mouth. I tasted salt, and instantly my stomach roiled—a painful reminder of just how hungry I truly was.

I spit, painting the snow scarlet at my feet.

Out of the corner of my eye, I could see Leo handing my blade over to Angela. She pulled her hood back up on top of her head, Grim Reaper style.

I wasn't afraid. I felt the opposite. A controlled calm had settled over me like a warm blanket.

It was only a moment before I felt her hand on my shoulder, and then she was pressing soft lips against my ear. "You're going to die knowing the truth about the cure—knowing that you could do nothing to stop it. You will take it to your grave with a scream on your lips, Nephilim."

I shook with rage and energy and fire—all of it coalescing inside me to create the perfect storm in which I could unleash. She had my dagger in her hand. Big mistake.

Her breath was hot and stinging against the deep gash on my cheek. "Do you like the throne I fashioned? I thought it a nice touch. And even though I erected it as a symbol of my strength, it also, fittingly, marks the spot."

Her throne. *Of course* ... the berries. The damn red berries. I knew I recognized them—Al and I had an had entire conversation about them. Rowanberries. Berries that marked a gateway according to the Druids. I should have known—

I felt the cold press of steel against the side of my neck. I didn't feel her cut me, only felt the slow trickle of something warm sliding down my throat. She'd been dying to gloat. I could hear it in her voice. She needed me to know she had won.

The end was what mattered most to her. She'd beaten everyone, and she had to make sure they knew it. I was also a symbol of everything she hated: weakness, humanity, emotion, birth, death, forgiveness, life, unity, harmony.

She leaned in close again. "The virus can only be eradicated in one way—by killing the aspens' root system entirely. If the aspens die, so dies the virus ... Unfortunately, the only person powerful enough to accomplish such a task is about to perish by my very hand."

The truth hit me hard, knocking the breath from my lungs. *Finally.*

And then an image surged up behind my closed eyelids. In my vision, I saw the crunch of skulls and bones beneath my feet once again. The nightmare that had plagued me for months. The one that held all of the death and destruction. Except this time I didn't see the dead bodies of my victims at my feet. I could plainly see that white bones weren't really bones at all—it was the crunch of bark and ash, remnants of what was left of the quaking aspens after I'd destroyed the curse.

Trees can be replanted—people, not so much.

It was a message meant only for me. This revelation changed everything.

I could control the power churning inside me. I wasn't going to slaughter hundreds of lives—well, I mean, only those who deserved it. Everything I'd put myself through. What my friends had endured because of me. Dave had given his life for mine. All the torment and pain and loss was about to be paid in full.

I laughed. It rang out shrill and harsh. Sleet and rain came down harder, painting my hair to my forehead.

Clearly, Angela had not been expecting this reaction from me, because she stepped back, hesitating.

"Why do you laugh?" she asked, a look of bafflement on her face. "You are about to die, and you find this amusing?"

I laughed louder, harder, and there was a madness in it that surprised even me.

Careful not to look at her just yet, I whispered, "You made a fatal mistake when you used my dagger against me. I knew *where* the cure was, but I had no idea how to enact it. No one knew. I couldn't get it from your memories—

they've been locked away and protected by these fools. If I tried again, the chances were pretty high that I'd kill myself in the process." I lifted my chin slightly, pointing it at Turiel, who was only a few feet away. "All I needed was a good old-fashioned confession out of you. Nothing fancy. Just a decent plan and a *whole* lot of acting. I admit my skills are subpar. I mean, you'd be surprised what you can do when your life depends on it, but Leo …" I shook my head, chuckling softly. "Leo should win an Academy Award for his performance."

Water and blood mingled together, dripping down my face and nose. Out of the corner of my eye, I could see Leo give a little shrug from behind Angela, as if he agreed with my assessment of his acting abilities.

Angela's eyebrows drew together as she lifted my blade, the tip brushing the hollow point at my throat. "*What is this?*" she hissed. "What's he talking about, Leo? Answer me. Now."

"Leo never switched sides," I answered for him. "He's always been a Watcher … Didn't Danel ever tell you what the *spear* does?"

I knew I had her on the hook when she spoke next. "I know it holds the power of seven angels. Look around you, Nephilim. There are twenty times that number here."

The tip of the blade scraped painfully against my throat. I would have tensed up had my body not already been as straight as a rod.

Still keeping my head down, I said, "All true."

She dug the tip painfully under my chin so she could raise my head up. "Look at me."

I ignored the sharp, lancing pain, keeping my eyes cast down. "Your people have been keeping me restrained, using up all their energy. The air is thick with it. This entire time, I've slowly been draining all these Grigori of their powers … and now that you have your hand on my blade …" I managed to lift my shoulders in a tiny shrug. "*Yours too*. By my count, that's fifteen behind me. Turiel, and you, Angela … plus twelve more behind my friends over there. What's twenty-nine plus seven?"

"Thirty-six," Leo piped up helpfully.

"*Liar*," Angela snarled, turning back to face Leo. "I still have your blade and you're dying, *hybrid*. All of what you just told me is a lie to delay your suffering. There is no way that you could possibly—"

I raised my head and looked her in the eyes.

Time slowed to an agonizing halt as I watched her mouth drop open.

She knew the truth as soon as she saw my eyes blaze bright with all that uncontained power coursing through me—with the power of thirty-six angels, and vampire *Sight* to boot. I was surprised I'd been able to keep it all contained until now.

I broke free from the Grigori's hold, slipping out of their grasp as easily as a stone skipping across a glass pond. At the same time, she began the terribly slow thrust to carve out my spine through my neck.

Lightning crackled across my skin, shot through my veins, exploded out of my hands, and I disappeared in a clap of thunder and wind, appearing behind her in an instant. A trick I'd learned from her, when she'd killed Ikari's wife and unborn child.

As soon as I thought it, my blade was in my outstretched hand.

Without a second to spare, I struck out, stabbing her in the back. The blade ripped right through her sternum, scraping bone on its way out the other side. *For Ikari.* She staggered forward, tripping on the end of her robe, and then turned to face me, her hood falling in ridiculous slowness off the crown of her head. Hard rain plastered her raven-colored hair to her scalp. Pale blue eyes stood out wide and angry. Suddenly wings unfurled at her back and spread out wide. Massive. Supernatural. Powerful.

I thought of *Grimm's Fairy Tales*, of a dragon instead of an angel. *Can she breathe fire?* She stood erect, unfazed by being skewered, and then disappeared in a whirlwind and clap of devastating thunder and lightning.

Okay, she was still pretty strong.

I threw my dagger into the air, calling for the elements right as I heard Leo shout, *"She's going for the throne!"*

The bolt came down from the heavens in slow motion—crystallizing. To me, it looked like azure fire, but to Turiel, I'm sure it looked like pure death.

He began pointing up at the sky, his mouth falling open. There was a sudden burning, pungent odor to the air as it threaded down in a deafening *CRACK* of retribution. There was a blinding flash so intense that I had to shield my eyes from it, and then nothing but black smoke. It lingered for a long moment afterward, and as it cleared, I could see the crater in the exact same spot Turiel had been standing in—with nothing left of him.

Most of the Grigori scattered to the wind, scrambling

this way and that, diving, squealing, and throwing themselves to the ground, hands to their heads in fright, effectively dropping all of the barriers they'd conjured to keep my friends held at bay.

I turned my supernatural gaze on Gabriel Stanton. He was crouched on the ground, his gloved hands over his ears, his dark eyes round as saucers.

I pointed my blade at him. "Are you with me?"

"Y-y-you," he stammered. "Yes. Yes. I'm with you." He still managed a small apologetic grin as he staggered back to his feet, his normally perfect hair flattened to the side of his face by the pounding rain.

Larna was barreling into me, her arms going around my neck before I even had a chance to look up.

I sucked in a deep, relieved breath and squeezed her tight, returning her embrace. A much-needed one. I drew back, planting a hand to my injured chest—now that I had used a considerable amount of energy, I could feel the aches and pains creeping back up once again. Everything hurt.

My lightning had signaled the others on the outskirts to start fighting. I could hear shouting. It sounded like waves swelling and subsiding on a stormy sea. Their charge was piercing and the clang of metal on metal deafening as the battle raged on.

I gave Larna a quick glance to make sure she was okay. There was black soot smudged under her eyes and across her cheeks. Her hair was a tangled mess, but she had a fire in her eyes, and that was all that mattered. The crease between her brows formed a perfect V as soon as she placed a gentle hand over my heart. Then she reached up to the cuts on my cheeks and neck, and winced in empathy. "Are you okay?"

"I've had better days," I said.

She walloped me across the shoulder—it did not feel as playful as I wished it had—and screamed, "*You idiot! Are you trying to get yourself killed?*"

Al stepped up beside me and put a supportive hand on my arm, thankfully placing himself between Larna and me before she could go at me again.

His eyes widened as he gazed back at the basin in the ground. "Did you just vaporize Turiel?"

Before I could answer, everyone else started to swarm around me. They looked exhausted, but I noticed they all had a vigor in their eyes that hadn't been there before. *Hope.* They believed in me, and that change made all the difference. It was enough to get me to trust myself. I could finish this.

"Everyone get close," I commanded, nodding at Tami and Sam and Vinson, and lastly Imani. Her eyes were glittering like beautiful diamonds.

They formed a tighter circle around me, obeying without argument.

The scattered Grigori were just now coming back to their senses. I felt the sudden surge of panic and fear—fear of the roar of a thousand people starting to fight. Anxious eyes darted toward the din of battle, but I shot a glance to the throne a dozen or so yards away to see a group of Grigori starting to form a protective shield around it— with Angela right smack in the center.

As soon as everyone was close enough, I thrust my blade into the air, using my newly acquired powers, and raised a shield around us all. The air shimmered and sizzled, and steam rose up, making it look like the inside of a rain forest sanctuary. Water hit the top of the dome and dripped down the sides. On the other side, skewed faces stared at us through the shimmering wall of light. Angry. Apprehensive. Twitchy. Several angels had stepped up closer to the barrier. I had to hand it to them, they were still ready to fight me even after what they'd just witnessed. It was good timing too, because as soon as I closed us off from the outside world, something bounced off it in a blaze of energy.

Knife.

And then other sharp, pointy things started to pelt off it: spears, arrows, and bullets … even a stray ax, I thought. My shield held, but I already felt the slow drain of power seeping out of me after each strike.

More Grigori raised glowing hands to throw lightning at us. Each strike rebounded off the shield in a dazzling display of light. I screwed my face up from exerting so much energy. Even after I'd drained a lot of it from the Grigori, I was still dying—I could feel myself waning by the second. Everyone had their limits.

Tami and Sam, seeing that I needed help, merged their angel energy with mine. Everyone outside the barrier was circling the dome, looking for the weakest point to attack. Leo came up beside me to help, letting loose a deadly stream of lightning that sounded like a whip cracking.

I gnashed my teeth and hissed, "I won't be able to keep this up for long. Gabe, does your clan know they're Team Watcher now?"

Gabe rolled his eyes at me in his usual smug fashion. "I have always been on your side, *Slayer*—even though you tried to kill me. I told you, I chose the winning side. Besides, I'll risk being human again, *for now*"—his eyes flashed with his *Sight*—"if it means I can live to fight another day. Ascended beings were created, which means they can be created again, even if you get rid—"

"Not on my watch," I growled.

"Not on mine either," Nan agreed vehemently.

Another barrage of lightning and bullets and knives struck the outside of the wall in a coordinated attack. I had to lock my knees and grab my elbow with my other hand to keep myself from buckling under the brunt of it.

Nan drew both curved swords from the sheaths at her back and held them out to her sides. Gabe eyed Nan up and down in silence, suddenly wary about how old and powerful she truly was. I wondered how much older she was than him …

"So, you're the *first*," I said slowly, still astonished by this news. "If I had known that, I wouldn't have left all those dirty coffee mugs in your sink."

Nan tilted her head to the side, clearly amused. "Vampire rule number one: never tell anyone your true age."

I looked to Leo, and then reached my free hand out to clasp his forearm. His fingers encircled my arm too, and then I pulled him into a one-handed hug. Surprisingly, his grip was warm and genuine. He'd sacrificed a lot, and so had Danel, in order to get me here.

"You had me going for a minute." I put a hand to the cut on my neck, and my face twisted with pain. It wasn't deep enough to slow me down, but it hurt worse than the other abrasions on my cheeks or chin. It must've been deeper than I'd originally thought.

Leo winced in apology as he pulled back. "Your wounds—they aren't healing … I wouldn't have cut you had I known you wouldn't be able to heal … Do you need blood?"

"I need a lot of things," I muttered. "But at the top of the list is getting me to that throne."

Sam interjected before Leo could. "Unless we get rid of the virus, and soon, there won't be anything any of us can do to help him."

Another volley of lightning bounced off the shield. I flinched. It was getting harder to hold together. I could see why angels didn't use shields all the time: it was seriously draining on the energy.

Leo reached out toward me, but I stopped him with a look. "Save your strength—you're going to need it. Besides, you can heal me later when I eradicate the virus. Hopefully, by then I won't even need healing."

With one hand still pointed at the shield, he used his other to start to unstrap his armor.

"What are you doing?" I asked him.

"My armor will help protect you—you need it more than I do."

"I appreciate the gesture, but I can't move in that heavy gear. I can deflect what they throw at me. I've got the strength of thirty angels now. Keep it."

"I can see that stubbornness and ego is genetic." Leo sounded half-annoyed, but he left his armor on all the same and then redoubled his efforts on the barricade, his face contorting with the strain of it.

We were surrounded. A sea of vamps and Grigori were all clamoring to get at us. So many, in fact, that I couldn't see the throne or Angela now. A boiling multitude. It reminded me of a scene in *World War Z*: zombies crawling over each other in masses to get to their food source in whatever form or fashion they could get. I'd taken too much time.

Imani laid a concerned hand on my arm. A jolt of electricity sparked between us. I could sense she wanted to say something. I studied her in that one long, stretched-out second, committing her to memory: red leather gear, tight pants, lots of pointy knives in sheaths wrapped tightly around muscular thighs. That silky black hair and smooth, dark skin … I imagined pulling her against my side and kissing her. How soft and sweet those red lips would feel against my own—

Sam interrupted my reverie. "Did you find out how to enact the cure?"

I raked a hand through my damp hair, combing it out of my eyes. "Yeah, the throne marks the spot. I need to get to it in order to kill the entire root system—one hundred acres of it. Leo, Sam—you're with me. Clear a path and keep them off my back so I can work. I have no idea how much energy or time it's going to take for me to destroy it. Everyone else … Tami, Vin, Larna, and Al … keep the vamps back … by the fence line—it'll be mass chaos if they get through it. Gabe, where are all your people and choppers and tanks?"

He tapped a hand to his ear, and I noticed the microscopic, almost-invisible earpiece. "They're coming, but there are a lot of vamps and Grigori between us. My aircrafts can't fly in this weather, especially with all that lightning you lot are throwing around. And tanks aren't part of my repertoire."

I glanced around at our group, meeting everyone's eyes. "Are you with me?"

Larna put her hand on top of mine. "Until the very end."

"Did you really just quote *Harry Potter*?"

She cracked a smile. "It felt right."

"That's my girl," I breathed.

Al popped his knuckles and then pulled a gun, not one of his regulars, from one of his many holsters. "No, that's *my* girl. And who's Harry Potter?" He stuck his hand on top of Larna's, flashing me that wide, charismatic grin of his. "I'm with you until the very end too, by the way."

Vinson appeared next to Larna and, in his thick Russian accent, growled, "*Please let this end.*" But in a totally unexpected move, he placed his hand on top of Al's, his eyes darting to mine, challenging me to say anything about it. I didn't. I was only grateful.

Tears pricked the corners of my eyes as we all pulled apart. "The day Vin makes a joke is the day we've already won." I looked at each of them in turn. "Is everyone ready?"

Gabe had his sword in one hand, but then he reached into his snazzy button-down coat and pulled out a cylindrical black object from the inner lining. He pushed a button at the end, and I heard a soft noise as it extended open to reveal a very severe-looking thinly curved sword. Two swords now. Just like the one he'd used at the cemetery when he'd killed Jack, except this time he was fighting with us, not against us.

Larna gave me one small nod, her lips pressed together in resolve. "Can you do this?" she asked me. Her voice sounded steady but thin.

"*I can do this.*"

I took note that she looked savage in her dad's brown duster, with dark leather armor laced at each wrist, and the hilt of a short sword sticking out of a scabbard sheathed at her back. She had drawn out the same type of gun Al had in his hand.

We all dropped the shield at the same time.

Chapter 54

Corinth

THE HUNGER AND PAIN and frustration spilled out of me in the form of vividly lethal lightning. Bodies pressed in around me, crushing. I extended my dagger and threw a concussive bolt at the tightly formed group of vamps surrounding us. Several of the luckier ones managed to dive out of the way at the last second, while the rest crumpled to the ground on impact. Fire lanced through my veins, and the heat seared my lungs. Every breath I took in felt like dragon flames unfurling inside my chest.

I closed my eyes and tried to transport myself directly to the throne, but my head exploded in pain. I sank to a knee, a hand going to my skull as something whizzed past my right ear and clipped me on the back of the shoulder.

Did you think I would make it easy for you? Angela's words slammed around my skull like a jackhammer. *You may be strong, but I have all of the Grigori working against you right now, Nephilim. Can you fight all of them at once?*

Leo was by my side, pulling me roughly to my feet. "You have to get up, kid," he said through clenched teeth. And I did. I felt the power crackling out of my fingertips once again. Angela's words in my head dissipated. I realized there was only so much energy my body could contain at one time. I'd have to charge it back up like a battery.

Directly in front of me was a large cluster of vamps who were all trying to use their own bodies to block my progress. The snarling and snapping of teeth sounded frighteningly close behind me now.

"Go!" I yelled at Leo over the clamor of fighting. "Keep them off me—I'm going to have to get to the throne the old-fashioned way."

The group behind me moved in unison to my coordinated attack, fortunately keeping the surging vamps off my back while I regained control of my powers once again. Something sliced at my side. I reminded myself that I needed to throw up a shield to block these sorts of things. Everything was happening brutally fast. I lost track of Vin, Larna, and Al as I moved.

Currents of energy arced off vampires and Grigori alike, but the lightning didn't stop there. Mother Nature had a mind of her own too as she poured out of my body, lashing out at those unlucky souls who got near me. I twisted and turned, moving with a fluid precision born of hours and hours of training.

Vampires flew at me in clumps, and I watched them tumble off my shield, looking a lot like dandelion seeds drifting apart in the wind, not caring whether they lived or died.

I gritted my teeth and shoved my shoulder into the throng. They surged forward as a single organism. Leo and Tami and Sam were behind me, all of them shouting their battle cries. I heard the clank of armor and steel striking steel, smelled the fresh scent of blood hanging in the air. Some of it, mine.

More bodies pushed in closer, restricting my movements—all hot, cramped, and heavy breathing. Inch by inch, I managed to shove them back, vaguely aware of how much strength I was putting into the process. Into moving the entire crowd back.

The rain had stopped.

There were so many flying fists and so much blood leaping into the air that I was drenched in it. I dug my feet into the mud and ice, my chest heaving from the effort as I pitched forward. I thought I screamed, but the rush of adrenaline was turning me into a snarling animal, exactly like the rest of the cadre of vamps. This was what madness looked like.

I dropped my shield, threw my blade out in front of me, and let loose a gigawatt of power. The energy plowed right through the remaining vamps, effectively clearing a path and leaving behind gory destruction in its wake.

I could now see the heavily guarded throne of black roses and red berries up ahead. Leo zipped past me to throw down some lightning and cover, while Tami and Sam followed closely behind him. They all worked in unison, but Sam was uncontainable. He was carving through vamps like Thanksgiving turkey. Slicing. Dicing. Chopping. His massive form blotted out the sun as he moved ahead of me, clearing a bloody path.

I reminded myself to stay out of his sword's reach as I crashed through and over rocks, shrubs, and sticks, jumping over an occasional body that he left behind, the air hammering out of my lungs in the form of great white puffs.

I skidded to a halt not ten feet from the throne, in front of at least twenty Grigori, who were all blocking me from getting to Angela.

Of course, Leo was trying to take them all on at once.

I watched in horror as several of the opposing angels took aim and fired at him. Without so much as a warning, a concussive bolt hammered into his chest. The combined lightning should have killed him upon impact, but the currents crackled and arced across his gleaming armor as it deflected the strikes back off him.

Leo stumbled back and then lost his footing, landing flat on his back as the group of Grigori launched another volley at him. He raised a hand up—

Ignoring the piercing pain in my head, I opened up a portal and flung myself into it, dropping down in front of Leo on a cyclone of wind and a horrendous clap of thunder. The combined enemy fire struck my blade and rebounded off it, splintering out across the gathered crowd instead, sending them dashing in different directions.

Leo's singed black hair was sticking straight up. He drew in a deep breath and exhaled, clutching a hand over his ruined armor. "I'm glad you didn't take it from me," he finally wheezed.

Lightning whizzed past my head so close that the resounding jolt sent a fizzle of electricity running through my entire body.

I bolted forward, too slow for my liking, batting aside a meaty fist that came out of nowhere. Then more fists. Rough hands seized hold of me, tore at my T-shirt, pulled my limbs, and scratched my sides.

I tried to portal away, but they clung to me like rabid dogs. Jagged nails scratched my skin. Teeth snapped violently at my neck. For a moment, the edges of my vision turned red as claustrophobia struck. A squat, brown-haired girl latched on to my arm. I didn't realize she'd sunk her fangs into my flesh until she dropped like a stone at my feet, foaming at the mouth. The sting in my forearm wouldn't seem to let up as I stumbled forward.

There were too many to fight. I prayed everyone was okay. A part of me had little hope that everyone would survive this onslaught. I couldn't even finish the thought before a vortex opened up right on top of me and a body shot out—

I conjured a shield at the last second, right as a kamikaze Grigori dropped down onto it with such force that my teeth rattled in my skull. He slammed into the mud-coated earth at my feet, his skin still sizzling as he flopped around like a fish on dry land.

A barrage of bullets ripped through the air, *POP-POP-POP-POP-POP*, in rapid succession. I had a fleeting thought that it was Vinson.

I flattened myself to the ground and threw my blade up on instinct as orange flashes flared up bright, rounds pinging off it with lethal intent. By the time the barking stopped, my ears were ringing. My nostrils were full of gunpowder and smoke. Sam was still out there. I could see his shield flaring up occasionally, looking like a bright beacon of light off in the distance.

Tami was fighting just as ferociously on the other side of me, trying to get closer, but she was swarmed by so many vamps, she couldn't even call up a portal. I caught a flash of Vinson's helmeted hair. Leo—well, I wasn't sure where he'd gotten to. My chest constricted with dread.

Through the smoke and haze of battle, four vamps rushed me. Still curled in a ball, all I had time to do was throw Thunderblade in the air and call for the elements' help once again.

The sky opened up, and out of the clouds, lightning came down, rushing to my aid in an earth-shattering rumble. It connected with my weapon in a blaze of glorious, almighty light, enveloping me and everyone around me too. I brought the charged dagger down, blasting all four vamps, and a Grigori, right before they got to me. The blast blew them all to ash and dust, their bodies drifting apart on a cloud and a gentle breeze.

Power drained out of me instantly, and something warm and sticky slid down my chest, which I knew wasn't sweat. I came up on a knee, scanning my surroundings, blade brandished.

The rest of the Grigori had already fanned out, forming a tight, yet cautious circle around me, too afraid to approach. It never ended.

I started to take aim but froze as soon as I saw Angela. So much for protecting their fearless leader. They had cleared a path right to her. She was sitting on the edge of the throne, legs curled underneath her. A small coy smile played across her lips as she watched the show. She didn't look like she was hurt after taking a knife to her back, she looked quite the opposite. Her eyes were lit up with a strange golden light.

She stuck a hand out and made some weird,

complicated motion with her fingers—

And then suddenly the sounds of the battle faded. All of the shouts and pleas for help, armor clanging and steel ripping into metal, the crash of thunder echoing unbearably loud in the distance from the angels fighting one another—all of it went away.

I tried to stand back up, but my chest felt like it was caving in. Everything hurt. I heard Larna shouting my name somewhere off in the distance, but then her voice was gone, and so was my vision—it tunneled around the edges just as Sam flew past me, along with Leo, who was right on his heels.

You are out of your league, little Nephilim. Her voice was in my head, harsh and grating as sandpaper across bare skin. *You are nothing. You are no one … In fact, it's time I finish this.*

A zigzagging arc of light hurtled through the air to recoil off the shield around Angela in an orange shower of flames.

My head spun as I gasped, taking in a lungful of sweet air. I staggered forward, a hand held to my chest, as someone landed behind me in a whirlwind of light and sound.

On pure instinct, I twisted around and executed a roundhouse, my foot connecting with the angel who'd landed behind me. The Grigori staggered back with a grunt as I turned to face him—I looked up … and up, craning my neck to get a good look at him. I didn't think anyone could look as dangerous or savage as this angel did. He was a giant—at least eight feet tall, with well-developed forearms that looked like bowling balls. He wore brown leather armor strapped across his broad chest—the same kind of armor I had seen them wearing in Ikari's memory, two intersected lines with four crosses in the corners.

His lips curled up on one side. He cracked his knuckles and then brought those knuckles down, down, down toward my face.

Someone collided with me from behind, hard, at the same time as Mighty Fists struck me. Bright splotches of agonizing light exploded across my vision.

I felt my cheekbone shatter under the pressure. The pain was debilitating. Somewhere at the back of my mind, I knew someone else was attacking me at the same time. I needed to address it quickly or I was toast. I caught sight of a blurred face with a dark goatee, sideburns, and all flashing pointy teeth. Vampire. He threw a punch, but instead of it hitting my nose, like he'd intended, his hand struck my shield, and he flew backward, landing in a broken heap, with one leg twisted up at an unnatural angle beneath him.

As soon as I turned back around, I found myself at eye level with the Grigori's chest. The sinews of corded muscle running down his neck were raised. His fury and hatred were on vivid display. A vein popped out and his pulse jumped, and the only, insane thought running through my head was how hungry I was. Starving, actually. I needed blood. Not *his* blood, I reminded myself—he was angel.

He slashed out with something sharp and metal. I jumped back, barely avoiding getting my head separated from my neck in the process.

I propelled a knee into his gut, threw a shoulder into his chest, and took a flying leap into the air to ram an elbow into the side of his neck. He staggered back and doubled over, dropping the steel out of his two-handed grip. Three quick jabs to his ribs with my blade only seemed to incense him more. Massive, hot-dog-sized fingers wound around my throat, but before he could squeeze the life out of me, I disappeared in a quick flash and reappeared behind him, driving my dagger up and into his chest.

My blade, still speared into his chest cavity, blazed up bright, and lightning exploded out of his whole body. The force sent him sprawling backward. He toppled over like a felled tree, landing face-down in a thick pile of powder snow.

Sweat and blood dripped into my eyes, blinding me. My breath felt raw and ragged at the back of my throat. The blood pumping through my veins seemed to throb in tune with the beating of my heart, and so did the bite on my arm.

Another robed Grigori stepped toward me, squaring up. This one was significantly thicker around the middle. He was wringing his hands together, his eyes darting from left to right as he realized he was all by himself. My blade sizzled with lightning—it crackled over my skin, tracing patterns down my hands and arms. I wondered if my eyes were just as deadly looking. I gestured at him to come at me.

He turned and ran in the opposite direction.

Someone called my name. *Larna.* Her voice sounded distant and panicked—I didn't know how I'd heard it through all the raucousness of battle, but I did. I took a moment to scan the wooded area and saw a cluster of vamps in a thicket of aspens.

Sam and Leo were still throwing bolt after bolt at Angela's heavily protected throne, trying to take her down.

Leo shouted, "*Corinth—now! We need you!*"

Again my gaze flickered to the surrounding trees, where I knew Larna and Al were fighting for their lives, trying to stave off the rest of the incoming vamps from getting to me.

Was Imani there? Vin? Nan?

"*Corinth—hurry! Finish this! She's right here!*" Sam shouted.

"*Corinth, it's now or never!*" Leo screamed. "*What are you doing?*"

Another of Larna's cries cut through the haze of battle, more insistent this time.

The decision was an easy one. I turned and went after her instead.

Chapter 55

Larna

EVEN THOUGH I HAD the power of vampire *Sight*, I still found it hard to see clearly through all the mist and rain. Corinth had demolished a long line of attacking vampires, paving the way for us to retaliate. While he had gone one way, we had gone the opposite.

Currently I'd used up most of the serum Pearl had made for us—having shot everything in my dart gun in a matter of seconds and then reloaded multiple times after that. Another vamp, who had the largest snapping mandible ever, dropped like a stone at my feet.

For every felled vamp, another one popped up in their place. It was horrific and bloody and gritty. As sure-footed as I was, fighting through a dense copse of trees over slippery, rough terrain wasn't helping. Even with Gabriel's forces behind us, there were just too many foes and extremely powerful angels to beat all of them—they fought furiously, knowing what was at stake. My goal was to keep as many of them off Corinth's back as possible.

I'd lost sight of Alastair somewhere along the way. Nan was out there somewhere too, and Gabriel had already plunged ahead of us while Corinth took on Angela.

I hoped Corinth was getting the job done—we could only hold them back for so long.

Off in the distance, I could hear the ominous crack of lightning and thunder echoing as the melee with Ikari and Diniel increased tenfold. It sounded like the end of the world. I wondered how many more Grigori were left. Sozo and his clan were fighting just as hard. We all were.

I ducked and then dodged over a downed tree right as a vamp wearing all red flew at me with such speed that she shredded some of the thin saplings near me like pulled pork. Even her red hair looked like flames.

She was holding a weapon in her hands. A multilinked chain with a metal dart at one end. I scurried around another aspen as it whizzed past me, feeling an agonizing sting on my right hand. My dart gun went flying through a thicket of bushes and shrubs in the opposite direction.

The wind whistled earsplittingly past my ear as she slashed out with the chain whip again, screaming, "*You killed my boyfriend with one of those darts!*"

I dashed behind another sapling right as the sharp point embedded itself deeply into the bark. I kicked out sideways, pinning her against the tree, and she cried out in surprise, pulling on the chain still clutched in her grasp. I was about to release the thin blades at my wrists when something heavy slammed into the back of my skull.

I rocked forward and crashed to my knees, suddenly too shocked to move, my vision fogging over. I could hear the slow fade of my heart thumping in my eardrums, and for some reason, the fingers on my hand where she'd hit me with the sharp end of the dart started to go numb.

The red-haired vamp wrenched the barb free and then slowly began twirling the chain in the air, taking her time as she approached me. I stared into her eyes and she stared back. They were dark and cold and deeply set. Blood slid down the side of my neck.

The person who'd struck me from behind, a dark-skinned kid who looked to be barely a teenager, pulled me roughly to my feet with surprising strength. He wrenched my arms cruelly behind my back. There was a desperation to his movements, and his eyes were lit up like lanterns, the tips of his fangs protruding over his bottom lip. He was wearing clothes that looked too small for his tall frame. He chuckled to himself as he pulled me backward, away from the girl with the heavy iron chain. He was all elbows and sharp angles.

Off in the distance, I could hear the sounds of people still fighting for their lives. Pleas for help, moans of the injured—the sounds of fight blurring together until my head felt like it might split in half. The prickly disconnect of brain from body was incapacitating.

"You want to use her for some target practice," the boy suggested, a light mocking tone to his voice. It came out sounding warbled and thick in my ears.

I glanced down dully to see a hammer tucked into the side of his belt and realized it was probably what he had clobbered me with.

The girl licked her lips and nodded, apparently loving his idea. "She's not going to put up much of a fight now. My weapon was laced with poison. We can drain her dry after we have a bit of fun … I've worked up an appetite."

"Sounds good to me," the boy agreed.

The girl began to swing the whip in wide, sweeping arches, edging closer. I wondered distantly how she kept the chain from getting caught in the tree limbs above us. Apparently, she was very skilled.

"Let's really savor this moment, shall we?" The girl's red hair looked like it was on fire as she threw the chain with lightning speed and accuracy at me. The weapon was already back in her fist by the time I even realized she'd thrown it.

A grim smile played across her lips when she saw blood spilling down the front of my duster. I sagged in the boy's iron grasp behind me, his grip increasing to a painful degree as he forced me to stay upright.

The girl coiled and looped the chain around her fist and then, in another lightning-fast movement, lashed out again—

But before the dart hit me for the third time, I saw a hand catch the chain up at the last second. There was a flash of blond followed by black leather.

Alastair.

He was winding the metal whip tightly around his fist at the same time as he shot forward, gathering up the slack and yanking the weapon out of the girl's grasp to pull her off-balance. All the while, I could feel the tension in the kid's body behind me as he held on to me, his grip unrelenting.

I couldn't help but be impressed by Alastair—catching up a fast-moving metal whip right out of vamp's hands was beyond extraordinary, especially from someone lacking preternatural strength.

The girl's eyes flew wide right as she went for another

weapon on her belt. It was too late for her though.

Alastair had thrown the whip into the air and kicked the spiked end back at her before she could react. It struck her right in the chest, point first. She let out a choked cry, ripping the blade out of her torso, and for one long, stretched-out second, all she could do was stare at the sharp end, and then she looked back at the kid holding me, tucked tail, and ran in the opposite direction, stumbling as she went.

I slammed the back of my head into the kid's nose behind me and heard a satisfying crunch. He lurched sideways as I faced him and rammed a fist into his stomach at the same time as I ejected one of my blades and jabbed it into his side.

His eyes bugged out of his head, his hand moving to his abdomen in a slow exaggerated movement. "*You bitch!*"

Alastair wound the chain up into his fist and rounded on the kid, his voice filled with a contained sort of rage. "I suggest you run."

The kid ran.

When Alastair was sure he was gone, he whirled back to me, concern filling his eyes. "You okay?"

I retracted my blade back into the armor at my wrist and clutched the back of my skull. "I will be." It came out sounding a little too slurred and breathless for my liking. "How did you move that fast?"

"Practice ..." he said, but his voice trailed off as soon as his gaze fell on the blood on my neck and fingers. I had started forward, but my head erupted in agony, and my knees buckled. Alastair dropped the chain and ran toward me, scooping me up into his arms before I could hit the ground.

While in his arms, I studied him for a moment, disoriented and fuzzy-headed. The rain was coming down in sheets, making his jacket look painted on. He had a black eye, and I had no idea how it had happened. I didn't think he had looked any more intimidating or beautiful or fierce in his entire life. Rain dripped off his nose and raced down his chin. I could see the rapid beat of his pulse at his neck.

His eyes frantically swept over me as his hands explored the back of my head. When he pulled his fingers back, I could see them slick with red. "You need blood," he said firmly. "To replace what you've lost."

I tried to say, "*Not yours*," but it didn't sound coherent—actually, I wasn't even sure I'd said it. His blood was just as toxic as Corinth's. He was right though. I *was* starving. "I'll be fine," I slurred. "I'm … already healing."

I stood shakily back to my feet at the same time as Alastair swore under his breath as the sound of thunder and lightning shattered the quietude close by.

An angel portal opened up right behind us, and Alastair spun around, picking the whip back up in one smooth motion, getting ready.

I flicked my blades free but stopped myself from attacking as soon as I saw who dove out of the open vortex. Tamiel, and she was supporting someone, her hand wrapped around their waist—an injured someone, I realized. Tufts of wispy hair poked out from her dyed-platinum braid, and her armor was crunched in on one side. She carefully helped the slumped figure down beside the base of a tree.

Momentarily caught off guard by the skirmish surging closer, I cast a furtive gaze around, listening. The shouts and cries grew louder, and rapid reports of gunfire sounded like bombs dropping all around us. A zigzag of lightning threaded the storm-darkened sky overhead. They were coming.

The air was thick with copper, gunpowder, and damp earth.

My breath was leaving me in ragged pants now. We were minutes away from being swept up in the stampede heading in our direction, and we were Corinth's last line of defense.

I heard a low growl come from the prone form on the ground, and I realized with a jolt who it was just by that one growl. Vinson had been wearing all white. Now his coat and pants were stained a solid gray from the dirt and blood and soot. *No. No. No.*

He tried to get up and then immediately collapsed back against the tree, his lips pulled back into a snarl at having been teleported or touched—probably both.

I retracted my blades, quickly sliding down to the ground beside him.

"He's hurt," Tamiel explained evenly. "Badly. I couldn't leave him behind, even though he wanted me to."

Vinson's eyes tracked the movement of my hand as I reached for his gear to check for injuries. He stuck an arm out to stop me, planting a hand on top of mine. I knew it was going to be bad before I even looked. He wouldn't have touched me otherwise.

Tamiel said, "Don't let the vampire fool you. He's lost a lot of blood. He took a lightning bolt to the gut—for me." She sounded annoyed. "It went right through him. I don't think he's healing."

I steeled myself and looked down.

Blood bloomed brightly against the other stains of his jacket. I tried to unzip it to see the extent of his injuries, but he gave a sharp protest in Russian and stopped me.

"Dammit Vinson," I breathed. "That's your signature move—jumping in front of things to save people's lives."

Vinson gave me a hard look. "I could say same about you."

"They'll be on top of us in about two minutes." Alastair turned to Tamiel, worry lacing his voice. "Can you protect him or try to heal him yourself? Send him out of here using a portal?"

She glared down at Vinson, who had slowly started to get back to his feet.

He gently but firmly pushed me away when I tried to help him up. When I attempted to bite into my wrist to donate some blood to him, his eyes narrowed, and he stuck a hand out, stopping me. "No," he said sternly.

Tamiel shook her head, remorse filling her eyes. "We can't heal vampires. Only humans or those who are part human—like Nephilim. I can send him away—"

"*No*," Vinson echoed.

I tried to stop him from moving, but he gave me a look that said, "Touch me and die." I knew not to go against one of those looks. He mashed his teeth together and then slowly got back to his feet, unassisted. Proud. Defiant. He was chalk white, especially with that slicked-back black hair pulled into a short ponytail. The shadowed outline of sharp cheekbones and sunken eyes made him look that much more severe.

He pulled out one of his multitude of throwing spikes from his vest pocket. Then he squared his shoulders and growled, "This is exactly how I leave world … in blaze of glory."

I wanted to make Tamiel take him away, but I knew if I did, Vinson would never forgive me. And it was just so him. This was what he did best … *fighting*. I almost couldn't stomach it. I tasted salt in my mouth, and I tried to push down the flood of raw emotion at the back of my throat, suddenly glad that my tears had mixed with the rain and no one could tell the difference. I loved Vinson.

Alastair wound the chain whip back up around his fist, getting it ready as he nodded at Vinson.

I drew my short sword out. It rang loud and clear—like one final bell tolling the end. I raised it high above my head in a two-handed grip, waiting for the battle to meet our entourage.

Chapter 56

Alastair

FALLING WATER DRIPPED FROM the canopy of trees above, splashing down onto Alastair's cheek. The rain had finally stopped, and even though it was still freezing out, sweat stung his eyes. The sky was a dark omen hanging over their heads, bruising the color of nightfall.

He had seen many wounds in his day; it was how he knew Vinson's would be his end. At least they were all together. Tamiel threw up a shield to catch a stray bullet or knife before it could take him out, but she had already moved on with the flow of the fight, heading back in the direction of Corinth and Angela, and, he thought, so she could stay with Vinson as long as she could. Those two made quite the pair—and Tamiel knew it. Maybe she felt guilty for not being able to repay Vinson for his heroics.

The woods were thick with vampires and Grigori alike. Some of Deimos had made it to this point and were helping, along with those left from Eleutheros—Sozo and John and Irwin and the rest of his crew. Gabriel, Ikari, and Diniel had joined the fray too, all of them swept up in the pandemonium of battle.

Alastair had forgotten how challenging it was to use a chain whip, especially while deep in the heart of a grove of aspens. This particular weapon was one of the hardest to control, because the linked sections had looser joints.

Still, it felt good in his hands.

With a flick of his wrist, he flung the whip out to the side. The links looped around a tree with a quick snap, and the dart pierced right through the thigh of a charging Grigori. It did nothing to slow him down. In fact, it only served to piss him off more, which Alastair didn't even think was possible. This particular angel looked almost albino. His irises were tinged bright red, matching the color of his face as he came at Alastair in a mindless fury.

Alastair yanked the chain back in a graceful arch and swung it back around, winding it up tightly around his shoulder and arm. It was time to switch tactics. A whip wasn't going to work against someone who had arms the length of jet wings.

The advancing Grigori was twice as tall as he was, and extremely fast, and his footsteps shook the earth as he moved. The giant barely broke stride, slamming into Alastair and tossing him backward with such force, the air left his lungs in a rush and his head bounced off something hard, like stone. He heard a crack that sounded a lot like an egg breaking long before the wave of dizziness washed over him.

Then the angel was smashing him against a boulder. The loops of the chain wrapped around his arm dug painfully into his back. There was no give or room to breathe—

Larna catapulted herself over the top of the rock wall

above them like a ninja, slashing out with her wakizashi at the giant's chest. It left a wide gash across his leather breastplate, forcing him to step back an inch, giving Alastair a tad more room to breathe. Larna moved as fluidly as an angel herself. *Impressive*, he thought distantly.

The ogre glanced down, his lips stretched wide, revealing teeth the size of tombstones. What should have been a deadly blow, though, didn't seem to have any effect on him at all. Larna pulled her sword back in a two-handed grip and stabbed the monster all the way through the chest, through muscle and bone and his armor in one fell swoop.

The Grigori disappeared in a clap of thunder, her sword still deeply impaled in his chest. Alastair dropped to the ground like a sack of bones, wheezing heavily, momentarily stunned into submission as Larna whirled around, her blades ejected at both wrists, trying to anticipate where the angel would reappear next.

A vortex burst open right beside her in less than a millisecond, the energy and wind whipping around so violently she lost her balance.

Alastair tried to move, or shout a warning, but the advancing Grigori had already wrapped a hulk-like hand around her throat, lifting her off the ground, her legs dangling. It gave him the mental image of a bully squeezing the stuffing out of a toy doll—and Larna was the doll. He forced himself to a knee, enraged and sickened—more angry at himself, because he couldn't seem to recover fast enough to help.

The angel pulled Larna against his chest, and she kicked out weakly at him … for all the good it did. Her face was already turning a frightening shade of purple.

Alastair staggered forward right as Larna, in an amazing display of dexterity and strength, grabbed the hilt of the sword still sticking out of the giant's chest and yanked it free. She meant to try to take another swing at him with it, but the Grigori's other hand, the one not clamped around her throat, swatted the weapon out of her grip as if it were only a toothpick.

The behemoth's gaze lit on the gaping hole in his chest, and his eyes widened in disbelief. And then he brought one of those giant hands down, clubbing Larna across her face. There was the sickening crunch of bone, and then she went sprawling backward over the boulder, vanishing from his view.

The blood in Alastair's veins turned to steel and ice and something worse. A primal scream tore out of his throat as he unwound the chain around his shoulder and launched it at the Grigori.

In a quick flash of light and sound, the angel darted into another portal, seemingly controlling time. In slow motion, the metal dart spiraled toward the spot the giant had been standing in only a second ago—

And he was vividly aware of the fact that the giant's shadow stretched on forever in front of him as he bounded out of the portal at Alastair's back in the next second.

There was nothing Alastair could do to prevent the Grigori from grabbing the whip out of his hands, looping it around his neck, and pulling it agonizingly tight in one swift movement.

He was now the child's plaything.

Alastair just managed to slip a hand between the

metal links, preventing the Grigori from completely cutting off his oxygen supply.

He thrashed wildly, his feet not even close to touching the ground, as the beast lifted him up by the chain—a fish dangling at the end of a pole. He'd fought many foes over the centuries, but no one had compared to this *thing*. It didn't respond to pain. But Alastair sure did. A piercing ache shot through his neck and shoulder. His fingers caught up in the metal loops felt like they were going to be ripped clean off his hand.

He could hear his own ragged pants echoing in his ears as he kicked out hard, his foot connecting with something harder. He heard a grunt of pain but no give. No air. Alastair clawed at the links with his free hand— his crushed windpipe.

The giant swung him around as if he weighed nothing, slamming him against the rock, and black spots erupted across his vision. The sound of mocking laughter drowned out everything else. His limbs felt heavy, and his eyelids began to droop.

"You fight horribly. No challenge." the Grigori hissed, and he was about to slam Alastair again when Alastair jabbed an elbow into the angel's stomach. He heard a satisfying grunt come from the back of the angel's throat.

Alastair writhed and kicked and swung his legs around, trying to force the giant back over to the rock— his plan was to launch himself off it. Find purchase. Grab a weapon. Kill him … *Get air …*

Except after another second, Alastair's arm, the one that wasn't pinioned between unforgiving metal, began to go limp. His head was spinning. If he passed out now, he knew he was as good as dead—*again*.

He thought of Larna and their life together. His promise to her that he was going to live. He wanted to survive, for her. He thought about everything he'd never gotten a chance to do with her. Paris. Cooking. Exploring the world. These thoughts immediately sent another bout of energy and much-needed adrenaline coursing through him.

Alastair raised his arm, scrabbled at the beast's eyeball, anything soft to tear into, and then he felt give as his fingernails ripped into soft flesh. The Grigori groaned and loosened his hold on the chain just a fraction, enough for Alastair to drag in one precious breath right as a dark form hurtled into the clearing. His head was still swimming. Everything was blurry, but he was sure he saw two black short swords slash out at the angel holding him.

His savior, the dark form, was slowly coming back into focus. The figure hacked at the angel's side, forcing him to let go of Alastair, and he sank to his knees, fumbling at the chain still wound around his neck, his fingers feeling rubbery.

As soon as he freed himself, he swallowed two sweet breaths of air through his swollen windpipe. There wasn't anything else he could do in that moment but reorient himself and let his vision come back to him in small, slow increments.

When Alastair tried to stand again, to go after Larna, his legs buckled and he started coughing uncontrollably.

When he was finally able to see who'd saved his life, his mouth dropped open and he froze in place.

Gabriel Stanton.

Alastair knew how much Gabriel hated him. *He* hated Stanton. Up until a few days ago, he had thought the billionaire wanted him dead. This chivalrous, *other* version of Gabriel made Alastair's eyebrows disappear into his hairline and his jaw go slack.

Stanton moved with expert precision, his arm slicing downward in a graceful arch as he sheared right through the Grigori's left arm, separating it from his shoulder. The limb flopped uselessly to the ground, and the angel's eyes traveled down to the severed arm at his feet, a frown marring his ugly features.

Those monstrous red eyes flickered back over to Stanton, assessing, incensed.

Alastair had seen Gabriel fight only once before, when he'd gone after Larna's father. This time Gabriel was on their side, and he looked fiercer than Alastair had ever seen him.

This version of Stanton got his hands dirty.

His eyes were blazing with his *Sight*, his scar was raised and standing out against his skin, and the tips of his fangs flashed bright. The fact that Gabriel didn't look quite so put together made him look that much more frightening. His wild, untamed black hair half flopped into his eyes, and his coat was unbuttoned, revealing an untucked silk shirt underneath and stylish suspenders. His slacks were stained with dirt and blood and grime.

The Grigori squinted down at his missing arm again as if in disbelief as Gabriel circled him like a vulture waiting for his prey to die, swords held at the ready.

Alastair noticed that no gore spurted out from the

exposed wound. A gruesome smile lit up the Grigori's features at the new challenge.

Stanton spun his blades, prowling closer to the giant, no evidence of fear on his scarred face.

Alastair wanted to tell him that a healthy dose of fear might serve him better in this fight, but for now, he had to admit that he was more than a little curious to see how Stanton would stack up against this guy in a fight.

The goliath only seemed annoyed, though, as he reached out with his one good arm to throw a bolt of lightning at Stanton. It struck Gabriel in the chest, and he went soaring backward into the trunk of a tree with enough force to break it. The crack resounded through the forest as Stanton landed in a heap at its base, face-down.

Larna appeared beside Alastair in a flicker of movement, her eyes widening in surprise at seeing Gabriel on the ground at the now-mangled tree. It hadn't quite toppled over yet, but it looked dangerously close. She helped him to his feet. There was blood on her jaw and a rapidly disappearing bruise that covered half her face from where the angel had bludgeoned her, no doubt knocking her out.

She put an arm on his shoulder. "You okay?"

Alastair nodded at the same time as he abandoned the chain.

Stanton was already getting to his feet again. As if they'd coordinated it, all of them went after the giant together—

Nan beat them to the punch, flying out of nowhere to jump at the one-armed Grigori. She kicked him square in the chest. He floundered back a step, tripping over his own mangled arm on the ground. He grinned at Nan, red eyes flashing, and then he beckoned her to continue.

Nan had one of those wicked-looking curved swords in her hand. Her leather armor was crispy fried and melted. One side of her face had scorch marks running down it in ashy streaks.

Alastair had seen Nan train with Jack. She had taught him how to use his weapons. He knew how proficient Nan was at fighting. She moved with the grace of a feline—elegant and stealthy in each step she took—her sword held above her head as she prowled closer.

"Get back," she ordered. "*This one's mine.*"

They obeyed.

When she stalked forward, Alastair could see each line of hard muscle and tendon in her back. Nan looked like an avenging angel, which was fitting, because Alastair knew she meant to get back at them for what they had done to her.

The Grigori nodded his gargantuan head, gave her another small smile of "Challenge accepted," and then disappeared in one of those spinning tunnels of light again. He dropped out of the portal, landing behind her with a heavy thud. The earth trembled.

Nan was already spinning around though, swinging her sword around like a baseball bat, chopping the hulk in half at his waist—armor and all—in one hefty stroke. The strength it took to split this demon in half as if he were nothing more than an apple was incomprehensible to Alastair.

None of them had very long to celebrate, because a swarm of vampires and Grigori spilled out into the forest, fanning out in a mad dash to get to Angela and Corinth and the throne. Suddenly bodies were everywhere, crushing.

They fought for their lives. Gabriel, Larna, and Nan at his back.

He lost track of time. He lost track of how many enemies he slew. He lost track of everyone. Something cut his face, and then he felt the cold slice of something else tearing at his jacket. A sharp object lodged into his thigh, and he screamed in pain. Arrow. He had a sword in his hand and no memory of how it had gotten there.

Alastair's lips curled back from his teeth as a vampire with braided bone-colored hair—no, that *was* bone in his hair—came hacking at him from out of nowhere. This vamp was long limbed and lithe as an alley cat. A rock crashed into the side of Alastair's head from behind. He saw stars as he snapped a flat palm against the alley cat's chest, ignoring the pain in his head. The limber vamp went flying and was subsequently trampled under the scores of others around them.

Then Alastair whirled around, slamming his broadsword into a second vamp behind him, the one with the rock, straight through his heart. There was a flash of red lips and white fangs. They fell. Lots fell. He didn't see faces anymore. Only bodies, hands, feet. Blurs. Blood blinded him. Hack. Slash. Chop. It went on like that until he found he couldn't lift his arms any longer. Alastair wiped a sweaty hand across his brow, and he caught sight of Vinson, who had joined their inner circle. He had no idea how Vinson was still on his feet. He could survive an apocalypse. This *was* an apocalypse. How any of them were still on their feet amazed him. They found themselves shepherded into a tight circle. With Larna at his back, he felt better. More capable. She didn't say anything. There was no time for speaking. She only fought ferociously, refusing to leave his side. Her vambraces were broken at each of her wrists. She was punching and kicking, keeping the horde back for now.

Ikari, Diniel, and Tamiel threw up a barrier around their group, trying to protect them from the last brutal barrage. Blessed light rained down around them like a translucent curtain. Alastair could see how tired they all looked, their energy drained out of them ages ago.

The barrier was taking a pounding. It wavered, steadily losing power.

Several more Grigori had joined forces to throw balls of lightning at them—and even more vampires had surged forward, hurling whatever they could find to help bring down their last line of defense.

Imani dropped down out of a tree like a stalking panther, landing agilely in the center of a group of vamps, just outside the shield. She threw two small round devices at the crowd surrounding their group and then dashed out of the way at the last second.

The devices exploded, taking out the vast majority of vamps in the process, and their shield flickered and almost vanished.

Alastair threw his hands over his ears and fell to the ground. He must have blacked out for a few seconds, because when he came to, his leg felt like agony. Someone had ripped the arrow out. He screamed. Blood gushed from the open wound. He hadn't even known it had still been in his thigh.

"I can't heal you right now. I'm sorry." Ikari's face swam in front of Alastair's. The world tilted around him, showing him a tableau of turmoil. Larna wasn't at his back anymore, and that was what gutted him the most.

"*Protect Larna,*" he croaked.

Ikari bolted back to his feet and tried his best to deflect another attack from several more Grigori and some Sangre members. Lightning rattled the atmosphere and the shield around them, sending his heart into his throat. It wouldn't hold.

Bits of aspen rained wooden shrapnel down around Alastair, mixed with snow and dirt. The smell of metal and gunpowder was thick in the air. His eyes settled on a body across the way—an angel with shining armor. *Diniel.* Fallen for good this time … She'd died fighting to save their lives. Her sandy-blond hair and caramel-colored skin were covered in scorch marks. Her armor had been forcibly ripped from her body. Savage beasts.

Vinson collapsed a few feet from him. Larna was there, beside Vinson in an instant, pulling his head into her lap. Alastair gave a shuddering sob in relief. She was still alive.

Larna cradled Vinson close to her body. There were tears streaming down her soot-stained face. She cried out Corinth's name. And then Alastair's. From only a few feet away, within an arm's reach, he met her distraught gaze. Everything melted away. The cries of the battle faded. Her eyes softened when she found his. She mouthed the words: "I love you."

All Alastair cared about was holding Larna one last

time. He tried to reach out to her but found he couldn't move. She reached out toward him, and their fingers brushed. A single touch was all they got.

His blood ran cold as Larna's eyes traveled to Vinson's still form.

This was what war felt like. This was what he'd been trying to avoid. That feeling of emptiness and desperation, losing someone you loved over and over again until there was no one left to love.

Vinson's eyes were closed, and he was as still as death, his hand curled in Larna's—and then the shield shattered around them, igniting everything back into a world of chaos and blood and devastation.

Chapter 57

Corinth

THE PORTAL I'D CALLED forth dumped me right into the middle of chaos. I jumped out of the spinning vortex, dagger held at the ready, and saw Larna on the ground, her arms folded around a very still form. For one excruciating long second, I thought the person she was holding was Al, but then I laid eyes on him a few feet away from her. He was on his back, arms splayed out by his sides—*alive*, but definitely down for the count.

The shield Ikari had erected had all but vanished, and their group was surrounded on all sides by a horde of vamps and Grigori who were about to lay waste to them.

I threw myself in front of my friends, calling for lightning, and it plunged out of the sky with lethal intent, connecting with my dagger. My head snapped back as the energy soared out of my chest. Power exploded out of the blade in the form of a single deadly bolt. It splintered and fragmented, whizzing in a thousand different directions to strike anyone standing within twenty yards of me.

It was invigorating, finally connecting with all that energy and fire and power. The hard metal of the hilt cut into my palm as I tightened my grip and let the blade do its work. Lightning hurtled back up into the sky, disappearing with a sharp *SNAP* and deep sonic boom, so loud that for a second, all I could hear was a high-pitched ringing noise in its wake.

I blinked rapidly, trying to clear my vision as a dark cloud of dust and debris drifted down in the still air, settling back to the earth in an eerie tableau. No flicker of movement. No glint of armor. No raised weapons. I saw only slack, haunted faces staring back at me, mesmerized and dazed.

Then, as if the Grigori and vamps had all been connected together, they all dropped, their legs going out from under them at the exact same time. Everyone still alive was staring at me or staring up into the sky, mouths gaping open as if they had never seen such a spectacle before.

The only people left in the clearing were Larna, Al, and Ikari. I didn't know where Imani or Gabe was, or anyone else for that matter. I assumed they had been separated in the fight. Leo crossed my mind, but I knew I'd left him at the throne.

A bright glint drew my eyes away from Larna. *Angel armor.* A form lay on the ground not too far away. My heart wrenched at seeing Diniel. Her broken armor and twisted body lay under a bush, just to the south of where I stood. She was staring vacantly back at me, just like Benny had when he'd been killed trying to save my life.

No. No. No.

Ikari appeared next to me, his eyes full of pain and sadness, but when he spoke, he sounded urgent. "Over there, on the other side of that path. Help them." He hunched over, clutching at his side in pain. He sounded out of breath and just as hurt by Diniel's death as I was—worse. A giant hole had been burned into the side of his armor.

"What about you?" I said.

"I'm okay," he reassured me. "I need a moment to gather my strength again. I'm depleted."

I heard a skirmish, metal striking metal, and then, in an instant, transported myself to the disturbance, leaving Ikari behind. A group of vamps was circling Imani like scavengers, ready to pick her clean. I caught glimpses of red leather and moved, throwing my hands out in front of me. Lightning crackled over my skin as my feet left the ground. Power lashed out of my fingertips like a cracked whip, slamming into the five vampires surrounding her. They dropped dead, falling to the ground almost simultaneously.

A spear came out of nowhere, and I batted it aside. I had never moved so smoothly or been so in tune with my powers. Sharp projectiles bounced off my shield as I crashed into someone wearing all red, their yellow eyes flashing.

I threw blazing palms against someone else's chest. They seized up, and lightning sizzled through the air, burned the ozone with its mad dash to destroy every living creature within its reach.

When I got to Imani, I extended a hand out. She took it with wide eyes and, without a word, let me pull her against my side. We disappeared in a flash of light and a tunnel of wind, and a second later dropped back down with the rest of our disheveled group.

Imani laid a hand on my arm, attempting to steady

herself. She was still trying to catch her breath and, I thought, was a little taken aback by my performance.

"*That was—*" she started to say, but I turned toward the raucous sound of humming and whirring steel to see Nan and Gabe fighting in a thicket of trees in the opposite direction. Sparks were shooting off their blades. They twisted and spun, slashing and hacking at another barrage of enemies surrounding them.

A vampire came springing through the air at Gabe, an ax glinting bright in his hands. Gabe reacted, twisting around with skilled precision to shear neatly through the metal tip of the hatchet in the vamp's hand. Almost graceful, as if he were dancing, he whirled back around again and cleaved through another vamp's heart with his sleek-looking sword. They dropped like a stone, legs thrashing in pain as they writhed on the ground. I had to admit, each of Gabe's movements was flawless and precise.

Nan, back to back with him, drove an elbow into a vamp's jaw. The girl floundered to the side, giving Nan plenty of time to launch herself into the air and kick her in the face—the girl fell away as another vamp stepped over her to take her place. Nan smashed a fist into the older woman's nose, flung a throwing star at another charging Grigori—it hit her with such force that it nailed her to a tree before she could call up a portal or a shield.

I heard the crunch of bone and saw Gabe strike out at another clan member, with a star inked on his cheek. He wore heavy-duty, dark armor—but it was still no match for Gabe's weaponry.

Nan and Gabe worked seamlessly together, as if they'd been a team this entire time.

It was an impressive sight, but not as impressive as me.

I called up another portal and ducked into the storm-ridden vortex, only to dive out of it a moment later into the tumultuous gale of wind and fire and mayhem.

There was a heaviness in my chest as lightning burst out from the heavens in a surge of all-consuming energy. It struck me once, driving down into my body. I aimed my dagger at the surrounding group and lit the world on fire—apocalypse orange. There were several screams of terror followed by eerie silence as I put one hand on Nan and the other on Gabe and transported them to the rest of our group before the cluster of Grigori and vamps had even fallen.

It looked like a bomb had gone off. Whoever or whatever was left of the enemy was either writhing in pain, separated into parts, or running in the opposite direction.

I turned wild eyes on Larna, shaking with the flood of power and adrenaline still coursing through me.

A slow, visible shiver worked its way through her, and I sucked in a sharp breath at seeing the shape cradled in Larna's lap, still as a corpse. She had them wrapped up in her arms, her chin pressed to that recognizable helmet of dark hair.

Al stumbled drunkenly to his feet to drop down beside Larna, landing hard on his knees, a hand going to his head. I felt what little moisture there was in my mouth disappear as soon as I realized who was missing from of our group.

Please, no.

Everyone was staring at me as if they'd never seen me before.

I tried to take inventory of our group: Ikari, Nan, Gabe, Imani … Tami was with Leo and Sam at the throne, fighting Angela … *Vinson. No, please, don't let it be Vinson.* I shuffled closer, suddenly overcome by a dark cloud of emotion, feeling like I'd been sucked directly into one of my waking nightmares.

Vin's limp hand was clutched in Larna's. It was so pale, and I could see the spider web of veins against his pallid skin. There were some images that would stick with me for life. This was one of them.

Larna gazed up at me briefly and turned her grief-stricken eyes back on Vin.

I listened as if in a far-off place as he rasped, "Don't worry little caterpillar. Everything will be okay. I am not worth crying over."

An overwhelming loss stabbed through me, sharp and aching. These were his final moments.

I can fix this. I can fix this. I will fix this. I will end this. Angels couldn't heal vampires—but they *could* heal humans. If I ended this right now … we might be able to heal him in time.

I clenched my jaw and threw a hand into the air as a yawning cyclone opened up behind me, and then, giving Larna and Al one last fleeting look, I stepped backward into it, letting it swallow me up whole.

For a moment, there was only the sensation of cold. A brutal cold that felt like someone had ripped my lungs right out of my chest, then taken a knife to my skull and scalped me. I wondered idly if this was what it would feel like to drift in space without a pressurized suit.

When I felt the weight lift, I opened my eyes.

It only took me a second to realize it had worked. I was inside the barrier with Angela. Just me, her, and the dark throne.

Sparks dripped like blood from the tip of my blade, illuminating a path of cobalt light beside me. Then the light dissipated like a flame being extinguished. It was oddly quiet and dark in this space—little light and no sound from the outside world penetrated her bubble.

I could barely make out the outline of Leo and Sam trying to take down the wall from the other side. Tami was fighting off the rest of the stragglers at their backs. They were throwing bolts of lightning at the barrier, all the while shouting something incomprehensible. Luckily, there weren't many more left to fight.

Leo could see me; of that I was certain. I saw his shouts increase exponentially as soon as he saw me appear inside the sphere with Angela. He was gesturing wildly at me now, and he had a look of panic on his features, his eyebrows drawn tightly together. There wasn't anything they could do to help me now though.

This was my fight to finish.

Angela threw the hood of her robe all the way back, eyeing me wordlessly with glittering eyes as she circled the throne made of twining white branches and obsidian-colored roses, flowers so dark they seemed to suck the light right out of this space.

She gave a little flourish of her hand, apparently not surprised to see that I had suddenly appeared inside the protective dome she'd erected. Finally she said, "Those cuts look deep."

I raised a hand to my face, having forgotten that I'd even been cut in the first place. That had been ages ago. Dried blood had crusted over the swollen gashes on both my cheeks. A trickle of it ran down the side of my neck. I thanked the adrenaline still running through my veins for not feeling any pain just yet.

"It's just the two of us now. Fitting, don't you think?" Angela inclined her head toward Leo and the others. "They can't break through. They handed over too much energy to you and that"—her eyes skimmed over the dagger clutched in my fingers—"*blade*. Unfortunately, power like that doesn't last. You've used up quite a bit of it portaling yourself inside here. This is no ordinary barrier. Not the brightest of moves on your end, I must admit."

I pointed toward Leo on the other side of the oddly glowing orange light. It was like looking through a stained glass window. "You wouldn't mind letting my brother in here too, would you?"

Angela laughed darkly and shook her head. "Your half brother," she corrected.

"You lost, Angela. Even your own son doesn't want anything to do with you. Your army is running for the hills. Literally. It's over. *Stand down.* I don't want any more bloodshed on my hands."

Angela padded closer, stepping lightly on the balls of her bare feet as she did so. "Don't you?" She perched herself on the edge of the giant throne, her hands on either side of the knobby and gnarled armrests. "Didn't you say my blood will run down your hands?" She giggled. "I never cared for Leo … not really. Now you, on the other hand, have grit—and *style*. Apparently, you have all the talent in the family." She cocked her head to the side, a small smile playing across her lips. And as if she'd changed her mind about something, she said, "You might still serve a purpose. I saw the way you annihilated all those vampires. There is much darkness inside you. All that vampire and Nephilim blood vying for control."

I didn't want to hear about darkness inside me. I already knew it was there.

"What do you know about family?" I asked, unable to hide the anger bubbling out of my voice. "You've destroyed more of them than you've ever built."

Angela's grin widened. It was like staring at a wolf in human form. "I could say the same about you, Nephilim. How many have you killed today? Vampire and angel? Hundreds."

I dropped my gaze away from hers, guilt twisting my stomach into knots.

"Do you know why I am not afraid of you?" she asked.

I shrugged, and then met her eyes once again. They were wide and round and perfect.

"I'll bite—and that's not a vampire joke."

She laughed softly as if she really did find me humorous. "Blood is seeping through that shirt of yours. You're dying. All those lacerations are coming back. The angel energy you stole helped keep you moving, but it is too late for you now. The Watchers merely expected you to sacrifice yourself for the greater good. As soon as you passed through that barrier though, you … hit your wall. Don't tell me you didn't feel it. It's made of something darker ... something *demonic*."

I felt myself blanch at hearing that, but I gave her a grim smile despite this news. "Demonic?"

She shrugged as if she were going to keep her secrets to herself. "No matter what happens to me—even if you turn every single vampire out there human once again—you'll still succumb to those old wounds of yours. The ones Sarah gave you. You thought that if you got rid of the virus, you'd magically heal right up?" She laughed scornfully, mocking. "No ... no, you are already on your way out, and there's nothing you or anyone else can do about it. Except for *me*, maybe. I could make it stop ... if you wanted me to. Swear fealty to me for the rest of your life—and I will heal you. You don't have to die today."

I licked my dry lips. I had considered the possibility that I wasn't walking away from this, and it still came as a shock to me, but it didn't make hearing it any less horrible. Something shiny and slick stained the front of my dark T-shirt. Suddenly all I could feel was the warmth oozing out of old wounds, just like she'd described. At least it didn't hurt.

"So ... you had help creating the virus—from *demons?*"

"You thought this was going to be easy? Taking me out with all that power you stole from angels? I've been around for eons. I was here at the beginning of this dreadful place. You've had, what ... eighteen years of life?" She laughed, and it echoed loudly in the domed chamber. "In here, I am stronger than you are."

She was right. I couldn't feel the connection with my power like I had before. It had vanished the moment I felt the cold hit me once again. She had wanted me to find my way inside this place. I knew that to be true. Her way of controlling me without outside interference too, I supposed.

"Maybe," I said finally. "But even Satan disguises himself as an angel of the light." She raised an inquisitive eyebrow as I said, "I would rather die than be saddled up with you for the rest of my life. Besides, I think you're way more scared of dying than I am."

"Pity." She raised her arms high in the air and made an elaborate motion with her fingers.

It happened quickly and without warning. I doubled over and then landed bruisingly hard on my knees. My eyelids lowered and then closed of their own accord. Something wet splattered onto my cheek and ran down my chin. My chest rose and fell steadily. It was as if she'd placed me in some kind of deep trance where I was aware of everything that happened around me but I couldn't do anything about it. Like sleep paralysis. My worst nightmare coming to life—and she knew it. I wasn't afraid of dying. Well, okay, maybe I was a little, but that didn't mean I wanted to go out in a painful way.

Angela had been in my head. She knew my darkest fears. I wondered if I could block her like Ikari had taught me to do. Something told me no—not in this place.

I felt someone crouch down beside me and tug my blade out of my fingers, and then I heard Angela's breathless voice reverberate inside my head. *How do you think I am so much stronger than you are? I am not doing this on my own ... I have seen what frightens you most. You—revisited by a ghost from your past. And it's not me, unfortunately.*

The blood inside my veins seemed to thicken. I called for my blade but nothing happened. I felt disconnected. I tried to wiggle my fingers or toes but found even that was too great a task. *Calm down. Clear your head, Corinth.* What had Ikari said?

But immediately my composure fled as soon as I felt the cold press of steel against my stomach. I knew what that object was.

A scalpel.

The person beside me was not Angela. She'd visited my nightmares often enough.

This isn't real. She isn't here right now. Breathe.

Sarah answered my fears as if I'd spoken them out loud. "Oh, I *am* real."

My heart launched itself into my throat, restricting my speech and breathing at the same time.

"Open your eyes," she commanded.

I did. It was just like the time I'd come out of my dream state. Bleary and dull. I could feel the loathing as she stared at me with those hate-filled, arctic green eyes. Trickles of dark blood trailed a path through the snow underneath me.

With the scalpel clutched between her fingers, Sarah moved a lock of damp hair off my forehead. This new version of Sarah didn't have any missing digits.

She was giving me the same pacifying look as the day she'd drugged me, stabbed me, and left me for dead. "I can see by the look on your face how much you've missed me."

"*No*," I gasped. "You can't be alive."

She gave me a coy smile. "Can't I?"

Chapter 58

Corinth

"SARAH." I SWALLOWED HARD, watching her every move with a growing sense of dismay. "You're looking a whole lot more … well … for lack of a better word, *whole* than when I saw you last."

"And it looks like you are still riddled *with* holes." Sarah teased my shirt with the tip of her scalpel.

I sucked in a sharp breath, dimly aware of Larna screaming just on the other side of the barrier, her mouth hanging open in complete shock. She was there to witness this. I felt the anger simmering inside me. They were all watching me from the outside, looking in. I had no idea when they'd shown up. Sam, Tami, Al, Leo, Nan, Gabe, and Ikari—everyone except Vin and Din—were all there, desperately trying to break the barrier down.

I couldn't hear a word of what Larna was shouting, or hear anyone else for that matter, but I could see the startled expressions on their faces. Larna had streaks of sweat and soot and blood entrenched into the creases on her beautiful features. By the looks of her, she could see Sarah too. Al appeared waxy even through the golden, glowing haze of the walls—I couldn't see where his blond hair ended and ashen skin began.

A part of me wanted to mirror Al's terror at seeing Sarah, but what would be the point? I was already dead. Fear was beyond me now. My powers were long gone, the energy having been sapped out of me as soon as I'd stepped foot in this place.

Speaking of dead, how many times had Sarah come back from the other side? I thought Al would have been used to her sudden appearances from beyond the grave. Technically, she had never died the first time.

The word *demon* came to mind immediately.

I didn't want to go out on my knees. I tried to get back to my feet, but my body refused to respond to even the simplest of commands, and my head opened up as if it had been split in two. I inhaled sharply and Sarah laughed.

"If I had known this was going to be a party I would have brought streamers," I wheezed. She flipped the scalpel and caught it by the handle, the well-sharpened edge glittering harshly, supernaturally, in the radiant light. "Did you at least bring cake?"

"Still deflecting fear with humor, I see. Do you know what's so funny about all this?"

"That you shouldn't wear blue scrubs after Labor Day?" I parried.

Her grin widened devilishly. She was giving me that same chilling smile as she had right before she'd stabbed me in the chest. My skin prickled in anticipation of being tortured all over again.

"That out of everything in this world you should or could be scared of … *I'm* your biggest fear." She scratched her forehead lightly with the tip of the blade. "I'm flattered."

The hairs on the back of my neck stood up as stiff as wires. Something was wrong—I mean, besides the fact that Sarah had miraculously come back from the dead. Al had come back, so I didn't discount it really happening. I remembered when I had been immersed in Ikari's memories, how Angela had winked at me right before slitting his wife's throat. Angela could be manipulating my thoughts right now. Feeding off my fears.

How could she know what scared me most in this world, unless she was inside my head? This was what she was good at—and it was why she had beaten so many others at their own game.

My eyes darted back to where Larna stood on the other side of the dark barricade. She was so close but so far away, walled off from me like that. A pang of regret welled up inside me. I was going to miss her the most. My gaze traveled to Al again. His mouth was pressed into a firm line, and he was pacing in front of the shimmering wall, pointing and shouting something unintelligible at Sam.

I turned my attention back to Larna. She was staring at me in resignation, as if she'd completely given up. That wasn't my Larns. She would never give up on me. Not in a million years. This wasn't real. It couldn't be.

And when Sarah knelt down in front of me, pulling my hand into hers, slowly lifting my index finger with the blunt end of the blade, I believed it *was* real.

Her bright green eyes met mine. I could see the triumph and delight dancing in them.

"I plan to cut off each one of your fingers ... in front of Alastair and your girlfriend, of course." Her eyes drifted back over to Angela. She was curled up on her throne like a cat, looking less than impressed. "How much time do I have to make him suffer?"

Angela waved a hand. "Time is something we have in pitiless abundance here. Months, weeks, or ... even years of it. Make it last. And when he's had enough, he'll join me. Defeated. I think I will keep him alive, tied to me, of course."

"Wait ... *Wait* ... I give up. I swear fealty," I said thickly, my voice cracked. "I can't take an eternity of torture. I can't even take the sound of your voice anymore."

At that, Angela perked up, perching precariously on the edge of her throne. "Wait."

Sarah gave a little huff of annoyance but turned stiffly around to look at Angela expectantly.

"Prove your loyalty," Angela pointed at Larna. "Kill your friend, and I will know you're truly on my side."

"There's something else I can do ... t-t-to prove my loyalty, I mean." I spoke the last part so softly Sarah had to lean in closer to hear me. "Trust me. You're going to want to hear this."

Sarah clucked her tongue in irritation, and even though she sounded annoyed, she inched closer. I could almost feel her pulse beating in her neck.

"*Closer*," I breathed.

Sarah barked out a small laugh, but did as I asked, almost as if she'd been compelled to do so.

Her lips were soft against my neck. Her sickly-sweet

breath caressed my cheek. "Do you remember our date?" she asked. "In the lab." Sarah was confident. Unafraid. Why shouldn't she be? She had me exactly where she wanted me. She sniffed my neck like a rabid animal might right before it ravages its prey's throat. Her vein was thumping out a slow, methodical rhythm that made heat flood through me. It was agonizingly enthralling, the sound of her blood rushing through her veins.

My eyes blazed up bright with my *Sight*. I ran my tongue over the sharpened tips of my fangs and hissed, "*I'm part vampire.*"

It didn't take much effort for me to clamp down onto her throat, which was a good thing, because I didn't think I could move any more than I just had.

Sarah tried to break free, pushing me away, but it was too late. She was mine. No amount of fighting was going to make me stop.

As the first drop of her life force entered my body, a semblance of warmth flooded back into me—enveloping—a life-sustaining substance that I had so desperately needed. I drank. And drank. And drank some more. All in the span of just a few short seconds.

It was amazing how quickly it happened. Her body quivered violently under my hands as I took every last drop from her. My head was reeling. My ears were ringing. My body shook right along with hers. Maybe it was all that angel power mixed with the preternatural vampire strength ... Whatever the case, she couldn't pull out of my hold no matter how hard she fought and squirmed against me.

Her cry of terror shattered my trance completely.

Then the world came suddenly crashing back together around me again, and I realized it wasn't Sarah who was screaming.

My eyes snapped open.

I was still on my knees, holding a pliant body in my arms in a death grip. Definitely not Sarah. Angela. I was strong—so much stronger than she was. I braced both hands against her shoulders, hauling her closer. Her eyes had rolled to the back of her head, and her hood fell back, revealing hair the color of raven's feathers, draped over half her face like a mask.

She shuddered, letting out a tiny gasp of pain, thrashing against me in one last attempt to free herself, but I had her in an iron grip, and I wasn't letting go.

I had never done this before, drunk straight from a vein. I could now see why this whole war between vampire clans had started in the first place. This was exactly how I should have had blood all along. There was something primal and invigorating about taking it right from the source. Every last drop. The feeling was addicting.

But I'd been deprived of sustenance for too long to stop now … I was starved to the point of anguish—

Angela laughed, and as she did, she choked on her own blood, gurgling, "You … just … sealed your … own fate."

A warning bell went off at the back of my mind.

When her eyes finally closed, I let her go, suddenly horrified. Her lifeless body fell to the frozen earth. She was flat on her back, hands splayed out by her sides, gray, by the time I realized what I'd done.

The good news was that I felt my power surging back

to life inside me like a geyser. The bad news: I knew what was about to happen next. Vampires weren't meant to drink angel blood for a reason. Blood dribbled down my chin, hers and mine mixed together.

All the lacerations on my chest, throat, and torso reopened. I could feel each and every one of the cuts as if Sarah had stabbed me all over again.

Now that Angela was gone, I called for Thunderblade. It appeared in my outstretched hand right as a molten fire lit up my belly. Pain lanced through my stomach, shooting up into my chest. I doubled over and retched. So, this was what it felt like to drink full-on angel blood. Something dark and black slid out of my mouth.

Not good—like drinking battery acid, maybe. It was the most pain I'd ever felt in in my entire life, which was saying something, because I'd been in a lot of it in my short span of eighteen years. I pressed a hand to my neck as something sharp and pungent and acidic filled the back of my throat.

The barrier had fallen down around me at some point. I gaped down at Angela's body at my feet, barely believing my own eyes as the blustery wind sliced through the thin material of my shirt, and the cold pebbled my skin.

My whole body burned. A current of electrical energy ran through me, searing, as a tornado of air rushed up around me, spinning straight up into the sky, blotting out everything else like a solar eclipse.

This was how the world ended.

I could feel the storm swelling up around me like a never-ending tunnel.

I knew my friends would try to come to me—to help—but I was beyond that now. Through a parting in the gale force wind surrounding me, my gaze settled on Imani for a moment. Her head of wavy black hair was full of white flecks of snow and brown dust. She tried to come toward me, but Leo threw a hand out, forcing her and everyone else to stay back.

He spoke to me, using only his mind. I felt the connection between us spark to life like a transistor radio turning on. *What do you need me to do, brother?*

I answered back almost as soon as he'd asked it, using only my mind to do so. *Transport everyone safely away from here. It's about to get really bad.*

He shook his head, and even though he was speaking only in my mind, I could still detect how offended he sounded. *We don't leave our own behind.*

I rolled my eyes, frustrated, but also I was immensely relieved that they weren't going to leave me to do this alone. *Keep everyone back. Combine your shields to protect everyone from me.*

I was dimly aware of Leo passing on my message to our gathered group. I could tell they all were insisting to say something, but I didn't have much time left to speak with everyone or even relay my last wishes. An unpleasant sensation washed over me as my throat swelled. I panted from the pain of it all, taking it in.

And then Ikari's voice filled my head. *What you did— you saved thousands of lives and future generations to come. You are a hero of the highest order, Corinth Taylor.* He nodded, his gaze falling on Angela's prone form at my feet. I could see the tears sliding down his face now. *For all of us. For Aiko. I know the sacrifice you are making.*

Leo piped up and said, *Corinth, I am so sorry for my part in this. Thank you for ending it.* I could feel his sorrow through our connection. I cut the link between us quickly, afraid that if any of them said anything else, that I might not go through with this.

Each of the Watchers began to form a protective shield around themselves and my friends—*Good.* I prayed it would hold up against what I was about to do.

Another round of debilitating agony rolled through me. I fell face-first, smacking my head against the frostbitten dirt, dizzy and winded. My throat closed up. I felt weak-kneed and drunk as I clawed my way slowly, inch by inch, my blade still clutched in my bloodied, swollen hand, over to the throne, determined to finish this.

The windstorm blazed up all around me, stretching into the sky, seemingly going on forever. My gut twisted in agony with each movement I took. After what felt like an eternity, I made it to the base of the throne and collapsed. It took a couple of tries to work my way up onto my knees. More dark liquid leaked out of the corner of my mouth.

I didn't look over at my friends, but I knew they were with me—and that was all that mattered.

I stabbed my dagger into the seat of the throne—it sunk into the wood, all the way up to the hilt. For one full minute, all I could do was try to control the unendurable amount of pain roiling through me, my breathing hard and harsh. Something warm and sticky slid down my cheeks. Blood mixed with tears.

With trembling fingers, I placed both my hands on the top of the spear and lifted my head to the sky, calling for lightning one last time—

The clouds parted in an earth-shattering crescendo of sound and light, and not one bolt but a thousand, lanced down around and through me, shredding the clouds, creating a whirlwind of lightning around the throne.

A million bolts drove their way down through me, the throb and impact of so much power made my back bow agonizingly. My fingers clamped down hard on the handle of the blade, cutting into my skin as sparks shot up around me in little stinging showers of fiery gold.

I couldn't have let go even if I'd wanted to as each strike ripped its way through my body, drilling down into the tortured earth. It cracked and hissed and groaned as the soil trembled and broke apart beneath me.

I guided the current of energy toward the interconnected root system of the eighty-thousand-year-old aspens—which connected me to it in the process. I felt everything. The trees growing at an abnormally slow pace. The ice water flowing through the roots. The worms digging pathways in the earth. I could even feel the sun soaking into the trees.

With each sweep of current, the ground bulged and bent beneath me. I stripped away at the network of inky darkness—just like I'd done when I'd brought Al back, except this time I used the power inside me to destroy instead of restore.

I pictured the ichor bleaching out of the gnarled and black roots, imagined the virus scrubbed and gone— eradicated. It was intricate work, and it didn't take long for sweat to stick my already-damp T-shirt to my back and chest. I didn't hold anything back as I put every ounce of myself into the task. This was what all that power had been meant for. Fire sizzled up and down my veins, and the earth rumbled its displeasure. The force of so much lightning hitting the earth blackened the clay to dust and ash at my feet.

My jaws ached from clenching them so tightly together. After what seemed like an excruciating amount of time, the last of the lightning finally stopped slamming into me. I slumped over. It was done. The virus was gone, along with the virus inside me. I no longer felt its presence.

I swallowed past the lump of grief lodged in the back of my throat as I stood, first to one leg, and then the other, getting shakily back to my feet. Through the haze in the clearing of smoke and fire from the storm, I could see Larna across the way.

She was gazing at me with wonder and admiration and a strange sort of detachment. She looked down at her hands as if they didn't belong to her anymore, her brows knitted together in concern. I understood how she felt. It was going to be hard for her to get used to being human once again.

All that was left of the throne was a smoking husk of a tree stump. Surprisingly though, all of the trees around me had survived. The dagger lay at my feet, glinting brightly, almost as if winking at me.

Chapter 59

Larna

THE FIGHTING HAD ENDED. The throne was gone, along with Angela's body, presumed vaporized in the cosmic lightning show Corinth had put on. I was suddenly glad the Watchers had held us all back from him. Without their shields to protect us, we'd all have been consumed by the rain of light and destruction.

Whatever Corinth had done to get rid of the virus had been of the mystical and divine variety. I had never seen so much lightning in one place before. A tornado filled with it. Somehow, out of all that madness, the trees had miraculously survived. It was strange and bewildering, Corinth having just ended the reign of vampires.

Imani, Nan, and Gabriel seemed to be affected the most by the change. Trying to come to terms with being human again after thousands of years must have been crippling.

Gabriel dropped to a knee, a frown marring his handsome features as he stared at the ground, seemingly a million miles away, processing.

I felt different too. The presence inside me was gone, and an overwhelming sense of loss settled over me.

Everything I'd just been through hit me all at once, and I bent over, cradling a hand around my stomach. I had not been ready to lose my *Sight*. It had been just as vitally important to me as my heart was.

Alastair pulled my hand into his, and I straightened back up.

"Are you okay?" he asked.

I nodded, too overcome with emotion to speak for a moment. It was finally over. All of it. Tears pricked the corners of my eyes as I breathed, "What about Corinth?"

Alastair pointed to the clearing about twenty yards away, where the white throne used to be. When he spoke, he sounded both awestruck and proud. "That kid has nine million lives."

Corinth was standing in the middle of a giant, charred hole in the ground. The earth around him had been shattered and quaked apart. His face was painted with his blood, and his hair was damp and curling around the sharp angles of his cheekbones. Most of the color had drained out of his face, which I attributed to shock, just like the rest of us. He looked like he'd been to hell and back—a vision of a true warrior.

Corinth must have sensed me staring, because his eyes locked on me from across the way. In almost ludicrous slowness, his lips turned up at the corners as he gave me one of those signature lopsided grins of his—the gesture felt so familiar and sweet and decidedly *him* that I clutched a hand to my chest, feeling suddenly overwhelmed. *He did it.* Corinth had saved everyone, *and* he was okay.

I stepped forward to go to him, but someone shouted

behind me, sending my pulse racing once again.

"*He's alive!*"

Leo was standing about fifteen feet from us in the opposite direction, his concerned gaze locked on the person who'd spoken behind us.

I twirled around to see Tamiel crouched over Vinson's prone form, not even ten feet away. Her head snapped around as she looked to Samyaza and Ikari. "I don't have enough strength to heal him on my own, but together … we might just be able to—he's human now."

It felt like I was stuck in quicksand, I was moving so slow. No more vamp speed or super strength to help with that anymore. When I finally arrived by his side, I threw myself down next to Vinson, winding my fingers through his, clutching a cold hand to my cheek. He'd called me his little caterpillar.

Alastair was beside me too. I heard his sharp intake of breath at seeing the extent of Vinson's wounds. They looked ghastly. Black scorch marks covered his entire midsection. The lightning had gone all the way through, exiting out his back, and he hadn't been able to heal—not even when he was a vampire. I wasn't even sure how he was still breathing with the gaping hole still in his torso. I knew he was tough, but this was taking it to the next level. It only proved to me that he was a fighter—and he didn't want to die.

Hope unfurled in my chest like the petals on a flower. They could heal him now.

Tamiel, Ikari, and Samyaza kneeled down, each of them placing a flat palm against Vinson's chest. They closed their eyes in concentration. I could see electrical currents arcing off their hands as the eerie light sank down into his body and dissipated.

"They can heal him …" Alastair whispered more to himself than to anyone else. "*They* can *heal him.*"

I closed my eyes, remembering how unnervingly similar this felt to the time I had held my father's hand in mine after I'd stabbed him with the blade, having been compelled to do so by Gabriel, unbeknownst to me.

I remembered Nan's soft voice as she'd sung over him. And then Nan was singing for real—her voice melodic and comforting. Fresh tears leaked out of the corners of my eyes. Vinson couldn't die. Not now. We'd already lost so much. I didn't want to lose him—even if he wanted to die gloriously in battle.

And then, as if he'd read my mind, Vinson's eyes fluttered open, and he growled something unintelligible, his gaze landing on my fingers clamped in his. He squeezed my hand in a firm grip. I let out a startled sob.

When I was sure he was blinking up at me, *alive*, I yanked him into a tight embrace. With a tenderness I didn't think him capable of, he patted my back, then slowly dragged himself into a sitting position, glancing down to his ruined clothing with a scowl.

Alastair planted a relieved hand against Vinson's shoulder, and surprisingly, Vinson didn't pull away from either of us. We sat like that for a second, all of us taking a moment to be thankful. My heart felt full for the first time in forever.

After a while, I realized Corinth wasn't beside me. Neither was Leo, for that matter. A part of me knew Corinth would never miss an opportunity to get a hug from Vinson—or any sort of sentiment.

I scanned the area, searching for him to make sure he was okay, but I couldn't see where he'd gone off to. Everything had gone eerily quiet. It was as if I'd put noise-cancelling headphones on with how hushed everything had become. The rush of blood was thumping loudly in my ears. A ray of watery sunlight broke through the clouds, and the cold, crisp afternoon air started to clear out the fog of battle.

That was when I saw Imani on the ground where Corinth had been standing moments before, her arms wound protectively around someone, rocking them back and forth. Leo was huddled over the form too, his hand planted firmly against the person's chest, his eyes squeezed tightly shut in concentration.

And my eyes took me where I didn't want them to … toward the person's legs—and then down, finally landing on red Converse.

Dread filled me to the core.

Gabriel was standing behind Imani, a look of regret on his face as he looked down upon her and the cradled form in her arms.

I shot to my feet, the trill of alarm tearing through me at the same time as Alastair's hand fastened around my forearm, hard. It felt like a tunnel collapsing in on me. My world went dark around the edges, and the air sawed out of my mouth noisily.

"*NO!*" I ripped out of his grip and ran—vaguely aware of everyone else running behind me too.

Leo's polished armor gleamed radiantly bright in a patch of sunlight. Sweat beaded his forehead. I didn't think angels sweat.

The rest of the Watchers had appeared out of their portals to land beside the prone figure as I bounded to a stop beside Imani. It was Corinth. I didn't need to confirm it—but I had hoped it wasn't him. One of his limp arms was draped across his middle. He looked like he could have been only sleeping. Peaceful. Timeless. Beautiful. A dark lock of hair curled up along his forehead, his skin porcelain smooth. It was like studying a video on pause in painstaking detail.

My lips shaped his name, but I couldn't get it out. *Corinth.* The metallic scent of blood was thick in the air. I whimpered softly as Alastair slid to his knees beside me.

He went as rigid and still as a statue, his face crumpled in the purest form of misery. "He was standing only a second before … He smiled at us …" Alastair's voice hitched.

Leo gently extricated Corinth from Imani's grasp and pulled Corinth's head into his lap. He closed his eyes and put his fingers on either side of Corinth's temples, completely focused as the others joined him, placing glowing hands on his chest. Now that I was so close, I could see how much blood covered his midsection and T-shirt. Blood smeared the snow all around him, pooled beneath his legs by Gabriel's feet. Through a rip in his shirt, I could see how much of it had soaked clean through.

The angels stopped working on Corinth, gently drawing their hands back away from his prone form.

Leo cracked his eyes open, clearly in anguish, and said, "Not today, Father. Don't take him today."

"God's will be done," Samyaza said quietly.

"What are you doing?" I dug my fingernails into my palms and focused on them biting into my skin. "Bring him back."

Samyaza's hand hovered over Corinth's chest, his mouth pressed into a thin line, while Ikari leaned down to lay a hand on Corinth's brow, but he wasn't trying to heal him now—he was paying his final respects. Tamiel had gotten back to her feet to put a hand over her heart.

Shallow air hissed out between my lips.

Leo muttered something in another language. Seeing Leo upset was what sent me spiraling. It could only mean one thing. They had all given up, and I couldn't understand why.

"What's the matter with y'all?" I gestured at each of them in turn. "*Bring him back.*" I let my anger buoy me, my voice trembling. "He's human. There's no trace of vampire or … virus left in him—"

"Ascended being," Gabriel interjected.

I threw a glance back at him, annoyed. His usually perfectly coiffed dark hair was tousled and windswept. It was chilly. I could see the raised outline of his scar running down his now-flushed cheeks. He reminded me more of the Greek soldier from Thermopylae than the vampire— or *ascended being*. Surprisingly, he did look remorseful and hurt. *Human.*

"Come on, Gabriel, you're always full of ideas …"

He shook his head in regret. "Not this time. I'm sorry, Larna. I truly am."

I whirled on Ikari and then Leo. "Dave—he brought Alastair back from the dead … So can you. You're angels." I enunciated each word slowly. "*Bring—him—back.*"

Samyaza's eyes darted to Alastair and then landed back on me. "Danel didn't do that—Corinth did. He was something"—he bowed his head—"*different*. Angels can't bring back those who have gone on to the other side … There's only one powerful enough to do that." He lifted his eyes to the sky, his meaning clear. God. God was the only one who had control over that.

"*Well, bring him back!*" I screamed at the sky.

Snippets of our life as kids melded together in a blur. I remembered the childlike wonder in Corinth's coffee-colored eyes when he'd gazed up at the stars, his mouth hanging open as he'd pointed out the Dog Star to me for the first time. The numerous times he'd picked flowers from my mom's garden and given them to me—those endless summer nights. I remembered the day he'd picked me up from school and helped me get rid of the gum in my hair after I'd been teased—all memories from a lifetime ago. That was him. Always helping people. Trying to right wrongs. He'd righted his last one and paid the ultimate price for it.

Imani clutched one of his hands to her cheek—his skin pale and hers dark, blended together and blurred as moisture shone at the corners of my eyes.

We crowded around him, silent—me, disbelieving. Everyone but Leo, that is.

Leo gently placed Corinth's head back to the ground and stood slowly, backing away from us, his head down. "My … brother—" his voice wavered "—counted on me. I promised I'd take care of him."

For some reason, Leo's reaction hit me harder than anything else had. His own brother was giving up on him.

My tears wouldn't stop now.

I felt a hand on my shoulder, and I looked up to see Vinson staring at me, his eyes full of sorrow and pride. Corinth had gone out the way Vinson had wanted to go. *Gloriously.*

Samyaza went over to Leo and put a hand on his arm. "You did what no one else could. You saw this through, just like your father wanted you to do. You should be proud. He is proud. The last Nephilim finished what none of us could. Corinth was brave—"

"Braver than *all* of us," Leo snarled.

Alastair shook his head in incredulity, his eyes swimming. "Corinth, he knew he wasn't coming back from this, and in the end, he saved us all anyway."

The admiration he had for Corinth was clear. I could see it in his expression. Corinth had done what Alastair would have done for any of us.

I laid a hand against Corinth's chest. My knees were wet with ice and his blood. With eyes half-closed, I listened. No heartbeat. No other signs of life left in him. Lightly I wiped a spatter of blood off his cheek with the sleeve of my dad's duster.

A cold hand touched mine. I looked up to see Alastair beside me. "Sometimes gone is gone." Alastair meant to pull me away, but I pushed him off me.

"Not today," I growled.

I could see the hurt in his eyes, but I couldn't give up on Corinth. I wouldn't. Vinson shouldered out of his white coat and then crouched down beside Corinth so he could drape it over his body. I didn't let him put it over Corinth.

Vinson took his coat back as I growled, *"Don't do*

that." My voice shook as I thought about losing my father, and Vinson doing the same for him. For Paul. For all those we'd lost. "Vinson, you can't."

A cold sort of numbness settled over me. His parents. His family. How would I break the news?

This can't be happening.

I heard Leo gasp and my head snapped up.

When I saw what he was looking at, I sucked in a startled breath. The Spear of Destiny, Corinth's blade, slowly began to rise into the air, glowing a soft red, like embers in a fire. My mouth fell open as it glided over to us and then stopped, hovering inches above Corinth's chest.

"Are you doing that?" I asked Leo.

He could only shake his head, looking as thunderstruck as I felt. "I'm not doing that."

I shared a quick glance with Alastair and the others, who looked just as stunned—

A brilliant flash of light burst out of the blade, and it shattered into a million tiny pieces. We threw our hands over our faces to shield our eyes from the light emanating from it. Shards that looked like sand from an hourglass—all pulverized metal—rained down on and around Corinth's tranquil form. We watched, marveling as the golden dust slowly dissolved and disappeared inside him. Gradually, Corinth's body began to glow golden with the heavenly light. I could see the complex pattern of his veins standing out almost black through his translucent skin.

I wrapped my arms around him, feeling a strange warmth running through his body. As the light faded and then disappeared, a deep rumble came from beneath his rib cage.

I shot another glance at Leo. His pale indigo eyes were wide and round. I could see the ring of violet surrounding dark pupils.

Then something stirred inside Corinth's chest. I laid my head against it, listening intently. It sounded like a delicate fluttering of wings beating against glass.

Suddenly cold fingers curled into my hair, and I let out a torturous moan born of grief and hope and faith, but I didn't dare move an inch. His heart was thumping away now—steadily. Strong. Machinelike. I didn't want it to go away.

It wasn't until I heard him speak that I finally managed to gaze down at him in wonderment.

"I need coffee and cheese enchiladas … stat … and a coat … and maybe … not in that order, or maybe in that order..." Corinth was slow-blinking up at me, the light in his doe-like eyes shining brighter than the Dog Star, glittering with life. I took in a shuddering breath, my brows drawing together with relief.

The cuts on his cheeks and neck had all vanished, and so had the wounds on his chest. I ran my hand along his forehead, brushing a stray lock of hair out of his eyes. We took a moment to study each other. He was shivering uncontrollably now—back to being part human once again. But even so, he took in his surroundings with wide, appreciative eyes.

He gazed around at everyone, his fingers still tangled in my hair. "I've never been so happy to be freezing my ass off in my entire life." His gaze zipped over to Vinson, who I knew was standing behind me. "I'm pretty sure nothing can keep Vin down—*ever*." He laughed softly.

"Good to see you alive and well, TL."

Vinson handed his coat over to Corinth, a low growl at the back of his throat.

With a little help from Leo and Imani, Corinth got back to his feet, and he immediately wound his fingers through Imani's.

I took note that she didn't pull away from him as she breathed, "Don't—ever—do—that—again."

"Do what?" He cocked his head to the side in feigned innocence. "Did something happen?"

Samyaza was staring at Corinth as if he'd never seen him before, his eyes glistening. He looked truly content, and it seemed to be a conflicting feeling for him—I could see all the different emotions flickering across his face. Finally he pointed up at the heavens and said, "Divine intervention."

Alastair reached out and hauled Corinth into a tight hug, pounding a solid fist against his back.

"It's good to see you too, Al," Corinth breathed. "But you're squeezing the life out of me—I'm part human again."

Alastair pulled back and gave him a warm, wide toothy grin. "I see being dead didn't take with you either."

Corinth laughed. "Just taking a page out of your book, brother."

Ikari strode forward and clapped a hand down on Corinth's shoulder. "You did good, my friend." He lowered his head. "Sozo didn't make it. I was with him at the end ... he fought bravely."

"He's a hero. He paid the ultimate price. So many lives lost." Corinth swallowed hard. "I'm so sorry, Ikari.

Sorry for everything. I wish I could have saved more … done more—"

Gabriel stepped up to our group surrounding Corinth, interrupting him. He was back to looking stoic and unhappy again, I noticed. The sharp bones in his soot-stained cheeks were standing out, and so were his dark eyebrows. His windswept hair could have its own Instagram account, I mused. He looked different. More vulnerable.

"You took something from me, Corinth." Gabriel smoothed down the collar of his coat with his gloved hand. "And I plan on getting it back."

A ghost of a smile played on Corinth's lips as he spread his arms wide. "Oh, come on, man—aren't you tired of all this arch-enemy stuff? You're human now. Go enjoy the rest of the life you have left. Grab a margarita. I know this great spot in Fort Worth, Texas … best patio on the planet—Joe T. Garcia's. You'll love it."

Gabriel rubbed a gloved finger across his mouth and scowled. "That sounds hideous."

Corinth lifted a hand and snapped his fingers. Blue sparks shot off his skin, crackling and sizzling a warning, and then the spear, his dagger, miraculously appeared in his hand once again. The light crept over his fingers, igniting his veins, trailing a path up his arms. Suddenly everything was bright, searingly bright. There was an outline of smoldering wings unfurling out of Corinth's back. Wings that looked like they had been left for far too long in a fire—scorched and torn.

I gasped, and everyone else did too, the Watchers looked just as stunned, I thought. When the fire finally faded, he was normal again and the wings were gone. His blade was once again strapped at his thigh—where it belonged.

Corinth said, "Behave, Gabe, or our paths *will* cross again."

Gabriel appraised Corinth with a glower before turning his gaze on Nan, who looked just as imperious and fierce with her burned and broken leather armor strapped across her chest.

"The first ascended being." He nodded at her in respect. "It was an honor." And then those black eyes slid to mine briefly. "Without a doubt, Miss Collins, I'll be seeing you again."

Off in the distance, I could hear the rotors of a helicopter lashing at the air, Gabriel's chopper coming to pick him up now that the weather had cleared. Without explaining what he meant by that, he turned and walked away, his back rigid and straight.

Alastair stepped in front of me and made a move to go after Gabriel, but Corinth stopped him with an arm on his shoulder. "Let him go. He'll hang himself soon enough."

"I really hate that guy," Alastair snarled. "Why must he be so infuriatingly evil?"

"And yet I sense something different about him," Nan said. "A light that wasn't there before. He did save your life."

Alastair could only shake his head at that.

We watched his retreating form dwindle into the distance without saying anything else about it. A fight for another day, perhaps.

Chapter 60

Corinth

THE ONLY TRACE LEFT of the rampaging storms was a gentle, albeit bitterly cold, breeze blowing in from the north, off the lake. The purpling of dusk was heavy in the sky. I felt different. Lighter. I rubbed my arms, glad for the warmth of Vinson's coat, thinking about how I had come back miraculously from the dead. I didn't remember anything, only waking to find my friends looking down at me as if they were attending my funeral. Which, technically, they had been.

I shivered, but not from the cold, and glanced around. Nan was already taking charge, as usual, organizing the cleanup after the battle, hopefully minimizing the chance of any outsiders witnessing the events that had unfolded around us. Always the leader.

I hadn't realized how bad it was until I saw all the carnage. Amazingly, except for the section of trees I'd wiped out, the aspens were all still intact. Everyone who wasn't injured or a corpse had cleared out or been healed by the Watchers.

Off to my left, I watched Larna and Al speaking conspiratorially to Vinson. They were giving me furtive glances, but I couldn't bring myself to care what they were saying. None of it mattered except for the fact that I was alive. And Thunderblade was back at my hip.

Imani came up beside me, her mouth pinched, making her cheeks dimple adorably in the process. She didn't look the same. I couldn't tell if she was happy or sad about being human once again. Probably both.

"You look like you could use a week's worth of sleep," she deliberated.

"That bad, huh?" I flashed her one of my, in my opinion, charming half grins. "How is it being human again?" I gave her a sidelong glance. "You okay?"

"Different," she murmured, but she didn't elaborate any further.

"That's what I like about you, Imani. There's no excessive talking. Well, that and those incredibly tight pants of yours ... So ... pray tell, what are you going to do now that this is all over?"

She quirked an eyebrow at me, her face still inscrutable. "I suppose I'll try out this place with a great patio ... cheese enchiladas, whatever those are ... They sound heavenly. I'm starving."

I smiled at that.

Her onyx-colored hair had little flecks of gray ash in it. I reached out, gently brushing some of it from her dark strands, my hand lightly caressing the side of her cheek in the process. For a moment, she closed her eyes, giving me an opportunity to step closer. I pulled her against me before she could protest, and then drew her hand into mine, weaving my fingers through hers.

Her eyes opened wide in surprise. "I'm not a handholder," she said coolly, glancing down, but there was a small smile on her face.

My gaze landed on our interlaced fingers. "I guess it's a good thing I am."

We stood in companionable silence for a moment longer until I said, "So, I guess I'll just give you my number, I mean, when I can get a new phone … and you'll text me cute little smiley-heart emojis …"

"Don't make it weird," she said.

I could only nod at that. I was weird.

Through a section of trees up ahead, I could see Leo heading back toward us, his long legs moving at a rapid pace. He had been off helping to heal Al, and anyone else who needed it. He wore a frown, but there was a spring in his step. It was weird, seeing him with the weight of the world off his shoulders. I noticed he'd exchanged his polished armor for a long navy-blue button-down coat that looked military-esque in style. The gold buttons flashed bright in the setting sun.

Had he been walking on the street, with that combination of dark hair and exceedingly pale blue eyes and those chiseled features, I knew he'd have gotten a lot of head turns from the ladies, and gents too.

I thought back to almost freezing to death in the mausoleum and how I'd felt a heavy weight on top of me like a blanket. I'd originally thought it was a blanket. I realized it had probably been Leo's coat. He'd at least tried to keep me from becoming hypothermic … which I thought was a nice, brotherly thing to do. I wanted to tell him he'd done a crappy job of it—just to mess with him—but something stayed my jokes as soon as he stopped in front of me.

For some reason, it felt like we'd known each other for our entire lives, even though we'd just met a few days ago. I found I could already read his facial expressions as easily as reading a book. He reminded me a lot of Dave. I felt a pang of regret well up inside me all over again.

"Why do you still have that strained expression on your face?" I asked.

Imani, sensing we needed a moment, took her hand back from me and said, "I'll give you two a minute."

After she was gone, Leo said, "So … I'm sorry."

I raised an eyebrow. "For which part? Abducting me, torturing me, or cutting me with my own blade?"

He scratched his head, glancing down. "All of it. I fear I've been an atrocious older brother from the get-go. I understand if you can't forgive my reprehensible actions … I would never have let you go through with what you just did"—he ran a hand through his hair, mussing it up on top, reminding me of my signature move—"if I had known your wounds weren't going to heal. I foolishly thought that if you got rid of the virus inside you, it would fix everything else. I promised I'd keep you safe … and I didn't, and for that, I *am* truly sorry."

I barked out an incredulous laugh. "Don't be, dork." His mouth turned down at the corners as I continued. "Get used to the name calling—we're brothers, and you're older, which means I get to give you a hard time. Look, I've already missed out on a lot of years with a half brother I never knew I had. I don't plan on losing any more. You've had to deal with a lot of crap for a very long time. The planning it took to get to this point …" I let my voice trail off for a second, thinking about it. Suddenly, I realized I didn't want to think about it anymore. I was just so tired. "Well, I can't even imagine. And Dave—Danel—I'm still trying to wrap my head around everything he did. How in the world he could get with Angela *ever* ..." I shuddered at the thought. "He was my biological father. You'll have to fill in some of the gaps later. I'm still angry with him, you know? I can't believe he's gone, and that he did everything for me ... and yet *not* for me. He's your father too, and you just lost your mother by my hands. I'm the one that should be sorry. This conversation is so strange."

He shook his head. "She was never my mother ... only a monster. Danel, he ... he tried his best. He was sorry he didn't get to know you in the way a father should know a son. Believe it or not, he loved you very much. I would like to tell you about him someday."

I nodded, feeling the tears sting the backs of my eyelids. "I would like that very much." After a brief pause, I said, "So, answer me this, the dyed-hair thing—everyone else going blond and you not falling in line—that was to show Angela that you were never *really* in league with the Watchers, right?"

"Nah, I just don't like blonds." His eyes sparkled in jest as he raised a finger to his head. "Being the outcast for centuries wasn't exactly fun."

"What you had to go through ... it sounds ... terrible. And here I was complaining about being raised as a normal kid."

"It was the only way." Leo toed the hard-packed snow with his boot as he said, "How *did* you kill Angela, anyway?"

"You didn't see?" I asked slowly, carefully.

He shook his head. "Oh, I definitely saw her fitting demise … I mean, what you told her to get her to come that close … I'm curious."

I took in a deep breath and blew it noisily back out. "Perhaps a conversation we could have, like, on any other day besides today."

He nodded, understanding lighting his eyes. "Let me take you home."

I didn't tell him I didn't need him to take me home. I knew it was his way of trying to look out for me.

We watched the sun dip below the outline of aspens. I was amazed that I was able to enjoy another sunset on this earth. Something I was not going to take for granted now.

After another long moment, I said, "This might be too much to ask … but, since we're in the States, would you like to come visit the fam in Texas with me? Is that weird? I've got a lot of questions for my mom and dad, and I'd love for you to meet my brothers and sister. They're your family now too—and since they already know about angels, it might not come as a shock to them, meeting you."

Leo's eyes widened, and he tilted his head to the side, I think caught off guard. "I would like that."

Suddenly I was barely able to keep my eyes open. I blinked and then forced them back open again, and when I did, I saw Larna and Al approaching, hand in hand, glowing like newlyweds. They deserved to be happy. They deserved a break. They deserved each other.

"Your father's coat suits you, Larns," I said, nodding

at her in greeting as they stopped in front of me. "Nicely tailored."

Larna grabbed my arm and hauled it over one of her shoulders, pulling me against her side. It felt familiar and right, feeling the warmth of her body pressed close to mine, strictly platonically speaking, I mean.

"That was the stupidest thing you could have done, and just because what you did was incredibly brave and self-sacrificing, doesn't mean I'm not upset at you for that letter you left me."

"Yeah, about that," I said, hanging my head. "Sorry."

She slapped my chest and I winced. I didn't feign it either. I was tired and sore, even after having been miraculously healed. We all had our limits, and I had hit mine days ago. Food and coffee were going to be a top priority for me.

"So, what are you two cats going to do?" I asked Al as I watched Vin loping up to join our group. The rest of the Watchers followed behind him, along with Nan and Imani, who surprisingly were talking animatedly to one another. Best buds.

We were ragged and worn, but there was a sense of unspoken pride and comraderie between us all now. Well, maybe not Imani and Vin just yet.

Al gave Larna a starry-eyed look that made me want to barf as he said, "For starters … visit Larna's mother— pick her up from the cruise terminal in Galveston. Then I think I'll show Larna Paris—at night after that."

I rolled my eyes, but a smile tugged at the corners of my lips all the same. "Sappy and predictable, Al."

He shrugged as if to say "Guilty as charged." "What

about you?" he asked.

I glanced to Leo, and then I let my gaze slowly drift to Tami, Sam, and Ikari before settling back on Al once again and then lastly Imani. "Go talk to my family. Eat. A lot. Drink. A lot—of coffee, I mean." Larna nudged me. My gaze stayed locked on the slush at my feet. "Honestly, I'm just going to take it one day at a time and enjoy every single one of the days I'm given, considering I wasn't even guaranteed a tomorrow." I looked up to Vin. "What about you, Vin?"

Vinson peered up at Tami, who was standing beside him, towering over his average height of five feet nine. "I like how Watchers fight. They are violent bunch. I go with them."

Sam tilted his head to the side and laughed. We all did. It was just such a Vinson answer.

I inclined my head at him, still chuckling. "Then I guess I'll be seeing more of you in the near future."

Vinson's answer was only a grunt.

I shared a glance with each of the angels in turn, looking to Sam first and then Tami and finally Ikari. I broadcasted a message to all of them at the same time. *If that's okay with you guys.*

Ikari ran a hand through his spiky platinum hair. *Picking up on the angel communication quickly, I see. Now that you know how to converse like a proper angel, you can give us a shout from anywhere in the world. We'll always be here anytime you need us.*

Thank you for everything, I answered, almost as quickly.

Al was staring back and forth between the Watchers

and me with an inquisitive brow arched. I'm sure it looked strange, all of us staring intently at one another without saying a word.

He said, "I feel like we probably missed out on an entire conversation."

Larna sighed and then wound her arms around me in a tight embrace. I could feel her body trembling against mine. I didn't think she was shaking from the cold, it was everything else—including the aftereffects of the battle. She was just as tired as I was.

"You always have a place at my dad's cabin whenever you need it," she whispered softly.

I drew back, placing my hands on her shoulders. "You mean your place," I corrected.

"No. I mean *our* place," she said evenly.

Chapter 61

Corinth

TEXAS WOULD ALWAYS HOLD a special place in my heart. Leo and I arrived back in my hometown of Fort Worth in a crack of thunder, landing in my parents' shaded, untidy backyard, away from prying eyes. The swing set was broken from one too many surprise ambushes from my brothers. A faded Barbie doll-house was lying half-buried in the dirt. Nothing had changed.

It was unseasonably warm in Texas for winter—which was the case most of the time. Fortunately, my siblings weren't outside, chasing each other, and we'd positioned ourselves behind the shed, which housed all the lawn equipment I'd never used.

Just a block away was Larna's home. Larna's mom wasn't there, I knew, but I would pop in and check on her house and maybe water the plants. I missed walking over there to pick flowers from her garden. A feeling of nostalgia rolled over me as I shucked out of Vinson's coat. Leo gave me a questioning look, watching me check the sheath strapped at my thigh. I'd worn it for the better part of eight months. The blade was still an intrinsic part of me.

"I realize it's not quite as cold as it was in Utah, but you're only wearing a T-shirt under that coat," he said slowly.

I held it up and pointed at the burned-out hole in the center of the material. "That's a very brotherly thing to say," I noted. "But I don't think my parents would appreciate me walking inside wearing something that looks like I've been in a war zone."

Leo lifted his shoulders in an exaggerated shrug. "I really don't think walking in there with your shirt covered in blood is such a good idea either. And your face is painted in it. Here." He placed a finger to the middle of my forehead, and just like that, my shirt was as clean and fresh as if I'd just taken it out of the package brand-new.

I reached a hand up and felt at my face. There was no speck of dried or crusted blood or injuries left on my now-smooth skin. I ran a hand through my hair—it felt the cleanest it had in ages, I think I even had some product in it. I missed my mint shampoo. "You're going to have to teach me that next. You come in handy—roommates for life now," I stated. "A snap of the fingers, and the whole place is clean. Did Larna tell you I'm kind of a slob?"

"She forgot to mention it." A tug of his lips at one side was all I was going to get out of him as he crossed his arms over his chest. "You know we could have waited to go see your mum and dad until you had time to eat and sleep."

"No," I interjected quickly. "I couldn't wait another second. Not after ..." I shook my head, and Leo nodded as if he understood.

I needed to see my family.

"Are you sure you want me to come with you?" he

asked hesitantly.

I nodded. "I'm positive. They know what I am—part angel. That's no surprise. My brothers and sister probably don't know, but Mom and Dad will want to meet you. Plus they're going to want to kill me since I haven't called them in forever … and having someone with me might lessen the blow. Also, can we keep the whole me dying thing between us?"

Leo let out a long sigh that I couldn't quite interpret. He'd been through just as much as I had … even more. I was throwing a lot at him.

I clapped him on the shoulder. "Let's go greet the fam, then."

At the front door, my hand hovered over the doorbell. I decided to surprise them and ring the bell. So I pushed the button once and immediately heard the scamper of little feet and children's shrill voices coming from the other side. My stomach did a flip of anticipation.

When the door flew open and I saw Zoey, my little sister, who was now five years old, she screamed and threw her arms around me. And then I was enfolded in a tangle of limbs and bodies. Jimmy and Peter were attached to my legs like barnacles on the underside of a ship.

I moved inside, dragging them right along with me, speechless for a moment as I pulled Zoey up and into my arms. I was sure she'd grown at least two feet while I'd been away.

Vaguely I was aware of Leo ambling in behind me to shut the door. My brothers were throwing their heads back, giggling. Everyone was talking excitedly over each other now.

Zoey reached out and touched my bicep and then looked down to the holster and sheath strapped to my thigh. "You look like a superhero in a movie."

I blinked dumbly back at her for a moment before I realized she was seriously comparing me to a superhero. I didn't think my outward appearance had changed that much—apparently, it had.

"Who's that?" Pete pointed to Leo. "He's tall."

Leo looked extremely awkward and out of place, standing in the middle of the foyer, his hands clasped together. It was really quite entertaining.

"That's Leo," I said, glancing back at him. "He's my half brother."

Jimmy said, "Why do you look so … *different?*"

Pete said at the same time, "*Half brother?*"

My mom came striding in from the kitchen, a dish towel in her hands. She started to say, "What's all this about?" but as soon as she saw my siblings clustered around me, she stopped speaking, her mouth hanging comically open in surprise.

She dropped the towel as my dad came wandering in from their bedroom at the back of the house. He did a double take, his wide brown eyes opening and closing as if he didn't believe I was standing there. A hand went to his mouth.

They both looked truly shocked to see me. A part of me thought maybe they didn't think I was coming back at all. It had been so long since I'd called or spoken with either of them. Maybe they thought they'd lost me when they hadn't told me the truth. I saw it in their eyes as they gazed at me in wonder.

I set Zoey down and slowly extricated myself from my brothers' embraces. And then I wasn't sure who moved first, but we were all wrapped up in each other's arms. I hugged them each for a solid two minutes before speaking. I had missed them so much. I hadn't thought I'd ever see them again.

My mom pulled back and her voice broke. "Corinth … you look so … *grown-up*. Different. Is that a dagger?"

"It's a long story, Mom." I peered back at Leo, who was still in the entryway. "This is Leo …" I swallowed hard. "He's my half brother."

My dad was the first to stride over to him. After a good long moment of him studying Leo without saying a word, he held his hand out. "I'm Jonathan. Everyone calls me Zeke though." He nodded at my mom. "That's Susan."

Leo took his hand warmly in both of his and, in his British accent said, "It's a pleasure to meet you, sir, Mum."

"It would appear we have a lot to talk about," my father said. "I'll make some coffee."

"*Oh thank heaven,*" I breathed.

Epilogue

Gabriel

GABRIEL MELTED INTO THE warm leather bucket seat of his private helicopter, annoyed at how cold he now felt. Being human once again definitely had its disadvantages. It was a good thing he loved his creature comforts. He took a sip of his sixty-four-year-old Macallan Scotch, enjoying the smooth bite at the back of his throat. Already he hated the feel of human hunger pains.

There was a strange tightness in his chest—right near his heart. He shoved that feeling down deep, ignoring it. He also ignored the flashback of disappointment on Larna's face when she'd realized he wasn't on her side. He ignored the grief-stricken feeling he'd gotten when Corinth was dead. They weren't genuine. They were residual feelings belonging to Larna. *Or are they?*

Gabriel swallowed the rest of his drink down in one gulp, annoyed at himself, and then filled it back up again.

The hooded angel rose up like a specter from the darkened shadows to sit beside him.

Gabriel pulled his gloves off, then his coat, plucked the earpiece out of his ear, and followed lastly by the thin, expensive armor strapped to his chest. He took his time, unafraid of the disfigured angel sitting next to him.

When he had finished, and he found he could breathe a little more deeply, he finally allowed himself to lean back in his seat. "Is he here?"

The massive angel moved his head slightly, turning to look to the other side of the chopper.

A small, thin form materialized out of thick black smoke and darted forward, moving with a speed and grace that was definitely *not* human. The creature was lithe and dangerous and wild—of that, Gabriel was certain.

If he hadn't seen how powerful this being was with his own eyes, Gabriel would have dismissed him, or *it*, immediately, just based on his looks alone. Demon. A real demon. And this one looked like a fifteen-year-old kid. His round, black-rimmed glasses, worn for style only, he thought, made him look like a bookworm instead of one of the deadliest demons on the planet. He wore corduroy pants and a plaid sweater vest. His thick brown hair was carefully styled with hair gel and swept to the side, making it look like a wave. A nerd if ever Gabriel had seen one. In fact, he was almost entirely sure this kid would get along with Mr. Taylor.

The black eyes behind those lenses glittered like an oil slick as they raked over Gabriel, studying him. "Is the Nephilim dead?"

Gabriel took another slow swallow of his drink and gave a tiny shake of his head. "Angela."

"*Ah ... I see.*"

Gabriel heard the sharp edge in the demon's voice, but it still came out sounding smooth and silky, as dangerous as a razor slice. He said, "Corinth is too powerful. He was raised from the dead, and he still has the blade."

"Do you have a contingency plan?"

Again Gabriel nodded. "I do."

"Who?"

He finished the rest of his drink, enjoying the feel of it hitting his empty stomach. "Alastair Iszler."

"Excellent," the demon hissed. "Shall we begin, then?"

Gabriel set his empty glass down. "*We shall.*"

AUTHOR'S NOTE

There comes a moment in time, as an author, when you finally come face-to-face with reality, and it sucks. I know, it's rare, like catching a glimpse of the Easter Bunny. "I'm done with my last book in this series!" I shout to no one in particular (well, technically, I shout it to my family and friends, repeatedly, but that's neither here nor there), "after seven long, painful, wonderful years." Reality slaps me in the face and says, "You'll never be done! Because you've created a world that you won't ever give up on."

It's true. I don't *want* to give up. That's why I am starting on a spin-off series from *The Blood Dagger*. (It shall not be named, because I don't have a name yet.)

Everything in this series is a work of fiction. There is no hidden meaning behind religion, or vamps, or angels. I just find all of this extremely entertaining. I wrote this series for the explicit reason to entertain. I hope I did my job. If I did, please reach out and tell me so. I'd love to hear from you.

If you want to know more, please join my mailing list to stay apprised of all the gloriously fun things happening, events, signings, and free stuff by going here: http://eepurl.com/dg029j

ACKNOWLEDGMENTS

I want to thank the loyal folks out there who have been with me from the beginning—you guys rock my world, and truly and in all seriousness, these books would not exist without you. Thank you to Becky Pruitt for always being there for me, and for all those endless hours of reading and rereading and proofreading and editing (like the wind too). You are indomitable.

Thank you to Paul Leonard for being my tour guide in London all those years ago. You set the course.

Thank you to my family, who are my constant support and guiding light: Christy Leonard, Sherry Daugherty, Annie Hayes, Robert Hayes, Oscar Pruitt, Susen Pruitt, Big Oscar Pruitt, and Jeremy Daugherty and all my aunts and cousins.

Thank you to Misty Spitzer for getting me to the finish line—I love you, sista. That time when we leaned over to each other in the movie theater and both said, "*I'm writing a book!*" Famous last words.

Thank you to my editor, Leonora Bulbeck, who never lets me down. She is a godsend and true talent. Don't ever leave me. Seriously. No, really.

Thank you to my cover designer, Mark Reid, who is

nothing short of a genius. You always seem to be able to read my mind. This last one was a doozy. Thank you.

Thank you to my formatter, Lorna Reid, who is as quick with lightning responses as Corinth is. Your attention to detail is unfathomable.

To my proofreaders, beta readers, and constant supporters, you are the foundation on which this book was built—and you know what they say about a good foundation: It's paramount. Y'all are my true clan.

To June Owens, Stephanie Hancock, Monique and Paul Irwinsky, Eric Skinner, Dean Toland, Michael Avery, and the folks at Discord Book Club, thank you for including me.

To all the men and women who put on a uniform, each and every single day, to protect our city. Heroes don't get the reward. They pay the price.

To all of you who believe in these characters—you are my inspiration, and they wouldn't exist without you. Much love to you all.

www.ingramcontent.com/pod-product-compliance
Lightning Source LLC
Chambersburg PA
CBHW031630130726
47900CB00019B/783